# DREAM COUNTRY

G·K
Hall
&Co.

*Also by Luanne Rice*
*in Large Print:*

Blue Moon
Secrets of Paris

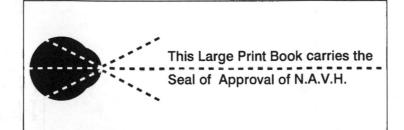

# DREAM COUNTRY

## Luanne Rice

G.K. Hall & Co. • Waterville, Maine

Published in 2001 by arrangement with Bantam Books, an imprint of The Bantam Dell Publishing Group, a division of Random House, Inc.

G.K. Hall Large Print Core Series.

The text of this Large Print edition is unabridged.
Other aspects of the book may vary from the original edition.

Set in 16 pt. Plantin.

Printed in the United States on permanent paper.

**Library of Congress Cataloging-in-Publication Data**

Rice, Luanne.
    Dream country / Luanne Rice.
      p. cm.
    ISBN 0-7838-9384-1 (lg. print : hc : alk. paper)
    ISBN 0-7838-9385-X (lg. print : sc : alk. paper)
    1. Mothers and daughters — Fiction. 2. Runaway teenagers — Fiction. 3. Missing children — Fiction. 4. Wyoming — Fiction. 5. Large type books. I. Title.
PS3568.I289 D7 2001
813′.54—dc21                                  00-067297

To Bob

# Acknowledgments

For twenty-one years of friendship and grace, I send my love and thanks to everyone at the Jane Rotrosen Agency: Jane Berkey, Don Cleary, Stephanie Tade, Meg Ruley, Ruth Kagle, Annelise Robey, Peggy Gordijn, and Barbara Goodwin, and, especially, Andrea Cirillo.

To Nita Taublib and Tracy Devine, with thanks for their boundless patience, insight, guidance, and support.

Many thanks to the Dutchess County SPCA and Animal Farm Foundation, Inc., who worked together to save the real Petal; to Dr. Kathy K. Clark, everyone at the Clark Veterinary Hospital, and Pet Connections, Inc. on behalf of Maggie, May, and Maisie, and to Amelia S. Onorato for the help and care she gives to all animals.

With deep gratitude to Dr. Elizabeth Moreno, Sherry Kohn, Mary Connolly, and Lynda Hunnicutt.

For a lifetime of inspiration in life, joy, compassion, and skiing, love to Betty Anne Whitney, Tobin Hagelin, Sam Whitney, Sarah Blanchard, and Palmer Whitney.

With appreciation to Rob Monteleone for his

commanding performance on the docks in Lunenburg, and his inspiring presence on the baseball field and hockey ice.

Thanks to Heather McNeil, for her warmth, generosity, humor, and for making me an honorary Cuckoo.

To Karen LeSage Stone, whose songs are deep and true, for sharing her art, spirit, and philosophy with me, for our talks at 104 and so much more.

Rosemary and Maureen: I love you.

# Chapter One

At seven A.M., Daisy Tucker paused at the foot of the stairs to smell the laundry she held in her arms. She had gotten up an hour early to wash her daughter's clothes, throwing an extra sheet of fabric softener into the dryer the way Sage liked it.

Mounting the stairs, Daisy wondered why her heart was pounding. She felt nervous, as if she were applying for a new job instead of waking up her sixteen-year-old with a pile of clean clothes. The house was quiet, flooded with thin morning light. While waiting for the laundry to finish, Daisy had gone to her spare-room jewelry studio to work on a bracelet that she hoped to finish that afternoon. But she had been too upset to concentrate.

Daisy and Sage lived alone. There had been no witnesses last night to hear Daisy screaming like a banshee, see her pulling her own hair like a caricature of a maniac. There had been no one present to watch Sage sit back in her inflatable chair, messy dark hair falling across her face, observing her frustrated mother with cool detachment in her wide green eyes, no one to watch that composure crumble under Daisy's words.

9

Sage had been wearing the clothes Daisy now held in her arms, and they had been mud-stained and sopping wet. She had been out with Ben Davis, her boyfriend, until midnight, even though she had promised to be home by nine. They had gone canoeing and capsized. In late October, Silver Bay, Connecticut, was frosty and cold, and all Daisy had been able to think about was how they might have drowned in the dark.

The phone rang. Still holding the clothes, Daisy walked to her bedroom. Wondering who it could be, ready to be stern to Ben, she picked up.

"Hello?" she said.

"How's my wayward niece?"

"Sleeping," Daisy said, relaxing at the sound of her sister's voice. "But it was touch and go last night. When she walked in all soaked and bedraggled, I wanted to kill her."

" 'Kill'?" Hathaway asked. "That seems like a strong word. Perhaps you mean 'maim.' "

"Oh, Hath," Daisy said, almost laughing. Talking to her sister could break the tension like nothing else. "She was bad, but I was worse. The mad twin took over. I was standing over her, slavering — truly, foam was dripping from my mouth —"

"Did you ground her until college?"

"Yes, and I told her only stupid girls go out canoeing with boys until midnight on school nights," Daisy said, cringing as she remembered her words, her tone of voice. "Stupid, slutty girls."

10

"I hope you told her she could never see Ben again," Hathaway said, knowing that, last night notwithstanding, Daisy liked Ben. He was polite, serious about his schoolwork, too mild to ignite any real passion in Sage.

"Of course I did." Daisy stared miserably at the clothes she held, knowing that the hour of truth was at hand.

"She did come home late," Hathaway said. "On a school night. Plus, there was ice on my birdbath this morning. Just a thin coating, but still. It was cold out — no wonder you lost it."

"I hate that I called her slutty."

"No, you just *compared* her to slutty girls. That's different."

"I feel awful." Standing over her sulking teen-ager, looking into those huge eyes, Daisy had felt as if her heart could break. She was an overprotective mother, and she knew it. Sage's twin brother, Jake, had disappeared when he was three, and that fact informed every decision Daisy had made ever since regarding Sage. All Daisy had ever wanted was to protect her children. With a slim body, full mouth, and wide, knowing eyes, Sage had lost the last vestiges of babyhood. Still, Daisy had looked straight past those features to see the infant she and Sage's father had brought home from the hospital sixteen years ago.

"I don't want her to get hurt," Daisy said.

"I know," Hathaway said gently.

"But I said some awful things. I could see it in

11

her eyes. I have to go wake her up now. I did her laundry, and now I want to sit on the edge of her bed."

"And tell her you love her."

"And everyone makes mistakes."

"But you'll ground her for life if she ever does it again . . ."

"Right," Daisy said, laughing.

Hanging up, she felt a little better. Talking to Hathaway had helped her put the situation into perspective. A single mother raising a smart daughter, Daisy was ultravigilant about keeping Sage's focus on schoolwork, away from boys. Generations of daughters had been staying out too late, falling into lazy rivers. That didn't make them bad children, and it didn't mean they had bad mothers. Many years had passed since Jake's death, time for Daisy to tell herself again and again she wasn't to blame.

Sunlight streamed through the bedroom windows, into the upstairs hall. The wood floors were waxed and polished. Walking toward Sage's room, Daisy thought about what a nice house they lived in. It was a small saltbox, safe and enclosed, with a sliver of view down the cove. Daisy had bought and paid for it herself, selling the jewelry she made and saving her money. Sage might dream of riding the range, living the ranch life, but Daisy reassured herself that she was doing a good job, making a fine home for herself and her daughter right here on Pumpkin Lane.

Taking a deep breath, Daisy took hold of the doorknob to Sage's room. She said a prayer, that she could stay calm no matter what, that she wouldn't rise to any bait Sage might float her way — intentionally or not. This only *felt* like a war, and merely because Daisy loved the girl so much. Forcing herself to smile, she entered her daughter's bedroom.

The room was empty.

Sage's bed had not been slept in. It was neatly made, the Indian blanket drawn up over the pillows. Daisy could see the outline of her daughter's body, where she had lain outside the covers. A drawer was partly open, and Daisy saw that clothes were missing.

Posters of Wyoming hung everywhere. Purple peaks — the Wind River Mountain Range, the Medicine Bows, the Big Horns, and the Snowies — filled the walls, along with blowups of cowboy corrals and galloping mustangs. Her father had sent her a rack of elk antlers, and she had turned them into a shrine: The single picture she had of him hung among turquoise beads, horseshoes, the pelt of a jackrabbit, and her brother's blue booties.

A note lay on Sage's desk. The second Daisy saw it, a small sound escaped her. She dropped the neatly folded laundry and touched her heart.

Her hands shaking, she picked up the note.

Sage had been upset when she'd written it. Daisy could tell by the spidery handwriting, the way the ink had blotched and trailed off, the terrible terseness of the message from a girl who had always loved to talk, more than anything.

Daisy stared at the words. She looked for "Dear Mom" and "Love, Sage," but there were only four words, and in the time it took to read them, Daisy felt the world cave in around her:

"I HAVE TO GO."

Daisy called Hathaway. As she waited for her sister to arrive, she paced around the house. She suddenly had so much energy, she felt as if her chest was going to explode. At the same time, she had a knot in her forehead from concentrating on where Sage might have gone. It was Thursday, a school day. Could "I have to go" mean simply "I have to go to school"?

Just in case, she telephoned the office at Silver Bay High School. Sage was in eleventh grade, her third year. She had finished off sophomore year with high honors, gotten A's on her first junior year tests — and had received two deficiencies last week. Daisy had stared at those notes from Sage's chemistry and history teachers, filled with worry and fear. Sage, her bright light, her brilliant girl, letting herself slip? "Hi, Mrs. Wickham," Daisy said to the school secretary. "It's Daisy Tucker and I was, um —"

"Hello, Ms. Tucker. I was just about to call you. If Sage is going to be absent, we really need to get a call from you, just to let us know —"

"I'm sorry," Daisy said, bending over from the waist, covering her eyes, dropping the phone. Of

14

course: Of course Sage had not gone to school. Hurrying now, she tried Ben's house and found no one home. The same for Zoe, Amanda, and Robin.

Hathaway walked in, looking tall and tough. She smothered Daisy in a hug before Daisy could get one word out. By then Daisy was crying, and she leaned openmouthed against the shoulder of her older sister's silk blouse. When she pulled back, Hathaway was regarding the spit-blotch with dismay. But she raised her eyes to Daisy.

"It was just a fight," Daisy said. "It was bad, but still . . . it was just an *argument*. We've had hundreds. Why would she say she has to go?"

"Where's the note?" Hathaway asked, as if it contained answers. Perhaps it did: Feeling renewed hope at her sister's arrival, and her sister's direct approach, Daisy's heart leapt.

"Here." Daisy handed over the blue-lined white paper, ripped from one of Sage's notebooks.

"That's a *note?*" Hathaway asked.

"I told you." Daisy would have been much happier if Sage had left her pages of complaints, grievances about life at home and school. She would have preferred spewings of anger and resentment. Being sixteen had moments of torture, and Daisy was a mother prepared to bear the brunt.

"Who have you called?" Hathaway asked.

"Ben, some of her friends, the school."

15

"What did Ben say?"

"I got the answering machine at his house," Daisy said. "I know his mother works at a bank, but I'm not sure which one. His parents are divorced, and his father lives in Boston."

"This note . . ." Hathaway said, frowning. She was big-boned and chic, very no-nonsense. She ran a small boutique on the wharf called The Cowgirl Rodeo, where she sold western jackets, suede skirts, and Daisy's jewelry. For some reason, people vacationing in their Atlantic coast town loved spending their money on items evocative of the Old West. Hathaway had gotten the idea back in the days when she would visit Daisy and James in Wyoming.

"It's short," Daisy said, trying to laugh.

Hathaway just stared at the scrap of paper. " 'I have to go,' " she read out loud.

"She ran away, that's all." Daisy was unable to keep the tremor out of her voice. "I did that when I was young, more than once. I was five the first time, remember? I packed a washcloth and my stuffed dog and went to live in the pine hollow. And I ran away again when I was nine, right after Dad died, so I wouldn't have to go to the cemetery —"

"She's sixteen; that's not five or nine," Hathaway said.

"She's a good girl. She wouldn't —" Daisy's mind felt crazy. Her thoughts were darting all over the place to avoid the fact that it was nine-fifteen A.M. and Sage hadn't slept in her bed and

16

she had no idea of where her daughter was. "She left a note. It's short, and she was obviously upset; we'd just had the worst fight of our lives. I was so mad. She knows how I felt after Jake disappeared. She wouldn't do that to me . . ."

"She sounds serious," Hathaway said, taking Daisy's hand.

"Oh —" Daisy said, making a moaning sound again, because she couldn't get out the next part: serious about what?

Serious about Ben, of course. Daisy called four banks before she got the right one. Paulina Davis managed the wharf branch of Shoreline Bank & Trust. Paulina was with a client, and the receptionist told Daisy she would call back. Daisy gave her ten minutes, then rang the bank again.

"Hello?" Paulina sounded very slightly annoyed.

"Hi, this is Daisy Tucker," Daisy began. Although the two women weren't friends, they had spoken on the phone several times since the previous summer, when Sage and Ben had started spending so much time together.

"I got your message," Paulina said.

"Did Ben —" Daisy paused. How could she word this without offending his mother? Did Ben skip school today, did he run away from home, did he leave you a four-word note that scares the hell out of you?

"Did Ben and Sage lose our canoe last night?

17

Yes," Paulina Davis said. "Did I just get a call from school telling me he's absent without my permission? Also yes. I'm furious, Daisy."

"At Sage?" Daisy felt the heat in her face. Was this supposed to be Sage's fault?

"Ben's a senior," Paulina said. "He's always been a good student, and this year he's captain of the soccer team. It's been his dream, and yesterday he missed the game. He should be visiting colleges, planning —" She had to stop, her voice shaking with rage. "I've forbidden him to see Sage before, but this time I mean it."

"When did you forbid him to see Sage?" Daisy asked. Her worry was instantly supplanted by defensive rage at this other mother's tone of voice regarding her daughter.

"A month ago," Paulina said. "Not that he listened."

"Listen, Sage is a good student, too. An honor student," Daisy said hotly. "I'm not wild about her spending every free minute with Ben, that's for sure. I trusted them all summer because they're good kids, especially Sage, she's always —"

"Look, I'm sorry." Paulina cut her off. "I'm upset. Seeing each other nonstop all summer was one thing, but now school has to come first, I'm sure you agree. It's just a matter of making some rules and sticking to them. I just think —"

"Have you been home since the school called?" Daisy asked.

"No, of course not. I work until — Why?"

"Because I think maybe they've run away."

"Run away?"

"Sage has, anyway." Daisy started to shake as she said the words. "Run away. She left a note."

"Did she mention Ben?"

"No."

"Ben wouldn't run away," Paulina said flatly. "Would not."

"I didn't think Sage would, either," Daisy said.

Ben hadn't left a note, but he had packed some things and taken his backpack and tent. Paulina had left work immediately to go home, and she called, upset, the minute she checked his room. Hathaway leaned against the refrigerator, waiting while Daisy held the phone and listened. Daisy was upset, but she wasn't surprised by the fact the two kids had gone off together.

"He doesn't have a car, she doesn't have a car," Paulina said. "What are they, hitchhiking?"

"Hitchhiking, yes, probably," Daisy said.

"This is great," Paulina said. "This is wonderful."

Paulina's tone said she was blaming the whole thing on Sage, and Daisy felt like screaming at her. "Should we . . ." Daisy didn't want to finish the question: "Should we call the police?"

"The police," Paulina said. "For one thing, they're teenagers old enough to play hooky, and your daughter left a *note*. So the police won't give this the time of day. For another, my son is seventeen, and I don't want them getting the wrong idea."

"What wrong idea?" Daisy asked.

"That this is *his* plan."

"Maybe it is!" Daisy said harshly, closing her eyes, picturing Sage cuddled beside her on the loveseat, wanting her mother to play with her hair.

"No, Daisy. It is not! One thing I know about my son is he would not run away from home. Would not, unless someone was coercing him. If this isn't Sage's idea, I don't know what. So don't give me *that*. We're a close family! My son wouldn't just disappear." Paulina choked back a sob.

"I want to call the police," Daisy said with her eyes closed. She felt Hathaway take her hand. She had a new pain in her chest, from saying it out loud, the fact that she wanted to call the police, and from hearing Paulina Davis say with pure and total conviction that her son wouldn't just disappear. Jake's image flooded Daisy's mind.

Only three years old, her son had been strong and solid. He had the same dark hair and green eyes as his twin sister, a brilliant smile and an amazing laugh, a way of scrambling up to his mother's neck and hanging under her chin, refusing to be put down. He would laugh, his lips against her skin, and she would start to laugh too, as if his happiness and good humor were

20

catching. Oh, God, she had never thought he could just disappear. She had never thought she would look into her husband's eyes while he told her he'd lost their son. Jake had been missing, presumed dead, for thirteen years. And now Sage was gone, too.

Daisy dialed 911. When the operator answered, Daisy had to concentrate on not losing it. "My daughter . . ." she began.

"Yes?" the operator asked.

"Go ahead," Hathaway urged.

"My daughter's missing," Daisy said. "That is, she left a note. We had a fight, and she was very upset."

The operator directed her call to a detective. He gave his name, but Daisy didn't even hear it. She started talking right away. "My daughter is sixteen," she said, her throat aching, filled with relief at the sound of this anonymous voice that was going to find Sage, bring her back home.

"You say you had a fight? And she left a note?" the detective asked. "That's what you told the dispatcher?"

"Well, yes," Daisy began. "But —"

"This isn't unusual," the detective said in a calm voice. "It's a gorgeous day out, and she's probably playing hooky. Sixteen is prime time for that."

"I know," Daisy said. "I called the school, and she hasn't been there. But — it's not like Sage."

21

"She's a teenager," he said calmly. "They like to hang around the orchards, go pumpkin picking this time of year. Whole groups of them do it, every Halloween. You're the third mother to call this week."

"The third . . ."

"See?" he asked.

Daisy tried to breathe. She almost felt lulled by the officer's tone, his non-panic. What he said made perfect sense. Daisy herself had played hooky at sixteen. She had skipped school more than once, gone to the beach with Hathaway and their friends. But Sage's note was too abrupt. And besides, Daisy had been here before: with one of her children missing, everyone telling her to sit tight, be patient, wait for him to come home.

"Please," she said. "When you see the note she wrote —"

"She'll be home before dark," the officer said.

"How do you know?" Daisy asked, closing her eyes.

"Because kids are kids. You say you and she had a fight. If she's not there by suppertime, call us back. Okay?"

"Oh . . ." Daisy said, her heart skidding out of control. But she pulled herself together. "Okay," Daisy said, after another thirty seconds. She had to tell herself she was overreacting because of what had happened to one child thirteen years ago. Sage was emotional, dramatic, and sixteen. She would come home on her own.

The day passed slowly, and Daisy spent it working. Sunlight streamed through tall windows overlooking her yard. Prisms hung on fine threads, throwing tiny rainbows on the floor and walls. The spare room had two parts, front and back: Daisy worked in the darker back half, which those customers who knew about it called her magic cave.

Daisy made jewelry that brought people love. She had never set out to do it, and even now she didn't understand how it happened. As a girl she had enjoyed stringing beads and twisting wire. She would drill holes in pebbles, coins, and shells, link them together with pine cones and acorns. It was just a hobby, something to fit in after homework. She would give the pieces to her sister or their friends, and they would get boyfriends. She had traveled to Wyoming, in search of inspiration, and there she had met James.

"Mail's in," Hathaway said now. She had called her assistant at the shop, told her she wouldn't be in. She walked into the room with a handful of letters.

"Oh." Daisy hunched over her workbench. Her heart was beating too hard, and she knew it wouldn't settle down until Sage walked through the door. She heard Hathaway rip open an envelope and sigh as she read the letter inside.

"Here's another one," Hathaway said. "You've done it again. Want me to read it?"

"Okay," Daisy said, desperate to be distracted.

" 'Dear Ms. Tucker,' " Hathaway read. She had quit smoking recently, and her voice was rough and low. " 'I'm writing to tell you about the miracle you have brought to my life. Friends have told me about your necklaces, but I had to experience this myself before I would believe. For so long, I had been alone . . .' "

Sitting in the darkened cubicle, Daisy kept working. Her gooseneck lamp cast a circle of light. The surface was covered with stones, bones, silver, and gold. Gold dust stuck to her fingertips. She concentrated, carving a disc of cow bone to look like the face of an Indian ghost.

Making jewelry, she used myths, family stories, western and New England Indian lore in her work. Using sharp tools, she etched fine designs in the bone, filling them with black ink like tattoos or scrimshaw. She used dot, circle-and-dot, and concentric circle designs to symbolize love, eternity, and spiritual vision.

When she set the carved bone faces in eighteen-karat gold or sterling silver, strung them together with polished granite and tourmaline for a bracelet or necklace, they looked like parts of a totem pole connected by a gold chain.

"Bring her back," Daisy whispered to the bones. Sometimes customers wanted to heal broken relationships, win back husbands who had left, sweethearts who had walked away. Daisy would pray for their wishes, whisper their intentions as she carved the faces, filled the finely etched lines and dots with ink. But right

24

now, her thoughts were for Sage.

" 'I never thought it could happen to me,' " Hathaway continued reading. " 'I never thought my life could be like this. I look at Bill, and then I look at the sky, and it's like something I've never seen before. I don't think I'll take your necklace off for as long as I live.' " Hathaway folded the letter. She took her time smoothing out the stationery, fitting it back into the envelope, examining the postmark.

"They keep coming," Hathaway said.

Daisy squinted at the bone face she was carving. She knew her sister was pulling herself together. The letters really got to her. They got to Daisy, too. There were so many different kinds of love in the world, and everyone wanted it. To fall in love, to heal broken hearts, to bring families back together.

"You don't have customers," Hathaway said. "You have devotees."

Daisy shook her head.

"You okay?" Hathaway asked.

"I don't know," Daisy said. "I don't think so."

"She's coming home," Hathaway said. "This isn't like Jake."

She just hugged Daisy, and Daisy closed her eyes, thinking of the truth: that her three-year-old son had disappeared in a canyon, that her daughter had run away, that she and her children's father were divorced. She had a family of bone ghosts. *This isn't like Jake,* Hathaway had said.

"What if it is?" Daisy asked, afraid to open her eyes.

Daisy and Hathaway waited all day, until the school bus passed by and Sage didn't get off, until Daisy had called Amanda, Zoe, Robin, Cale, and Billy to ask if they had seen Sage or Ben, heard about any groups playing hooky at the orchard. No one had. Then they waited until suppertime. Sage had been gone for three meals: breakfast, lunch, and now dinner. Hoping that hunger would bring her back home, Daisy made Sage's favorite: tuna noodle casserole.

The kitchen smelled good. The October evening was still and cold. Opening the back door, Daisy gazed into the garden, through the pine trees to the bay. Trying not to think of that other waiting time, when the search parties had fanned out over the range and into the canyons, while she had stood on the front porch, in case Jake would somehow wander home. Daisy now imagined Sage hiding nearby, nursing her anger over the fight, over her mother's injustice. Smelling her favorite supper, she would finally come home.

"Are you going to call the police or am I?" Hathaway asked.

"Should I give her a few more minutes?" Daisy asked, looking at her watch. "Sometimes we don't eat until a little later . . ."

"It's getting dark," Hathaway said.

That did it.

# Chapter Two

"She's sixteen," Daisy told Detective Barbara LaRosa and her partner, Detective Adele Connelly. "This isn't like her. I know you probably see kids who do this all the time, leave notes and run away, but Sage isn't like that. She's never done it before."

They were standing in Daisy's kitchen. This time when Daisy had called 911, the officer had said someone would be right over.

"What's she like?" Detective LaRosa asked.

"Well," Daisy said, "she's incredible. She loves to write, essays and stories. Poems. She wants to be a writer —"

"What does she *look* like?"

"She's about five three. She weighs one hundred and fifteen pounds. She has reddish brown hair down to" — she touched her own shoulder and, again, her collarbone — "here. Her eyes are green. Hazel. More green than brown."

"In certain light," Hathaway said, "they're gold. She can look like a little cat sitting in the dark."

"Yes," Daisy agreed, seeing Sage sitting on a bench in the garden at twilight, writing in her journal, looking up at the sound of her mother's

27

footsteps. "They can be golden."

"She looks like her mother." Hathaway handed Detective LaRosa Sage's school photo. "Like Daisy did at her age. Very pretty."

"Yes, she is." The detective regarded the photo.

"We're alike in lots of ways," Daisy said.

"Emotional," Hathaway said. "Like opera."

Daisy couldn't deny it, picturing how quickly Sage's face revealed her feelings, the way joy registered in her eyes, the way sorrow showed in her lower lip. Knowing that she was the same way.

"What about her father?"

"He's not in the picture," Daisy said.

"May I see her room?" Detective LaRosa asked.

"Of course." Daisy's throat ached as she led the way.

Sage loved animals. She worried when she saw crippled children or blind people. Daisy gave her money every month to send to Save the Children, the organization that sponsored children of war and poverty. Beautiful music, especially opera or pop music with string sections, could make her cry. Daisy told Detective LaRosa all those things.

"She's at the top of her class," Daisy added. "She gets all A's." But as she spoke, she caught herself. Was that a different Sage? What about the grades slipping, her sudden disinterest in school?

Detective LaRosa was about fifty, with handsome gray streaks in her dark hair. She had deep-set eyes that seemed compassionate and alert, and she caught Daisy's hesitation.

"Any recent change in habits? Does she use drugs or alcohol?"

"She's very straight," Daisy replied. "She's totally against drinking and drugs. We talk about everything.

"She's a very cool kid," Daisy added, her voice catching. "She tolerates other people doing whatever they want, but she knows what's for her and what's not. Her schoolwork has slipped since the beginning of the year, but —"

"That's often a sign of drugs," the detective began. "Even the best kids —"

"Not Sage," Daisy insisted, shaking her head.

When they entered Sage's room, Daisy's knees went weak. Her daughter should be here right now, sitting at her desk, doing homework after dinner.

"She likes the Wild West," Detective LaRosa commented, gazing at the mountain posters, the elk antlers and everything hanging from them, the collection of arrowheads.

"She loves it," Daisy said.

"Why is that?" The detective was staring at the photo of red mesas against a bright blue sky. "Did you take a trip there once?"

"She was born in Wyoming," Daisy said. "We lived there until she was four years old, and we haven't been back since."

"Her father lives there," Hathaway added.

"You said he's 'out of the picture,' " Detective LaRosa said.

"We're divorced," Daisy said. "He lives on a ranch, and he sent her those antlers for her tenth birthday. She covers them with things like they're a Christmas tree." Stepping forward, she looked at the photo of James dangling from a blue ribbon. He was a stranger to her now, older, still lean and tan and unsmiling.

"That's him?" the detective asked.

"Her only photo of him," Daisy said. "He hates having his picture taken. She must have begged him — he sent it to her a couple of Christmases ago."

"They're in touch?"

"Not very much."

"He doesn't visit?"

"No."

Hathaway stepped forward, as if she sensed Daisy needed protection. Staring at James, Daisy's throat closed up. She felt tears coming, and she lowered her eyes. She had gone to Wyoming because she wanted to find inspiration in the wilderness. Instead, she had met James Tucker, a man with the wilderness inside him.

"Why hasn't he seen his daughter since she was four?" Detective LaRosa asked.

"Because he won't leave the ranch," Daisy answered. "And I wasn't going to send my daughter out to Wyoming alone."

"Blue booties?" The detective touched Jake's tiny knitted shoes.

"My son," Daisy explained. "He was Sage's twin, and he died when he was three."

The detective's head snapped up.

"How did he die?"

"We don't know," Daisy said quietly.

The detective waited.

"James — my husband — took him out riding. It was a roundup, lots of men. James, his father, and their foreman were there. He always took Jake with him — Jake loved it. He was a little cowboy, always wanted to be with his father. James put Jake down for one minute, told him to sit still and watch —" At the detective's expression, Daisy shook her head. "No — I know you think that was crazy. But we did it all the time. We lived on a ranch — there was always so much going on. We thought the kids were so lucky — all those wide-open spaces. The air was so clean, they loved the animals. Jake was such a good little boy. He'd do what he was told —"

"So, your husband told him to sit still," the detective prodded.

Daisy nodded.

"What happened next?"

Hathaway stepped closer. Daisy swallowed. The words were so hard to get out. "We don't know what happened next."

"Was there an investigation?" Detective LaRosa asked.

"Yes," Daisy said. "Oh, yes."

The canyon was vast, the natural dangers obvious and brutal, but the police had seemed to

31

count those out. They immediately focused their attention on James. Daisy thought of the detectives with their hard eyes, their suspicious voices. She was insane with worry, and they were treating her like the wife of a murder suspect. They kept James from joining the search party those first critical days, bombarding him with questions.

"They never found anything," Daisy said. "No sign of my son. The area where he'd been waiting was covered with prints — boots, horses — we couldn't find Jake's tracks at all. We had search parties, helicopters, a Shoshone shaman. The police questioned my husband for hours and hours —"

Detective LaRosa nodded. Everyone knew the father was the first suspect, no matter how much he — or the rest of the family — protested.

"By the time they let him go," Daisy said, spinning back, "he was like a tornado. He told me he wouldn't come home until he had Jake — he promised me. He went out searching." Daisy swallowed. "And I didn't see him again for fifteen days, until long after the search party quit. He was sick and dehydrated — his father and the foreman had to go find him, bring him home."

"And he didn't find Jake?"

"No."

"What about Sage? Where was she in all this?"

"With me," Daisy said, remembering how her daughter hadn't left her side all that time. How quiet the little girl had been, as if she'd sensed that her mother needed calm, that no question she might want to ask could be answered just then. Daisy had made a necklace for Sage that week, praying while she worked, sending all her love for Jake into the stones and bone. Sage wore it still: She never took it off.

"James will never leave Wyoming," Daisy said. "In case Jake comes back."

"Is there any reason to believe —" the detective started to ask.

Daisy shook her head. Hathaway's hand rested on her shoulder. Daisy stared at the detective, thinking of the things that had run through her mind during all these years of not knowing where her son had gone: buzzards, bears, coyotes, rattlesnakes. The fissures in the red rocks. Chasms and caves. The vast open space. The sound of his voice calling for help, no one hearing.

"There's animosity between the two of you?" the detective asked. "You and your ex-husband?"

"Maybe so. I'm not sure animosity's the right word," Daisy said, wondering what was.

Detective LaRosa nodded. She just stood there, examining the things on Sage's desk. She flipped through a pile of notebooks, looked in drawers. Opening a plastic film canister, she looked inside and sniffed. She touched the top of Sage's wooden box. Dark mahogany, it had a cowboy riding a bucking bronco carved into the lid. This was where Sage kept her jewelry, her ticket stubs, her father's notes — all her most important mementos. Daisy bit her tongue: She knew the detective was searching for drugs.

"This is beautiful." The detective held up a bracelet Daisy had given Sage last Christmas. She touched the delicate carving, examined the finely inked etchings. "Very unusual."

"Daisy made it," Hathaway said.

"I know your work." The detective smiled, glancing at Daisy. "My sister has a pair of your earrings. 'Moon Goddesses,' I think they're called."

Daisy nodded. She named all her pieces. The bracelet Detective LaRosa held in her hand was called "Pine Ghosts." It came from the voices Daisy heard whispering in the wind, rustling the pine boughs, saying the word "love" over and over, telling people to love their families. The pine ghost faces were wise and knowing, old women who had lived forever in the trees' bark and needles. Wherever Sage was right now, Daisy wished she had taken the pine ghosts with her for protection.

"What are these?" the detective asked, staring at a tiny series of concentric rings etched on the face of one of the ghosts. "My sister has them on her earrings, too."

"Just symbols," Daisy said.

"Daisy often uses circles in her work," Hathaway said, stepping in because Daisy was staring at the bracelet, momentarily unable to talk. "They're an ancient image of protection —

the clan gathering around to keep out intruders, evil spirits, wild animals . . ."

"Intriguing," the detective said.

"Just let her be safe," Daisy said out loud.

"Is there anything she always does, a place she always goes?"

"She loves nature," Daisy said. "She hikes, canoes . . . she knows all the parks. I've taken her camping in Vermont and New Hampshire. We've rented a cottage the last three summers in Maine."

"Where in Maine?"

"Near Mount Katahdin," Daisy said. She had chosen the wildest place she could find in New England, the closest in spirit to Wyoming. They had seen eagles, moose, and black bears. The roads were unpaved. The night sky was black velvet. The stars were great globes, low and luminous. Standing on the ramshackle porch while Sage slept inside, Daisy had talked to Jake, and she could swear she'd heard him talking back.

Detective LaRosa took more notes.

"She loves that spot," Hathaway said thoughtfully, as if she was considering the possibility of Sage having run away to Maine. She had come to visit last summer, and the three of them had spent five wonderful days together.

"It's so far," Daisy said. "She couldn't get there by herself —"

"Do you really mean that?" Hathaway asked kindly, and Daisy's eyes filled with tears, to think

35

of how resourceful her daughter was. Sage had been a Girl Scout for ten years. She could start a fire with two sticks, locate north without a compass, find her way home on an unmarked trail.

"Mount Katahdin," Detective LaRosa said. "What town's that near?"

"Millinocket."

"Tell me more about her." The detective sounded like someone who really cared, who really wanted to know.

"She worries about her weight," Daisy said. "That she doesn't look 'perfect.' She hated her braces when she had them. I made her a necklace when she was four, and she never takes it off. She has a birthmark on the top of her right thigh that her father said looks just like a mustang. She was thrilled. She used to say she wanted to be a cowgirl when she grew up."

"So did you," Hathaway said, smiling. Then, to the detective: "Daisy won a Nestlé's Quik contest when she was little — she got a red cowgirl outfit."

"What does her necklace look like?" the detective asked, ignoring the part about Daisy, writing down everything about Sage. Daisy liked that.

"It's long, down to here." Daisy touched her own breastbone. "It's a circle of bone set in white gold, with four gold nuggets dangling below on a white gold chain. I carved the bone on both sides, a two-sided face. The only one I've ever done."

"What's it called?" the detective asked, looking up.

" 'The Twins,' " Daisy answered.

She could hear the detective's pencil scratching on the paper, along with branches moving in the wind. The windows were open. The sun was down, and the birds had stopped calling. Daisy could picture Sage touching her necklace. She always kept the boy's face, her brother, turned to face her heart.

"Tell me about her boyfriend," Detective LaRosa said.

"His name is Ben Davis," Daisy told her. "They've been friends since Sage got to high school. He's a good kid —" Nothing like James, she was thinking. Not at all dangerous. Not a quiet cowboy with stormy eyes and a rock-hard stomach. Just a nice suburban kid who excels in science and plays the trumpet in band; no threat whatsoever to the future Daisy had in mind for Sage.

"A good kid," the detective repeated, writing.

"They're *both* good kids," Daisy continued, starting to feel better as she talked about them. "They went canoeing last night and lost track of the time. They were having an adventure! I lost my temper, pushed her too far. It's my fault. I've always been overprotective. That's all — she's . . ."

But Detective LaRosa was staring into the jewelry box. She pushed some rings and the pine ghost bracelet aside, the gold and silver jingling lightly. Daisy felt like shouting at her. There were no drugs to be found in there. Frowning, the detective removed something from under Sage's jewelry that looked like a white plastic Popsicle stick. At one end was a small square window, colored blue.

"Oh, no," Hathaway said.

Daisy's hand went to her mouth. She stared at the white stick. It was a home pregnancy test. She remembered as if it were yesterday. Daisy had used one herself, over sixteen years ago. Way out on that Tucker ranch, in the privacy of her bathroom, she had used the stick she'd bought at a drugstore in Dubois. Not wanting to get James's hopes up, she had been positive her missed period was a false alarm, just wishful thinking — but she had taken the test anyway.

"She's pregnant," Hathaway whispered.

"I can't think of that now." Daisy sobbed. "Just let her come home to me." She bowed her head, going back in time to Wyoming.

The way Daisy had found out she was pregnant with the twins had been by peeing on a white plastic stick, waiting for the little window to turn blue.

Blue as the big sky over the Wind River mountains, blue as the unknowable depths of James Tucker's eyes, blue as the ocean she had missed back home.

And as blue as the window of this other pregnancy test, the one Sage must have taken, the one that told Daisy Tucker the reason her sixteen-year-old daughter had run away.

# Chapter Three

James Tucker rode down the fingerbone ridge, dust swirling up from beneath the horse's hooves. A few stunted cedars clung to these red rocks, sloping down to the bare brown rangelands. The Wind River mountains rose around him, and he galloped through their purple shadows on his way home for supper.

He followed a dry creek bed over the barren desert-brown land. This was blood-soaked territory, the heart of Wyoming's cowboy, Crow, Shoshone, and soldier history, and James had never lived anywhere else. His mind was on cattle and water: All summer they'd had the worst, longest-lasting drought he'd ever seen. Here it was the middle of October, and the streambeds were as dry as they'd been in August. It had been a long day riding the range, and he was hungry.

Thousand-foot cliffs rose to his left. He swung through the dark canyon, where it was cool and lonely. The setting sun turned the rock pinnacles bloodred, but down here in the shade the summer heat dissipated. The horse ran fast and steady. They clambered up an incline, the trail wriggling across a narrow pass, emerging into the river valley.

The land was different here. The slow river carved sharp red cliffs, flanked on both sides by huge cottonwood trees and dry pastures. James had six miles to go, but he felt the hot wind in his face and knew he was close to home — the DR Ranch, named for his parents, Dalton and Rosalind.

Getting close, James felt his breathing change. His horse knew it, too. This was how it was to understand a bit of land, to be just as much a part of it as the red rocks and riverbeds. Newcomers never got that. Like the sheep owners who'd come in when his father was a child, ignoring prior claims of cattlemen, nearly ruining the basin land for cattle grazing. His grandfather had barely held on.

In Tucker lore, cattle were good and sheep were bad. Instead of a teddy bear or woolly lamb, James's father had given the twins toy brown cows the day they were born. James had told them bedtime stories about their great-grandpa slaughtering those overgrazing sheep, driving them straight over rimrock precipices. True tales: The Tuckers had defended this land against the sheepherding Rydells. His wife hadn't liked those stories much.

Daisy was a New Englander. She had the deep blue sea in her blood, and she didn't understand the measures people took to keep their land out here. James would take her on the most fantastic rides, showing her red rocks, searching for bones and gems to use in her jewelry. He had given her secret canyons, glowing skies, sagebrush trails, and ancient cave drawings. They'd given each other twins — Jake and Sage — and that had been enough to keep her out west awhile.

Some people were born home, James thought. They might move to the next valley or even another state, but it was another story to pick up and transplant themselves into a whole new landscape. Daisy had tried. She had found inspiration for her jewelry, and for a while she had seemed to find something larger — different or deeper — with James and his country.

But when the nightmare came, Daisy didn't have enough comfort inside her to withstand the loss of Jake, and she had to leave. This was the country that took her son. James couldn't blame her: New England was her home, just like Wyoming was his. Sometimes he imagined following her and Sage back east to the Connecticut shoreline, but that would be like trying to plant a cactus in an apple orchard. Wouldn't take. Besides, there were other reasons why James couldn't leave this land.

Jake was here. He was three when James had lost him. They'd ridden down to the spring grazing lands on a roundup, father and son in the same saddle. Twelve cowboys altogether had ridden along, plenty of eyes to keep watch on one tiny kid. Sage had cried because Daisy had wanted Sage to stay home with her. James had felt so bad that day, hearing his daughter wail as they'd galloped off, but soon he felt grateful. At least he had one child left alive.

They had never found Jake's body, so they'd never buried his bones. There wasn't a grave to visit. His spirit dwelled in the canyon, near the rock where James had told him to sit, in the thirty seconds he'd left him alone while he'd ridden off to rope a steer. After all this time, James knew Jake wasn't coming back, but he wasn't going to abandon his son to the canyon, with no one to look after him, no matter what.

The ranch buildings were visible now. James had a log cabin out back, but wanting to check on his father, he rode up the trail toward the big gabled stone house. The land was bone dry. He'd spent the day watching the sky, thunderheads forming without letting out any rain. Riding to the headwaters of the creeks that fed his ranch, he'd seen rocks that hadn't been above water in his lifetime. Tomorrow he'd go out to burn the irrigation ditches, ready to catch whatever rain might come.

Reining in his hard-ridden horse, he stepped down from the saddle and led him to the corral. He could smell Louisa's cooking. She wasn't quite his stepmother — she and Dalton had never seen fit to get married — but she'd lived with the old man for over twenty years. Louisa Rydell was as different from James's mother, Rosalind Tucker, as any woman could be. James had never been happy about the idea of seeing his mother replaced, but with his father losing ground, lately he'd been almost glad of Louisa's presence.

Slapping his hat back and forth across his chaps, he shook off the trail's dust. It covered his clothes, his skin, the back of his throat. His hands were brown and dry, and his fingers ached from holding the reins, not a lick of moisture in the air. He'd paid to have water trucked in, so the troughs were full. Bending over, he scooped up a careful handful of water. He drank one, soaked his neck with another. Locusts hummed in the trees, and some bird was squawking.

James knew all the wildlife, and he hadn't heard a bird like that before. It stopped him in his boots. Standing still, he looked around. Most birdsong came from the chaparral, and he turned to survey the dense, dry thicket of dwarf evergreens and cactus. But this song was coming from the ranch house, and it reminded James of an ancient sound, one he had rarely heard for over fifteen years.

After all this time, he still heard a baby crying every time he turned around. But two juncos flew out of the porch eaves, onto a cottonwood branch. They chattered noisily, dipping into the water hole, then flying back onto the porch. Shaking his head, James let out a big breath. Inside the house, he heard the radio playing and pans clattering. The cooking smells were strong.

"What the hell's that noise?" Dalton Tucker asked, walking out onto the porch. Small-framed, he had a limping, pigeon-toed gait. He had had polio as a child, and it left him with one leg shorter than the other.

"Birds, Dad."

"Building nests in the goddamn eaves? In October?"

"Beats me."

"Snowbirds, at that. In the middle of a drought. We're in for a bad winter. I'm telling you, son," the old man said, shaking his head, "the birds know. This dry patch'll look like child's play compared to what's coming. Snowbirds nesting on the porch . . . did you see the frost this morning?"

"I did."

"No water in the streams, but frost on the pumpkins. And birds in the eaves. It's gonna be a blizzard year. Mark my words — drifts up to the roof." Dalton coughed and walked over to the rail to spit.

Standing there, he looked confused. His face was red and leathery, as dry as beef jerky, and James pictured his eyes lively and laughing. That image — his spirited cowboy father — was most often in his mind these days. Dalton spit into the dirt again, then turned around. Seeing James, he jumped.

"Jesus, you scared me," Dalton said.

"Didn't mean to," James said slowly.

"What are you doing home?" Dalton Tucker asked, as if he was seeing James for the first time.

James just stood there. He was six inches taller than his father, his shoulders twice as wide.

Dalton squinted his blue eyes, as if he was trying to remember something, attempting to weave together the facts of James riding home, the time of day, and the snowbirds in the eaves. The more he thought, the more frustrated his expression became. James saw the clouds in his eyes, wondered what was going on in there.

"Suppertime, Dad," James said. The old man's face registered the memory, and James looked away just as he started to look confused again. "Where's Louisa?"

"Louisa?"

Again, James just waited. There'd been plenty of times he wished his father had forgotten all about Louisa Rydell, but right now it scared him. Dalton looked afraid, too. Fear always made him angry as a bear, flashing in his eyes and knotting his hands into fists. To cover himself, he always struck out.

"Why don't you speak plain English," Dalton snapped. "Don't talk gibberish when you know I don't understand. Start over, will you?"

"I asked you —" James began slowly.

"Goddamn it," Dalton said, sniffing. Inside, the cornbread was burning. The odor was sharp and sweet, like sugar turning to caramel: James ran past him, found the kitchen filled with smoke. A pan in the oven was on fire: James grabbed a mitt, reached inside, threw a flaming brick of cornbread into the sink.

In the next room, a child began to fret. Louisa sometimes baby-sat her daughter Ruthie's young girl, Emma. Swearing at himself, Dalton clomped out of the room to check on her. He must have been minding the stove, watching the girl, and forgotten both in the commotion of the bird.

"What's this? Where's Dalton?" Louisa Rydell asked, running in with an armful of sunflowers.

"Cornbread caught fire," James said, "looks like to me. You left Dad in charge of cooking and Emma?"

Louisa looked from James to the black pan, and her face fell. Handing James the flowers, she began to scrape the charred and sodden bread into the garbage.

"You lose that tone with me, James Tucker," Louisa said. "I just stepped out to pick some flowers."

"Yeah, well, you shouldn't let her out of your sight," James said sharply. "Not for a minute. The house could have burned down."

"You telling me how to be a grandmother?"

"My father can't take care of himself, much less a baby."

"Now listen, you —" Louisa began, her eyes blazing.

"Forgot, that's what I did." Dalton came to the door with Emma on his hip. She was a sweet little girl, all pink and blond. Smiling in Dalton's arms, she seemed unperturbed by the fire and fight. "Goddamn it. Smelled the cornbread burning and forgot I had this little angel to look after."

James didn't say anything. His father had forgotten the sequence, but it hardly seemed important right now. Emma held Dalton's ears, trying to look him straight in the eyes. *That's how it used to be with Sage,* James thought. She had loved her grandfather, and he'd adored her.

"Don't worry, darling," Louisa said. She was still a fantastic-looking woman, tan and tall. She wore a full denim skirt, lavender washed-silk blouse, and purple boots. Silver earrings dangled, and turquoise beads hung around her neck. Her auburn hair hung in a long braid down her back. Raising her head, she flashed a big smile to reassure Dalton Tucker.

"No?" Dalton asked, enthralled by Emma. She was about two and a half, as fair as Sage had been dark, and James wondered whether he still missed his granddaughter. Whether he still remembered her . . .

"Don't worry about a thing," Louisa said, her voice full of love, throwing a hard look at James. "We're all here. Emma's fine, you're fine, we're all fine."

"Could've been a disaster," Dalton said, stroking Emma's blond head. "The ~~god~~damn house could have burned down. This little one . . ."

James walked away. He had ten thousand head of cattle on the spring range, thirsty and in need of water. Why wait till tomorrow? Tonight he was going to ride back, start burning irrigation ditches. He liked Emma, but right now he

didn't want to watch his father pouring attention on someone else's kid. The Tuckers had had two of their own, once upon a time. . . .

Maybe he could go out and catch some rain in areas he hadn't gotten to yet. Ready new ditches, burn away the summer's growth of briars and sagebrush to clear the way. Dig out more rocks, roll away bigger boulders, watch for the rattlesnakes that multiplied in drought summers. His irrigation shovel was sharp, and he hoped he'd hear the rattle before he felt the strike.

Ranchers lived in a perpetual state of hope. They hoped for rain during dust season, dry spells after deluges. They hoped for smart horses that didn't need much spurring, good stock dogs to heel the cows. James knew something he hoped most men would never find out: Men who lost their sons didn't have much left in the way of hope. Hope to James was scarcer than this season's rain. But when the skies finally opened up, damned if he wouldn't be prepared. Then he thought of what his father had said about blizzards coming, and shook his head.

Maybe Daisy had known what she was doing, leaving. Wyoming was one goddamned hard place to try to live.

# Chapter Four

The train jolted along the tracks, making Sage feel as if she was going to throw up again. It took all her concentration not to. Staring at Ben helped. Ben loved her, and they were going to be together forever. He had said so, and he kept saying so. Sage loved Ben so much. She could hardly believe he was her boyfriend. So many girls at school liked him, but it was Sage he wanted to be with.

Their hands were touching. Well, their fingers, actually. The tips of their index fingers. Ben was asleep, lying in his bedroll on the hard wood floor, facing Sage. The boxcar was dark and cold. It wasn't heated, and last night the temperature had been so low they could see their breath. Sage stared at their fingertips, as if she could actually see the connection she had with Ben, keep it as solid as it was in that moment, preserve it forever.

"Oh!" The word just popped out of her mouth as a terrible wave of nausea went through her.

"Huh?" Ben asked, waking right up. He rubbed his eyes with one fist, just like a very small boy. "What's wrong — you sick again?"

Sage nodded miserably.

Ben linked his fingers with hers, his eyes filled with sympathy. Sage knew he was concerned about her, but there were so many other things to be worried about, too: their mothers, missing school, having to ration their water, being cold, being railroad stowaways.

"If only the train wasn't so bouncy," she said.

"It's pretty weird without windows," he said. "Even I feel kind of sick."

"Bet you wish you were safe and warm at home," she said, afraid he'd say yes.

"Coming was my idea," he reminded her.

Sage wanted to smile, but she felt too sick. Ben amazed her. When she had tried to say good-bye to him, he had refused to let her go alone. She had never thought she was very pretty, wonderful, the kind of girl someone would want to be with. Her mother always praised her, told her to be confident, but no matter how much Sage wanted to believe her, she couldn't. If she was so great, why would her father stay so far away?

"Oh," she moaned again, holding her stomach.

"Hang on." Ben stood up. "I'll see where we are."

She nodded, watching him go to the door. He couldn't help her nausea, but she could feel him wanting to do something. They were in the seventeenth car of a freight train, chugging west through New York State. Their car was carrying bins of machine parts manufactured in New London, Connecticut, and bound for Boise,

Idaho. Sage had checked and rechecked the destination labels, and she could smell the grease the parts were packed in, heavy and sweet as old perfume.

Sage and Ben were heading for Wyoming, to see Sage's father. They had to go somewhere. Sage had vague memories of the ranch being huge, endless, with barns and cabins everywhere. Even if her father didn't want any part of her, he could let her and Ben stay in a cabin hidden off in the mountains till the baby was born.

"Can't see too much," Ben called, peering through the narrow gap in the sliding door. The car was old, made of wood and iron. People had carved their initials in the panels. "Fields and trees covered with a little snow, or maybe just frost. Looks like farm country, haystacks everywhere."

"Are we still heading west?"

"Yep. Following the sun," Ben said, coming back to hold her. He was an Eagle Scout with many badges, as knowledgeable and comfortable in nature as anyone Sage knew.

"Good." Sage leaned against his thin chest.

It had been her idea to jump this train. When she was little, after she and her mother had moved back to Connecticut, her mother had told her stories of the Old West. Even though Sage was so young, she had noticed that all her mother ever talked about was the place they'd just left. But the stories had made her feel closer to her father, so she'd never said a word. They were about cattle drives, roundups, square dances, and powwows. They told of cowboys, cowgirls, medicine men, very good guys and very bad guys, and hoboes who rode the rails.

This train line ran all along the shoreline, right through Silver Bay, and from the time Sage could remember, she had imagined becoming a hobo, hopping a freight back to Wyoming to see her father. If people could do it in the olden days, why not now? Sage had dreamed of going so many times over the years, not because she didn't love her mother, but because she needed her father: hearing that long train whistle leaving Silver Bay in the middle of the night, holding on to the ancient dream of being her father's daughter again.

But even Sage had been shocked by how simple getting aboard actually was. Six cars had been standing behind the old depot. With Ben hiding behind the station, Sage had watched men loading crates with forklifts, and she'd asked straight out which ones were heading west.

"This one, little lady." One old codger had laughed, spitting tobacco juice. "Why, you want to make your way to Hollywood?"

"No, I'm just doing a report for social studies," Sage had replied.

"Good for you," the man had said, nodding encouragingly. "What on?"

"Freight trains," she'd answered. "Where they

53

go, how long it takes."

"Well, this car you asked about," he began, "heading out to Boise, Idaho, with a load of engine parts. Later today the old 4:52 is gonna swing down from Worcester, and these cars are gonna hook aboard. It'll take around a week, going straight through Chicago and over the Great Plains, through the Rockies . . . engine parts, limestone, traprock, and fish meal. Wish I was going for the ride."

Sage had been leaning on her bike, her hair in braids, trying to look younger than sixteen so he wouldn't guess her motives. She knew the man was about her grandfather's age, and she listened to him tell her to work hard in school, that trains were ten times better than trucks, that if she wanted a lesson on cross-country transport, he was her man. He said he'd come right to her school and lecture to her whole class. Thanking him, Sage had ridden away.

She had circled back, and while the men were taking their coffee break, she and Ben had wheeled their bikes right up the ramp they'd left in place. They had knapsacks full of supplies, bedrolls, Ben's tent, and their bikes. Stowing everything had been no problem: The boxes were stacked four high, creating instant hiding places. She and Ben had curled up in the dark, listening to the men talk when they finished loading the car, waiting until 4:52, feeling the ground shudder as the train started to move.

"Third period," Ben said now, checking his

watch. "I'm missing history. Good."

"We'll see more history than you can imagine," Sage said, trying to make him feel better. She knew he liked school, but she was thinking of the tales about cowboy and Shoshone battles fought right on her family's land. Her father sent her arrowheads he found on the ranch, rising through the soil in the paddocks and corrals like ghosts with stories to tell.

"Yeah?" Ben asked, kissing her lightly on the lips.

"Yeah." Sage closed her eyes so he wouldn't see them fill with tears. She didn't know what she was doing. Sixteen and six months pregnant: This seemed to be someone else's life. Just three years ago she'd gotten her first period, and here she was ruining two futures.

"Do you think our mothers got the letters yet?" she asked.

"They will today."

"I'm sorry I made you leave home," she said. "Leave school."

"I don't want you to go alone," he said. "And I wasn't going to stick around to hear my mother's shit about you being pregnant. My dad got his girlfriend pregnant, and that's why they had to get married so fast, why I had to go to Boston in August for their wedding. My mom talks about it so much, you'd think it was her about to have the baby. I don't want to lay this on her, too."

Sage nodded, wishing he hadn't said "lay this on her, too." She let him kiss her some more,

55

even though she still felt sick. She didn't want him to notice the panic in her eyes, certain it must show.

He loves me, she told herself. She wished he'd say it again. He hadn't spoken the words enough that day. Sometimes he didn't need to: Sage just knew. They had met during Sage's freshman year, but they had fallen in love thirteen months ago, when they had crossed paths on a mountain hike. Ben had slipped away from his friends to follow her.

*It was meant to be,* Sage told herself, then and now. *We were made in heaven.* Way up on that mountaintop, that very day, they had kissed. Ben had taken her hand, and their fingers had interlocked. Their hands had been a perfect fit, and so had their hearts. Ben joked that they had never once had a date. Although they went many places together, there had never been the usual nervous phone-calling, waiting and wondering, awkward silences. Their time together flowed naturally; it was the hours spent apart that felt unreal.

"Touch me," she whispered now, her eyes filling with tears.

"Sage," he whispered back, taking her in his arms. The embrace unlocked her heart, and Sage started to sob.

"I'm sorry," she cried. "So sorry, Ben."

"For what?" he asked. "I love trains."

She laughed, choking on her tears.

"I do," he continued. "My cousin had this

whole model train setup when we were little, and I was so jealous, I took a big section of his track and hid it in his garage."

"But you didn't want to quit school just to take a train ride."

"No, but I wanted to be with you," he whispered into her ear. The feeling of his warm breath made her shiver, and she pressed harder into his chest. He stroked her back, making all her fear drain away.

They had been virgins when they met. Sage had always wanted to save herself for marriage, to wait until she and the love of her life made promises to be together forever. Ben had felt the same way. They told each other last Christmas, lying in each other's arms on an old mattress in the attic of Ben's house.

"But you're the love of my life," Ben had said, smoothing Sage's hair back from her eyes.

"And you're mine," she had whispered.

Even now, feeling him push the hair back from her face as he kissed her forehead, cheeks, and nose, she knew those words were true. Last Christmas, knowing they were years too young to get married, they had decided to make love. Their love was real. It was building so fast, they couldn't keep up with it.

The time came: during school vacation, during the week between Christmas and New Year's. They were so excited, so positive of their love. Taking off their clothes in Ben's attic, with his mother at work, they had all the time in the world. Sage had loved the way their skin felt, so hot under the thick quilt, as if their bodies had been born to be together.

Ben had bought condoms. Ripping open the foil package, unrolling the latex sheath, had made them laugh. What business did foil and latex have under the covers of their magic bed? Sage and Ben loved nature, and the coming together of their bodies seemed pure and right. Condoms got in the way.

They used them for a while. Ben bought them at the drugstore. He kept them in his wallet, along with his driver's license and high school ID. Other boys in school carried them as badges, proof of having sex. Not Ben. He considered condoms private, personal, rude but necessary. And then, one day last spring, he and Sage had made love without putting one on. The sensation had been incredible, intense, so different from anything they had ever felt before: heat, skin, dark wetness, passion.

"Too many clothes," Sage whispered now, jolting along in the train, wishing she and Ben could be under the covers of their magic bed, skin touching everywhere, their hearts beating together.

"I know," Ben said.

"I want to feel you closer," she said.

"Me, too," he said. Unzipping her jacket slightly, he slid his arms inside. She still had on layers of shirts and sweaters, but it was better than nothing. Sage craved more contact, just as she needed to hear him say he loved her. More and more, she needed his reassurance, his closeness, his words, his body.

"Do you —" she started to ask.

"Do I what?"

*Love me?* she wanted to whisper, but she stopped herself. She felt needy and pathetic. Hadn't he just told her that morning? How many times did he have to say the words in order for her to be convinced?

It was so hard to believe that people's love for each other could last. Just look at her parents — they had been so madly in love. She could tell by the pictures, the way her mother talked, the secrets her aunt had told her — and for the past thirteen years, they'd been apart for good.

Surreptitiously, she touched the spot between her collarbones. Slipping her fingers under her shirt, she felt for her two-faced necklace. There was love in the stones and bone; there was power in all the jewelry her mother made. Her mother said she didn't know why, but she couldn't deny it. She had taught Sage never to be falsely modest. If you had a gift, you had to bring it forth, not pretend it didn't exist. And her mother had told her there was more power and love in Sage's necklace than any other she'd ever made.

Sage wondered. With all her problems, she couldn't deny that she had love. Ben was with her, wasn't he? She had a wonderful aunt, a grandfather and step-grandmother in Wyoming, but what about her father? Cards and letters and boxes of arrowheads were one thing, but why wasn't he sending her plane tickets, begging her to come out? And all Sage and her mother did these days was fight. The sudden thought of her mother was so strong, so vivid, Sage actually swooned.

She nearly passed out, but instead she knew she was going to be sick. Tearing herself from Ben's arms, she flew across the car. She retched, holding her stomach, throwing up into another plastic bag, one from a roll she had in her knapsack, being as totally prepared as a Girl Scout on the run was supposed to be. Sage couldn't stop the tears rolling down her face.

*Mom,* she thought. This was the first time in her entire life that Sage had ever gotten sick without her mother there to hold her head. Why couldn't it be simple like before? Why couldn't she have stayed a child? Couldn't she be her mother's little girl and have Ben at the same time?

"You okay?" Ben asked gingerly, from across the swaying car.

"I'm fine," Sage called back, leaning against a crate of nuts and bolts. She twisted the plastic bag, placed it carefully inside another. There was a trapdoor in the middle of the car. She and Ben had opened it, pulling back the thick bolt, watching the tracks fly by underneath, needing to know they had an emergency escape hatch. But she felt too weak to pull it open right now.

She found a small hole in the corner of the car,

where the wooden floor met two walls. The hole was ragged, as if a rat had once gnawed its way through. Careful not to tear the bag, Sage pushed it out onto the tracks. She felt bad about littering.

She cared about the land. She had distant memories of her father teaching her to respect wildlife, to exist alongside other living creatures. He had built her a bird feeder, and she would sit on his shoulders to fill it every day. Touching her two-sided necklace again, she thought of her twin brother. Jake had loved the land so much, he had wandered off into it forever.

"Jake," she whispered.

That had been her first word, her brother's name. Most babies said "Mommy" or "Daddy" first, but Sage believed that all twins called for each other before anyone else. She touched his face — the tiny eyes, nose, and mouth her mother had carved, smooth against her skin — and said a prayer.

She didn't want to be running away from home, but she had to. The other night, her mother had been so crazed, so furious, just because she'd fallen into a river. She had called her "slutty," just for staying out late with Ben. How would she feel when she found out Sage was going to have a baby? Sage couldn't hide it much longer.

She had thought of the trains going by, her mother's stories about people riding from town to town, and Sage had known she had to head west. She had left that stupid note, afraid that if she took time to write any more, she'd lose her nerve and stay.

Pedaling her bike through the moonlit streets, her eyes swollen from crying, she had felt an odd sense of relief. At least she wouldn't have to see her mother's face once she realized what a horrible girl she'd been. Heading over to Ben's to say good-bye, she had climbed up the stone chimney to his bedroom window. And she had been so surprised, happy, and guilty to hear he was coming with her. Love was one thing; sacrificing high school, his home, his family was another.

Sage wished she wasn't pregnant, but she was. She had a new baby growing inside her. It was going to change everything; it already had. When she'd missed her first period six months ago, she had thought it was stress over school. When she'd missed her next one, she'd blamed it on her new diet. She had thought getting sick every morning had to do with nervousness about Ben, wanting to keep him so badly it was tearing her up inside.

Morning sickness was supposed to last only three months. For Sage, it had been going on for nearly the whole time. She knew some of it had to do with guilt and anxiety, keeping this secret from her mother, living in a constant state of hiding: the sounds and smells and fears and her size. She had started showing, her belly popping out so far that even her biggest jeans wouldn't fit. Her mother hadn't said anything, but one morning Sage had found the raisin bread and ice cream gone, replaced by whole wheat bread and fat-free yogurt.

So Sage needed a lot of prayers. She said one now, to her brother Jake. With the train rattling west, with her boyfriend anxiously waiting across the dark, hot car, she touched her twin's carved face and prayed her heart out:

"Let me have a boy," she said in the tiniest voice.

Her brother had been lost in a canyon, and her father had disappeared from Sage's world. Even before her mother had made the decision to move east, her father was gone. Sage had a long memory, and she remembered the day her big, wonderful cowboy father had become a ghost.

For years, Sage had prayed for Jake to return. If he did, maybe her father wouldn't stay a prisoner on his ranch. He told her he was herding cows, growing feed, but Sage knew otherwise: Her father was riding trails, scouring the long hills, searching for the little boy he had lost.

"A boy," Sage prayed, touching her belly with one hand and her necklace with the other. "Let it be a boy."

"What?" Ben asked. "I can't hear you."

"Nothing," Sage replied from across the car. "I'll be right there." She stayed where she was, crouched in the corner, concentrating with all her might on the medallion she held in her hand. She could feel the small bone face pressing hard into her palm, and her lips kept moving in prayer.

Maybe if she brought a boy into her family, everyone could be happy again.

# Chapter five

The morning after she'd found Sage gone, Daisy stood on the back porch watching gold leaves shower down from the birch trees on the hill. They sparkled in the shadows, a constant flow of tiny leaves falling down to the cold ground. She hadn't slept much. Now, as she stared at the leaves, she thought of Sage out there in the world.

The sugar maple at the end of the driveway had turned scarlet, as bright as Daisy had ever seen it. The colors were late this fall, owing to an especially cool, rainy summer. She and Sage waited for "the peak" every year: the day when the fall colors were the brightest, the most spectacular. She held herself tighter. Today was the peak, and Sage wasn't here to see it, and the sharpest pain she'd ever felt stabbed Daisy in her chest.

"It's cold out here." Hathaway came to stand beside her sister. "What are you doing without a sweater on?"

"I'm warm enough," Daisy said.

Hathaway took her hands and rubbed them. They were numb and stiff, and Daisy hardly noticed her sister's warm fingers, the gentleness with which she put her arm around Daisy's shoulders and led her through the kitchen door.

"Where is she?" Daisy asked. "I can't stand not knowing, Hath. What if she's cold?"

"She's taking care of herself," Hathaway said. "That's what this is all about. She had to run away so she could figure out what she's going to do. When she's clearer, she'll come home."

"But where *is* she?" Daisy asked, feeling thick, not hearing. She had called the ranch to ask James if he had heard from her, but the telephone had just rung and rung. He didn't have an answering machine, but someone — Dalton, Louisa — should have been there. "I thought maybe she'd try her father. Whenever she's this mad, she talks about going to him —"

"She wouldn't go to him right now," Hathaway said gently.

"Because she's pregnant," Daisy said, holding her head in her hands.

"Yes," Hathaway said.

How had Daisy not known? She and Sage had always had such a strong connection, sometimes Daisy would know what was happening before Sage told her. The night Sage had come down with chicken pox, Daisy had walked into her dark bedroom and known that when she turned on the light she would see spots. The time Sage had rescued a skier caught in the rope tow at Sugardust Mountain, Daisy had had a premonition of her saving a boy's life.

"I wish she knew she could have told me,"

Daisy said. "I wish she didn't think she had to go off on her own to figure it out."

"She's so independent," Hathaway said. "It's a good thing. I'm telling you, she'll be back any minute now. What she's doing is like Outward Bound. Of the emotions, you know? Testing her own limits. I wish I'd been more like her. And you —"

"Me?" Daisy stared out the window.

"You paved the way for her," Hathaway said. "Going out west by yourself, making your way cross-country, finding new ideas for your work. She's your daughter, and she wants to live up to your life. She wants to live adventurously."

"But I wasn't adventurous." Daisy watched the driveway, wanting to see that brown head bobbing along the boxwood hedge, just like the thousands of other times Sage had come home to her. Then, turning to face her sister, she said, "I was scared of everything."

Daisy and Hathaway had been raised by quiet parents. Their world had been books and stories. Their father had been a drama professor and their mother an English teacher — soft, gentle, and as eccentric as a person could be who'd died as young as she had, at thirty-six. She had named her daughters after Anne Hathaway, Shakespeare's true love, and Daisy Buchanan of *The Great Gatsby*. There hadn't been much room for adventure in their scholarly household.

"Being scared of everything makes some people brave," Hathaway said. "You went out

67

west because otherwise you might have been too afraid ever to leave home."

"How do you know?"

"Because I never left," Hathaway said. She brought her fingers to her lips, as if there might still be a cigarette in them, and when she looked away, she had tears in her eyes. She was big and tall, with a brassy Broadway voice like some of the actresses their father used to teach about, but inside she was the most gentle and timid soul around. "She's full of fire," Hathaway continued. "We couldn't hold her back even if we wanted to."

"I've always tried to teach her to trust herself," Daisy said. "Trust her instincts, her good sense. When we lost Jake, I was so —"

"I know." Hathaway held her tighter.

"— so afraid that Sage would see the world as a bad place. Full of dangers."

"You've protected her, too," Hathaway said. "It's a balance . . ."

"But she's pregnant," Daisy said, the shock hitting her again. "She's missing and she's pregnant."

The mail truck pulled up, and the letter carrier climbed out. He began stuffing envelopes into the box by the road, and Hathaway gestured for Daisy to wait. Daisy was grateful. She wanted to pick up the phone if it rang. She watched her sister walk down the driveway, exchange a few words with the mailman, begin flipping through the letters and catalogues. Hathaway had been walking slowly, head down, but suddenly she began to run. The other envelopes fluttered to the ground as Hathaway held one out in front of her.

Daisy knew even before she saw: Sage's handwriting. Hands shaking, she tore open the blue envelope.

*Dear Mom,*

*I'm sorry I worried you so much. Ben and I didn't mean to upset you with staying out late and tipping over the canoe. I never want to upset you. But I love him. I know you say I'm too young to know, but I do anyway. I love him like you loved Dad and don't say about the divorce because that was just because of the tragedy. Because of Jake. When we capsized last night, Ben saved me. He swam right over and pulled me out. Not that I wasn't swimming fine myself, but I thought you'd like to know that he put me first. He always does, and I do the same with him. That's how love should be.*

*We're running away. Don't worry about school. This is the part that's hard to write. We're going to have a baby. I can almost see your face. You're mad. I know, and I'm sorry. I wish I could take it back, or I mean, turn back time. We are together, and that's what matters. I'll go crazy if I stay here. I will. In fact, I almost am already. Right now, just writing you this note, I feel dizzy, as if I'd just eaten pencil lead. I'm dying of love for Ben, Mom, and we have to be*

*together. He's dying, too. Don't worry. I'll call
and write a lot.*

*Love, Sage*

"Oh, God," Daisy said, when she'd read it
through a second time.

"Where's it postmarked?" Hathaway asked,
checking.

"Silver Bay. She must have mailed it before
she left."

"She's smart, our baby." Hathaway sounded
almost admiring.

Daisy stared at the back of the envelope.
There, pressed into the paper, were the imprints
of two faces. They were almost invisible, like
ghosts staring out of the trees. Daisy could make
out the eyes and mouths she had once carved
into a disc of cow bone; she could see which was
the boy's face and which was the girl's.

Touching the spot where Sage had pressed her
necklace into the paper sent electricity through
Daisy's body. She closed her eyes and let the
current flow, and when the telephone rang she
knew it wasn't Sage. Caressing the imprints of
her children's faces, her fingertips tingled and
burned. The phone rang again, and Hathaway
hurried to answer it. Her voice drifted across the
kitchen.

When Hathaway turned around, Daisy felt
calm. She opened her eyes and saw tears brim-
ming in Hathaway's light blue eyes.

"They have a clue," Hathaway said, a hopeful,

70

terrified smile reaching from ear to ear. Her lower lip trembled as she spoke. "That was Detective LaRosa, and she said they questioned some men who work at the railroad depot. A girl who looks like Sage was asking questions about some freight cars, about which ones were going west."

"Going west —"

"She asked about the train's route, the man said."

"She wants her father," Daisy said. "She's going to James."

Ben had watched his mother's cat circle round and round just before she had kittens, building a nest out of scraps of paper towels pulled from the garbage, old socks dragged down from the bedrooms, the chamois Ben used to polish his mother's car. Sage was acting just like that now.

She was pacing around the boxcar, tidying up their sleeping area, plumping up their bedrolls, trying to make a nest from a bundle of rags she'd found in a wire basket. From his seat on a crate off to the side, Ben watched her and wished she would stop moving.

"Sage, hey. Come over here."

"In a second," she said. "This floor's so hard — maybe you'll sleep better if I pile up some of these old cloths under your bedroll."

"Don't worry about it." Ben yawned again, wishing he hadn't told her he couldn't sleep. Whenever he mentioned any discomfort, any

71

problem, Sage always tried to fix it. He'd been amazed, at first, that anyone would be so concerned about his comfort. Back in Silver Bay, when things were still normal, she would always give him the best seat at the diner, buy him cranberry muffins from the bakery, sew buttons back on his shirts, draw him cards and write him poems.

But now he wished she'd just stop. It was making him crazy, watching her try to improve something that couldn't be fixed. She could pile a thousand rags — calling them cloths only made it worse — on that hard, cold floor, and he still wouldn't be comfortable. He was sore and hungry, a thousand miles from home and getting farther away every minute.

"Sage, will you stop?"

She turned to look at him. She'd been smiling, her freckled face radiant as she tried so hard to please him, but at his sharp tone, her face fell. He wished he could say it again, take the impatience out of his voice, put the smile back on her face.

Crushed, she knelt down. She pretended to be plumping up his pillow, but she was crying. Ben could tell by the way her shoulders were quaking. Sliding off the crate, he went to her, wrapped her in his arms. Her sobs were silent, the tremors running through her body the only sign that something was wrong.

"Let's go back," he whispered into her ear. "This is too much for us." *Too much for me*, he thought.

"I just wanted" — she gulped — "to make your bed a little softer." As if she hadn't even heard what he'd said. Ben held her tighter and gave her a small shake. He had fallen in love with Sage last year. Sage had been climbing a rock face, green eyes narrowed in concentration as she'd gripped each crevice, found each toehold. Ben had gone after her, surprised by how hard it was to catch up. They had paced each other the last twenty yards, and when they'd reached the top, they'd lain on their backs in the sun. Kissing her had been as natural as his next breath.

"We should go home," Ben said.

"I can't."

"Your mother won't be mad." Ben thought of his own mom. She'd been so disappointed in his last grades, the fact he'd been missing soccer games. She wanted him to go to Trinity, her father's college, and they had an appointment with the admissions office next week. "Not for long."

"But we're going to live on the ranch," Sage said. "You, me, and the baby."

Ben held her tight, pressing his lips against her neck. His heart was pounding hard. When she'd come to his house in the middle of the night — just thirty-six hours ago — he had freaked when she'd said she was leaving. Being with Sage made him do things he'd never done before — his feelings for her were like a whirlwind inside his body, slamming him in and out of situations he couldn't believe were real.

73

But now, after a day and a half in a sour-smelling boxcar, reality was waking him up. Sleepless all night, he knew he couldn't keep this up. Sage was sick constantly. She was trying hard to make everything seem fun and adventurous, but she couldn't manage to disguise the fact that they were tossing away their lives. Ben had college in his future. He wanted to be a geologist, study the rocks he'd climbed on his hikes. Being cooped up on the freight train was making him lose his mind.

"The ranch is beautiful," Sage said. "The Wind River mountains are all around. We can ride horses to the summit and see forever."

"You haven't even seen your father in all this time." Ben wanted to talk some sense into her, make her decide to turn around on her own. "How do you know he'd let you stay? Why do you think this'll be any easier for him than for your mom?"

"I was born there," Sage said. "Me and my brother. My father would never kick me out."

"Then why haven't you ever seen him?" Ben asked softly, not to be mean, but to make her face reality, get her to see the truth and not just how she wished it was.

"He's keeping watch." Sage started to cry again. "In case my brother ever comes back. It's not that my father doesn't want me, it's that my mother would never let me go . . ."

"Sssh," Ben said. "It's okay."

Ben stroked her hair, wishing she would calm

down. He knew about mothers hating fathers: His own mother despised his father so much, she'd get bright red and start spitting any time his name came up. He thought of his baby, growing inside Sage, and he wondered whether someday the baby would say the same thing of him and Sage.

Because Ben couldn't do this.

He loved Sage, loved her still, even though she was acting wild and talking crazy, even though her hair was dirty and her belly was round under her baggy brown wool sweater, even though she smelled like barf. But Ben wasn't going to live with her on the ranch in Wyoming. He had made up his mind, he realized, sometime during the night before.

He'd get her as far as he could, put her into the hands of her father, then call his mother to send him the airfare home. It made him sick to know he'd gotten her pregnant. He had hurt her already, and he was going to hurt her worse: That dream of her, him, and the baby on the ranch wasn't going to come true.

The thought sent a shiver through his body, and Sage felt it.

"Are you cold?" she asked, pulling her head back.

"No, I'm fine."

"Are you sure?" She rubbed his forearms. "Because I have an extra sweater on. I'm boiling hot, you can have it —"

"I'm fine, Sage," he said again, trying to keep

the weariness out of his voice. It tired him out to have her trying to make him so happy all the time. Especially because he knew that before too many more days, he was going to let her down. He thought of library books, soccer balls, milk shakes. He thought of cheerleaders calling their stupid cheers, teachers yelling for quiet in the halls. He heard his mom's voice asking him whether he wanted pepperoni or sausage on their pizza.

Ben Davis thought of all those normal things, and then he looked around the dark freight car and realized that all he'd had to eat for nearly two days was beef jerky and gorp. He knew that this wasn't his real life, that Sage Tucker would never be his wife, that he thought of the child inside her as a mistake, not someone he wanted to live on a ranch with. Holding the trembling girl in his arms, he still felt love, and in that moment Ben learned something terrible: that love wasn't always enough.

# Chapter Six

The bar was dark and smoky, and Loretta Lynn was singing on the jukebox. Elk horns hung from every single inch of the wall, and license plates from all fifty states dangled by wires. James stood alone, drinking a beer. The couple beside him was fighting, snarling like wildcats. Wilton Stickley, a rancher from down south, had laid his health insurance card on the bar, atop his pile of money.

"What're you doing there, Wilton?" James asked. "Planning on getting carted off to the hospital tonight?"

"Nope." Wilton smoothed down his bushy mustache. "Got my reasons."

James nodded. He had come to the Stagecoach Tavern that night to drink beer and get away from his own thoughts. Lately his mind had been a bad neighborhood, dangers lurking in every corner. Blame, guilt, resentment, and recriminations. Worrying about the herd not having enough water got him thinking about others he'd let down, failed to provide for.

A young woman James hadn't seen before walked over, stood between him and Wilton. She had strong shoulders under her fringed suede jacket, a long blond braid hanging halfway down her back. When she stood close, James could smell her perfume, and he found himself leaning closer so he could smell it more.

"Hi," she said.

"Hi," James said.

"Buy you a beer?" Wilton asked.

The woman smiled, turned back to James. Although he hadn't made the offer, he pushed five dollars across the bar and told Joe to pour her a draft. She took the mug in her hands and took a long drink. Her eyes fell on Wilton's insurance card, and she gave Wilton a closer look. Life was hard out here, and ranch life didn't come with comprehensive health plans. Thanking James for the beer, she drifted toward the pool table.

"Usually works like a charm," Wilton said.

"You figure you let them know you're covered and they'll want to marry you?" James asked.

"At least for tonight." Wilton gave a big grin.

James nodded, went back to his beer. He'd come to town because he felt like talking, hearing some laughter, but now that he was here, he wasn't at all sure he wanted to stay. His work held him apart from others, and sometimes he felt that solitude had gotten into his bones.

No one except Daisy had ever gotten it out of him, he thought. But thinking of Daisy never did him any good anymore, so he twisted toward the pool tables and looked at the blonde, who was still smiling at him.

James had always gone his own way, even among all the people on the ranch. He needed the meadows of sweet grass and riotous wild-flowers, the massive mountains of craggy red rocks against blindingly blue sky. He needed a lot of open space just to begin to dissolve what it was he carried inside of him.

He did lonely work with solitary creatures. Moving across wide territory, cows trekked single file. They'd straggle off, fall back, stop dead. That's why herding cows was much harder than tending the more community-spirited sheep. Cowboys were assigned positions, front-back-center, to keep the herd together and moving. Working flat-out, with no one to talk to, they'd start thinking of the sound of their own voices as strange.

The door swung open, and James turned away from the blonde. His father and Louisa walked in, dressed as if they were going to the rodeo — his father all in black with a string tie, Louisa in a tight cream-colored top and full red skirt, her auburn hair bigger than ever. Dalton looked bewildered, as if he wasn't sure of where he was. James hadn't seen his father at the Stagecoach in many months, and neither had anyone else. A buzz started at the bar and spread back to the pool tables.

"Dalton!"

"Hey, man, where've you been?"

"Where are we, Louisa?" Dalton asked. James heard the fright in his father's voice as he watched the old man seem to shrink before his eyes. His father scrunched up his neck, eyes wild. Louisa linked arms with him and proudly marched him into the bar. James started over, but held himself back.

Louisa surveyed the room. Her eyes fell on Todd Rydell, her nephew, over at the dart board. James watched Todd start to turn away, but once he realized he'd been seen, he waved and began walking toward his aunt. He was lanky and fair, the kind of cowboy who rode with a Walkman and used sunscreen. He was descended from the Rydells who'd grazed their sheep on Tucker land and nearly started a range war — so was Louisa. But Dalton loved her, so James had to respect her. Todd was another story.

"Dalton, good to see you." Todd shook the old man's hand. He kissed his aunt's cheek, let her pull him against her in a big hug. James watched them whisper to each other, wondered what they were saying.

"It's Todd," Louisa explained to Dalton.

"Why are we here?" Dalton asked, checking to make sure his hat was on his head.

"For a good time, man." Todd laughed, slapping Dalton on the back. " 'Cause it's Friday night and the music's cranking."

"Music?" Dalton asked.

"Hi, Dad," James said quietly, standing between his father and Todd.

His father's hard brown face softened. Smiling

up at his son, his cheeks curved into a thousand more wrinkles. Nodding, he shook his son's hand.

"Jamey," he said.

James didn't say anything. He just stood there silently while the noise rose around him. His father's eyes were cloudy and blue, but as they stared at James, they looked happy. James watched his father take a long breath, settle down a little.

"What brings you down to the Stagecoach?" Louisa asked coolly, arms folded across her chest. "Haven't seen you here in a long time."

"I don't come here much. You?" James asked, unable to resist the jab, knowing his father didn't.

"To sing, son," Louisa said, hurt but proud. "You know I've got an open invitation on Friday nights."

James hadn't forgotten. Louisa sang country western, and she'd been holding court here for over thirty years. That's how Dalton had met her — drowning his sorrows the winter after James's mother had died. Louisa had drifted to his table between sets, offered to buy him a drink, moved in before the spring thaw.

Daisy had loved to hear her. Once or twice a month they'd leave the twins with Betsy March, the wife of James's foreman, come down to the Stagecoach, and sit right in front of the stage. Louisa would forget singing to Dalton or the men at the bar, sing straight to Daisy. Daisy had

81

lost her mother young and Louisa had never had a daughter; their bond had been thick and strong.

"C'mon, Dalton." Todd handed him some darts. "Let's have a game. I'll beat you fair and square."

"Can't beat me." Dalton was laughing like his old self. "I can knock the tail off a swallow with my eyes closed."

"Show me, man."

While the two men headed down the bar, James felt something in his stomach tighten. He didn't like Todd, and not just because he was a lousy cowboy. Todd had worked for him years before, and he'd been there the day Jake had disappeared. James had ridden off to rope the steer, leaving Jake to sit on a big rock. Todd and a few others had been riding drag — picking up defectors who'd stop to graze on the sweet grass around Jake's rock — and James had trusted them to watch his son.

"What are you doing, Louisa?" James asked now.

"Doing?" Louisa's eyes widened.

James stared down at her. It wasn't her fault her nephew hadn't seen where Jake had gone. It was James's fault. He hadn't asked the men to help; they hadn't known they were supposed to. Half a minute. That was all it had taken for Jake Tucker to disappear from the face of the earth. It wasn't Todd Rydell's fault, but James hated him anyway. He hated himself worse, but that was beside the point.

"Yeah, doing. What're you thinking, bringing my father here?"

"Well, I'm thinking of showing him a good time," Louisa said. "If that's okay with you."

"He's sick, Louisa."

"A little confused, that's all."

"He's got Alzheimer's disease," James said. "The doctor told us both."

"So what?" Louisa asked, her golden eyes flashing.

"He gets confused. He's embarrassed when people come up to him and he can't remember their names. It's loud in here, and the doctor said he does better with quiet. I feel sorry for him, watching him —"

"I don't feel sorry for Dalton Tucker," Louisa snapped. "I feel sorry for this *disease*. I don't think Alzheimer's disease has ever come up against anyone like Dalton Tucker. And another thing, young man —"

"Whoa," James said, stepping back.

Louisa stepped forward, tilting her head back so she could stare into his eyes. She grabbed him under the chin, shook it hard.

"You ought to take a lesson from your father. You hear me? He's not giving up. He knows what's happening to him — you think he doesn't? You think it doesn't break him up every time he calls me by your mother's name? But he's full of life, and he's not quitting until he's taken his last breath and I lay him in the ground.

That's something you should try."

"What I should try —"

"Damn right. You're a walking zombie. It's a holy miracle you don't fall off your horse, riding herd. Hit your head, bleed to death out in the canyon. You lost your son, we all lost him." Louisa was tearing up, drying her eyes with both index fingers to keep her mascara from running. "But you act like you were the only one. You chased Daisy and that baby girl away."

"Leave them out of this," James said.

"Don't you tell me who to leave out of anything. I've got love in my heart, James Tucker, but you wouldn't know that if it bit you on the ass. You don't give anyone the time of day — it's you and your boy's ghost. That's about it. Even your father — you act so high-and-mighty concerned about him, but you've been pushing him away for thirteen years, just like everyone else."

"You done?" James handed her a handkerchief.

Nodding, she blew her nose noisily. Together, they watched Dalton draw the dart back even with his ear, throw a perfect bull's-eye. The young men standing around went wild, and Dalton bought a round for the whole bar. Todd glanced over at Louisa, then at James. James held his gaze hard, trying not to show his dislike.

"Look at him," Louisa said.

"Your nephew?"

"Your father!"

"He's still got it," James said.

84

"Mean as a cougar with the eye of an eagle," Louisa said.

"Dead aim," James said. "I remember seeing him shoot the head off a rattlesnake hanging out the beak of a flying hawk." As he spoke, his father scanned the crowd, looking for Louisa. At the sight of her, he smiled and looked proud.

"I never claimed I could tame Dalton Tucker," she said, breathing lightly. "I just asked God for help on how."

"Louisa!" the sound man called from the stage. People turned toward the door, clapping and calling her name. A young man came forward, handed her her guitar. Being run through sound checks, the microphone gave off feedback. James backed away. He glanced toward the bar, saw that a middle-aged woman — skinny, bleached-blond, missing teeth — had gone to stand beside Wilton, caressing the back of his hand.

It was time to go.

James grabbed his jacket. He glanced at his father, to say good-bye, but Dalton was concentrating on throwing another dart. People had come from all over for Friday night at the Stagecoach, and the room was warm and full. Turning to go, James heard Louisa call his name.

"What?"

"Same goes for you," she said.

"What's that?"

"What you said about your father, what you said yourself, in your own words."

James wrinkled his forehead, trying to remember. "I don't know what you're talking about."

"He's still got it." Louisa was smiling.

James turned and walked out of the bar.

It was a long ride home, Louisa's words ringing in his ears. He drove his truck along state roads, then veered off at Split Tree Pass. *Got it,* he thought. Got the ability to ride a horse, birth a calf, shoot a coyote. To smile at a girl, buy her a beer, take her to bed when you both knew you'd be gone before sunup. Bumping along dirt roads for ten miles, he swirled up a storm of dust and thought about how there was more than one kind of drought.

Driving through the gates of DR Ranch, he passed the big stone house where his father and Louisa lived and pulled around back to the narrow drive that took him home. He lived in a small log cabin behind the other ranch buildings. He had built it himself sixteen years ago, from cedar logged on the mountain. It had been a belated wedding present for Daisy, started the same week she'd told him she was pregnant. He'd finished it just in time for the babies to be born.

Running his hand along one smooth log, he stood outside the front door and smelled the sage. Night birds were calling, and the stars were on fire. James stared at the sky. The mountain made a black hole against the glowing stars, and that seemed about right to James; it was the place where Jake had disappeared. He tried to look at the sky, but his gaze was always drawn back to the mountain. Just across the pass was the canyon where —

The telephone rang. James let it go. It was the same line that rang at the main house, probably one of Louisa's nieces or nephews calling. But the bell wouldn't quit, snapping him into the present. He walked into the house, his boots sharp on the hardwood floor.

"Hello."

"James?" She said his name, and he heard her voice.

"That you, Daisy?" he asked.

"Yes."

He waited, trying to get his breath back again. He heard from her once or twice a year, always telling him something about Sage — her good grades, her artistic prowess, the essay she'd had published in the town newspaper — and informing him in none-too-kindly tones that he should send his daughter a telegram, a letter, a bunch of flowers. That he should get on a plane and visit her. But every single time, the sound of Daisy's soft voice shocked him to his bones, as if he was hearing it for the first time or as if he'd never gone a day in his life without it.

"How is she?" he asked, knowing Daisy had to be calling about Sage — there wasn't ever any other reason.

"She's . . ." Daisy gulped, and then there was something like silence, broken by the unmistakable sound of her breathing into the receiver. James could practically feel it on his ear. "I don't know how to tell you this. Sage is missing. She ran away."

"Missing?" James focused on the only word he'd heard.

"She left a note," Daisy continued. "Two notes, actually. The police have been looking for her, and we think she's heading out to see you."

"So you know where she is?" he asked, feeling relieved.

"No, we don't know. They have a clue, and I'm pretty sure she's on her way west, but —"

"By herself?" James asked, wondering how a young girl of sixteen could make it all the way from Connecticut to Wyoming without getting hurt.

"What's that supposed to mean?" Daisy asked.

"It means —" James started to explain himself.

"She's with her boyfriend," Daisy said hastily, backing off.

James didn't reply as he thought about his daughter having a boyfriend, how the last time he'd seen her she'd been just ready to start kindergarten. But silence on a telephone line between two people — with as much between them as he and Daisy — worked in strange ways, and he could hear Daisy getting agitated.

"She's always wanted to go to you," Daisy said. "I know you think I should have sent her.

You probably think this is my fault, that if I'd let her spend summers with you this never would have happened."

"No, I —"

"But I didn't want her traveling alone, and I didn't want her on that ranch. I couldn't stand thinking of her going to the place where Jake —"

"I know, Daisy."

"You could have come here," Daisy said.

"No," he said. "I couldn't."

"He's not coming back, James." Daisy's voice was shaking. "We've known that since the third or fourth day. Our son is dead, but your daughter's needed you all this time."

"He might." James stared out the window at the black mountain against the sky, milky with stars. "He could walk out of wherever he's been, come home looking for us . . ."

"No," Daisy said, as she'd said a hundred times. "No."

"I'm here," James said, "and I'm staying here. In case he does."

"You're crazy, James," Daisy snapped with impatience. "It's been thirteen years! And now our daughter . . ."

James closed his eyes. When she called him crazy, he couldn't disagree. He held back from defending himself the way he used to. But he wasn't going to change his plans or his ways, even if he had gone slightly insane. Daisy had, too. What parent wouldn't, losing a child?

"Meanwhile," Daisy continued, "your daughter's so starved for your love, she's on a freight train heading out to see you!"

"You know that for sure?"

"No! I said no already." Daisy sounded frantic. "But she was asking questions at the depot. That part's for sure — they identified her picture."

"Which picture?"

"What's the difference?" Daisy asked, her voice rising with the strain.

But it did matter. James was standing by the stone mantel staring at the gallery of Sage's photographs from birth onward. He picked up her tenth-grade picture and looked at her green eyes, her hesitant smile, her brown hair.

"They've alerted police departments all along the train line," Daisy said. "People will be checking the train at the next stop."

"Good." James didn't put the picture back down. His eyes stung, and even after he wiped them, his vision was blurry.

"If she calls you —"

"I'll call you right away," James said.

"Thank you." Daisy's voice was clipped, as if she'd said everything she needed to say. James held on to the receiver for a long time, wishing she'd think of something else. Instead, she just said good-bye, and so did he. Still, he didn't hang up the phone.

Replacing the school portrait on the mantel, he picked up an older, much more familiar one.

The picture was small — just a snapshot. It

stood in an ornate frame, made by Daisy from silver, gold, and stones gathered by the children from the river. The picture had been taken fourteen years ago, and it showed Daisy and James on horseback, each holding a two-year-old twin on the saddle in front of them.

Daisy was dressed in chaps, a blue chambray shirt, and a white Stetson. Her skin glowed from a summer in the mountains, but not half as bright as her smile. She embraced Jake from behind, pointing so he'd smile at the camera. James held Sage. He'd been afraid she might fall off the horse, so he was looking straight down at the top of her head, gripping her so tight his biceps and forearms were flexed. That's how it had been back then — keeping hold of his family in this vast country had been the most important thing on his mind.

"Little one." He said the name he had once used for his daughter.

She was on a freight train, heading cross-country to see him. Daisy had called the police, and they were going to intercept her, make sure she got back to her mother safely. That's what James wanted, what he prayed for now. But holding the picture, unable to put it down, he knew he wanted something even more.

For his daughter to come home. He wanted Daisy's mind set at ease; he wanted his daughter to be safe. But his arms ached to hold her, just as they'd ached for his son all these years.

If she made it to Wyoming before getting

caught, he'd give her the biggest talking-to a daughter ever got. He'd warn her against all the maniacs you could meet and all the accidents that could happen, against worrying her mother half crazy. James Tucker shivered to think of his daughter *out there,* and he shook his head, telling himself it was wrong to wish she'd slip through the dragnet and come to the ranch.

Before he sent her straight back east.

# Chapter Seven

Four days without Sage passed. Daisy found the waiting torture. What would Sage eat? Where would she sleep? What kinds of people was she encountering out there? How far along was her pregnancy? The thoughts swirled around and around her mind. She worked to dull them, to keep herself from replaying her talk with James. She had held back from telling him Sage was pregnant: She wanted to protect her daughter from that hard reality for as long as she could.

When word got out about Sage and Ben being missing, it was as if a stranger had come to Silver Bay. There was a feeling of curiosity, danger, and sorrow all mixed together. Not everyone had heard about the notes, but most people had seen the state police with their dogs sniffing along the railroad tracks long into the night.

Silver Bay was a postcard-pretty New England town. It had two white churches that artists came from all over the country to paint. The garden club placed stone pots at most intersections, cascading with ivy, petunias, and white geraniums all summer long. The schools were excellent, the crime rate almost nonexistent. Daisy had grown up about ten miles down the

93

shoreline, and she had chosen to come here after the divorce because Silver Bay seemed like the place least likely to pose a threat to her only surviving child.

Other mothers felt the same way. They checked their own children's eyes for signs of drug use, smelled their breath while kissing them good night. Talking about Sage Tucker and Ben Davis, they paid extra attention to the differences — the characteristics that set those children apart from their children — proof that the same thing couldn't happen in their homes.

When people stopped by Daisy's to drop off casseroles, homemade preserves, frozen lasagnas, she was working in her back room. Hunched over her worktable, her long-necked lamp trained on the bone she was carving, she ignored the doorbell. The persistent ringing reminded her of how it had been after Jake disappeared, how people equated grief with hunger, as if there was any food in the world that could fill that dreadful space.

Hathaway let herself in with her key. Daisy looked up when her sister came through the door.

"I just met Felicity Evans on your porch," Hathaway said, carrying in a basket of apples. "She told me you were inside working, and she asked me to give you these."

"How do they know I'm here?" It was just a question; she was past cringing. People had watched her work during Jake's ordeal, thought she was cold-blooded. They'd be saying the same thing now. She knew that she was in the category of "other": a woman who had lost one, and now another, of her children.

"They see your car, figure you're waiting by the phone."

Daisy narrowed her eyes, carving the left cheekbone on the disc of bone. Her latest piece was called "Lonely Girl." It was a simple face, open and innocent, distant as the moon. Daisy would set it in eighteen-karat gold, to show that it was precious. She would link it with pebbles of polished tourmaline, each stone representing a virtue the lonely girl carried within herself, so that even though she might be alone, she was still blessed: courage, kindness, intelligence, grace.

"Daisy." Hathaway took hold of her sister's wrists, making her drop her tools.

"It's Sage," Daisy said, staring into the small bone face, no more than an inch in diameter, yet full of her daughter's spirit.

"Stop working," Hathaway said. "Talk to me."

"It's just that —" Daisy began, her voice in control but her hands beginning to shake. "I can't stand it, Hathaway."

"I don't see how you could."

"I called James. I just told him about her being gone . . ."

Hathaway just stared, giving Daisy that silent support her sister was so good at giving, when she understood to the depths of her soul without

95

saying a word. Daisy let herself fall apart. She needed to be held, and her sister pulled her into her arms, stroking the top of her head. Hathaway knew what to do.

"What did he say?" Hathaway asked after a long time.

"You wouldn't believe it."

"Go ahead. Tell me."

"He's still waiting for Jake." Daisy pulled back so she could see Hathaway's eyes. "Now he thinks Sage is coming to see him, so he's waiting for her, too. We don't know for sure, though, do we? I mean, I'm just guessing. We don't have any definite proof. She could be anywhere —"

"Calm down, Daisy."

Daisy took a deep breath. "But James believes me. He's ready for her, if that's where she's going."

"Vigilant," Hathaway said, her neck long and her head held up. Daisy knew her sister thought James was noble in an insane sort of way. When Daisy would rant and yell about his not accommodating the inconveniences of divorce, not coming east to see Sage so Daisy wouldn't have to send Sage west, Hathaway could always see James's side.

"It was hard to tell him," Daisy said.

"It couldn't be easy for anyone, but especially not for the two of you."

"We don't see eye to eye on anything," Daisy said, trying to breathe. "How were we ever married?"

"I think . . ." Hathaway began, but she held herself back.

"I was nuts," Daisy said. "That's what. Moving out west, marrying him. I was trying to be someone I wasn't, pretending." She trailed off.

"Pretending what?" Hathaway asked. "To love him?"

Daisy shook her head. No, she had never had to pretend that. "Living a life that wasn't mine. I'm from New England; this is where I belong. I like things safe. We couldn't last, you know? I see that now, but no one could have told me then."

But even as she spoke, her words didn't quite ring true. She had loved the West, found depth and meaning there that she still felt today. Her jewelry proved it, and so did her dreams. At night she dreamed of red rocks, long trails, big sky, the scent of cedar and sage, the feeling of James's arms around her shoulders.

"Americans marry Frenchmen," Hathaway said gently. "Italians marry English. Why be so hard on yourself because you married a cowboy? You always loved horses, loved to ride. To me it seems natural, especially knowing you and James together."

"I was living a fantasy," Daisy said, as if trying to convince herself. "That's all. It wasn't real."

"You had two kids," Hathaway said. "That was pretty real."

"Did I somehow curse them?" Daisy asked,

tears pooling in her eyes. "Being selfish, doing what I wanted to do?"

"No, Daisy. No, you didn't."

"I wish the police would call," Daisy said, staring at the phone. "They must have located the train by now. They must have found Sage. Or not found her. What if she's not on it? What if it's a wild-goose chase, and she's somewhere else instead?"

"Trust yourself, Daisy. You told me you know she's heading west."

"I do know it." Daisy closed her eyes.

"Just think of how many miles they have to cover, how many trains there are crossing the country at any given time. Sage is in one little car, and it'll take them some time to find it. But they will."

"I can't wait till she gets home," Daisy said.

"Me, neither."

Daisy bent over, holding the small bone face that reminded her of her daughter. People said her pieces were magical, that they were filled with love; if that was so, Daisy was pouring everything she had into this one small, flat carving. When the other mothers looked askance that she would be working on a day like this, they didn't understand that carving bone ghosts was the way Daisy prayed. Just like James rode into the hills and Sage went hiking in the woods. This was Daisy's way.

The train stopped well after midnight in a

cornfield outside of Lone Tree, Iowa. Sage was lying on her side, curled into Ben's body. She had been dreaming of cantering across her father's ranch on a white horse, its mane and tail flowing out behind. The sky was blindingly blue, and she was riding easily homeward, so happy she felt as if her heart might burst — until the train began to stop with a screech, metal grinding against the tracks.

"What's happening?" she asked, terrified.

"It's . . . we're crashing!" Ben said.

Ben held her tight from behind, and for a long, jolting thirty seconds, they were afraid they were going to die. The train hurtled forward, the pressure of the brakes trying to hold back several thousand tons of locomotive and freight cars. Sage closed her eyes, both arms instinctively clutching her middle, to hold the baby inside her. Shuddering as if it was going to explode around them, the car kept flying forward, then slowed, then came to a complete stop.

The silence was deafening. Ben and Sage looked at each other, then got up and moved quickly to the sliding door. It was dark in the car, and when Sage pressed her cheek against the metal door, it was freezing cold. Through the narrow crack she could see a midnight-blue sky, luminous over the cornfields. They had to be almost all the way through Iowa. Several police cars were parked along a road running parallel to the tracks, their blue strobe lights flickering.

"What are they doing?" Sage asked. "Are we at a station?"

"I don't think so," Ben said.

Sage knew he was right. They had been traveling aboard the train for four days, long enough to know the rhythm of station stops. The engineer would start putting on the brakes gradually, slowing the big train bit by bit instead of all at once. Sage had felt nervous the first time, her stomach lurching as the weight of the train worked at coming to a complete stop. She and her mother had taken a train only once — from Old Saybrook to Boston — and there hadn't been half as many cars as this one.

"Start at the front and work back!" someone yelled from outside.

"Two teams," a different voice called back. "One takes the rear, the other goes forward."

Sage pressed her face harder against the door, trying to see what was going on. Police officers with flashlights seemed to be everywhere. The light beams swept across the train, pointed low, as if to look along the tracks. Sage tried to tell herself maybe the train had hit something — a cow or a deer or even a person — and the police were trying to see if it was still alive. But deep down she knew: They were looking for her and Ben.

"What should we do?" she asked.

"I don't know," Ben said.

Sage stepped back from the door. She gazed up at her boyfriend. He kept his cheek glued to the door, peering out the crack. The last two days he hadn't said very much, and when she'd wanted him to hug her, she had felt he didn't want to. She had a nervous feeling all the time, waiting for something to happen; maybe she already knew what it was, but she was afraid to tell herself.

"I love you," she whispered.

"They're checking the cars," Ben said, as if he hadn't heard her. "Half the guys are up front, the others are back here."

"They're looking for us."

"Yeah," Ben said. "Probably."

Sage held herself tight. She wanted Ben to tell her everything would be fine, he'd take care of them, they could hide among the crates and keep going to Wyoming. Her heart was pounding so hard, she'd never known she had so much blood in her body. Opening her mouth, she realized it was too dry to talk.

"You think they'll arrest us?" he asked, twisting his head to see more.

Sage hadn't thought of that. She tried to take his hand, but she couldn't pry it off the metal door. "Ben?" she asked. "Ben?"

"They're two cars back," he said. "Maybe three."

"I love you," Sage repeated.

"Oh, Sage."

"We have to get to the ranch."

"That's just a dream," he said without looking at her.

"No," she said, holding her stomach. "It's real."

"Real . . ." he murmured, as if he'd never heard the word before.

"There's a cabin for us there. The sky is so big and blue . . . the stars fall right down to the ground. We'll fish in the streams . . ."

"Our mothers called the police." Ben's voice cracked. "That's why they're looking for us."

"I know," Sage whispered. Sitting down where she stood, she pressed her face against her knees. Tears spilled over as she thought of her mother. Picturing her mother's eyes, she actually felt her mother's hand brush her cheek. She remembered nights when she couldn't sleep, when her mother would sit on her bed and tell her stories of mustang families galloping through the canyons. She knew that her mother would have called the police the first day she was gone, that she wouldn't rest until Sage was somewhere safe.

"I think we should go home," Ben said, crouching beside her.

"I am going home," Sage said hoarsely, and she meant Wyoming, not Silver Bay. With her eyes squeezed tight, her knees drawn up to her chest, she was picturing the West. She saw red rocks and fields of grain, mountains against the bright sky. She felt her mother's touch again, and she saw her father's eyes — the way they looked in the picture he had sent her — and she cringed with pain.

Sage wasn't running away from home; she was going *to* home. She had a mother in one place and a father in another, and something she didn't understand was pulling her west. Even with the policemen waiting to take her back, probably ready to give her a free plane ticket back to comfort and safety, she knew she couldn't go.

"We can work this out," Ben said, holding her hand. "We can do what we should have done before. Tell our mothers and get —"

"Not an abortion," Sage said hotly. "Don't say that."

" 'Help.' I was going to say, 'get help.' "

Outside, the searchers were closing in. Sage heard them sliding train doors open, clanging them closed. Two state policemen stopped outside their car to light cigarettes. Holding her breath so they wouldn't hear her, Sage crawled over to look out. They stood back, surveying the scene as if they were the head officers.

"Whose brainstorm was this?" one asked. "Five more miles, the damn train would've been in the station."

"Element of surprise," the older guy said. "Where're two kids gonna run to out here? Into a cornfield? We take 'em in town, they could slip off, hide anywhere."

"Engineer's mad as hell."

"Tough luck."

"What are they, teenagers?"

"Yeah, boy and girl."

"Romeo and Juliet," the younger policeman said.

"Yeah, well, Romeo's old enough to know better. We got him for kidnap, statutory rape, the whole nine yards. He's looking at real time."

"The report says they're schoolmates, their families know each other. It's probably just young love —"

"The court doesn't give a shit about young love, true or not. You don't stop a freight train, get two police forces out in the middle of the night, and not pay for it. The kid's going to jail, and we both know it."

"Yep," the other guy said. "I know."

Sage snapped her head to look at Ben. His mouth was hanging open with shock. *He didn't kidnap me,* Sage wanted to scream. *This was my idea!* And rape! They were in love!

The two men ground out their cigarettes, drifted back toward the car being searched. Sage grabbed Ben. "We can't let them catch us."

"They think I did that." He sounded bewildered. "I'm going to jail —"

"No," Sage said firmly. "I won't let them. I'll tell them it's all my fault, that I love you so much that —"

"Let's turn ourselves in." Ben's voice was shaking. "Let's explain the whole thing."

"Didn't you hear him?" Sage begged. "He said he didn't care about the truth."

"I can't go to jail," Ben said. "I'm supposed to go to college."

"Let's sneak off," Sage said. She began trying to pry the door open. They'd been inside for over four days, their plan being to stay hidden till the crates were off-loaded in Boise, Idaho. From there, they were going to ride their bikes to Wyoming, camping out along the way.

"They'll believe us." Ben looked her in the eye. "I know they will."

"I don't want to go back," Sage said, panicked.

"Sage," Ben said. "I do. I do want to go back."

"No." She shook her head.

"I want to go home."

"Ben, please . . ." she said, gulping down a sob.

"You do, too," he said, softening his voice. "I know you. You think your mother'll be mad, but —"

"It's not that." She squeezed her eyes shut. "I want to go to Wyoming —"

"You can go later," he said quietly. "The right way."

"This is the right way," she whispered, her heart breaking because she knew it was already over. Their journey across country, a new family together, had come to an end. Ben was leaving her — had left her already. She could hear it in his voice, and she could imagine the future: The next time she saw him, he'd be cool and distant. It would be a breakup like other kids' she'd seen, with the girl crying by her locker and the boy sitting with his back to her in the cafeteria.

If he didn't go to jail first.

"No," he said, holding her hands. "It's not."

The police were in the car behind them. The train walls suddenly seemed as thin as paper. Sage could hear voices — talking and rough laughter. She was sobbing quietly, holding the sound inside. Staring at Ben's hands clutching hers, she blinked away tears. If only she could make it last forever, this moment with Ben. Why did God give people love, then take it away?

"Sage?" he asked.

She could feel the strain, see him pulling toward the door. She knew he wanted them to turn themselves in, and the truth spread over her like a cold wave. This was one of those times she'd heard about in songs: If you love somebody, set them free. The idea seemed so cruel, so impossible. *It will never happen to me and Ben,* Sage had thought. But now she knew: She couldn't make Ben come with her, no matter how much she wanted him to.

"I love you," she whispered.

"I love you, too," he said, his eyes sharp with pain.

"Will you do something for me?"

"Yes," he said gruffly, wiping tears from his eyes.

"Tell them you're alone. Tell them I got off in Chicago or somewhere. Give me a little time . . ."

"A head start . . ." He glanced at the door. The policemen were getting closer; he could hear their voices in the car behind them, laughing as they scuffled around.

"Yes." Pulling her hands away from his, she moved over to the trapdoor. They had spied it their first day, known they could use it as an escape hatch in an emergency. Now that she had made her decision, she knew she had to move fast. She grasped the bolt and tugged. It was thick and rusty, but Ben moved her aside and yanked the door open.

The trapdoor itself looked heavy, but she knew she could have lifted it. Sage could accomplish just about anything when she had the will. It was about a yard square, big enough to push her bike and backpack through. Ben helped her, and Sage was thinking she'd slip out, lie on the tracks under the train, waiting for everyone to move away. Ben would distract them for her, and by the time the ruckus died down, she'd be hiding in the field.

"I think you should come with me," Ben said.

"I know," Sage said. "But I won't. Don't even try to talk me into it."

"But —"

"Please, Ben," she said, the tears rising again. "Don't. For me."

"Shit . . ." He shook his head.

"You'll be okay, won't you?" She'd heard the men talking about arresting him, but she couldn't believe they would. Ben was so gentle and good. "I'll tell them you didn't do anything. As soon as I get to my dad's —"

"I'll be fine. I promise."

Sage nodded.

"I know how much you want to get there," he said, stepping toward her.

"I do." Sage knew nothing else could part her from Ben.

His eyes were wide, his brown hair falling into them. He wore the rawhide she'd given him, a bear claw hanging from it. Her father had sent the necklace to her years ago, and it had always been one of her most cherished possessions. She touched it with one finger, as if she could get strength from the bear, her father, and Ben. She glanced at the trapdoor he had helped her unlock.

"Will you do something else for me?" she whispered.

"Yes."

"Hold me." His arms came around her, and his breath was warm in her hair. She felt their hearts pounding together, and she felt her belly pressing against his, their baby inside. "Tighter, as if you'll never let me go," she gasped.

"We're too young," he said. "I didn't want this to happen."

*But it's happening,* Sage thought. She memorized the feeling of his arms, the smell of his sweater, the sound of his breath, the dampness of his tears on the top of her head.

"You have to leave."

"I know."

"Fool them," she said. "Don't let them see

you near this car —"

"I'll try."

He backed toward the trapdoor. She knew it was important that he leave the car, roll out, go running down the train as fast as he could, to lead them away from her. Blindly, she turned away. She could cling to his side, watch him leave her, or she could stick to her plan, make her own dreams come true.

"Sage . . ." he said, as if maybe he was reconsidering, or as if he just wanted to see her face one last time.

"Go!" she said, sobbing, without turning around.

She heard his side brushing against the opening, the thump of his feet as they hit the ground. Crossing the car, she looked into the open space where Ben had gone. It was small, thirty-six inches wide, but to Sage it looked bottomless. Her eyes were blurry with tears, and she couldn't make the ground come into focus.

She heard Ben running away, and her heart squeezed smaller and smaller as she wondered whether she would ever see him again. She thought of how much she had loved her father and brother, and how one day they had disappeared from her life. Kneeling down, she stared — now it was coming into clear view — at the dusty earth between and outside the tracks, and she saw Ben's footprints. She heard voices, men starting to shout and hustle from all over, pounding past her car like a stampeding herd.

Cradling her belly, she told the baby everything would be fine. They would be in Wyoming soon, on the ranch, in their own log cabin. She would take care of them both along the way; she wouldn't let anything happen to them. She made her voice brave, to sound as convincing as she could. The strange thing was, the more she talked, the more she believed herself.

Hearing the hubbub several cars forward, she knew that this was her chance.

Heart pumping, she took one last look around the car. It was the first home she, Ben, and their baby had shared together, and she hoped it wouldn't be their last.

Bracing herself with stiff arms, she dropped through the opening. Landing softly on her pack, she lay on her back and tried to get her bearings. Voices came from her left, and she glanced over to see a crowd of officers standing in a circle. She knew they were surrounding Ben, and although she strained to hear, she couldn't make out his voice. This was her chance, and Ben was giving it to her.

Scooting out from beneath the train, she hauled her bicycle out behind her. The air felt dry and cold. Lungs aching, Sage strapped her pack on her back, tightening the harness even as she began to mount her bike. The police cars were on the other side of the train, but she could see their blue strobe lights reflected in the low clouds. Dawn was breaking.

A line of red showed above the horizon. Sage

stared at it for a moment. The sun was there, even if she couldn't see it yet. The sky was dark blue, lightening from the bottom up. Sage caught her breath, gazing east at the sunrise: She knew that the sun had already risen over Silver Bay, that her mother was back there in Connecticut, that every minute of her day so far had probably been filled with thoughts about Sage.

Taking that as a blessing direct from her mother, Sage pointed her bicycle away from the rising sun and began to pedal west. Her legs were stiff, but they loosened as she moved. She rode into the dark cornfield. Half the corn had been harvested, and it was stubble: Sage ducked between rows of dry cornstalks, tall and brown. Her tires bumped over ruts in the ground. Her shoulders hit dry leaves, and they sounded like playing cards in her spokes.

Ben was back there, protecting her as she got away. The police voices grew fainter and fainter. After a minute, all she could hear was the beating of her own heart and the whisper of wind through the rows of cornstalks. She wobbled a little, riding over the uneven ground, but her legs were strong and sure as she straightened out and headed through the field into the last traces of night.

# Chapter Eight

The night before, James had been burning irrigation ditches in the Red Mine Canyon. Standing upwind, he had watched the smoke blowing through the steep ravines of the Wind River Range, crimson in the firelight. He had heard a wild snarl, and when he looked up, he saw a bobcat drive a calf off a cliff.

Climbing down, he had found the calf with its back broken, lying at the foot of the trail. The animal struggled, trying to stand, still thinking it could run away. James crouched beside it. He petted the calf's long neck, trying to calm it down. The calf's eye was wide and dark, and it stared up at James with terror. Any creature not its mother was the enemy right then.

"I'm sorry," James said.

Kicking its front legs, the calf was paralyzed in its hindquarters. It squealed, and its mother called back from above, a long lowing that sounded grief-struck.

"You're not alone," James said, because he thought it was important for creatures to know that. More than anything, he hated to think of anyone or any animal suffering alone.

Standing up, James had drawn his gun and

fired, killing the calf instantly.

Now, saddling up the next morning, James tried to think about anything but the look in that calf's eye. He wished he hadn't seen the fear, known that the calf was still nursing and wanted nothing more than its mother. He wished he didn't think of his own children with that same look.

"Rain's coming."

At the sound of his father's voice, James turned. He peered into the darker part of the barn, saw his father standing by the stalls. The old man stepped forward, dressed for work in chaps and boots.

"Morning, Dad," James said.

"Seen those thunderheads over the basin? We'll get rain for sure today. Where you heading?"

"Down to the east pasture. Thought I'd check on the herd out there."

"Want some company?"

James hesitated. The last time his father had come with him, he'd gotten disoriented and upset. He'd thought James was his father instead of his son, spun back fifty years to a time when they had been driving the Rydells' sheep off their land. Dalton had started sputtering about the family's enemies, the importance of tradition, how cattle were better than sheep. James had brought him back to reality, set him straight on the father-son relationship, reminded him that he was living with Louisa Rydell — grand-

daughter of his archenemies — that peace had been made a generation ago.

"Sure," James said now. "I'd be glad to have you."

"Wouldn't want to be in the way," Dalton said gruffly.

"You won't be."

They finished saddling up, led their horses outside, started riding east. James still had the scream of that bobcat in his ears, and he couldn't stop thinking about Sage. Several days had passed since Daisy's call, and he hadn't gotten much sleep since, waiting for the phone to ring. He wanted to hear Daisy, her voice clipped and cool, telling him the whole thing was a mistake and Sage was back sleeping in her bed.

"Damnedest drought I ever saw," Dalton said, cantering alongside past a stand of cottonwoods. "Lasting clear into October."

"Well, you're predicting rain," James said.

"Your father can call the weather, can't he?" Dalton asked, chuckling.

James didn't reply. He'd been praying for rain all summer. He had cows so thirsty they were trying to drink dirt. They were moving close to the cliffs, hoping to catch a trickle of runoff. Last month he'd trucked in water. Dumping it into tanks, he'd watched cattle trampling each other to get to it. Thirst was a killer.

The drought called forth rattlesnakes. By night, their rattles sounded all through the Wind Rivers, that ominous *tch-tch-tch* coming from

rocks, ledges, the chaparral, rafters in the barns. Dust covered everything, a fine brown film shading the animals, ranch buildings, people's skin. But now his daughter was out there somewhere, and he couldn't bear to think of her getting rained on.

"Taught you how to irrigate," Dalton said. "The old way, the right way."

"The hard way."

"You complainin'?" Dalton asked testily.

"Wouldn't do that, Dad." Neighboring ranches had fancy irrigation systems with pumps and sprinklers, everything on timers. When the well ran dry, they paid to have water trucked or freighted in. Everything was automatic, computer-operated, error-proof.

The Tucker way suited James. It wasn't the easiest or most efficient, but it felt real to him. When it came to his herd, he knew what was what. He had to climb on his horse twice a day, ride out to the pastures to change the water himself. He had to walk the land, know every rock and crevice. His herd knew the pitch of his voice, the sound of his horse's hooves. It gave him comfort to know that he was part of the land, closer to Jake. It was a small thing, but it gave him a little peace.

"Louisa said Daisy called."

"Yeah, she did." James had passed Daisy's message on to Louisa, just in case Sage tried to call the ranch and she happened to answer.

"Your girl's gone missing?"

"That's what Daisy says." James felt his stomach drop.

"She's a teenager," Dalton said, guffawing as if that was explanation, joke, and curse all rolled into one.

"I know."

"Well, teenagers hate staying home. You think I don't remember the time you decided to borrow my pickup, drive all the way to Lander after supper one night? You were all of fifteen — no license, no nothing."

"I remember," James said. It was the year his mother had died and Dalton had started seeing Louisa. He'd spent it acting half-crazed, drinking till dawn, skipping class, taking his father's truck every chance he got. When Louisa moved in, the half-crazed became full-blown.

"Well, there you go. Don't waste your time thinking anything bad. Nothing's wrong with your daughter that growing up won't fix. She's not lost, she's not disappeared. She's just a damned pain in the neck, like you were, and she's runned away. Give her a week, and she'll be home again."

"A week?" James asked.

"Yep," his father said. "Seven days."

The thing was, James found himself counting as if his father had the inside story. Sage had been gone for five days now. If his father was right, he only had two more to wait. Then he'd hear from Daisy — or Sage herself — and he could rest easy. James had taken his father's word as the gospel truth on everything when he was young. That had changed with Louisa. And it changed even more now, day by day, as his father grew less alert and sharp, as James caught himself treating his own father like a child.

"Hey, Dad —" James didn't know exactly what words he wanted to say, but he knew the subject had to do with his children and Daisy, the losses they'd suffered in life — things he never talked of to his father.

"Clouds are movin' in," Dalton said, looking at the sky. "Hope Louisa remembers to take her wash in early, because the sky's gonna open up."

James didn't say anything. His father had sensed something coming and saved them both from James saying something stupid. James spurred his horse's flank, took off on a dead run. The ground was flat here, dusty and dry. Sagebrush had withered in the summer heat, and it lay in bundles of dead twigs. Dalton was right behind him. James could hear his father calling out, telling about the time he'd plugged an irrigation hole with a rusty refrigerator, but James just let his horse run harder.

Tuckers didn't talk about love. They didn't cry about the past or speak of dreams about the future. They didn't express fears or doubts. They just got the job done. They talked of nature, weather, horses, and cows. The ability to predict rain was a talent, and Dalton had it.

James had calves tumbling off mountainsides, being attacked by parched bobcats. The ranch needed rain. But right now, James didn't want it. He'd sacrifice the whole herd if he could keep his baby dry. James Tucker would let every single four-legged animal on his land weaken and fall if he could ensure his daughter would be okay. He wished his father was able to predict something like that. Truly predict it, the way he could rain.

He thought back to how Daisy had acted when Jake was missing. One day, after he had been gone for a month, she had ridden into the canyon and tried to feel his presence. She had this gift with stones and bones — the way she could touch things cold from the ground and sense life inside them. James had watched her kneel in the dirt where Jake had last sat, sift sand and pebbles through her fingers as she said his name over and over.

"Stop," James had said, grabbing her roughly.

"I want to know where he is."

"You're not going to find him in the dirt."

"It might be my only chance." She pressed her face into the earth. Mud clung to her eyelids and nose. She licked it from her lips.

"Daisy, stop."

"He's here," his wife had said. "My baby is here."

It had rained for two days before, and the ground was soft and wet. Dirt had turned to mud, and the underbrush was thick and green. James remembered feeling sick, knowing that the earth teemed with life. Things were living all around him, but Jake was gone.

Daisy made a terrible guttural sound, as if she was reverting to some primitive beast. James had wrapped her in his arms, rocking her back and forth. "He's here, he's here," she had cried, and only then had James realized that the noise she'd made was that of weeping, of grief bubbling up from some part of her they hadn't known about before.

"Daisy —"

"He's here!"

"Daisy, stop. You don't know —" James had said, powerless to stop her from crying, clawing at the earth, making that terrible sound. All he could do was hold her, let her weep. He had rocked her back and forth, listening to the wind in the rocks overhead, feeling the rhythm of their bodies moving together. After a while she had stopped crying. James had kept rocking her.

Riding hard now, he thought back to that time with Daisy, of the silent promise he had made while she wept for their boy. That James would never, for as long as he lived, abandon their son. No matter what else happened in life, he would stay there for Jake. Daisy had raked the earth, eaten the dirt where Jake had played. James would never leave the land.

But what could he do for Sage?

When he was young, his mother had told him, "If you're going to pray, don't worry. But if you're going to worry, don't pray."

James couldn't stop himself from worrying, but he couldn't stop himself from praying, either. He just galloped east toward the dry pasture, his father right behind him. He felt the wind in his sunburned face, and he pulled his hat lower over his eyes. The dust was blowing in, and he couldn't see straight.

From the ridge, he could see so far. Canyons, pastures, ranch, and range. The Wind River mountains ringed the scene. Whenever he stood here, he felt as if he mattered, as if he had a place to come home to.

He also felt very alone. No one knew he was here, and no one cared. Sometimes he saw the ranchers tending to calves, and his eyes would burn with tears. That's what fathers were supposed to do: look after their own.

*Mothers and fathers, mothers and fathers:* What did it all mean? Out on the range he saw so many parents and young: deer and fawns, cows and calves, coyotes and pups. The babies deserved a chance to grow up, but plenty didn't make it. The ranch was a brutal place to live — or die.

He didn't care anymore. He'd sit up here while the storms passed, wait forever if he had to. Thunder cracked, but to him it was a dream song. This was his mountain, and he'd been rocked to sleep by the sounds of nature so many times before. In the land of the wild outside, comfort had to come from within.

Hugging himself, he felt the tears pouring down his cheeks. *You're a good boy.* The words came from far away, in another voice. Someone had told him that once, and he told himself now. Hoofbeats sounded below, and he shrank against the rock ledge. He wasn't ready to be seen. Yellow leaves were falling now. Maybe when the snows came, when the houses were warmed by fire and the mountain was covered in ice.

Maybe then he'd show himself. Maybe then he'd claim his mountain home. Another thunder crack, and he inched closer to the ledge. He'd always needed something to believe in, and he'd always found it here, on the ranch.

Growing sleepy, he curled up in a dry spot and let the dream songs come. *You're a good boy,* he heard. *You are a good boy.*

Louisa Rydell stood on the wide porch, drinking a cup of coffee as she watched a line of antelope climb the side of the mountain. She tried to count them, lost track after twenty-five. She watched the big clouds billow over the valley. They were purple, biblical, like cups of blood. Dalton was calling for rain. She knew how badly the ranch needed rain, and she hoped they'd get it — only not yet.

Not with Daisy and James's daughter out there. Louisa hadn't seen Sage in years, but there had been a time she had considered her her own grandbaby. She had baby-sat the twins every chance she had, letting Sage sit on her lap and play with her big earrings and beads while they watched Jake toddle around the grass between the house and paddock.

Back then, they'd all been one happy, crazy, extended western family. Louisa and Dalton, though not married, had been matriarch and patriarch of the whole clan — Rydells and Tuckers on the same ranch. Louisa's father would never have believed it. She'd watched Dalton hire her nephews Larry and Todd as hands; she'd seen Dalton escort her daughter Ruthie to the father-daughter square dance.

Even James had come around. After a decade of despising Louisa for — as he'd probably put it — taking his mother's place in Dalton's heart, he suddenly seemed to respect her. A woman good enough to be liked by Daisy was good enough to be tolerated by James. Louisa certainly missed that younger woman's presence on the ranch.

Louisa sighed. One of the cow dogs had smelled her breakfast roll, and he came nosing up the porch steps.

"What do you want?" she asked, as if she didn't know.

The dog licked her hand, then rolled onto his back so she'd scratch his belly. Louisa thought of all the kids she'd sat with on this porch, all the cow dogs whose bellies she'd scratched. Clouds covered the sun, and she heard the far-off rumble of thunder. She shook her head. The only moisture this side of Gannet Peak was in her eyes, and she hated what crying did to her mascara.

"Damn it all," she said, and she meant it *all*.

She wished they could go back to a happier time. There had been so much love on this ranch. The couples, the babies, the growing generations. *Back when this family wasn't falling apart,* she thought. That had started thirteen years ago, the day Jake had wandered off the face of the earth.

The more she tickled the dog's belly, the more he wanted. His left leg was kicking the air like a jackrabbit's. Louisa tried to laugh, but that just made the pain in her heart feel bigger. Her eyes were going to puff up, and that was going to be hell. She and Dalton were supposed to meet friends for supper down at the Stagecoach, and Louisa harbored a secret hope the manager would tempt her up on the stage. Although she wasn't booked for a show, she loved to be asked.

No, tickling this old dog wasn't doing the trick. Louisa straightened up. She wore a flowing blue dress, the color of mountain gentians. Her eye makeup matched. Around her neck hung "Bear Mother," the necklace Daisy had made for her. It came from the bones of a dead grizzly, shot by James one summer night when it had attacked the tent where he, Daisy, and the kids were camping.

Louisa held the necklace in both her hands. It hung between her breasts on a chain of gold. The beads were polished jasper, turquoise, and bear bones. Teeth and claws hung around the medallion, guarding it. When James had seen it, he'd made the comment that it looked too aggressive and wild, like nothing Daisy had ever done before.

Louisa had understood that his words were directed at her, that James had been suggesting that no one less out-there than Louisa could have inspired the delicate Daisy to make such a violent piece, fanged and clawed. But Louisa hadn't cared. She and Daisy knew and loved each other, and they understood there wasn't a more aggressive creature in the world than a mother. A mother would do anything to protect her babies; they both knew that.

The medallion told another story.

It came from the bear's rib, closest to her heart. Daisy had cut a smooth slice, carved it with the grizzly's face. It was the visage of death, not attack. The expression was peaceful, restful, loving, of the spirit. For after the attack, after James had shot the bear dead, he had found the cubs waiting down the hill. The mother had sensed her babies were in danger, and she had done what she had to do.

Daisy had understood. She had wept for the bear, and for weeks afterward, she had made James ride into those northern hills to search for the cubs, make sure they were surviving on their own. He'd spotted them twice, but after that he'd seen only one. The other had disappeared.

Louisa's necklace was meant to symbolize the mother bear's great spirit. She reigned over the ranch, the mountains and canyons, protecting the young of mothers everywhere. Daisy had intended for her to protect Louisa's daughter Ruthie, Daisy's own children Sage and Jake, all the Tucker and Rydell children from here to Dubois.

Having worn it every day since Daisy gave it to her, Louisa had taken it off after they lost Jake. It had seemed futile to wear an amulet of protection that had failed to protect. But this morning, thinking of Sage, Louisa had put the necklace on again. Just in case. That little girl would be sixteen by now, growing up without her father. She was the spitting image of Daisy. And Louisa knew the bad things that could befall a fatherless young woman in her first bloom.

Some of them had happened to Louisa herself.

With that in mind, she let out another great sigh. It dissolved into the heavy air as more thunder drummed down the canyon. The first drops of rain fell: big and fat, hitting the ground and raising dust.

Shooing the dust-covered sheltie off the porch, Louisa knew what she had to do. Sometimes young families needed all the help the universe could offer, even coming from a spurned quasi stepgrandmother. She walked inside, ready to make a telephone call that wasn't going to be easy.

# Chapter Nine

Wrapped in a shawl, Daisy huddled in her work-room. Five days after Sage's disappearance, it hurt to breathe. Detective LaRosa had just called and reported that Sage wasn't on the train. Ben had told them a story about how she'd gotten off in Chicago.

Although the police had not believed him, they hadn't found her yet. Sage hadn't been kidnapped, nor was she a criminal: Therefore, the FBI had not been called in. The investigation depended on the efforts of many small jurisdictions, none of whom considered a pregnant runaway their top priority. Daisy had called the Davis home every day since the kids had run away.

Paulina had been frantic, but now she was just cold. She told Daisy she'd have Ben call her when he could. Daisy had lost it then. "Look," she'd said, her voice rising, "I know you blame Sage for this, but I don't care. You have him call me the minute — the second!" — by now she was screaming — "he gets home. Do you hear me? The *second!*"

The telephone rang.

Daisy stared at it with red eyes. Sitting on a

rocker, arms wrapped around knees drawn up to her chin, she got tangled up in the shawl as she lunged for the receiver. Maybe it was Ben, maybe it was Hathaway calling back, maybe it was James, maybe it was bad news. But as she fumbled the phone to her ear, Daisy shouted the name:

"Sage!"

"No, darlin', it's me," came Louisa's low western voice.

"I thought you might be her," Daisy said, her heart falling even farther than it had before.

"Have the police called yet?"

"They can't find her." Daisy squeezed her eyes shut. Her intuitive sense that Sage was headed for the ranch had grown into a conviction, but that didn't sway the police. "I don't even know how hard they're looking. If only she'd call . . ."

"Yes, yes," Louisa said. "That's a hope I'm harboring myself — that she'll pick up the phone and call you and just get herself home."

"God, I hope that's what happens," Daisy said. "That she calls me or James. I just know she's on her way to him . . ."

There was silence on the line, and in those few seconds Daisy had a vision of what life would be like if Sage didn't come home. It would be like a black hole, so vast and terrible she wouldn't want to go on. If she thought it had been bad before, with Jake, this time her despair would be unbounded.

"Daisy, ever since you called James with the news, I've been thinking," Louisa said. "We were close, once upon a time, you and I . . ."

Daisy gripped the receiver. The older woman's voice was thoughtful; full of affection and something like nostalgia. But Daisy didn't have time to get sentimental. Sage was missing. She was trying to keep the line clear, and Louisa wanted to talk about old times?

"I . . . I can't talk right now," she said.

"But I —"

"Louisa!" Daisy screamed, lurching forward so hard she sent a bowl of unpolished garnets flying to the floor. "I'm waiting for my daughter to call!"

"I want you to hear me out," Louisa said, her voice suddenly so stern it shocked Daisy.

Hathaway must have just arrived, because she came running into the back room, still wearing her plaid jacket. Daisy felt that her face had gone pure white, and she thought she was going to faint. Hathaway put her arms around her, eased her back into her chair.

"It's Louisa," Daisy said, looking into Hathaway's eyes.

"Okay." Hathaway looked as if she'd aged ten years in the last few days.

"Is that your sister?" Louisa asked from half a country away. "Good. I'm glad she's there. You shouldn't be alone right now, and when you hear what I'm about to say, you'll want to run it by her. You might want to rip my eyes out, too, and

I'll be glad to have her there to talk you out of it."

"What do you want to tell me?" Daisy asked hesitantly, holding Hathaway's hand.

"It's this," Louisa said. "I want you to come to the ranch."

Daisy felt the blood pounding in her ears. Had Louisa said what she thought she had?

"You're joking."

"This is no joke, young lady. If you think that I'd speak lightly at a time like this, you don't know me as well as I thought you did."

"I can't go to the ranch . . ." Daisy hadn't set foot on the DR Ranch in more than a decade. It was the site of her worst nightmare. She wouldn't be able to see those jagged rocks, smell that sage-scented air, without thinking of her little boy. James lived there now, and with all that had happened between them, there was nothing but bad blood. Besides, what did this have to do with Sage? "I can't," she said. "I won't."

"Don't you want to help your daughter?" Louisa asked.

Daisy felt her blood boil. "Help my daughter?" she said. "Is that what you said? How dare you!"

"That's right, help your daughter," Louisa said. "You heard me right."

"Louisa." Daisy's voice was shaking. "You were my friend once, and I loved you. You were part of our family, and now you —" She'd been holding Hathaway's hand, but now she yanked it away to hold the phone steady. Hathaway looked worried.

"Settle down," Louisa said. "You're out of your mind, Daisy, and don't think I don't know it. I would be, too. I'm wearing the 'Bear Mother' you gave me, thinking on that old grizzly James shot, trying to imagine how I'd feel if life ever ripped me away from my cub."

"Both of mine," Daisy wailed, bowing her head. "Both of them!"

"Hang up, Daisy." Not understanding what was going on, just seeing her sister's unimaginable distress, Hathaway tried to take the phone out of her hand.

"Oh, God." Daisy shuddered.

"I know, sweetheart," Louisa said. "Oh, I know."

"Both of them," Daisy said again.

"That's why . . ." Louisa began, but Daisy hardly heard her. She was thinking of her two babies. She would rock them to sleep, one in each arm. Jake always took longer to fall asleep than Sage, and he would talk and coo, staring into his mother's eyes, while his sister slept against Daisy's other breast.

"What?" Daisy asked. "That's why . . . what did you say?"

"That's why you have to come out here."

Something inside Daisy had just broken like a dam, and all her anger flowed out of her, like a river to the open sea. She felt washed out, completely empty. The memory of her babies had

been so strong her breasts and arms ached.
Hathaway rubbed her head, but all of Daisy's
attention was on what Louisa had to say.

"Why?"

"Because this is where you belong right now.
Not forever, but for this waiting time. This ranch
is where you had your babies. It's the first home
Sage knew. Something's pulling her here, something powerful. I don't know what it is, but I
don't believe she's going to stop — or be stopped
— until she gets here."

"So many things could happen to her before
that."

"I know, sweetheart." Louisa's voice was
steady, sure, and warm. "But they won't. She's a
strong woman, just like her mother. The world
has handed her some hard times already, and
look how she's stood up to them."

"I want her back home."

"I know you do, and she'll get there eventually. But she's coming here first, and I want you
to be here when she arrives."

"I can't stand the ranch."

"That doesn't matter much, does it," Louisa
asked, "when it's Sage we're thinking about
right now?"

"What good will my going there do?"

"It'll show her she's worth it."

"Worth it?" Daisy asked, confused.

"That you and her father can set your differences aside for now. Put Sage first. Be at the
ranch waiting for her with open arms when she

131

comes walking through the gate. She's a troubled little girl, and she needs her parents. Both of them."

"She's pregnant," Daisy said, the words spilling out along with the tears. She had wanted to keep it secret, to protect Sage's privacy till they had the chance to talk, to decide what she should do; but Louisa's tone was so calm and maternal, Daisy could almost believe she was talking to her own mother.

"Well, I figured that might be the case," Louisa said. "Her running off so fast and dramatic. It's just what I did."

"What you did — ?"

"When I got pregnant young."

"Young?" Daisy asked, trying to remember the details of Louisa's life.

"Just a girl. Barely older than Sage — seventeen."

"I hadn't known . . ."

"My father had died a few years back. I'm not saying that fact alone made me get pregnant, but it contributed. I missed him so, wanted his love so badly, I went running off with the first boy who came along. I just needed to be filled with love, if you can understand that."

"But you were married when you had Ruthie," Daisy said, remembering the story about Louisa's husband, Earl, how he had died right after the baby was born.

"That's just what I told people."

"But you said Earl died —"

"In my heart he died," Louisa said. "I killed him off in my heart when it came clear he wasn't going to marry me and give our baby a name. When I realized he didn't want any part of her life. Guy's dead as a doornail to me."

"But —"

"Daisy, my lying about Earl's neither here nor there. I just did it to protect Ruthie. The point is, I got pregnant when I was seventeen years old, and all I wanted was to go home. My daddy was dead. My mother'd remarried an oilman in Cheyenne, but their house wasn't a refuge to me. All I wanted was home. *My* home."

Daisy thought of Louisa's father being dead, of Sage missing her own father so much she kept a shrine to him in her bedroom. She closed her eyes and pictured James's picture hanging from the elk rack, right where Sage had placed it.

"The ranch," Daisy said. "Sage's first home."

"The only home where you all lived together as a family."

"Us all . . ."

"You and Sage, her daddy and her brother."

The Seth Thomas clock across the room chimed the hour. Daisy and Louisa had been tying up the phone a long time. Confused and hurting, Daisy shook her head. Some of what Louisa said made sense, but still — how could Daisy go back to the ranch? Daisy's gaze fell on the new piece she was working on: "Lonely Girl." She thought of all the love she had for it, and she realized why she had chosen that title.

There was so much in what Louisa was saying, the hidden truth about Sage needing her larger family. Sage had been a twin. She had had a loving father, grandfather, and Louisa. When Daisy had moved them back east, she had ripped Sage away from everyone who loved her most. How that must have felt to Sage . . . Daisy had been so busy trying to stay alive, to survive her own grief, she had made some selfish decisions. Needing to keep her only living child away from the ranch, she had kept her from her father.

"Thank you," she managed to say. "For being so honest with me. I'll think about it. I really will."

"That's all I'm asking you to do," Louisa said kindly.

"Louisa, will you keep this between us? I mean, don't tell James about Sage being pregnant."

"Never, Daisy."

Carefully, Daisy hung up the phone. She turned to Hathaway, and suddenly the ranch melted away. *This* was home; this was where Sage belonged. Daisy would be waiting right here on Pumpkin Lane when the police finally found her.

"Louisa thinks I should go to Wyoming," Daisy said, waiting for her sister to laugh, scoff, shake her head in disbelief.

Hathaway waited. She touched Daisy's shoulder, tilted her head as she listened for her to say more. Today she wore a red western shirt, turquoise beads, silver earrings, a Sioux beaded bracelet: the stuff she sold at the Cowgirl Rodeo.

"She thinks Sage misses her father so much, it's what this is all about," Daisy said.

"All about . . ." Hathaway said, trailing off.

"Getting pregnant, running away, everything."

"Missing a father's a very big thing," Hathaway said slowly. "I haven't stopped missing Dad, not even after all this time. That smile, his sense of humor, the way he'd read to us. Oh . . ."

"Dad . . ." Daisy said, thinking. She and Hathaway had lost their own father to a heart attack. She could hear his good-natured laugh, see him perusing his books with half-glasses perched on the end of his handsome, aquiline nose, remember the distinctive scent of his library: leather, furniture polish, the flowers her mother always arranged on his desk. She missed him so much, her eyes filled with tears, and she understood a little more about Sage's journey.

"I've never doubted Sage loved James," she said carefully. "I'm positive that she's on her way to see him. The thing is, I just don't understand what my going out there would do. I just don't get that part."

"That part's for you," Hathaway said, her eyes liquid with warmth and love.

"For me?"

"You see," Hathaway said gently, holding

both Daisy's hands, "I agree with Louisa."

"But why?"

"To be waiting at the ranch when Sage gets there. You already know she's on the way. She has her reasons for going back there, and so do you."

"Me?" Daisy asked. "I can't imagine what they are, what you're thinking. I was born in Connecticut and I love it here. You're here —"

"I'm with you wherever you are," Hathaway said. "You must know that by now. We're in each other's hearts."

"I don't want to go to the ranch," Daisy heard herself say, the words sounding like echoes in a deep canyon.

"But I think you're going to go anyway." Hathaway squeezed Daisy's hands as she smiled into her eyes.

Daisy had always felt lucky to have a sister, especially an older sister like Hathaway.

"Really?" Daisy asked.

"I do," Hathaway said. "I think that."

"Tell me why again."

"Because it's meant to be. Because you love the West much more than you ever let on. You think New England's in your blood, but you're more cowgirl than Annie Oakley."

"How do you know?"

"Because I'm the oldest sister," Hathaway said, smiling widely, kissing Daisy on the top of her head. "I know everything."

Eleven hours after leaving the train, Sage stopped to check her map. She was exhausted, and it felt good to stop. Digging through her pack, she pulled out the travel kit she had made before leaving home: flashlight, matches, pictures of her father and the ranch, and the map.

It was a Rand McNally map of the United States that she'd bought at the drugstore years ago. For a long time, it had hung on her wall, with one thumbtack in Connecticut and another in Wyoming. As time went by, she began tracing the route she imagined taking to the ranch.

Now the dream was real, and she had made it partway through Iowa. Luckily the roads were pretty straight, so as long as she pedaled toward the setting sun she'd be okay. By late afternoon, as she traveled country roads through field after field, she felt exposed in the wide-open spaces. She thought of stone walls, hills and valleys, oaks and pines: the landscape of home, with places to hide around every bend.

She realized how near she had come to being caught, sent back home with that close call with the police. One part of her wished she would be found. She pedaled along, thinking of Ben, wondering where he was. She kept remembering that moment when his voice had cracked, when he'd said he wanted to go back to Silver Bay. The memory made her cringe, tighten her shoulders. It made her feel alone and ashamed in ways she had never felt before.

It made Sage know that he would have broken up with her eventually. It made her picture herself alone with the baby. Had the authorities called Ben's mother, put him on a plane home yet? What if they'd put him in jail? Riding along, Sage wished on every hay wagon she saw that he was okay. The hurt she felt was shocking, searing, like a just-skinned knee. She felt as if they'd been ripped apart, and she couldn't quite believe it yet.

Even though she knew it was what Ben wanted. That made it worse. She thought of how she had known he wanted to go back: When he had held her on the train, it wasn't the same as before, nothing like the magic bed. His arms had been around her body, but she'd felt him wanting to push her away. He didn't even have to say.

As she rode her bike past empty cornfields, the stalks shorn down to foot-high stubble, Sage's stomach rumbled. A few miles back she had found some unharvested ears, and she'd eaten the dry kernels, trying to pretend they were unpopped popcorn. Watching low clouds blowing across the endless sky, she tried to comfort herself, telling the baby they'd be there soon.

*There.* What a strange word for little kids. She remembered her own mother saying it all the time: *"We'll be there soon."*

The trick was not what her mother had meant, but how Sage had taken it. There wasn't a time, from the age of four on, that Sage hadn't hoped that "there" meant "the ranch." They might be going to the A&P, the aquarium, the wharf, Aunt Hathaway's — but if her mother said, *"We'll be there soon,"* Sage's mind would click into some bizarre mode, and she'd think — or at least hope — that her mother meant the ranch.

*There,* Sage thought. *There.*

A pickup passed, going in her direction, and she saw the driver check his rearview mirror. He hit his brakes, slowing down slightly. Sage sat upright, feeling her stomach lurch. What if he came back? She was way out in the middle of nowhere, and she knew full well to be leery of strangers offering her rides.

At the same time, she was exhausted. It would be getting dark soon, and she didn't know where she was going to sleep that night. Besides, it looked like rain.

The pickup truck's brake lights went off as the driver sped up again. Sage watched him for a long time, until the truck was no bigger than a fly.

The wind blew harder, getting dirt in her eyes. She saw tractors in the fields, their yellow wheels like big eyes watching her pass by. Thinking of owls hunting, she shivered all the way down her spine. That had been one of her worst nightmares of childhood, the dream of an owl swooping down on Jake, carrying him into a tree hole, tearing him apart like a squirrel.

"We're almost there," she said to her baby,

just to let him know they were safe, that they'd sleep soon. "I promise."

There were no twists in the road, no hills. She could see two houses up ahead, two red barns. The first house had a tricycle parked by the lamppost. A neatly trimmed hedge ran around the yard. There was a flagpole surrounded by chrysanthemums, the American flag standing out straight in the stiff wind. Aunt Hathaway loved the flag, always flew it from the white porch outside her small shop.

And the ranch had had a flag. Sage had forgotten all these years until this very moment, but now she remembered her grandfather giving her a ride on his shoulders, letting Jake pull the line that hoisted the flag up the tall white pole. Stopping her bike, Sage took a deep breath. She thought about going right up to the front door, asking for a place to stay that night.

They'd call the police in two seconds flat.

Instead, Sage wheeled her bike around the barn. She watched the house windows, to see if anyone was looking. Night was falling, and the sky was getting dark. Gentle shadows coated the brown yard. Pushing the heavy barn door half open, Sage thought of the familiar shadows of home: her house, the pines, the grape arbor. Since she had begun seeing Ben, she had sneaked into her own house many times at night: Not once had she ever appreciated the warm feeling of knowing that her mother was right down the hall.

Here she was in Iowa, hiding in the barn of strangers. She felt cold and alone, furtive as a criminal. Pushing her bike behind a rusty old tractor, she looked around. The day's fading light came through cracks in the walls. A horse whinnied, and she jumped.

It was the children's pony. Small and shaggy, it tossed its head as she approached. She saw a pile of apples and carrots on a low shelf, and she ate some hungrily. The pony nickered, and she fed it an apple. Bone tired, Sage wanted to curl up in the pony's stall. She wanted to feel the animal's warmth, curl her stomach against its spine. As she fed it another apple, hoping to make friends, the pony kicked.

Its hoof struck the stall, the sound loud and echoing. Sage jumped away. Her eyes filled with tears. She felt rejected, unwanted even by this gray pony. His ears were flat, and she knew that wasn't a good sign. Sage remembered horse-lore from her childhood. Her father had taken her riding every day of her life until she was four, let her sit high in the saddle, hold the reins. She had a knack for horses, he'd told her. She remembered that still.

With the pony watching her, Sage climbed a narrow ladder to the hayloft. It was dark, and it felt warmer than downstairs, as if the straw generated its own heat. Too tired to look for more food, Sage crawled into the pile and pulled hay around her like a blanket. Snuggling into a ball, she felt her belly.

"We're safe now," she whispered. "We're not there yet, but we're safe for the night."

She heard a truck whiz by on the road outside. A night bird screeched. Way up above, a jet engine droned, and she wondered whether the flight was going east or west. She pictured her mother's face, and she pictured her father's. The baby felt warm and cozy inside her. The hayloft was dark. They might not be *there,* but they were here. Sage slept.

David Crane loved the car because it took him away. He stepped on the gas, and he sped east. The car was ancient, with rust holes and missing trim. Inside, springs poked through the torn vinyl upholstery, and tufts of white stuffing and foam fell onto the floor. The car smelled of wet fur.

Animals huddled everywhere. Their eyes were wide open, alert in the night. They caught the glare of passing headlights — circles of yellow, all through the car.

Driving east through the Black Hills of Wyoming, he neared the Nebraska border. He hesitated, rolling down his window to listen to the wind. Here the ponderosa pines were dark and thick, and their boughs brushed against each other telling him which way to go: *Turn left, take the highway, drive fast:* as specific as that.

He got his directions from nature. The sun, the moon, the stars, the wind: Nature spoke to him the way a mother was supposed to. He got signals he couldn't explain, followed them without too many questions. The directions always led him to animals, creatures who needed to be rescued.

One of the dogs barked, and he knew it was time to give everyone a walk.

"Want to go out?" he asked.

Two of the dogs whimpered in response.

Glancing into his rearview mirror, he saw a big semi barreling down the road. He pulled over to let it pass, and then he opened the car's rear door to let the dogs out. They tromped into the trees, without any of the joy or freedom of normal dogs. Doing their business, they kept close watch on their driver.

When they had finished, he whistled long and low — like an owl hunting over the chaparral. The dogs dutifully marched back to the car, their heads hung low, one clenching an old stuffed toy in her teeth.

"Inside, Petal," he said, giving her a gentle pat. "That's a girl."

Petal was his first rescue, and he loved her more than any other creature on earth. A white, black, and brown pit bull, she gripped her toy in her massive jaws, drool soaking it wet. He had given her the toy himself, something ancient from his own childhood, to help her feel secure.

With everyone safe in the old car, he opened the glove compartment. He had dropped out of school years ago now — if he had ever really gone. School had never meant anything to him, but traveling did. Nature taught him better than any teacher. Right now it — nature — was pulling him so hard, he couldn't breathe right.

Mostly his work — saving things — kept him in Wyoming. Plenty of barns filled with stray cats, hundreds of puppy farms run by cruel owners. But right now he felt the tug — like a fish on a line — toward Nebraska. He had never felt such a compulsion. His eyes watered, and his mouth was dry.

Something needed him. Rifling through the glove compartment, he found his kit. Inside, he had sewing needles, a fine-tipped fountain pen, and ink. For now, he left the needles alone. But dipping the pen-point into the bottle of ink, he shook the loose drops onto the dirty floor of the old car.

Pen-point nearly dry, he adjusted the rearview mirror. It was dark, but he could see by the moonlight slanting through the pine boughs. Very carefully, he drew on his left cheek. Then on his right.

The marks symbolized protection, things to be saved. He knew he had something big ahead of him. It might be a hurt dog, a litter of abandoned kittens, an owl with a broken wing. David didn't know; he'd have to wait till he got there.

That's how it felt to him, starting up the car, driving through the Black Hills into Nebraska: as if he was heading into danger, as if whatever needed him this time was bigger and more intense than anything he had ever handled before.

# Chapter Ten

Dalton Tucker's prediction came true: The rain came. And once it started, it fell in torrents. Sheets of silver rain blew down the Wind River mountains, filling the lakes and riverbeds. Bison, moose, elk, and antelope drank alongside cattle. Draws filled up with water, and armies of rattlesnakes slithered up the crevices. Dust turned to mud, making the ground slippery underfoot.

On horseback, James was moving cattle down from the summer range. He wore his hat, chaps, a boot-length green slicker, and a bandanna around his neck, but none of that mattered: He was drenched through. The brim of his hat acted as a spout, pouring water straight into his crotch. At least it kept his mind off the worst of what might be happening, off the six days his daughter had been missing.

The calves scrabbled in the mud, trying to get closer to their mothers. The younger ones wailed and the mothers moaned. James and his crew had been working for six hours and in the move, families tended to get separated. Cow babies would stay with their mothers the rest of their lives if he'd let them. They wanted their mothers' milk and protection, and they'd keep it as long as they were allowed.

He cared for the cattle and hated to see them suffer, but that went with the territory. The calves had to learn to survive — graze, find water — on their own. Each head on the range was worth money in its own right, and it was days like this that made James remember he was in the beef business, not the veterinary business. There were parts of ranching he hated, and this was one of them.

"James!" Paul March called, riding after a pair trying to run away. "Got a stuck one over there."

James turned to look. The rain had transformed parts of the pasture into a bog, and a calf had gotten caught. He galloped over. The calf had sunk up to its chest, all four legs mired in mud. Its eyes had the look of a child lost in the grocery store — helpless and frightened. James didn't let himself feel anything. He just drew back his rope, threw a loop around the calf's neck, took his dally.

"She's stuck good," Paul said, riding over.

"We'll get her out," James said. With a half-hitch around the saddlehorn, he kicked his horse forward. The calf wouldn't budge.

"When it rains, it pours," Paul joked.

"No one's thirsty today," James said, rain trickling down his collar. As the horse strained more, the calf began to move. It popped out of the mud like a cork, found its legs, ran to its mother.

"Heard about Daisy coming out," Paul said. "That true?"

"That's what Louisa says." James had heard the news last night.

Seems Louisa had taken it upon herself to stir the pot, call Daisy for a woman-to-woman talk. Daisy hadn't mentioned anything about coming here when James had talked to her. The opposite had seemed true: that she hated the place with a passion, wanted to stay as far away as possible.

"Well —" Paul began.

James cleared his throat to cut Paul off. His eyes narrowed, watching his father. Across the pasture, Dalton sat tall in the saddle, seeming oblivious to the rain. For that matter, he seemed to have forgotten that he was on a horse in a downpour. He just turned his head from side to side, as if he was watching the world go by.

"Been a long time since she was here," Paul said, not getting the message.

"Hmm. Yeah," James said, not wanting to think about Daisy. It was a thought that picked up emotion as it passed through his mind. Long time ago, it might have been attached to hope. Now he found it was linked to dread. "Where'd you hear about her?" he asked Paul.

"The Rydell boys," Paul said. "Talking at the bar last night."

Louisa's nephews, James thought. She must have told them, getting the word out. He wondered whether she'd included the part about Sage running away from home. Paul March was

147

his ranch foreman — a good man, and a real friend. But James didn't want Todd Rydell talking about Daisy or Sage.

"Nothing's definite," James said. "She might come, she might not. Don't think she's decided yet."

"Look, I know about your daughter being missing," Paul said, removing all doubt about what Louisa had said. "That she's on her way out here. You've got to be worried shitless."

"That's a good word for it."

"She'll show up."

"Yeah." James wiped rain off his face with the back of his hand.

"She will, James."

James nodded, peering at a cluster of cows, mothers and calves gathered together for protection. He thought of the calf stuck in the boghole, how the earth could just swallow your offspring without warning.

"James. Talk to me, okay? I was there, remember?"

"There?"

"When Jake went."

"Went . . ." James repeated, considering the word. For some reason, it made him think of Daisy. He wondered what she would say if he tried using "went" on her, as in "Jake went away." A mild, gentle word for the whole world falling apart.

"You've got to be going crazy. Why haven't you said anything?"

James looked Paul straight in the eye. The foreman was big and stocky, going bald under his hat. He had pale brown eyes, the color of the land. The men had grown up together, right here on the DR Ranch — Paul's father had been foreman to Dalton, just as Paul's grandfather had been foreman to Dalton's father, Asa.

James had gone to school with the March kids — Paul, his sister June, and their brother Luke. He and Paul had had their first beers together at a bar in Lander. They had played ranch Little League; they'd gone fly-fishing on Torero Creek. Attended each other's wedding. Paul and his wife had baby-sat for the twins. James had no brothers, and Paul was the closest he had to a best friend. But in a million years, James wouldn't have considered telling him about Sage leaving home, about Daisy maybe coming west.

"Nothing to say," James replied after a long minute.

"I don't know." Paul shook his head. "Seems like there's a whole lot to get off your chest —" His jaw was set, his eyes scrunched up with hurt and frustration.

"My chest's fine," James said.

"Whatever you say." Eyes flashing, Paul seemed about to add something more, but then he wheeled on his horse and rode away.

It was hard being James's friend. Daisy had told him that a thousand times. The thing was, James could give out — no problem. He could sit by a campfire and listen to another man's woes

149

about money, wife, kids, the roof of his house blowing off. But James couldn't take kindness. He didn't know why, but love, friendship, tenderness — whatever you wanted to call it — made him so uncomfortable he wanted to crawl out of his skin.

"Mind your own damn business," James said once he was sure Paul couldn't hear him. Even as he spoke, he felt a pain in his chest, the pain he got all the time, ten times a day. It came when he thought of his kids, when he pictured Daisy. *A lot to get off your chest,* Paul had said.

Okay, maybe. But where would it go?

The horse beneath him reared. A rattlesnake had somehow failed to heed nature, find its lair; it was there in the middle of his path. Coiled, rattle going, it opened its fangs to strike.

"Goddamn snake," James said.

The big bay reared and whinnied and James brought it down to kill the snake. The bay's front left hoof struck the rattler's head, cut it right off. The long, thick body straightened out, jerking in spasms. The horse rose again. James felt its weight slam down again, jarring against the earth. Taking care of business, James thought. Killing a rattlesnake that might have bitten his horse.

Time was, he'd wanted to kill every rattler in the Wind River Range. He'd wanted to shoot every grizzly, drain every deep water hole, wipe out any possible danger to his family. After Jake disappeared, James had lain awake every night for months, thinking of all the threats that could befall him. Daisy had blamed him for losing their son. The least James could do was annihilate all the predators.

One rattlesnake, dead.

Now, maybe Daisy was coming west.

Daisy Tucker. Those big eyes, the way she'd look at nature — the mountains, the animals, the big blue sky — and have it come out her hands in the jewelry she made. Daisy had love in her hands, along with magical powers. The first time she'd held James, he had felt himself come alive. Every hair on his body had stood on end. She could kiss him and make him whole. When she touched his skin, he believed in heaven.

Heaven had been Daisy's gift. For their five years together, James had lived with more peace and bliss than he'd ever dreamed possible. The mountains were the clouds, the land was endless sky. James and Daisy were above the realm of earth, the struggles and pains of being human. They hadn't had to work at being happy, at loving each other, at having a good marriage. Heaven didn't require such things.

Suddenly he heard his father cry out, then call, "I'm all wet!"

"Dalton, hey —"

"I'm soaking wet," Dalton yelled again.

Shaken from his thoughts, James looked across the field of cattle. Dalton had climbed off his horse in the middle of it all. Trying to dry himself off with a red bandanna, he stood among the confused herd, getting jostled around.

"It's raining, Dalton," Paul said. "We're all wet."

"Why am I all wet?" Dalton asked, as if he hadn't heard him.

Some of the young cowboys were laughing. They tried not to show it, and James turned away from them. He didn't want to remember who to hate, to resent for making fun of his old father. Senility in a cowboy: No one wanted to think it could happen to them. The laughter got louder, and James snapped.

"Shut the fuck up," he shouted.

"James —"

"Sorry —"

"You got fathers?" he asked. "Any of you?"

"Sorry, boss —"

James was past hearing. He shouldered through the herd. His father had no business being here. He had ridden out on his own, after James and the other hands had left the barn that morning. Now Dalton was trying to get his sopping clothes off, stripping off his slicker, unbuttoning his shirt. James felt the pressure of so many worries: Sage, Daisy, now his father. He wanted to explode, yell at Dalton for coming along where he wasn't wanted, screwing up the day's work.

"Jesus Christ, Dad," James yelled.

"I'm all wet." Dalton's eyes were as wide open as a child's.

"I know, it's pouring rain," James said, his

face hot and flushed.

"All wet," Dalton said sorrowfully. "Soaking wet."

James bowed his head. He could hear his son's voice. That's what Jake had said every time James had given him a bath. With the same regret and dismay in his little voice, the boy had looked trustingly up at his father and said the same words: *"All wet. Soaking wet, Daddy."*

"You're okay," James said to his father now, as he had once said to his son. Swinging down from his horse, he stood by his father in the middle of the swirling herd. Cattle stepped on their feet, bumped against their bodies. "Don't worry, Dad."

"I don't like it," Dalton said, panicked. He was naked, having pulled off all his clothes.

James picked up the old man's yellow slicker, wrapped it around his father. Dalton was skinny as a bird. Leaning into James's chest, he was shivering. His face was leathery, wrinkled, but his expression was childlike. He breathed in panic. James thought of Jake. Wanting his son to be tough, at first James would try to ignore the child's cries. Daisy had helped him come up with words of wisdom and comfort to soothe his son. He held his father, and he used Daisy's words now.

"It's only water," James said as he held his father in his arms. The cows closed around them, and the rain pelted their heads. "There's nothing to worry about. Nothing at all."

Daisy rang the Davis house twenty times before noon. Half the time it was busy, the other half she got the answering machine. When both kids had still been missing, Paulina had answered Daisy's calls screaming that she would like to kill Sage; she had known she was bad news from the minute Ben had brought her over. Daisy had hung up on her.

But Daisy had kept calling. The parents had to stay connected, to report any new developments. With Ben on his way home, Paulina was smug and cold. At least he was safe. Paulina had promised he would call, but still he hadn't.

Once again, Daisy tried the line. She had left three messages, asking Ben to call her when he got in. She began to suspect that Paulina had lied, that she wasn't going to tell Ben to call after all, so she kept calling. It worried her, tying up the line when Sage might be trying to get through, but she had to know — she had to ask Ben where she was, *how* she was. Just about to dial again, she heard a knock at the back door. Telephone in hand, she pulled it open.

Ben stood on the porch. He wore a parka that made his shoulders appear huge. Looking scared, he hung back. Daisy's mouth dropped open. Very slowly, she hung up the phone.

"My mother told me you called," he said. "It seemed better that I come over than call you."

Daisy nodded. "Come in."

"You probably don't want to see me," he said.

His eyes were red, his face pale. His brow was screwed up with worry. He was one year older than Sage. Staring at him, Daisy knew he had gotten her daughter pregnant, helped her run away from home. Her eyes filled with tears.

"I do want to see you," she heard herself say.

"I'm sorry," he said.

"Tell me," Daisy said, swallowing. "Where is Sage?"

He stared down at the floor. It was pine, polished to a high sheen. Daisy and Sage had stenciled a border around the edges many years ago: white daisies and silvery sage leaves entwined together on vines.

"Ben?"

"I don't know."

"You must."

"No," he said. "Honestly. We were together until —"

There was a green glass pitcher standing on the kitchen counter. It contained a bunch of yellow chrysanthemums Sage had picked a week ago, before she'd disappeared. Daisy had promised herself she would keep them until Sage came home. With one sweep of her hand, Daisy sent the pitcher flying against the refrigerator, where it shattered into a hundred pieces.

"Don't lie to me!" she yelled. "You lied to the police, you lied to your mother. But goddamn it, Ben, you're going to tell me the truth." Choking on a sob, she stared down at the dead flowers lying in slimy brown water, then into

155

Ben's shocked eyes.

"Tell me," she breathed, holding herself. "Tell me."

Ben started to pick up the biggest pieces of broken glass, but Daisy grabbed his arm. "I'm sorry," she said. "I'm not violent. I didn't mean to scare you. But I have to know. I have to hear what's happening to Sage."

"She —" Ben started, his mouth too dry to talk.

"Go ahead, Ben," Daisy said. "You can tell me."

"She was in Iowa, Mrs. Tucker," Ben said. "Just like I told the police —"

"After you said she'd gotten off the train in Chicago? I don't understand that. I don't get it."

"She told me to."

Daisy's heart was pounding. His voice was shaking, his eyes sunken like a raccoon's. "She told you to lie to the police?"

"Yes."

"Why?"

"She wanted time to get away —"

"Get away from what?" Daisy asked, her eyes filling again. Was home so bad? Was she such a witch?

"From the train."

"But where did you last see her? What was she doing? What did she say?"

"She was going to shove her bike out the train door," Ben continued. "She was going to ride through the cornfield and hide. The police fig-

156

ured out I was lying right away. They searched the fields around the train, but she was gone. I think she went backward for a while. She didn't want to get found. I don't think she will be, until —"

"Until what?" Daisy asked, so desperate to hear.

"She gets to Wyoming," he said.

Daisy tried to breathe. Wyoming. She broke down with the relief of finally knowing for sure. Her instinct had been right: Sage was going to James. Using the back of her hands, she wiped her eyes.

"What was her route? How was she planning to get there?"

"She had a map. It was all planned out, side roads all the way."

"Do you know which ones?" Daisy asked, staring into Ben's eyes in an attempt to see the truth. Even before he replied, she could see he had no idea.

"I don't," he said. "She had the map."

Daisy shuddered. She walked over to the telephone, silently told it to ring. All the women in Silver Bay thought she could conjure love out of old cow bones, and she couldn't even keep her daughter at home. She couldn't will her to call, no matter how hard she concentrated.

"You won't find her before she gets there," Ben said. "That's what I came over to tell you. I'm not sure how I know, but I know. She's determined to get to Wyoming — the ranch —

and I'm positive she's going to get there."

"Is she pregnant, Ben?" Daisy asked.

"Yeah."

Daisy heard herself moan. She clenched her fists, digging her nails into her palms, picturing the blue stick in Sage's jewelry box. Ben had just confirmed what she'd already known.

"Is she okay?"

"She's feeling sick."

"Then she's not very far along . . ."

"Six months," Ben said, as Daisy's heart fell.

*"Six — ?"* How was it possible that she hadn't noticed? By six months, expectant mothers were starting to show. She hadn't seen her daughter's bare stomach in all that time?

"She's been throwing up since the beginning," Ben said, sounding miserable. "I'm sorry. I didn't mean to hurt her. . . ."

"Oh, Ben," Daisy said. She wanted to hate this boy as much as his mother hated Sage, but she couldn't. He looked so crushed, so upset about what was happening to Sage. The way he said she'd been throwing up, Daisy could hear that he cared.

"She wanted me to stay with her," he said, his voice cracking. "I couldn't. I want to go to school, not to live on a ranch in Wyoming."

Daisy listened.

"My mother told me not to come over," he said. "She's ballistic. I know she thinks Sage should have gotten an abortion."

"Did Sage want that?" Daisy asked, knowing

158

she didn't, feeling bizarre talking about this with Ben Davis. Sage was sixteen; she should be playing soccer, carving pumpkins, planning her Halloween party, thinking about college.

He shook his head. "She thinks she's having a boy."

*The blue stick*, Daisy thought. *A sign.*

"I love her," Ben said, his voice breaking again.

Daisy nodded. She believed he did, but what did he know? He was just a kid himself. When even adults couldn't stay in love, withstand the pressures of togetherness, she knew she was glad that he and Sage hadn't eloped, that he hadn't married her. She and Sage would figure this out. She would do whatever it took to make sure Sage and the baby were taken care of.

"What are you going to do?" Ben asked.

"I'm going to go to Wyoming," Daisy said. Until he had asked the question, Daisy would have said she was going to stay right here and wait. In spite of Louisa's call and Hathaway's encouragement, Daisy had thought her place was home by the phone. But something about the way Ben had said Sage was going to get there — to Wyoming — about picturing her daughter six months pregnant — still sick! — made Daisy know she had to leave right away.

"I'm sorry," Ben said again.

"I know." Daisy took his hand. It was cold, and as she looked out the window she saw that he had ridden his bike.

"My mother won't let me use the car," he said,

following her gaze. "The police said they were going to arrest me, but they didn't. I guess they believed me when I said I didn't kidnap her."

"I know you didn't, Ben."

"No one could kidnap Sage," he said, trying to make her smile. "She's amazing. She's strong, she knows what she wants. She's going to be fine, Mrs. Tucker. Honestly, she will. She won't disappear."

Daisy pulled her hand away. She looked down at the floor, gleaming in the late-October sun. Her gaze fell upon the painted flowers and leaves, white petals and silver-green leaves entwined. Decorating the floor together had been her idea, the year after she and Sage had moved east from Wyoming. She had handed Sage a brush, shown her how to twist the bristles as she stroked, making a perfect sage leaf. For the three or four days it had taken to paint the floor, Sage had never left her side.

Daisy thought of Jake, of the reason she and Sage had moved east in the first place. She looked Ben straight in the eye and said coolly, "Anyone can be kidnapped. Anyone can disappear."

*Mothers and fathers, mothers and fathers. Oh, what a perfect world. Hold me tight, and sleep will take me, all through the night.*

*All through the night, through the night, through the night.*

*Sweet dreams, sleep tight, don't let the bedbugs bite.*

Happy families, what a joke. He cleaned his nails with a hunting knife and nicked the skin. A big bubble of blood came up, and he sucked it and spit it out. Blood never bothered him. He'd gotten used to it long ago, living where he did, growing up around ranch land. When he skinned his knees and ran to mama, well, she was just a little too busy to kiss it better.

He got used to cleaning up his own cuts. You might say he knew where the Band-Aids were kept. He'd rummage under the sink for peroxide and gauze, even the worst time, when he'd snagged his behind on a rusty nail. Jesus, trying to clean that wound by himself, half turned around, looking over his own shoulder while his mother slept in the other room. His father? Who knew where his father was?

Who ever knew where his father was? *All through the night . . .*

*Poor little lamb,* his mother had said when she saw the jagged cut across his buttocks, down the back of his leg. *Poor little lamb.*

More like poor little cow, he thought now. The range was endless, dotted with cattle. Cows grazing on land too vast for the imagination to comprehend, yet too small for other varieties of stock. Sheep, for instance. Lambs.

The knife was large and sharp. He had sharpened it himself, using age-old methods, with spit, oil, and a whetstone. Back and forth, back and forth. Hiding had its boredom. One way to pass the time was to keep his equipment in top condition.

Another way was to eavesdrop. From his hiding places, he watched the cowboys. He knew the trails they took, the places they liked to rest. Sometimes they talked, and sometimes their voices carried.

A girl was coming.

Making her way west, just like the wagon trains. There's gold in them thar hills. There's grass for grazing and ground for planting and trees for cutting into fat, handsome building logs. Dreams come true out here; that's why people came west in the first place. Happy families, everywhere you looked. Just look.

The knife was sharp, the rain had stopped falling, the cows were grazing again, and a girl on her own was coming west. Wild, wild west.

*Sweet dreams, little lamb.*

# Chapter Eleven

Flying across the country, Daisy watched the ocean and cities of the East give way to the flat Midwest. She saw the Mississippi River flow, the boundary waters glisten, the Rocky Mountains rise, the badlands darken.

Looking down, Daisy's throat ached. She and Sage were on their way to the same place. Was it really possible they hadn't been back in twelve years? "Let her be safe," she whispered, her forehead against the window.

She felt pressure in her chest, like a hand on her heart. She thought of Sage on her bike, looking up at the plane flying overhead, following the white trail all the way to Wyoming.

Louisa had offered to pick her up at the Riverton airport, but Daisy had said no. She wanted to be as independent as possible, so she had decided to rent a car and drive to the ranch on her own. As the plane circled the airport, the sky seemed hinged to mountaintops. The land itself was red, rust, and purple, as bright as sunsets back east. It would be beautiful to anyone, spectacular to an artist. Daisy closed her eyes, moved and excited by the view. Something inside her stirred, a part that had been asleep for a long time.

*Heaven is wide,* she thought. Remembering Wyoming, she saw the big sky all around. It had spread outward from their little house, and she had believed that she and James had found the very center of heaven.

"There's a place for everyone," she had told him one cold night when the sky was deep and beautiful, when the aurora borealis painted fire and ice over the stars, "and this is our place." That night she had felt she could touch the wind.

Flying westward, she felt like howling. She didn't want to be seduced by the land, by the big sky.

Sage would show up soon, she told herself. They would be in and out of the state quickly. Many years ago Daisy had come west here, looking for inspiration for her work. She had found true love, given birth to two children. Then Wyoming had taken everything from her.

As she waited at the Hertz counter, the airport seemed to be full of pregnant women. Daisy stared at them all, trying to gauge how far along they were. One stood in the line behind her, staring at the ceiling while her husband talked trout fishing with the man behind them.

"When is the baby due?" Daisy asked, hoping her voice sounded normal.

"End of December." The woman wore jeans and a bulky plaid jacket. Close to Daisy's age, she had curly red hair, lines around her eyes and mouth.

"So, you're . . . seven months pregnant?" Daisy asked, trying to imagine Sage nearly this big. Was this what all those bulky clothes had been about? Daisy thought back to summer, how Sage hadn't wanted to spend any time sitting on the beach.

"Just about."

"Your first?" Daisy wished the line would move faster before she did something stupid. She felt the mad urge to reach out, touch the woman's protruding belly. Her fingers actually tingled.

"At my age, can you imagine?" the woman asked. "You have kids?"

"Twins," Daisy heard herself say, just as the man ahead of her took his keys and rental agreement, and went out to the parking lot.

"Two at once." The woman laughed. "Hope you had 'em young."

Daisy pasted a polite smile on her face and wondered whether she was going insane. She stepped up to the desk, found the slip of paper bearing her reservation number. "I did," Daisy said.

As the clerk processed her reservation, another pregnant woman passed by, pushing a stroller, and Daisy followed her with her eyes. That gave her two pictures to consider: Sage pregnant, Sage as a new mother.

She grabbed a road map of the area. It had

been many years since she'd been in Wyoming. She didn't want to waste any time losing her way. *In and out,* she thought. She walked out the terminal door into the cold, fresh air.

Daisy threw her bags into the midsize Ford and began to drive. She kept both hands on the wheel, her eyes on the road. She wanted to stay as focused and contained as possible. Anytime she raised her gaze, she saw mountains. There they were, the Wind Rivers: majestic and rugged against the blue sky. She kept her eyes trained low, straight ahead.

There was nothing between the road and the mountains but range. Sheep and cattle grazed. Wind-stunted cedars grew along straight ridge-lines; silver sagebrush covered the rolling ground. Although the air was cold, Daisy kept the car window open and the perfume of the West blew in: sage, spice, fur, and dust.

Emotions filled her chest. She tried to push them down. Memories returned, beginning with the first time she'd been in Wyoming. Born and raised in New England, she had been amazed by the things she saw here. She had been bowled over with inspiration. The size of the mountains, the expanse of the sky; she had known that everything in Wyoming was bigger, that any love that existed here was too deep, too consuming, too overpowering for a girl like her to understand.

She passed a rock formation spray-painted with the name "Sacagawea." Graffiti Wyoming-style, a tribute to the Shoshone girl kidnapped in a tribal raid. Jamming on the brakes, Daisy pulled over. She stared at the boulder, reading the name. From Daisy's first days in Wyoming, Sacagawea had intrigued her. Many of her first western necklaces had been inspired by her: carvings depicting courage, mother-love, living in nature, stepping into the unknown.

Taken from her people, from everything that was familiar, Sacagawea had been so brave. Horrible things happened to her, and she'd just gone on. Kidnapped from her family, she was sold as a wife to a fur trader. Daisy could think of nothing more disgusting than being forced to marry someone she didn't know or love, to have his baby.

But Sacagawea had loved her child. She and Baptiste, her infant boy, survived their three-thousand-mile journey with the Lewis and Clark expedition. She protected him, no matter what. People always thought Daisy had named her own daughter Sage after the beautiful sagebrush so common to Wyoming soil, and it was partly true; but Daisy had named her, also, after Sacagawea, the Shoshone girl of courage and endurance.

Getting strength from the sight of her name now, Daisy pulled back onto the road. She found herself raising her eyes, looking around. *You can't ignore mountains, especially not these,* she thought. The Wind Rivers were already capped with snow. She stared at the purple peaks, the brown cliffs. Once she started looking, she couldn't stop. The mountains were filled with mystery and magic, wind and spirits.

By the time she reached the gates of the DR Ranch, it was getting dark. She drove through the tunnel of cottonwood trees. With her windows open, she heard the creek flowing over stones and fallen trees. The main house was warmly lit, the stone and logs glowing like a jewel box. Smoke curled from the enormous chimney, vanishing into the dark red sky. Daisy saw horses in the corral, watching her as she came around the last bend.

Louisa was standing in the window. She stepped outside onto the porch, the wind blowing her red shawl. Parking the car, Daisy felt her heart beating in her throat. Her skin tingled, as if she was trespassing on haunted land. She hadn't been to the DR Ranch since the day she and Sage had left for the airport and their flight east. Looking around now, scanning the barns and the paddocks and the house itself, she felt dislocated, as if she'd gone back in time.

"Hello, stranger," Louisa called, coming down the wide porch steps.

"Hi, Louisa."

"You made it."

Daisy nodded, about to say something about the flight or the drive or some other conversation-making comment, when Louisa swept her into her arms. She smelled of wood smoke and Wind Song. Holding Daisy very tight, she seemed unwilling to let go. Daisy didn't want to step away; she clung to Louisa as if for dear life. *Jake and Sage,* Daisy thought. *This is where my babies used to live.* When Louisa finally stood back, Daisy saw that she was wearing the Bear Mother necklace.

"Has there been any word?" Daisy asked. "I've been out of touch since early afternoon, and I told Hathaway to call here if she heard from Sage. I also gave this number to Detective LaRosa, she's coordinating the search —"

"No word yet," Louisa said.

Daisy nodded, feeling dizzy again. A burst of wind came around the barn, blowing bits of brush. It fluttered Louisa's shawl, and as she drew it closer around her body, her fingers jangled the bones and metal of her necklace. She met Daisy's eyes.

"I'm wearing it for Sage."

"Thank you," Daisy said.

A pack of cowboys rode in, and Daisy tensed. She looked for James among them, but he wasn't there. Recognizing Paul March, Victor Lansing, and some other ranch hands, she watched them ride around the barns to the back pasture.

"The Marches and Lansings are still here?" she asked.

"Yes, they are. James runs a good operation, just like his father did. I'll say that for him."

"How is Dalton?" Daisy asked.

"He's my mountain," Louisa said. "That's how he is."

Daisy nodded, wondering about the pain — fleeting, hardly apparent — in Louisa's eyes. Louisa hadn't changed a bit in the twelve years since Daisy had seen her last. Her hair was still red and lustrous, her skin nearly unlined, her makeup dramatic. Beneath the scarlet shawl she wore a low-cut black velvet top over a flowing patterned skirt. Daisy wondered whether she was booked to go onstage that night.

"We'll have time to catch up later," Louisa said. "But right now you must be dog-tired. Let me take you to your cabin. That sound good?"

"Sounds very good." Daisy knew that all she wanted was a hot bath, a chance to close her eyes and get used to the idea she was back here. The sensation of being in a time warp was intense: She would look up and see James loping down the trail, holding the twins on his saddle.

"I've put you out back, down by the river. Remember that little house, the one that used to have green shutters?"

Daisy's heart lurched. "I remember."

"Well, it's all ready for you. With the old shutters, it's the closest thing we have to a seaside-looking cottage. Like it belongs on a sea cliff on Nantucket or somewhere. But don't you know, someone took the shutters off to paint and didn't stick 'em back on?"

Daisy knew that little house very well. Although she and James had lived in it together only briefly, some of their most important history had taken place there. She felt like asking for a different house, telling Louisa she'd sleep in the attic, the basement, anywhere. She wanted to jump into her rented car, drive to a motel in Lander, speed east across country, find Sage along the way. But she was polite, and Louisa had gone to all this trouble.

"Don't worry about the shutters," Daisy said.

"Good," Louisa said. "I won't."

How bad could it be to sleep in that little house after all this time? Daisy could stand it. She was here for Sage, and she didn't have to let the past get in the way.

"Does James — ?"

"He knows you're coming," Louisa said. She paused, as if coming up with something more to say. "One of the hands came back to say he had some big crisis down on the spring range, so —"

"You don't have to apologize for him," Daisy said. "I didn't expect him to be here."

"I put you as far from James as possible," Louisa said confidentially, wrapping her right arm around Daisy's shoulders. "You know he lives at the way-other end of the ranch."

"In our old house," Daisy heard herself say.

"Yep. He's still there. I picked the little house so you won't be running into each other every ten seconds. I know this reunion, under these circumstances, can't be easy for either of you."

"Thank you." An animal scurried through the chaparral, and Daisy jumped. She felt so uncomfortable being back here, as if she was wearing someone else's skin. *It won't be this bad tomorrow,* she told herself. *The feelings will pass.*

They always did. Daisy knew from experience. A lazy hawk circled overhead, riding the updrafts above the setting sun. Daisy tilted her head back to look. She wished she could fly herself, lower than any plane, looking in every corner for her missing daughter. She wished Sage would come through the ranch gates today, tonight, tomorrow, soon.

Standing beside Louisa on the land that used to be her home, Daisy looked up at the sunset sky over the Wind River mountains and wished with all her might for something that didn't have a name.

Making headway, Sage had ridden her bike for twenty-five miles, through more cornfields than she could imagine. Iowa seemed endless. She'd slept in a barn the night before, eating grains and vegetables left for the animals. Twice she'd milked cows, relying on vague memories from a lifetime ago: Her grandfather had sometimes taken her and Jake to the barn, filled their cups with milk warm from the cow.

Alone on the road, she could not imagine food more filling and soothing than milk. She coasted into a small town with three stores, a post office, and a bowling alley. The parking lot was crowded. Sage hadn't eaten since dawn, and she was so hungry and weary, she didn't think her feet could pedal one more time.

Some little kids were at the bowling alley for

an after-school birthday party. The mothers were standing around, helping them tie their shoes, showing them how to hold the balls. Sage felt a lump in her throat, remembering the bowling party her mother had thrown for her ninth birthday. But she swallowed it away. Her eyes were on thick slices of birthday cake with fluffy white frosting.

The children were circled around, watching a little girl — about seven — open her presents. They had already eaten lunch but not yet gotten to the cake, and the tray of half-eaten hot dogs and french fries sat off to one side. Sage inched toward the tray. Her stomach growled with anticipation. The french fries were golden brown, crispy on the crinkled edges — just the way Sage liked them. Her mother always cooked frozen fries longer than the package said, to get them exactly like this.

Staring at the girls' half-finished lunches, Sage was just about to grab a fry when someone spoke to her.

"Well, hello," one of the mothers said. Not many years older than Sage, she held an infant in her arms.

"Hi," Sage said.

"Which one's yours?"

"Mine?" Sage thought the mother meant which hot dog, and her heart raced because she realized she'd just gotten caught.

"Which child. Aren't you here for Jenny's party?"

"No," Sage said, pointing at some boys in another alley. "I'm with them. With . . ." She thought for three seconds flat. "Jake."

"So, that's your second?"

Sage just stood there. The woman was talking a language Sage didn't understand. But she saw her smiling down at her stomach, jutting her chin out at the pregnancy. Sage blushed; the woman was the first person to have noticed her showing. "Oh," she said, strangely thrilled and proud, "yes." Once again, she glanced over at the french fries.

"Hardly even touched," the woman said, taking a handful. "My Megan's over there, next to the birthday girl. She eats six fries at a sitting, it's all she can handle, and she'll take half an hour to do it. She's a little bird. Go on, have some. You're eating for two."

"Okay." Sage ate a french fry, then another. She gobbled two nearly whole hot dogs, even though they both had ketchup on them. Sage had never liked ketchup before, but right now it tasted so delicious, she saw stars. A feeling of fullness came over her for the first time since leaving home.

"I'm Deenie," the woman said.

"I'm Sage."

They gave each other wide smiles. Deenie was very pretty, with big brown eyes and flower-pink lipstick. She was heavy, even bigger than Sage, and she wore embroidered jeans and a bright purple sweater patterned with suns and moons.

"You from around here?" Deenie asked.

"Not really," Sage said, hoping that didn't sound too weird. But it must have, because Deenie just stared at her. What would she be doing at a bowling alley in the middle of nowhere if she wasn't *from* there? If this was a small town like Silver Bay, everyone knew everyone. The kids played together, the parents took turns carpooling . . . there were no strangers, only neighbors. Sage felt her face get red.

"What're you doing, visiting in-laws?"

"Um, sort of," Sage said.

"Oh, in-laws!" Deenie laughed. "Mine live all the way in Des Moines, thank God. It's just me and Harley most of the time. Who's your husband?"

"Ben Davis," Sage said, thinking of how happy Deenie sounded saying "just me and Harley." Saying Ben's name pierced her like a lance. She felt her shoulders curl over, and tears popped into her eyes. Deenie shifted the baby onto her other hip, leaned closer to Sage.

"You okay?" Deenie asked.

Sage tried to nod, but she couldn't. Bowling pins clattered; children screamed with joyful abandon. Sage gulped, the sobs caught in her throat. Knowing she was going to be sick, not sure of where to find the ladies' room, she ran full-tilt toward the front door. There in the parking lot, she threw up between two pickup trucks.

Deenie had followed her out. "Morning sickness all day long?"

Sage nodded, holding back the sobs, missing Ben and her mother so much she thought she might die.

"Is Ben understanding?" Deenie asked.

"The best," Sage whispered, staring at Deenie's feet. Her boots were old. Sage could see a line of glue-pearls where Deenie had tried to glue the old sole back on.

"Megan's probably wondering where I am," Deenie said.

Sage nodded.

"Jake's probably looking for you — ready to come in?"

Sage lowered her eyes. She had noticed a bread truck pulling into the parking lot: bright blue, with the words "Cinderella Baked Goods. Serving Western Iowa" stenciled in yellow. Sage heard the driver call hello to the alley's cook, say he was running late on his trip back to Nebraska. Her heart started beating faster.

"I think I'll stay out for one more minute," she said.

"Breathe that fresh air," Deenie said, standing up. "You'll feel better."

"I know," Sage said.

"Come sit with me when you get inside. I'm kind of new around here myself — I'm from Macksburg, and Harley had a little run-in up there . . . oh, never mind. Anyway, we're living behind my aunt's farm up the road here, and the other mothers have known each other forever, so

come sit with me. Okay?"

"Okay," Sage said, feeling sad.

Because she knew she wouldn't: The minute Deenie walked into the bowling alley, Sage went for her bicycle. She retrieved the pack she'd hidden under a bush. The deliveryman had left the back of the bread truck open, a little silver ramp tilting up from the pavement. Sage pushed her bike straight in. Nebraska was one state closer to Wyoming.

The truck was filled with shelves of bread. They were wide and deep, and right away she saw a good hiding place: under the bottom shelf. It was low to the floor, and Sage had to take the front wheel off to shove her bike underneath. By twisting and pushing, she got it well hidden. Standing back, she made sure.

Now she scanned the shelves. She saw cookies, muffins, doughnuts, bread, and rolls. Craving sugar, she saw a raspberry coffee cake and held herself back. She didn't know how long she would be riding, whether she'd be able to keep anything down. But she knew the baby needed nourishment. Carefully taking a snowflake roll from one box, she held her breath and rolled under the low shelf opposite her bike.

The truck door clanged shut a few minutes later. The engine started up. The floor was hard and cold: Sage lay on her back, enclosed by metal shelves and the truck's wall and floor, holding the roll. Her heart ached, and she told herself to stop. She missed Deenie already, and

177

she'd only just met her. She thought of the loneliness in Deenie's eyes, and she wondered if it
was always there — for everyone. On the floor,
nibbling her snowflake roll, Sage pictured her
mother's face and missed her with all her heart.

David tried to stay warm. The night was so
cold, frost had formed on the pinecones that
hung from the tips of the trees. His breath was
white, and his eyelids were heavy. The dots on
his cheek had faded, but they were still there. His
tattoos kept him company. The dogs slept
beside him, all crowded into the front seat. He
knew he should stop to get some rest, but the terrible thing was pulling him onward.

*Terrible:* That was the word that kept filling his
mind. Something brutal, a creature who needed
him being hurt, violated, possibly killed unless
he got there. He had never felt this way before,
this sense of urgency, so he didn't dare stop the
car. He knew he wasn't there yet.

Nebraska was a lot flatter than Wyoming. It
seemed like a lot of farmland, a lot of barns and
houses. He had a list of puppy farms he'd taken
from his parents' office, and at certain times he
thought maybe he should be heading to one of
them. But nature seemed to be telling him otherwise. He headed southeast, the car windows
open to keep him awake, hoping he'd know
whatever it was when he saw it.

Petal stayed awake beside him. She gnawed
her toy, feeling it in her mouth. He knew she

needed something to bite on, to hold, to take the place of all the puppies she had lost.

He had been passing farm after farm, but suddenly his headlights caught a long flash of white along the road. White dots, one after the other, low to the ground: a speckled snake, a huge white caterpillar. Slamming on the brakes, he steered onto the shoulder, trying not to hit the bizarre creature.

The dogs sensed danger, and they all dove onto the car floor. Through the open windows came the beating of wings. *Maybe this is it,* he thought. *Whatever it is I'm here to save.*

Leaping out of the car, he ran after the slinky white creature into the field. It twisted through broken-off cornstalks, hiding in the ruts and furrows of bare earth. Overhead, he heard wings beating, and he saw yellow eyes: an owl on the hunt. He saw that the owl had prey in its sights, watched it swooping down again and again.

As his own eyes became accustomed to the total darkness, he saw that the white dots were in fact paws: He was chasing a family of black cats. The mother was leading a pack of six white-footed black kittens, trying to hide them from the owl.

"Yah!" he yelled, waving his arms to chase the bird away. "Yee-hah!"

The owl flew so low, it brushed his head with its wings. The eyes were golden fire, blazing in the black night. He knew owls — he loved them for reasons he couldn't explain — but he knew

179

they were brutal, that they meant death to small animals.

"Get away!" David screamed, chasing the owl. He ran in a big circle, keeping the cats safely inside. He heard the owl calling as it flew, and for a minute, he thought he had been successful, that he had saved this big family of small creatures. The mother poked her head out to check. The kittens mewed, and she batted them with one big paw — to keep them quiet and hidden.

But the owl came back. It appeared out of nowhere, diving down with feet extended. Grabbing the mother cat, it lifted her into the sky. She twisted and snarled, and as the owl flew her into the treetops, the last sound he heard was pure grief, washing through the branches.

He remembered the cave. Owls had filled the dark space — burrowing owls, scores of yellow eyes watching over him when he was all alone. They had called, low and wise, telling him that soon he would be found. He had tattooed himself for a reminder.

David was crying now. The sob welled up from deep down inside his chest, and it spilled all over everything. Crouching down, he buried his head in his hands. He cried so hard, his tears washed off the last of the marks on his cheeks. Seeing the mother ripped apart from her babies had reminded him of himself: Right now, most of the time, he felt yanked in half. The mother's screams filled his ears.

Something scratched his leg through his jeans, and he felt claws on his skin. Then he felt fur on his face, and he realized that the kittens had climbed up his pants and wanted to slide down the neck of his shirt. Fuzzy black balls with white paws, scrambling down his chest.

More wings beat overhead. He heard them, and then he felt the cold wind. A pair of owls were here, circling the field, searching for the kittens. He felt the furry bodies snuggling into his body, trying to hide, looking for food. They started trying to nurse on his skin, searching everywhere for their mother's milk.

"Okay," David said, wiping his eyes. "I'll find you guys a bottle somewhere." A drugstore, he thought. A doll's bottle and a can of baby formula. He'd keep the newborn kittens alive. He wouldn't let the mother down.

He couldn't hate the owls for being owls, but his heart ached and he felt a long and raw scar of sorrow. He couldn't stop thinking of that mother — hearing her cry, knowing she'd tried so hard to protect these babies.

Maybe this was why he'd come to Nebraska.

These kittens had needed him, and he had been here to save them. Drying his eyes, lighting a cigarette as he started the car, he told himself that was it. He had come east to rescue this litter. Petal stuck her head out from under the seat: Leaping up beside him, she sniffed his shirt, wondering what was inside.

She held the toy in her mouth. It was torn and

chewed, soaked with her saliva. Her toy now, no longer his.

David Crane had dragged it with him everywhere he went, long ago. Sometimes he thought that was what he really wanted to find: the way this old stuffed animal had once made him feel. His home had been unhappy and violent; this toy had been his only comfort. Well, nothing could be softer and more comforting than a litter of tiny kittens inside his shirt, purring against the beating of his heart.

So why the hell did he keep driving east? If this was his big moment, why didn't the feeling of terror stop? He had it still — that awful pounding in his head, the slamming of his pulse, telling him to drive faster, get there or else.

There: where?

He didn't know, couldn't imagine. Trying not to think of the mother cat, what the owl was doing to her right now, he smoked harder and planned to stop at the first store he found: The map said he could be in Twin Lakes by dawn. They'd have baby supplies — from growing up on a puppy farm, he knew what it took to keep motherless baby animals alive.

He knew very well how to do that. Meanwhile, the compulsion raged inside him, and he knew he had to keep moving. That time was getting short.

# Chapter Twelve

The afternoon of Daisy's arrival, James had been checking water holes when he came upon a dead calf. Buzzards circled overhead; two black crows perched on its head. Dismounting, James had gone to check — expecting to find teeth and claw marks. Instead he found a bullet hole in the calf's back, the letter X carved on its side.

"What do you make of this?" Paul March asked, crouching down beside him.

"I don't know." James stared down at the calf.

"Some sick jerk off the highway?"

"Someone sick, that's for sure," James said. His ranch land lay in a notch of the Wind River mountains. It slanted west, but a narrow pass led eastward to the Indian reservation. Tourists passed by on the so-called highway — a two-lane road running toward Dubois — and James knew Paul was referring to them.

James hoped a stranger had done this, but he didn't know. Bad blood ran thick and deep around here. In past generations, grandfathers and great-grandfathers had killed each other over grazing rights. Paul's great-uncle had taken a bullet in the side, trying to protect the land from the sheepherding Rydells. Sheep ate faster than cows — they'd uncover a whole hillside in less than a year — and that had caused a near-war long ago.

"This look like a warning to you?" James asked.

"That's what I was thinking myself," Paul replied.

"Killing a calf's one thing," James said slowly. "Cutting it up's another."

"It was left here to be found, that's for sure. Different from the other times, though."

"Not different enough," James said grimly. He had hoped the bad things had stopped; they hadn't happened in months.

James studied the range and the hills. This was the trail he rode most often, through the pass leading toward home. All the local cowboys knew he came this way. Just around the hill, in the red canyon, was the spot where Jake had disappeared. And today Daisy was arriving from the East. Whoever had killed the calf might have known that, might not; it wasn't the first time something like this had happened.

One morning nearly a year ago, James had ridden down the long slope and found a grisly sight: a cow head stuck on a fence pole. Three riders, Paul among them, had come galloping across the range and told him they'd found three more. All together, four cows had been slaughtered.

Last July, someone had poisoned the water tank. It was nearly a quarter acre in size, crystal clear and calm. Twenty head of cattle had drunk from it, taken sick. Eleven had died before nightfall, and James had had to have the others put down. Town, county, and state police had investigated that one.

Suspicions in both cases had ranged from antibeef people to folks with grudges against the Tuckers. That made a long list. Their family dated back a hundred and fifty years here, and they'd been fighting off rustlers ever since. People wanted their land for sheep, gold, cattle, and now subdivisions, and the Tuckers had always held on. There were people who whispered about retribution, about payback, who said the Tuckers deserved everything bad they got. James thought about Daisy being here, Sage on her way, and he felt his muscles tighten.

"Where's Todd Rydell?" he asked.

"Where is he?" Paul sounded confused. "Working, I guess."

"Still driving a truck?"

Paul nodded. "Think so. Last I heard he was delivering packages for one of those freight companies. Couldn't make it on a horse, had to get himself a truck. He was the sorriest cowboy I ever saw. But you're not figuring him for this, are you?"

"I don't know what I'm figuring." James didn't like coincidences, and it bothered him that someone would butcher a calf the day Daisy was due in. He knew that Todd carried a resentment over the way he had been questioned about

Jake, that he held against all Tuckers the fact that they still had the ranch while his family had lost their land, that he was still ashamed about the time James had caught him spying through a window at Daisy.

"Todd's not vicious," Paul said.

"He likes a grievance, though," James told him. "He sticks it in the bank, hoards it like the family fortune."

"That *is* his family fortune," Paul said. "The only Rydell living on a ranch these days is Louisa, and it's your ranch she's living on."

"Take a look at him next time you're downtown," James said. "That's all."

"I'll do that." Paul stood beside the calf, looking down at it. He was marking the spot, James knew — in case of later trouble, or just because he wanted to keep good track of what happened where on the DR Ranch. Then Paul raised his eyes to James, shading them against the sun. "Seen Daisy yet?"

"Not yet."

"Gonna?"

"Don't see how I can avoid it," James said. "Seeing as how she's staying on the ranch."

"Huh." Paul scuffed his boot in the dust.

"You seem mighty curious about me seeing Daisy," James said. "Guess I wonder what makes that so."

Paul frowned. He squinted into the sun, which made him frown harder. Spitting behind him, he turned back to look down at the young calf. His expression was — fleetingly — one of sorrow, as if he was seeing a dead child instead. When he glanced back at James his eyes were hard, but his voice was soft.

"Could just be that I care," he said.

"About Daisy."

"About all of you."

Two weatherbeaten cowboys standing over a dead cow, talking about "caring." James wanted to smile, treat it like a joke, but he couldn't. All he could do was nod his thanks, because he knew Paul meant it.

James had that in mind a few hours later when he galloped through the notch toward the stone house. The DR Ranch sprawled among cottonwoods and chaparral, but the big house, a series of smaller houses, a huge old barn, and the water tanks were centrally located.

Louisa had told him she was putting Daisy in the white cottage, a fact that had stopped James cold. He had thought about suggesting somewhere different to Louisa, but he'd held his tongue. Daisy had probably done a better job of setting the past to rest than he had.

The sun had slipped behind the mountains, and all the lights of the ranch were coming on. James felt the evening chill in his bones: There had already been frost two mornings this week. He rode toward the corral to leave his horse, but then he changed his mind and circled around back.

Not much happened in this part of the ranch,

behind the main house. Louisa had her gardens here — vegetables and flowers. Right now she was growing pumpkins and squash, and they glistened as orange as the rising moon. James scanned the flowerbeds for something to pick, and that's how he knew he was heading to see Daisy. But everything was frostbitten, dead and brown.

James heard his horse's hooves clopping on the hard earth, sounding as loud as gunfire. His own heart was beating just as hard. Twelve years was a long time: They'd been apart over twice as long as they'd been together. Unsure about what he was doing, he steered his horse down toward the narrow river. The harvest moon shimmered between two peaks, lighting his way.

Looking over his shoulder toward the white cottage, he saw her. James pulled on the reins, stopping in the shadows. The big bay lowered his head, and James let him drink from the river. Daisy came out the doorway to stand on her porch, moving as gracefully as a deer. Her brown hair looked coppery in the moonlight; as she gripped the porch rail, tipping her head back to gaze at the moon, her face and throat had the luster of a pearl.

Oh, that posture: James knew it well. Holding the rail, her forearms were braced and taut — as if she might fall off the world itself, as if she were steering toward something better. She stared up at the moon, tilting toward it, her neck curved back, watching it with all her might. Her body looked full and beautiful under her pale robe, and James had to sit deeper in his saddle just to keep watching.

Now she reached out. Her index finger pointed, as if she could direct the moon to do what she wanted it to. Daisy had magic inside her, James knew. He didn't doubt she could command many things from nature; you only had to look at her jewelry, at the things she did with rocks and bone, to see that it was true. And James knew her well enough, even after all this time, to imagine what she was telling the moon right now.

*Light Sage's way.* Wherever she is, however dark her path might be, show her the way home. James closed his eyes, and as if the words he imagined Daisy saying were a prayer, he said them along with her. *Hold her in your hands, in your light. Keep her days long and her nights short. Ease her way. Bring her safely home to us.*

Daisy's arm fell to her side. She gazed at the moon for another few seconds. Then the intensity went out of her. She seemed to shrink in on herself, and he heard her crying. James wanted to jump down from his horse, go to her and hold her. Of course she wasn't his to hold. She hadn't been for a long time.

Daisy hesitated in the doorway. She seemed to be looking at something marked in the boards, and James knew what it was. He watched her, the way she raised her hand, traced the wood with her fingertips. His heart beat harder, and he

189

had the feeling she had to know he was there. His horse felt it, too: Raising his head from the stream, he perked his ears and let out a whinny. When Daisy turned, peering into the night, James felt her eyes pass across his body. He shivered as if she'd actually touched him, but he couldn't move out of the shadows.

Again she touched the door. The little cottage was old, one of the original ranch buildings. It had served as a one-room schoolhouse, a potting shed, and James's mother's music studio. Built one hundred years before James had built the log cabin for his family, its walls held a lot of secrets. James knew his share of them, and so did Daisy.

She paused, holding the doorframe, staring up at the moon again. Her eyes swept the black mountains, the dark cedars. An owl called from across the river, low and long. Daisy seemed to listen, and then she cupped her hands around her mouth. Right away, James knew what was coming.

"Washakie!" she called, as loud as any animal on the range or in the hills, the cry like lightning through James's veins.

"Washakie," James said back, in a voice too low for her to hear, the word ringing in his bones.

When Daisy went inside, she closed the door behind her. She must have thrown dry branches on the fire, because suddenly sparks flew up the chimney and melted with the smoke. Then she closed the curtains and turned off the lights.

James watched until the house was dark, and then he gave his horse a kick and headed for home.

He had pitched his tent near the ranch buildings, just to watch for the young girl. A lady had arrived: pretty and sexy, but no young thing. She had Tucker in a stir, the way he was snapping at everyone, riding home hours earlier than his usual pattern. Especially given the destruction that had been visited on the old DR Ranch.

*Mothers and fathers. Sheep and cows.*

The world turned differently here than anywhere else. He felt drawn to this place. He marked his brown leather belt with another notch. The DR herd was a little smaller tonight, and that notch proved it. His knife had done its work — cutting cowhide, making belt leather — and now it was time for the whetstone.

Drawing out the stone, he slicked it with spit and oil. The blade flashed in light from the kerosene stove, and he began to slice it back and forth across the stone. He enjoyed the rhythm, and he liked the sound. *Sssh, ssssh,* it went. A real cowboy lullaby.

His gun gleamed on the tent floor, dark, dangerous steel. He liked looking at it. The tent enclosed him, and he felt very safe here. He was armed, protecting himself. If anyone attacked him, they'd get a big surprise.

*Washakie.* The name reminded him of something. Wasn't there a legend, some Shoshone chief . . . ? Didn't matter, he thought, shaking his head like a dog trying to get rid of a burr.

Her voice rang in his ears. Jesus, he hated mournful women. Women who took care of themselves, coddling their own hurt feelings while everyone else suffered. Men were out, trying to protect what was rightfully theirs — their family's — while the women cried at home.

*Happy families, home on the range.*

# Chapter Thirteen

Daisy woke up at first light the next morning. Her cabin was one small room, and as she lay in bed, she could see mountain peaks out the windows on all four sides. The gray sky was streaked with high thin clouds, and flocks of geese flew in dark V's down from the north. Very slowly, she put her feet on the cold floor and looked around.

In daylight, the room looked exactly as she remembered it. The walls were rough and silvery, covered with old barn board. A bearskin rug lay on the floor in front of the stone fireplace, and bright Shoshone blankets covered the old armchair and sofa. Shivering, she opened her suitcase and pulled on clean clothes. She craved a cup of coffee, and although the room had a small kitchen at one end, she didn't want to stay there one minute longer than she had to. Louisa would have a pot brewing up at the big house.

Coffee and more: Daisy walked up the sage trail, around the corral, through the kitchen door, to find Louisa cooking away. A fire crackled in the kitchen hearth and coffee perked on the back burner. Louisa stood at the stove, sexy even at breakfast, wearing a satin nightdress as she fried eggs in bacon fat.

"Look who smelled breakfast cooking!" Louisa said, smiling without turning from the stove. "She's up early, same as ever."

" 'Daisy, Daisy, give me your answer true,' " Dalton said. He sat at the big table, already dressed for range work in his chaps and wool jacket. At the sight of him, Daisy felt a lump in her throat. He looked so old!

"Dalton," she began. Her eyes filled with tears. She hadn't known what to expect, but looking at him in his usual spot at the head of the table, she realized she still considered him her father-in-law: The divorce was between her and James. Quickly crossing the large room, she kissed his wrinkled cheek. "How are you —" she started to ask, but he interrupted.

"What's keeping James?" he asked, setting down his coffee mug to look into her eyes.

"James?" she asked, confused.

"Eat your eggs," Louisa said, pushing a plate in front of him. "They're nice and hot, the bacon's crispy, I buttered your toast, all you have to do is eat. What'll you have, Daisy?"

"Toast," Daisy said. "I'll get it myself."

"You'd better wait for James." Dalton reached for a crock of huckleberry preserves. "You know how he likes to have his meals with you no matter what. Once we were out stringing fence, and he wanted to leave a hole the size of a bear in order to get home for dinner. I had to —"

"That was a long time ago," Daisy said quickly, wondering why Dalton wanted to

194

remind her of those old, happy days.

"Long time ago?" Dalton chuckled. "Yesterday, today, tomorrow. 'T'sall the same when it comes to you snow geese."

"Snow geese?" Daisy was pouring a cup of coffee, but Dalton's use of the old nickname made her spill all over the counter. Louisa hustled over with a dish towel, and she began mopping the coffee up. She reached for Daisy's wrist, giving it a gentle shake. Daisy met her eyes, but the confusion welling up inside made her look away. Was Dalton trying to be cruel?

Snow geese . . . "Madly in love and mated for life, just like snow geese," Dalton used to say about Daisy and James. Daisy had loved the comparison. She'd watch the pairs that came to the ranch every year, how they'd stay together season after season. She and James had married in January, under the first moon of the year, the time of snow. And Dalton's friend Louis Shoulderblade, a Shoshone shaman, had told her that geese take love seriously and want to build a nest with only one other . . . that was how Daisy had seen life *before* . . .

"Where is he?" Dalton asked now, his mouth full of toast. "One of the kids sick?"

"The kids —" Daisy slammed down her cup as she turned around.

Louisa had her face in her hands. Dalton held a half-bitten piece of toast, his blue eyes filmed with worry. Daisy's anger suddenly washed away, replaced by concern.

Age wrinkled the old man's face and clouded his eyes; it had obviously transported his heart back to a time when they were all together, when Daisy and James were the snow geese. Old age had stolen over him.

" 'Daisy, Daisy, give me your answer true . . .' " Dalton began singing the old song again. Daisy looked down, waiting for her toast to pop up. Louisa sat with a plate of food in front of her, untouched and pushed away. She sipped her coffee and drummed her fingers, the worry lines deep between her brows.

"When did it start?" Daisy asked as they were cleaning up the breakfast dishes.

"Started two years ago." Louisa swirled coffee mugs through the soapy water. "Thereabouts."

"He seemed to think —" Daisy began.

"Sometimes he's sharp as an eagle," Louisa said, as if she hadn't heard. "Remembers every single detail about some rodeo ten years ago, things I never noticed in the first place. He has a pair of eyes on him, Daisy . . . sees everything. Recalls stories from his childhood, from the days when his daddy and mine were at each other's throats . . ."

"But today . . ." Daisy said.

"Today he got a little mixed up," Louisa said. "Seeing you and all. I told him you were coming, of course, and he understands about Sage running away, but seeing you . . ." She placed a dish in the drainer, and Daisy dried it.

"Seeing him, too," Daisy said. "It makes the years slip away."

"The years slip away for Dalton all the time," Louisa said, staring out the window. Her eyes looked hard and set as she watched a hawk fly over the field in wide circles. "It doesn't change who he is or how I feel about him."

"No, I know that," Daisy said, unsettled by Louisa's expression.

"His son questions my motives," Louisa said.

"Hmm." Daisy was careful not to say too much, thinking *he always has.* James had lost his mother young, and he hadn't liked or trusted Louisa from the start.

"Snow geese," Louisa said, trying to laugh. "I used to be so jealous when Dalton'd call you that. As if you and James were the only lovers here! I grew up around those Shoshone stories. Oh, I know about the totem of snow geese — the symbol of fertility and marital fidelity. How they soar together in pairs and cover great distances, how they belong together . . ."

Daisy's stomach clenched as she thought of James, of the distance they had covered, of their abrupt end. The kitchen reminded her of a thousand breakfasts together, and as she closed her eyes she felt the hot tears.

"We only thought we belonged together," Daisy said. "Look what happened."

"Fate was cruel to you and James. But you know, I thought you belonged together anyway. I wish you had never left."

"I did what I thought was right. I didn't want to raise my daughter on the same ranch where my son —"

"I know that," Louisa said quickly. "I'm in no position to criticize, and I don't. But I've missed you, Daisy. It's not easy, being the only woman with two Tucker men. Having you here balanced things out."

"I missed my own mother so much," Daisy said, wiping her eyes. "You got me dressed on my wedding day. You were my mother-in-law, my children's grandmother. Sage still thinks of you that way."

"Snow geese don't need paperwork." Louisa tried to smile, but her voice sounded bitter. "They don't need marriage certificates to prove they're together for life. So I guess I can be Sage's grandmother without marrying her grandfather."

"Yes," Daisy said, holding the sound of her daughter's name close in her heart and mind.

"I'm glad you're back," Louisa said.

The DR barn was deep and cavernous, and as Daisy walked through, barn swallows flew in crisscross patterns through the darkness. The horses whinnied at her approach, and her heart was pumping — she knew so many of them! There were Ranger, Chiquita, and Piccolo. Stopping by each stall, Daisy touched her head to theirs, said hello, caressed their velvety muzzles. Their eyes were so wide and alert — did they recognize her, too?

"Hi, boy," she said to Ranger. "You're the biggest one here, same as ever. Why aren't you out with the cowboys?" The enormous bay tossed his head, looking down, as if her question shamed him. He had always been James's horse — his favorite by far. Daisy saw the white whiskers around his mouth, the dry skin behind his ears. He was still the largest horse here, but he had aged. It made her sad to see, but grateful at the same time, as she realized she hadn't expected to see him — or any of the old horses — at all.

She greeted some new horses, ones she had never met before. A black barn cat leapt down from a rafter and a mouse squealed from under the hay. A flurry of bats swept through the shadows. Daisy jumped, as if the air was full of ghosts. Her heart racing, she paused to breathe. She wanted fresh air and open spaces. She wanted to chase this nightmare away — this visit to the past, the emptiness where Sage should be.

Her years back east had taken away her confidence as a rider, but right now she wanted — more than anything — to get up on a horse and gallop into the hills. Years ago, James had kept some gentle horses for her and the children. Silver Star, she remembered, and . . .

"Scout!" she said out loud.

Could it be? The yellow quarter horse stood in the same stall, midway down the row. Her coat looked matted and dusty, as if she hadn't been properly brushed in a long time. She faced into the corner, head down.

"Scout . . ." Daisy tried to whisper, but her voice wouldn't work. Scout had been Daisy's horse. She had held Daisy's children on her bare back and walked them through silvery fields of sage. A glossy palomino, she had made Daisy proud to ride her. Broad and strong, she had carried her down steep mountain trails, across icy rivers, over narrow rock bridges. Scout had brought her home from trail rides and night rides and camping trips and roundups. Daisy had brushed and curried her, the way James had taught her to care for the horses they loved.

But this animal looked uncared for. Her white mane and tail were brown with barn dust. Her head drooped with weariness, and Daisy took it for dejection. How could James have let her get like this? Or was it another horse entirely — a different palomino in Scout's old stall?

"Scout," Daisy said quietly, holding her hand through the bars. "Hey, Scout. It's me. Remember me?"

Most of the horses had stand stalls — narrow cubicles just big enough to hold a horse standing up. But the family horses had box stalls, large enough for them to move around in. This old mare stood where she was, frozen in place.

"Washakie," Daisy whispered.

Was it her imagination or had the old horse moved her head? She gave a half-look over her left shoulder, then turned back to the corner.

200

Daisy peered into the dusty gloom, looked for signs of the horse she had known. She found her voice, and it grew stronger. "Remember the river? How we used to follow it into the mountains? You loved it the colder it got, when the snow would melt . . ."

Daisy held her breath, reaching deeper into the stall. She kept talking . . . "Remember me? Remember us? Me and Jake and Sage? James would be up on Ranger . . . remember your friend Ranger? Washakie, Scout. Washakie . . ."

Just saying the name made Daisy's heart stronger. She kept talking, reminding the old horse of high trails and bright skies, wildflowers growing through the snow, blue ice on red rocks.

The horse moved her feet. Daisy heard her hooves shuffling through the hay. They connected with the wood floor, and the mare began to turn around. Her head was down, as if gravity made it too hard to look up. She lumbered across the big stall, clopping quietly. Daisy's hand trembled as she held it out. The mare began to raise her neck and smell Daisy's hand, and Daisy felt warm breath on her fingers. Then Scout lifted her head and looked Daisy straight in the eye.

"It's you . . ." Daisy whispered, her throat thick.

The white forelock hung across her face. Daisy's eyes flooded as she reached out to brush it away. The mare's eyes were dark brown pools. They stared back at Daisy with wisdom and love and recognition. Tossing her head gently, Scout let out a long, low whinny. Daisy unlatched the creaking stall door. The brass rails and hinges had been left unpolished for a long time.

She held the old horse in her arms. She reached around her broad neck and rested her head against Scout's. The horse quivered under her skin, as if she was coming alive again. Daisy's tears were nothing new to her. Daisy had cried into her mane the first night Jake hadn't come home, and every night afterward. Scout knew her scent and voice, and she knew her tears.

Daisy led Scout into the barn. She wanted to groom her, untangle her beautiful mane and comb the dust from her coat, but both Daisy and the horse needed something else first, something more. Walking her through the wide doors, Daisy blinked at the bright light of day — and so did Scout. They stood by the corral, and Daisy used the split-rail fence to mount her.

Facing into the wind, Daisy began to ride. She hadn't been on a horse in twelve years, not once since she'd gone back east. She had been afraid of the thought, certain she would need a saddle and bridle and someone helping her through the paces. Any woman incompetent enough to lose a child needed reins and stirrups and holding on to. But Scout saw it differently.

The old horse was taking it slow. She moved like a riverboat, rocking back and forth across the clear water. Daisy tangled her fingers in her long mane, letting her carry her. She stumbled once, nearly tossing Daisy over her head. But Daisy held on. Scout felt familiar, her gait slow and cautious.

Daisy and Scout rode past the barn and the bunkhouse, into the back pasture. The field was gold and brown. White clouds scudded through a steel-gray sky. A flock of starlings swooped down like a black cape, then flew away again. Daisy clutched the horse, afraid she might be spooked, but she just kept steadily on.

Scout was carrying her into the hills. Daisy nearly pulled back — James was out there, and she wasn't ready to see him. She wanted to be near the telephone in case Detective LaRosa called, near the ranch gates for the moment when Sage would come walking through. But something made her let go inside, give up her tension and worry, just let the old horse carry her where she wanted to go.

Looking around, she surveyed the ranch in broad daylight. Some of the buildings and fences needed paint. A tree had fallen in the near pasture and hadn't been cleared. The children's playground had been cleared away — no swings, no jungle gym, no slide.

A few snow flurries started to fall, and Scout tossed her head. Moving onto the gravel-strewn trail, she faltered as her back right hoof caught on a rock. Daisy patted her neck, and she stopped to steady herself. Whispering encouragement, Daisy felt the horse shake herself off. Her muscles tightened and shook, and when she started off again, it was with new confidence and strength.

"Good girl," Daisy said.

Scout trusted her. Daisy could feel it in the mare's gait, her sureness of foot. And she trusted Scout: She felt it in her heart, in the way she was riding her up into the low hills, into the big sky. Many things on the ranch had changed, but not that. Daisy's fingers were cold. Her heart beat steadily now, and she leaned down to hold her arms alongside the horse's neck and feel her warmth through her body. Closing her eyes, she rode her horse. Her horse.

Sage had a flat tire. She was somewhere over the Nebraska state line. Storm clouds were gathering, and her bike had a flat tire. There were no two ways about it. She had tried using her portable pump, and the tire had inflated, but only for a few seconds. Then *tsssssss* — the air escaped again.

Last night, after hours on the road, the bakery truck had driven to a hospital, and when the driver had gone inside to drop off his last load of rolls, Sage had wriggled out from under the bread trays. Stuffing her backpack with a box of day-old cupcakes, she had hauled her bicycle out from its hiding place and coasted down the metal ramp.

She had locked her bike to a rack and gone inside. The hospital had been bright and warm, and Sage had felt safe there.

The hospital seemed to have several types of rest rooms: visitor bathrooms in every corridor, patient bathrooms adjoining every two rooms on the ward, and large shower rooms for disabled patients. Slipping into an unoccupied shower room, she took off her clothes and took a long shower, drying off with paper towels from a wall dispenser.

Feeling a hundred times better, Sage had wandered through the halls. In the hospital cafeteria she had counted out three dollars of her precious money and dined sumptuously on beef stew, noodles, and Jell-O.

Trying to find the ground floor, she had pushed the wrong button and emerged in the basement by mistake. It felt warm, and she heard the throb of washing machines. Following the hum, she had found the hospital laundry. Dirty linens were piled in canvas carts. Looking around, Sage saw no one. She'd stopped one of the dryers, pulled the load of towels into an empty cart.

The white towels were hot and fluffy. Sage climbed in, falling asleep before they had started to cool. Her dreams had been full of parents and babies, walls of glass between them. She was the parent and then she was the baby. Either way, in her dream, she was going to be taken care of.

But now she was back on this lonely road. Somewhere between the hospital and here, she must have ridden over a nail. She could stick her finger through the tear in the rubber, even if it was getting too dark to see. She had been riding along back roads, and now storm clouds were gathering. On the outskirts of a small town, she had followed the signs pointing west for Wayne.

This wasn't a main road, and there weren't any stores around. She had dreaded this moment, but she had known it might someday come: To get to Wyoming, to reach her father, she was going to have to hitchhike.

The traffic passing by was sparse. Sage laid her bike on the side of the road, hiding it under a low juniper bush. She felt a lump in her throat: Her mother had given her half the money to buy the bicycle — a brand-new green Trek — for Christmas when she was thirteen. The rest Sage had earned from baby-sitting and snow-shoveling. She dreaded leaving it behind; her mother had held her hands over Sage's on the handlebars and blessed all her future rides: "Ride safely, my love," she had said. "Smooth roads, low hills, no bumps . . . and always come home."

"Always come home," Sage said out loud, into the cold Nebraska air, her eyes bright with tears.

A battered old car drove by, and Sage just watched it go. Crouching beside her bike, she reached under her jacket and touched the amulet her mother had made her. At least she had her necklace. Her fingers traced the boy's face, then the girl's. Leaving her bike was the hardest thing she had done since riding away from Ben. In some ways, it felt even harder.

Rising unsteadily to her feet, she looked around. The sun had completely disappeared into a bank of dark clouds. Pine trees stood along the horizon like hostile sentries. Sage shivered, planting her feet firmly in the dust. Her bike, her fallen friend — her childhood — lay under the prickly bush. *Always come home,* she thought.

Her baby kicked. She felt it, just a tickle under her ribs. He needed food and shelter, and Sage was going to give it to him. *Are we there yet?* she could almost hear him ask.

"We'll be there soon," Sage said out loud, seeing headlights in the distance. The road was long and flat, the car a long way away. Taking a deep breath, she stuck out her thumb. The cold air stung it. The car got closer and Sage felt her chest shrink. Her baby jostled her a second time. "We're almost there," Sage said.

# Chapter Fourteen

Nearly a full day now. That's how long Daisy had been on the ranch, and still James hadn't talked to her. Wasn't for lack of effort, either: He had set himself a slew of jobs as far from the houses as possible. With the temperature dropping and snowflakes falling, he'd ridden up to the north promontory to survey his herd.

The range looked cold and bleak, a thousand shades of gray. Last week's rains had brought relief from the drought, and now it looked as if Dalton's prediction was going to come true: Winter would be early and hard. Cows huddled in clusters, grazing on brown grass. He'd be shipping five hundred head of cattle soon, and he and Paul would have to start driving them to the big sorting corrals. He tried to count the calves he saw, but his mind couldn't stay focused enough.

Daisy was here.

James could feel her in the air. It was as if she had flown into Wyoming on her own wings, stirred up the atmosphere all around him. He hadn't seen her since last night, when he'd stayed in the shadows like some spying voyeur. But he could feel her presence — all up and down his spine, under his hat, in his hands. He could hear her voice, the way she'd yelled that word into the night — primal, yearning, blood-curdling, full of rage and resentment and desire. James knew, because he carried the same stuff inside himself.

He had told Paul he was riding the perimeter, searching for traces of whoever had killed that calf. So far they'd turned up a few things — beer cans, a stomped-out campfire, boot prints in the dirt along the sandstone ridge. James wanted to catch the bastard who'd done it and rip him apart.

Most of the time he controlled his rage, but Daisy's presence had stirred him back up. If he could catch one bad man and make him pay, he'd be free of something. He could keep the fire at bay. For whatever had been done to his boy. For the turns his life had taken. He tried to breathe. But his chest was so tight, not even a big Wyoming sky could dissolve the knot. He kicked his horse, once, twice. They took off down the chute, a living landslide. Rocks dislodged and rolled away. He kicked again, needing more speed. Maybe they'd slip off the cliff, maybe they'd soar into the gorge.

James glanced down at the black mane of his horse — Chieftain, the animal's name was. He'd named him himself four years ago in honor of an old secret, but he never really thought of horses by name anymore. Not for a long time. They helped him get the job done, that was about it.

Louisa had told him Daisy had been shocked about Scout, her old palomino, that she had spent over an hour this afternoon grooming the burrs from her mane and tail. It had been years since James had stopped to show his horses the same gentleness he'd once shown his family.

Down to earth again, James flew on Chieftain across the flat land. This ground held all the secrets of the universe, clues to every mystery, bones with stories to tell. James galloped his horse so hard they drank the sky.

As he entered the red rock canyon, James's eyes were blazing. His skin was still on fire, and his heart was pounding. This was where it had happened, where his boy had disappeared. James had to see. He had to check. Just in case, just in case . . . Jake's mother was here. She was on the ranch, in the house where it all began. He had to look with his own two eyes, just to reassure himself . . .

He swept the area with his gaze. Sagebrush grew from rock crevices, and ribbons of amber and jasper ran through the dark red canyon walls. Under clouds, the canyon was dark as dusk. Shadows fell across hard ground.

A pebble dislodged from the west rim above, making him jump. It clattered off the eroded cliff, setting more pebbles loose.

"Who's up there?" James yelled.

He stared up the water-cut rock, shifting his eyes over every shape. The canyon was deep and silent, leading to a labyrinth of endless smaller canyons and crevices. James gazed at every boulder on the rim, watching for movement. Under his Stetson, the hair on his head tingled. The black shadows looked alive.

Keeping to the rocks, to the canyon wall, he thought he heard something moving on the rimrock. He had the feeling of being watched. Another pebble fell, then more silence. Someone was walking up above. Using stealth, not moving freely, trying to get away without James seeing. Staring up, James looked for a way to climb. Stunted cedars and junipers grew straight out of the rocks — he could use them for handholds, wedge his feet into the cracks.

"Show yourself!" he yelled. He felt crazed, the way he had in the first year after Jake's disappearance. He had come here constantly, searching every crevice. Back then he had felt the presence of humans in the canyon, and he had seen ghosts swirling through the air.

Another stone fell, and a crow hopped to the edge of the rim. It cawed loudly, like a giant sawing chains. James looked up and wondered whether that was what he had heard. The crow swooped down, flying around the corner into the next crevice. James nudged his horse with one knee, and the animal walked on.

Bones from a kill lay against a rock pile. Mouth dry, James rode closer. This was western life: finding dead rabbits, elk, cows. Crows eating the dead. But discovering it here in this spot made him nervous. Bending down to check, he saw the bones bleached nearly white, yet still connected by fur. Gray fur with rusty brown glints. A wolf: James stared down at the skull, saw the fangs. Something bigger had gotten him — a grizzly, maybe.

Slowly dismounting, he crouched by the dead thing. The stench was gone — more crows and buzzards and other wolves had been here before him. He could have left the carcass alone. Ordinarily he would have. But something made him take out his knife and slice away a piece of the pelt. Then he cut off the animal's left front paw — the bones and claws nude of fur and gristle — and a section of its spine. He was glad it was an animal of prey. As he worked, he thought of the wolf's fierce spirit. The sensation of being watched from above was gone.

He heard the clamor of wings and looked up. A flock of geese was pointing south, pairs and pairs and pairs. Sometimes seeing the migrations made him feel lonely and left behind, but not today. That was because Daisy was nearby.

He sheathed his knife. He thought of a place down the Wind River, Crowheart Butte, where a century and a half ago the Shoshone and Crow chiefs had fought in single-handed combat to the death. Two fierce and brutal warriors ripping each other to shreds over land rights — the old Wyoming story. When Chief Washakie won, he'd honored the bravery of his dead enemy by cutting out his heart and eating it.

Daisy had called his name last night. She had always loved the story of the chiefs, the myth of gaining strength from other creatures — from respecting your enemy enough to eat his heart. It had given her courage many nights in the wild, including the time the grizzly had nearly attacked her and the twins in their tent. She had taught the word to their children, to say out loud whenever they were scared of the dark. James knew that Daisy's bone ghosts, her jewelry and artwork, came from the same deep belief that powerful spirits lived on.

And so, with the echoes of his own voice still murmuring through the empty canyon, James opened his saddlebag and stuck the wolf bones and fur inside. A peace offering, he thought, and for the moment the fire was out. His rage was gone, taken by the wind and the thought of Washakie. Chieftain drank from a narrow stream of clear, cold water.

James looked around. It was hard to believe these canyon walls contained the source of his family's torment. It looked so peaceful now. The stream trickled over golden rocks. The horse drank his fill. James could breathe without thinking he was about to die. The echoes of his voice blended into the tops of cedar trees rustling in the autumn wind. The crows cawed. And snow flurries fell upon the ground where Jake Tucker had once waited for his father to take him home.

The fires were starting up again.

Kick, kick. One pebble, then another.

Tucker looked up, and the Guardian stepped back from the cliff edge. That's how he had started to think of himself: the Guardian of what should have belonged to him and his family all along.

"Show yourself," the rancher had called.

Show this, the Guardian thought, giving him the finger. Two feet back from the edge was a rock. A big, round, wheel-sized rock, nothing like the pebbles. While the rancher busied himself cutting the foot off a stupid dead wolf, the Guardian dislodged the large rock with the toe of his boot.

New boots, they were. He'd bought them at a store in Lander. They had cost over a hundred dollars, and he couldn't remember ever having anything this nice before. When he was growing up, his clothes had been hand-me-downs. His boots had always been worn by someone else. That's why, when he kicked the toe under that rock, he had stopped himself from pushing it right over the cliff.

He'd scuffed his toe.

"Motherfucker," he swore, bending down to spit on the scratched leather, rub the scratches out with his thumb. By the time he cleaned the spot, Tucker had moved along. The Guardian breathed harder. He could have really gotten his licks in that time: sent the rock tumbling, scared the living hell out of the cowman.

Too late.

He packed up his camera, knife, stove, and gun, and moved on.

Sage had gotten picked up by a woman driving home from work, a truckdriver delivering chickens, and a life insurance salesman in a Ford. Ten cars passed by for every one that stopped. The three people who'd picked her up had seemed friendly, but shy. They hadn't said much except that Nebraska winters were hard.

Only the salesman had been weird. He wore a suit, for one thing, which struck Sage as a little pretentious — considering the only places around seemed populated by people in jeans, corduroys, or overalls. He also dyed his hair — Sage could tell by how the unusual shade of cordovan failed to blend with the stripes of white along his part and temples. It seemed so sad and vain, she didn't know whether to laugh or feel sorry for him.

But then, talking about the coming winter, how snow in Nebraska was denser than that in any other state, all confusion was removed: He was driving with his hand over his crotch. The instant Sage saw that, she'd jumped in her seat. This was one of the perverts her mother had always warned her about! *Oh, God,* she thought. Checking the door handle, she yanked so hard it flew open at full speed. A friendly little bell started dinging, a built-in reminder to close the car door after carrying in the groceries or something. The man had been more shocked than Sage, and she'd told him to let her out at the next mile marker — right in the middle of no-where — saying her father was meeting her there in ten minutes.

And there she'd been standing for the last ten minutes. Eight o'clock and no cars in sight. Across a rutted field occupied by a falling-down red barn, she saw a parallel road. Cars were zooming happily along *that* road. Watching them from a quarter-mile away, Sage imagined them filled with happy families on their way home to dinner. She could almost hear their loving voices, smell the good food.

Sage's breath came out in white clouds. The sky had been dark all day, threatening to rain or snow. Her feet were cold and her hands were numb. A car approached, and she tensed up so badly — afraid it was the creep — the baby gave her a double kick straight to the bladder. Oh, God, she had to pee.

Luckily, the car — a non-Ford — passed by. Looking around for a bush or a tree, Sage spotted a row of poplars near the falling-down barn. There was a rusty old car there, too. Things to hide behind. She started off, but immediately she knew she wouldn't make it that far. Now she was glad of the dark. Standing on the side of the road, so exposed she might as well be naked, she squatted in the dust. She heard the pee hitting the tar.

She fumbled for tissue in her pockets, trying to

keep her balance. When would life be simple again?

She was midway through air-drying — her calves cramping from the prolonged squat — when she heard a car. *Wouldn't the pervert just love this?* she thought as she struggled to stand. Oh, why had she ever started this trip? She saw herself, as if from above — pregnant, alone, hitchhiking, going to the bathroom on the side of the road . . . Her father probably wouldn't even want her. He'd send her home to Silver Bay, tell her mother to keep her.

At the thought of her father's disapproval, Sage bit her lip. Her eyes filled with tears, and as if on cue, so did her bladder. She had to go again already! The baby tickled her insides as if he thought it was a big joke. The car slowed down, and even without streetlights, Sage could tell it was the pervert.

"Couldn't leave you here all alone," he said, rolling down the window. He smiled, revealing perfect teeth. His tie was knotted so tight, it made his face puffy and red. "I got to thinking — her father's not gonna find her *there*. Why don't you climb in and let me drop you off someplace proper?"

"Um, no, thank you," Sage said politely. "My father knows exactly where to find me."

The man opened his door. He'd been busy since letting Sage off fifteen minutes earlier — although his tie was knotted and his shirt was all buttoned up, his shirttails were untucked. And

217

there was a definite opening where his zipper was supposed to be.

"You're with child," he said, making a statement.

"My father's coming —" Sage said, scanning the horizon. Could she make it across the field? She'd have to leave her backpack behind. She might have to pee as she ran, but she didn't care.

"You started having sex young," he said, getting out of his car. "You can't be much older than fifteen or sixteen. What are you, fifteen?"

Sage dropped her backpack. She turned to run, but he caught her arm. He felt it with pudgy fingers, just as if he was testing a chicken for plumpness. He squeezed up and down her bicep, pulling her toward his car. Sage screamed. She tried to kick him in the open zipper, but she slipped on the roadside sand. She heard him breathing harder, and she felt him embracing her with both arms. Screaming her head off, she kicked her feet.

Just then a car started up. She looked wildly around, struggling against the man. He was dragging her now, urgently, toward his idling Ford. The man grunted with effort, trying to throw her into the front seat. Tires squealed, burning out on sand and pavement.

"My father," Sage sobbed, trying to tear away from the man. He yanked her hair. She looked for the other car, but it was a phantom. It didn't really exist, except in the roaring engine sounds banging in her ears. "My father's coming for me," she cried. "Daddy!"

"Shit," the man said, still holding her hair.

Out of the field, a big black car appeared — no lights on. It was a long Jeep-style vehicle, old and low, like some sort of official-looking highway maintenance car. Its pipes and axles and oil pan clanked against ruts in the field. Sage saw the rust holes and realized it was the broken-looking vehicle she'd seen parked by the ramshackle barn. The front door opened even before the car had come to a complete stop, and the driver came tumbling out.

The driverless black car coasted slowly by, cruising down the road a few yards before coming to a gentle stop against a hump of grass, while the driver got to his feet. He brushed himself off, then came striding over to Sage and the salesman, who had released his grip on her.

"This is a family matter," the salesman said.

"No," Sage tried to say, but her teeth were chattering. It didn't make a bit of difference — the stranger wasn't waiting to hear what she had to say. He just wound up his right arm and punched the pervert right in the mouth. Sage heard the pop of skin and the breaking of teeth.

"Mmaaateeeffff . . ." the creep said through fingers clamped over his now bleeding mouth.

"You're done with them," the stranger said.

"Mmaaateeeffff . . ." the salesman said again, as if he couldn't believe it. His teeth had been perfect, Sage thought as he scrambled into his Ford and roared away. But she stopped herself short of feeling sorry for him. Instead, she turned to the stranger — to thank him. But he had run a few yards down the road, to where his car had stopped.

She would have expected a hero to be older and bigger. From several yards away, she could see that he was about five six, just a few inches taller than she, and thin. He had brown hair, and he wore faded jeans. Sage heard dogs barking and she realized the sounds were coming from inside the car. When her rescuer came walking back toward her, she could see that he was no older than she was — about sixteen, seventeen at the oldest.

Thank you, she wanted to say. But instead she just stared.

"You okay?" he asked.

"I think so," she managed.

"That guy hurt you?"

"He tried." Sage's teeth were starting to chatter again.

"I heard," the stranger said. He gestured toward the collapsing barn. "I was in there, and your scream scared every bird in the rafters. You see them fly out?"

"No, I was a little busy," Sage said. "Is that your barn?"

"Nah," he said, reaching into his breast pocket. He took out a pack of cigarettes, shook one out. "Want one?"

Sage shook her head. She stepped closer to him. Something about his voice made her want to hear him talk. The sound was soft and low, a little gravelly. It sounded like a man's voice. Darkness shaded his face, so Sage waited for the match light to see his eyes. They were pale green, and they looked hooded — as if he'd been hurt or hiding or both. He took a long, deep drag off the cigarette — just like a man who'd been smoking for twenty years.

"Where you going?" he asked, blowing the smoke out.

"Wyoming."

"Yeah?" he asked.

"I'm hitchhiking," Sage said. She tried to laugh, sticking out her thumb. But something about the way he just stared at her without smiling, with his pale green eyes glowing in the smoky light from his cigarette, made her feel like crying instead.

"I'll give you a ride," he said. "I'm going there."

"To Wyoming?"

"That direction, anyway," he said. "West. My name's David."

"I'm Sage."

She had forgotten about having to go to the bathroom again, but now the feeling came back full force. The baby swished around inside, just as if he was playing with a hula hoop.

"Um . . ." she began, trying to think of a polite way to tell David she had to pee.

"Go ahead. I won't look," he said, turning his back as if he'd known exactly what she was going to say before she'd even said it. Sage crouched down again, steadying herself with one hand, staring at his back. A dog in the car wailed, loud and heartsick. Sage could see the animal, frantically leaping from the front seat to the back, rubbing its nose all along the windows to get closer to David.

He touched the glass with one finger, and the dog stopped. Inside the car, nose to the front window, the dog was motionless against the glass as if it could smell his scent. As if calmed and held steady by his presence. Sage still didn't have any tissue, but this time she didn't wait to air-dry. She wanted to get into the warm car and hear the sound of David's voice again.

# Chapter Fifteen

Dalton and Louisa had stopped down at the Stagecoach to have supper and audition a new guitar player to replace Marty Hamlin, who'd just gotten thrown in jail for a parole violation.

Sitting onstage, the lights right in her eyes, Louisa sang softly while listening to the young man play "Gentle on My Mind." He had a beautiful playing style, sweet and poignant, and Louisa was relaxing into the thought that her problems were solved, her show would go on even better than before — Marty had always played so tense and angry though what Louisa had wanted from his guitar was *romance* — when she heard the crash.

Everyone surrounded Dalton. He lay on the floor, moaning in pain. Louisa burst through the crowd of men, crouched beside him. At first she thought he'd had a heart attack, but his eyes were wide open and he was breathing fine. Writhing hard, his face was pale as death.

"Darling, what happened?" she asked. "What is it?"

"Think I've been shot," he said.

"Shot — my God!" Louisa actually looked for blood.

"He fell," the waitress said into Louisa's ear. "He was headed for the men's room, and his legs went right out from under him. My grandpa broke his hip last year, happened the exact same way . . ."

"Call the ambulance," Louisa said calmly.

"We did, they're on the way," the waitress said, but Louisa had already stopped listening.

Louisa gripped Dalton's hand. His eyes were open so wide she could see the whites showing all around the irises. He was terrified, so she covered him with her shawl. She leaned down, kissed him on the lips. They felt cold, and she was afraid he might be going into shock.

"They shot me," he said. "A gunfight, just like when my daddy . . ."

"You're safe," Louisa said quietly. She heard the others talking behind them, laughing with discomfort at Dalton's confusion. Wanting him to be quiet, to protect him from their pity and derision, she covered his body with her own.

"They shot me," he said again, looking into her eyes for the truth. "No one believes me, but that's the truth. I've been shot. Haven't I, Louisa? Haven't I?"

"Whatever you say, my love," she said. "I believe you."

An hour later, Dalton was having X rays at the satellite medical center off the highway. Louisa hadn't smoked for many years now, but she found herself craving a cigarette. Waiting had never been her strong suit. She called the ranch, and James answered. Louisa could tell from the way his voice fell, he was disappointed it wasn't Sage. But he snapped to the moment Louisa told him about Dalton.

"What happened?"

"They don't know what's wrong," Louisa said. "He was healthy as all get-out this morning, and after supper he just collapsed. Fell down hard, James. He must've broken something, but we just don't know what."

"What are the doctors doing for him?" James asked.

"Tests. Trying to keep him comfortable."

James was silent, but Louisa could hear his boot heels pacing the floor. "You just caught me," he said. "I just stopped in to check for news on Sage."

"The roundup, I know."

"Yeah, and I can't leave," James said.

"You don't have to. I'm here."

"I know, but he's my father —"

"I'm here," Louisa repeated.

"Thanks. Tell him I'll get to the hospital as soon as I can. Okay?"

"I'll tell him."

When Louisa hung up, she felt her throat stinging. James had thanked her, as if he knew his father was in good hands. That Louisa was with him — she always was. Kindling that little resentment like a damp campfire kept her busy for the next few minutes. So much so, she hardly noticed when her nephew Todd came walking in — dressed in his navy blue package express service uniform, as if he'd come to deliver something.

"Aunt Louisa," he said, standing there with a worried look in his eyes. "Mel at the Stagecoach told me you were here. I came straight up, didn't drink my beer, didn't drop my truck down at the depot."

"Oh, Todd," she gasped, pulling him down to kiss his cheek. She felt so relieved to have family there, she held his hand and didn't want to let it go. "Dalton fell. They're doing X rays right now —"

"Man." Todd shook his head. "A fall . . . is he okay?"

"I don't know yet. They haven't told me anything." Louisa cast a dark look toward the treatment rooms, trying to see around the curtain. "I tried to go in with him, but they wouldn't let me."

Blood is thicker than water, her father used to say. Louisa hadn't always believed that was true. Her relationship with her parents had been strained after she'd gotten pregnant, and her own daughter didn't come to see her half as often as Louisa wanted — her husband wanted her all to himself, a possessive and selfish man. So when Todd put his arms around her, she was surprised by the deep, primal sense of care and family connection she felt.

"Mrs. Tucker?" a young man in a white lab

coat asked. He introduced himself as Dr. Middleton.

"I'm Louisa Rydell," she began.

"She's Mrs. Tucker," Todd interrupted.

"Well," the doctor said, oblivious to the shock on Louisa's face. "Your husband has suffered a fractured femur — the thighbone of his right leg."

"Like a broken hip," Louisa said. "Happens to everyone when they get on in years. Gonna happen to me someday."

"It's not quite that simple," Dr. Middleton said. "It's more painful and, in Mr. Tucker's case, more serious. He's had some significant bone loss, and his femur . . . well, to put it simply, it just crumbled. Disintegrated, if you will."

"His thighbone *crumbled?*" Louisa asked, horrified, picturing it just turning to dust.

"Yes. Imagine an old wall with mortar —"

"Hey!" Todd said, stepping forward. "Do you have to be so insensitive?"

"I'm sorry," the doctor said, bowing his head and steepling his index fingers in apology. "I just want Mrs. Tucker to understand — his convalescence will not be easy. He'll need round-the-clock care. Getting in and out of bed, to the bathroom — the most basic things will be impossible for him to do on his own. Coupled with the dementia —"

"Oh, God," Louisa cried, unable to control her distress. "Maybe if you were the head of some hospital instead of working in this little backwater bivouac . . ." The young doctor was regarding her with compassion in his eyes, and that made her feel even worse.

"Maybe we need a minute to absorb this," Todd said.

"Yes," the doctor agreed. "I was thinking that myself. I'm going to send Mr. Tucker up to Dubois, get him admitted to the hospital until he's stabilized. And then . . ."

"We'll talk about 'then' later," Todd said sharply.

"Thank you for being here. James has the roundup," she said to Todd when Dr. Middleton had walked away.

"I'm just glad to help," he said.

"Especially for what you said at the beginning. That I'm Mrs. Tucker."

"That's how I see you," Todd said.

Louisa nodded. She hated getting upset in public places — she never liked having anyone see her act weak, and she couldn't stand having her makeup run.

"I just hope he's taken care of you," Todd went on. "Looking toward the future, I mean. Treated you on paper like the wife you've always been."

"You'd better not be talking about anything like a will," Louisa said, hardening her eyes. "I hear you or anyone mention 'Dalton' and 'will' in the same breath, that person's gonna need one of his own. And quick!"

"I just want to see you taken care of."

228

"Don't worry. Dalton's a man of integrity. He does what's right," Louisa said, smoothing down her hair. If the doctor had the diagnosis, that must mean the tests were done and Dalton was ready to see her.

"I'm sure of that," Todd said.

"Mmmm," Louisa said.

"I'll help you handle anything needs handling," Todd assured her. "Tammy's sister's a nurse's aide. She works at a convalescent home up Dubois way. Does private duty, too. I'll give her a call and ask about broken femur bones."

"Thank you, dear." Louisa suddenly felt so tired and old, as if all the mortar was crumbling inside *her*. Sitting down, she stared at her feet. She was wearing red high heels. This morning she'd felt she could dance up a storm, and right now the love of her life was lying on a stretcher with his bones turning to dust.

Todd had gotten her thinking. She was just a visitor on the DR Ranch — the initials stood for "Dalton" and "Rosalind," his first and only wife. Dalton loved Louisa — of that she had no doubt. But he had never changed the name of his ranch. He had never married her. James's dislike of her had carried too much weight, and Dalton had never wanted to risk upsetting his son.

Where would Louisa go when — if — Dalton were to . . . she shook her head hard, not even wanting to think the word. The ranch was her home. That's how Dalton had always wanted it, and he wouldn't leave her high and dry. He wasn't that kind of man. Letting out a long, low breath, Louisa rose. She said good-bye to Todd. And then she walked, straight and tall in her red high heels, down the antiseptic white corridor to be with the man she loved.

After climbing into David's rusty old four-wheel drive, Sage felt exhausted and relieved. His hand was bleeding from punching the man's teeth, and he wrapped his fist in gauze — he had a roll in a first-aid kit, which Sage thought was impressive. In the wide-open Nebraska dark, the moon threw silver light on endless frost-covered cornfields. David drove slowly, as if the car was too old to make it going fast.

Sage wanted to thank him, tell him how amazing his rescue had been, but she couldn't bring herself to talk about what had just happened. Her teeth were chattering, and she wished she could take a bath and get the feeling of the man's hands off her skin. Instead, she looked around.

The old car rattled as it drove, looking like something that belonged in a black-and-white movie. The seats were torn, their stuffing coming out. The reason why was obvious: The car was filled with animals. Sage saw a dog curled in a ball, a spaniel with bandages over its head, a broad-faced dog with a shredded toy in its mouth, and at least six tiny kittens. The kittens were going wild, running across the seat backs, across the old-fashioned door handles, hanging upside down from the fuzzy white headliner.

"It's their busy time," David apologized. "They get active after dark."

"What are you doing with six kittens in your car?" Sage asked, oddly comforted to be talking about cats instead of what had just happened. "Wouldn't they be better off at home?"

"Not the home they came from," David said.

Sage glanced at him, mulling over his answer. Maybe he was running away from some terrible home — the opposite problem from hers. Sage's trouble was that she had two good homes in very distant places. "Are you running away?" she asked.

"I don't think of it that way," he said. "I just don't live there."

"Interesting way to put it," she said.

"Why, are you? Running away from home?"

"Running to home, actually."

"Interesting way to put it." He grinned.

He lit a cigarette and held it in his unbandaged right hand. Sage saw tattoos on his forearm — a hawk, an owl, a star, the moon, and three wavy lines that reminded her of how a little kid would draw a river.

Sage looked around the car, counting the animals. She looked at the stout, tricolored dog — just making eye contact — and it cowered in the corner of the backseat. It wrapped itself around its toy and tried to hide its head.

"Don't hide," Sage said, holding out her hand.

"That's Petal," David said, looking in the rearview mirror. "She's a pit bull."

Sage withdrew her hand. "Aren't they attack dogs?"

"Only ignorant people think that. Petal came off a puppy farm. You know what that is?"

"No, what?"

"A place where they stick dogs in crates and breed them until they die. The mothers spend their whole lives having puppies, one litter after another. The puppies get yanked away before they're finished nursing. The mothers get bred immediately, pregnant with another litter. They never get over missing their puppies. It's a bad place."

"Petal lived there?"

"Yeah. She was one of the mothers. She thinks she's pregnant all the time, even though she's not. Hasn't been since I took her away."

"Oh, God." Sage looked back at Petal again. She had arranged her small stuffed animal between her paws, licking it tenderly. "She likes that little toy."

"She thinks it's one of her pups," David said. "In her mind, she's always pregnant, always nursing."

Sage quietly touched her own belly. The baby was still, resting for now. It seemed strange to hear a young man talk so knowledgeably about pregnant, nursing dogs, just as it seemed incredible that she should be so far along herself. In three months she'd have a baby, and she'd know just as much as Petal. "You took Petal away from that place?"

"Yeah," David said. "And I took the others from places like it."

Again, Sage turned to look into the backseat. The other two dogs were just as docile as Petal. The one with the bandaged face — a brown-and-white spaniel — lay at the opposite end of the bench seat from the pit bull. In the middle, curled up in a tight ball, lay a Scottish terrier. Sage's mother and aunt had had Scotties when they were young, and she knew the breed was feisty and curious — but this dog wouldn't even lift its head.

For the first time, it struck her as odd that six tiny kittens should be romping around the car like mad — sitting on the dogs' backs, using their heads as springboards, while the dogs just lay still instead of chasing them. In fact, the only time the dogs had moved was when David had gotten out to help her.

"What's wrong with the dogs?" she asked. "Why are they so quiet?"

"Their spirits are gone. That's what happens to animals from those places."

Sage swallowed. She didn't know why the next thing was so hard to ask. "How do you know about them?"

"Nebraska and Wyoming have a lot of puppy farms," he said, not quite answering the question. The moon had risen directly overhead, flooding the road with light. Sage stared at

David's face, the way he kept a cigarette in his mouth all the time as if he wanted to hide behind the smoke.

"They're lucky to be with you," Sage said. "Instead of the farms."

David didn't say anything.

"Why do you have them?" she asked after a long silence.

David just kept driving, staring at the moonlit road through the smoke. Sage usually didn't like to be in closed spaces with people who smoked. Before Aunt Hathaway had quit, Sage would roll down every window in the car when they took rides together. But right now she didn't mind it. The old car smelled of smoke, exhaust, damp fur, and cat pee, and she didn't feel sick at all. She thought David had forgotten all about her question, or that he'd just decided not to answer it. But then he did.

"I save things," he said. "It's what I do."

"You saved me," Sage said. Her throat tightened up, and as she gazed across the long front seat, she saw David nod. He glanced over. She tried to smile, but he didn't smile back. He looked angry, as if she'd said something to make him mad. Three of the kittens were striding back and forth across the front seat, meowing for food or affection. "That guy would have —" Sage began, but her teeth began chattering again.

"Some people are bad," David said.

Sage nodded, biting the back of her knuckles. It began to sweep over her, the terror of being attacked by a normal-looking insurance salesman on a farm road in Nebraska.

"You okay?" David asked, glancing over.

Sage tried to nod.

"Don't think about him," David said. "If you can help it. Think about anything else. Here —" Picking up one of the kittens — a tiny one — he handed it across to her. Sage held the cat on her lap, stroking it gently. Then the kitten sprang away, onto David's shoulder. All six kittens were surrounding him, meowing loudly.

"Food break," he said.

He stopped the car. They were on the side of a long, empty road. Clouds seemed to be moving in from the west, hiding the moon. David opened the two car doors on his side and let out a long, eerie whistle. Sage huddled in her seat, watching all nine animals file out the open doors.

David opened the trunk of the car. Sage heard pellets of food being poured into metal bowls. The road was so empty, the sound clattered through the silence. Pale, filmy moonlight sifted through high clouds. Reluctant to leave the car's safety, Sage felt too curious not to watch. She climbed out and walked back.

The Scottie and spaniel ate hungrily from separate bowls. David finished filling three more bowls with fresh water from a plastic jug. Then he separated Petal from her toy, allowing her to eat. Reaching into the trunk, he pulled out a shopping bag.

Shoving a stick of rolled fruit in his mouth, he handed another to Sage. She chewed, thinking of camping trips with her mother. He removed two toy baby bottles and a can of Enfamil. Sage watched as he filled the bottles with baby formula. Then he crouched down in the cornfield as the six kittens scrambled to be first to be fed.

"They like it warmed up," he said, two kittens sucking noisily from the bottles. "But I didn't feel like lighting the stove."

"Can I help?" she asked.

"There are more bottles in there," he said.

Sage felt him watching her as she opened the bag. He had enough bottles and formula to feed an army of hungry kittens. She filled two bottles and settled down on the cold ground beside him. Their breath billowed out, white and ghostly. Sage felt the remaining four kittens climb all over her, and as she started feeding two, she felt sorry for the two who were left out for the moment.

"We'll get to them, don't worry," David said. "I'll be glad when they're ready for solid food."

"What were you doing in that old barn?" Sage asked.

"Back there?"

She nodded. Surrounded by animals making noises of contentment, she felt safe enough to visit *back there* in her mind. "I didn't think anyone would come," she said. "I thought he was going to drag me into his car —"

"He would have," David said without feeling

in his voice, as if he was stating a simple fact.

"And you came zooming out of the field . . . with your lights off . . . all I could hear was your engine . . . and I hoped . . . I prayed . . ." Sage gulped. Tears were running down her nose, but she couldn't wipe them because both hands were busy feeding hungry kittens. "I prayed someone would save me."

David didn't speak. He just stared down at the two kittens in his lap. They had drunk their fill and were lazily tapping the baby bottles with their paws. Gently he laid them on the frosty ground and let the other two — ravenous now — climb onto his knees. The bottles were still half full.

"All I could think of was my father," Sage said.

"Why?"

"That he'd somehow know. That he'd save me."

"Parents aren't God."

"I know," Sage agreed. "But I thought it anyway."

"Sometimes parents can't do shit. Sometimes they hurt more than they help."

"And sometimes they don't," Sage said.

David fell silent again. Sage stared down at his hands. Blood was seeping through the bandage on his left hand. But the things she couldn't stop staring at, couldn't look away from, were the tattoos on his right forearm. They were beautiful, like works of art. The owl's eyes were yellow — steady and alert. They looked alive, as if the bird might take off and fly into the night.

Sage had spent most of her life in the Connecticut suburbs, and had considered tattoos scary and gross. Whenever she saw girls at the mall with tattoos on their shoulders or ankles — even if they were of roses or butterflies — Sage thought of the girls as tough and hard. But for some reason, the pictures on David's skin brought tears to her eyes, and she didn't have a clue why.

"What were you doing back there," Sage asked for the second time, "in that old barn?"

"Bedding down," David said.

"Is it where you live?"

"No."

"You were going to spend the night there?"

"Yeah. It's not good for the dogs to spend too much time cooped up in the car," he said. "Reminds them of their pens at the farms."

Sage lifted her head. She saw that two of the dogs had finished eating, were slurping at the water bowls. Petal had picked up her toy again, and she was walking along the side of the road, looking for a place to relieve herself. She didn't stray too far, continually glancing over her shoulder for David. More clouds obscured the moon, making it hard to see.

"It's going to snow," David said, staring up at the sky.

"It's only October," Sage said. "Or November." What was the date, anyway? She'd been gone for a week now.

"November fourth," David said. "Lots of winters start around now."

"They don't at home, in Connecticut."

"I thought you said Wyoming was home."

"They both are," she said. "My mother's east, my father's west." Sage stifled a yawn. It was getting late, and she hadn't really slept in days.

"You're going to your father?"

Sage nodded. Her two kittens had finished drinking. They started to purr, nuzzling the nipples of the toy bottles. Sage remembered having a baby doll when she was little, playing with a bottle exactly like this. "I can't wait to see him."

"That's good," David said. "What made you leave the other place? Where your mother lives?"

"I don't know." Sage felt the baby stirring inside her, but she felt too shy to tell David she was pregnant. Thinking of Ben, she tried to picture him feeding kittens with baby bottles. But the picture wouldn't come to her: All she could imagine was him carrying his backpack through school, hanging around the playing fields with all his friends.

"Is this your car?" she asked.

"It was my uncle's. It has four-wheel drive, goes through mud, snow, anything."

"Did your uncle give it to you?"

"He gave it to my mother," he said. Then, changing the subject, "We should find a place to sleep tonight, before it gets too much later."

Sage nodded, yawning again. They looked around, but there were no barns in these fields — nothing but dry, chopped-off cornstalks. Her two kittens had fallen asleep on her lap, but the other four ran madcap through the field. The three dogs snuffed around in the milky moonlight, Petal keeping her toy gripped in her teeth.

"Aren't you afraid the animals will run off?" she asked. "And you won't be able to get them back?"

"No," he said. "They won't."

Sage watched him rise slowly, stretch toward the sky. He was thin, with a long, narrow waist — she saw his ribs when his shirt untucked. His stomach was covered with tattoos, too. She could see the dark shapes, but she couldn't make out what they were. The sight disturbed her somehow, but she found herself wanting to look at the pictures more closely.

David opened the car doors and let out that same long, unsettling whistle. It reminded Sage of a night owl hunting over the salt meadows on Pumpkin Lane, and she felt a pang of homesickness. The animals came charging back from their hunts, piling into the car as if they feared it might leave without them.

Sage tried to stand, but her legs were too stiff to move. Her baby felt heavy inside, and she rocked back and forth. Sage felt David watching her, and heard his boots crunching on sand as he came around the car. He put out his hand. Taking it, Sage pulled herself up.

"Thanks."

"No problem."

When they'd both climbed in, she counted the

animals just to be sure. David didn't even glance around — they were all there. Sage's heart was pounding. David's hand had felt rough and dry as leather, and it had brought back a memory Sage didn't even know she had. Her father's hand had felt that way, too: covered with scars and calluses from working the ranch.

From holding reins, raking out stalls, pulling rough rope, climbing red rocks, digging in dirt and dust. Western men's hands were tough. When Sage was small, she held her mother's hand, smooth from the work she did and the objects she handled: bones, stones, metal. And she asked her mother why men's hands were rough and women's hands were smooth.

"You'll find out," her mother had said. "As life goes along. But you might be surprised. Some girls are just as good at being cowboys as the boys are. Girls can have rough hands, too. You just never know."

"You never know," Sage said out loud now.

"What?" David asked.

"Oh, nothing," Sage said.

He nodded, accepting her answer. He drove slowly along, down the straight road pointing into the dark night. The moon was gone, and the first snowflakes had started to fall. Were those mountains in the distance? Or were they driving into the low clouds of a storm? Sage snuggled deeper into her seat while David drove, watching the landscape for a barn where they could spend the night.

# Chapter Sixteen

Daisy's third morning on the ranch, she pulled back the curtains to look outside. Snow had fallen during the night, and the ground was covered by a thin layer of white. Paul March, riding by, saw her and circled back to wave. Slowly, she opened the door.

"Howdy, Daisy," he said. "Long time since . . ."

Daisy hugged herself, shivering in the cold. *Since she'd left the ranch, since Jake had been gone.*

"Good to see you, Paul."

"You too. Any news on Sage?"

"Not yet." Her heart skipped, just saying the words. The ranch was still the same: News traveled fast.

"Don't worry too much. She'll be fine."

Daisy tensed. How would he know? Glancing down to compose herself, she noticed a package on the front porch.

"Did you hear about Dalton?" Paul asked.

"No, what?" She looked up.

"He fell. Broke his leg or something — we don't know yet. Louisa's with him at the hospital."

"Oh, no," Daisy said, biting her lip.

"Sorry to bring you more bad news." Paul

sounded concerned, and for a minute she thought he might climb down off his horse to console her. She flashed back to the day after Jake's disappearance, when she had cried against his shoulder more than once. He had been a good friend then, and she appreciated his kindness now.

"It's not your fault," she said, trying to smile.

"Hang in there, Daisy. If there's anything I can do . . ."

"Thanks, Paul."

Waving again, he kicked his horse and rode away, sending up clouds of snow. Daisy picked up the package at her feet and looked at the ground: Big footsteps led back toward the corrals. Shivering, she stepped inside and closed the door behind her.

Untying the parcel — a square of old red cloth — she found a bundle of bones. She sat at the oak table to examine them more closely: the paw of something — a dog or fox, or a coyote or wolf. Someone else might have felt alarmed, frightened by the intent of whoever might leave a bag of bones on a woman's doorstep, but not Daisy.

Seeing the bones calmed her down. She knew James had left the bones for her, and although she couldn't have said why, she understood that they were his gift. She had passed a restless night, hearing snow tap against the window-panes. Imagining her daughter somewhere *out there,* unprotected and all alone, almost drove her insane. She had paced the small house, stirring the fire, looking out the windows, trying to see through the snow to where the dark ridge and tall pines were supposed to be.

• Daisy had thought about Sage's future last night, dreading what it would be. Set apart in school, different from everyone else, having to endure the gossip and whispers? Daisy loved her own daughter so much, she already resented the tiny baby who was about to rob her of the rest of her childhood.

Eager suddenly to gather materials for a project, she pulled on boots and a jacket. She felt glad to be leaving the little house. Being cooped up inside with such intense memories couldn't be good. The cottage's four walls told stories that only James and she knew.

Wanting to see whether Louisa was back from the hospital, she veered up to the house. The big kitchen was empty, so Daisy dialed Hathaway.

"Any word from her?" Daisy asked as soon as her sister answered.

"No — nothing there?"

"No."

"I thought you'd never call," Hathaway said, exhaling.

"It's only been three days."

"Only three days! Wow, feels like longer. How's James?"

"I haven't seen him yet. Everyone's protecting us from each other."

"Probably an excellent bet," Hathaway said. "Call me the minute you need me."

"I always need you," Daisy said.

"That's what I wanted to hear," Hathaway said quietly.

The bracing air felt good as Daisy hurried across the field. Smoke swirled into the white sky from chimneys in every building. She kept her head down against the wind, hands deep in her pockets. Seeing hoofprints in the snow, she knew the men had gone out to the range — this weather wouldn't keep them in. She'd visit Scout in the barn, clip some strands from her tail. Brushing her yesterday, Daisy had been happy to see some of the old sheen return to her yellow coat.

Sliding the barn door slightly open, Daisy slipped inside. She stamped her feet, closed the door behind her. The horses tossed their heads at her approach. Used to the darkness now, Daisy worked her way down the row. She said hello to every horse, scratching their noses as she passed.

The barn felt cold. Her breath showed in the air. Music played in the distance, and Daisy recognized it as country western. Just like Louisa, she thought, smiling, to pipe Patsy Cline into the barns to make the horses happy. The stable was shaped like a cathedral, like a cross. When Daisy reached the transept, she felt the heat. Someone was working around the corner with the kerosene heater going.

Scout was clipped to the tie-offs. She stood in the center of the north aisle, a long line holding each side of her halter to opposite walls, exactly where Daisy had groomed her yesterday. It hardly seemed possible that this was the same horse: She glistened yellow as butter, and her mane and tail were flowing creamy white. Daisy hung back, standing in the shadows.

James stood with his back to her. Currying Scout's coat, he had both arms spread along her flanks. He wore tight blue jeans under dusty chaps, and he'd worked up a serious sweat from vigorously brushing the horse in the heated space. His plaid shirt was thrown on the straw-covered floor, and his muscles strained under his faded black T-shirt. Daisy stared at his broad back, and she gazed at his bare arms.

He had held her, once upon a time. James was grooming the horse he had given her when she'd come to live on his ranch. He was brushing the yellow coat with intensity and — Daisy could see — love. He was making right what he should have kept up all along.

"Pretty horse," Daisy said.

There was a moment of silence.

"Palomino mare," James said finally, without turning around. "Registered quarter horse."

"Strong." Daisy took a step closer. "She sure is strong."

"I know," James said.

Daisy went to stand beside him, to stroke the horse's thick neck. Scout whinnied and bent her head. Daisy rubbed her ear. She picked up a brush from the tack bucket, and James caught her wrist.

"I had to come," she said, staring into his eyes.

"I can't believe I'm seeing you." He kept holding her wrist. He shook his head once — hard — as if he thought he might be dreaming.

"I can't, either," Daisy said, forcing her voice to be steady. "James Tucker."

"Daisy Tucker," he said. "It's sure good to see you."

"Scout's so old . . ." Daisy gently pulled her arm away, petting the horse.

"She's going to be okay. She's going to make it out of this fine," James said, and Daisy knew he wasn't talking about Scout.

"Sage," Daisy said, her voice cracking. She kept brushing Scout, and then she stopped.

"You said the horse is strong? Sage is strong. She sends me pictures, letters. She's an outdoor person. Camping, canoeing." Talking about his daughter, he looked proud, his eyes brighter. "She's taking care of herself."

"She's only sixteen."

"Daisy . . ."

Daisy's chest was caving in, like a hill after a landslide, and she had to step back. As he touched the side of her cheek, she flinched.

"This is on me," he said. "That's what you're thinking?"

"I'm not thinking anything," Daisy said. "I just want her back safe."

"Well, it's what I'm thinking."

They stood there, face-to-face. Daisy saw the lines in his tan face, the slashes of worry around his blue eyes. His hair was shot with gray. She looked for the young man, the brash young rancher she had once loved, but he wasn't there.

"Sage." He whispered the name.

"Oh, James." She shook her head.

He pulled her tight and close in an embrace so hard every bone in her body ached. She cried out, and he hugged her tighter. She knew he meant to comfort her, to give her solace, but all she could feel right now was hate for herself, for failing to forgive after all these thirteen years.

"I thought . . ." she tried to say. "I thought . . ."

"What?"

"I thought time softened things," she said into his hard chest.

"Daisy . . ." he whispered. "No, you didn't."

"I did."

"You couldn't think that," he said. "You know time only makes things harder. Bones and stones, Daisy. You work with them every day. That's the truth, and I know it. Don't think I'm fooling myself. I know why you're here."

"Our daughter," Daisy said, clutching the front of James's old T-shirt. "That's all."

"I know," James said.

James rode across the range, shouting to the herd. He, Paul, and the others were driving them all toward home. This was his money-making time of year, and usually the most fun. Fall was when a cowboy knew why he wanted to be a cowboy. With the weather they'd had the last few days, the ground was all mud and snow. The feisty cows tried to run away; the horses reared up and knew they were kings of it all.

Trying to dodge a stubborn straggler, James fell with his horse and banged his thigh against a rock. It tore the outer edge of his chaps like the merest flick of a knife, but the mud was so soft and deep, no real harm was done. They just clambered up and started riding again. Distracted by thoughts of Daisy and Sage, by the fact that his father was in the hospital, James forced himself to concentrate. Cows pressed against them from all sides. Paul zigzagged through the herd, the adrenaline in his veins taking ten years off his face.

"You okay?" Paul asked.

"Fine," James said, putting the old "What are you talking about?" look in his eyes.

"Daisy looks good."

"You saw her?" James snapped his head up. Then he caught himself and squinted back toward the cattle.

"Snow squalls up ahead," Paul said, pointing toward the mist-shrouded purple mountains.

"Make this a little more fun," James said.

"Three feet by tomorrow," Paul said. "That's my prediction."

"You and my father."

"Really?"

"Yeah, he's been saying 'early winter' for a month now. Good — we can truck these guys away in a blizzard. Up the ante a little."

"Dalton's saying 'told you so,' " Paul said. "Looking out the hospital window, watching the snow clouds build. He's laughing because he knows we're gonna go snow-blind before this herd gets shipped."

A steer took off from the herd; the stock dogs saw it before James. They took off barking, and James just rode away without another word to Paul. He thought of his father, lying in bed with shattered bones, and he kicked his horse into a gallop. Fall roundups had been Dalton's favorite time. He had taught James everything he knew about ranching, and James had never shipped a herd without him. James could feel his father with him now.

The aspen and cottonwoods had turned pure gold, their leaves shaking in the wind like coins: branches full of money. The leaves fell and blew. Migrating herds of elk crossed the land. The fields up north had been cut for the third time that year, but not baled yet. The hay lay in the mud, waiting to be snowed on. James didn't think of the wet hay, and he didn't think of his father lying in a hospital bed. Ranchers weren't supposed to fall down, standing on a solid floor. They weren't supposed to be motionless, unable to help themselves, lying in a sterile white room with windows that didn't open.

James chased the steer hard, his eyes streaming in the wind. Every muscle was working, and he lost track of where he ended and the black horse beneath him began; he felt as if he *was* the horse. They pounded over wet ground, quarterback and tackle in a close game. Someone was going to go down hard, and James didn't care who it was. This was the ranching he'd grown up with. He didn't want to think anymore. Daisy was home, keeping another vigil: He couldn't get away from the fact even if he wanted to.

He chased the steer into canyon land. The animal veered around the corner, a truck on two wheels. James had his rope ready, arm back and prepared to throw. His horse wasn't even breathing hard, but James was. The canyon was wide at first, but it narrowed down into a hundred skinny ravines. James had been here just yesterday, cutting the foot off a dead wolf. The steer was going to get caught, or it was going to get lost.

The canyon was empty.

The steer had disappeared. James stopped his horse, looking around. He felt the tenseness of muscle fiber flooded with adrenaline. The thrill of the roundup, he told himself. But he knew he was lying to himself — it was the canyon itself. Creatures disappeared here. The rock walls ate them up. Cattle, children . . .

Sitting stock-still in his saddle, James listened hard. Far up the east rim, a hawk took flight, beating the air with sharp wings. Then nothing but eerie, brooding silence. James swore he heard his own blood pounding. Steers didn't vanish. The canyon was just a place — it wasn't evil. James had spent years surrounded by people who believed in spirits — Louis

Shoulderblade and his family. And Daisy, the way she coaxed something spiritual out of things she found on the ground. Although James was just a simple rancher, he couldn't deny the shiver down his spine.

Pebbles scrunched underfoot fifty yards away. The steer must have found its way into the labyrinth of crevices. James felt himself wanting to follow the sound, but he made himself stay put. He stared at the ground, looking for tracks in the mud. Plenty of them to read: deer, wolves, elk, coyotes, birds, the steer. A human.

This wasn't a place where people walked. There were no campsites or hiking trails. James bent over the saddle horn to see better. Size ten boots, from the look of them. The steer's tracks went straight into the deepest part of the canyon; the man's veered right. He had kept to the rock walls, using the overhang to shield him from the weather. Although the mud wasn't so deep there, his tracks were easy to read.

Staying just outside the man's trail, as if he was riding beside a ghost, James followed the footprints. They were fresh — hours, not days old: Time and weather hadn't caved them in. Their depth, considering the relative dryness of the sheltered ground, told James the man had been carrying something heavy.

The canyon twisted around a long rock outcrop, splitting into five narrow chasms. Each crack was wide enough to enter, but James couldn't freely see inside. They were too dark and constricted. At the same time, he lost the trail. The tracks disappeared mid-step, and James quickly saw why: Growing from the red sandstone were clumps of sagebrush and stunted cedar. It took him five minutes to find the broken twigs.

Someone had clipped a low branch. James found the fresh cedar wood, a white spot the size of a quarter, oozing sap. He saw where the tracks left the mud, climbing onto the rock ledge. The person had used the cedar branch to brush away footprints, hide his direction. James saw the trail branch off into five different crevices.

His muscles were so tense he thought he might crack. Again, he stopped to listen. Pebbles scuttled down from up ahead, as if someone was trying to climb the rimrock. But when James tried to tell which direction it came from, the sound stopped. The storm clouds were sliding down from the mountains, throwing the canyon into near darkness. James strained his ears, tasting primitive fear.

Someone was here. He felt it again. Suddenly James felt a deep, terrible blackness, the empty part inside himself that was missing two children. He thought of how this canyon had eaten his son, and he thought of how his daughter was supposed to be on her way home — here to the ranch — right now.

Were those tracks deep enough to have been made by someone carrying a sixteen-year-old girl? James felt wild, his eyes burning. He was

253

panting hard, fighting to keep his breath from being too loud. He jumped off his horse and started scrambling. The chances of finding someone might have been slim, but James refused to think that way. He was ready to tear the sneaking bastard apart with his bare hands.

He skinned his wrist raw, just getting up the first rise. Thunder cracked down the valley, and from the top of the rim, James could see the snow coming. Paul was driving the herd home, half of them obscured by driving snow. James saw the dark lines of cattle, the men on horseback doing the work James should be taking care of, but he turned away. He shifted his weight on the unstable ledge, moving deeper into the crevice.

Unbelievably, he found the tracks again. The cedar broom had missed a print — James caught the outer edge of the left boot. Panting, he started to run. His left shoulder brushed the rocks, hugging tight to the inside. The ledge narrowed again, giving him a two-foot path. The cliff fell sharply to his left, a two-hundred-foot drop. James felt the altitude in his knees, and he touched his pistol as he ran.

James came to a bend in the trail, where he couldn't see what came next. The cliff dropped straight down, and he dislodged pebbles that took a long time to hit bottom. Now he did pull his gun, because he wasn't about to round a blind corner empty-handed. Edging around the protruding red rock, he burst into the last crevice before the trail ended.

Someone had been here. James found a dead campfire built deep under a jutting boulder. The ashes were warm, and the last smoke wisped up the rock chimney. From the pile, James pulled out three old Polaroids. They were charred and smoke-stained, but he could make out the images of his grazing herd. He found an empty can of beans and a folded road map. It was a gas-station map, folded open to the land around the DR Ranch.

"Jesus Christ," he said. The camper had been furtive enough to brush his tracks away and build a fire where the smoke wouldn't show. But he'd left other signs behind. James searched the ground for evidence that more than one person had been there. He felt frantic, tearing the rocks apart for signs of Sage. He checked the three pictures again, for hints of a sixteen-year-old girl.

Down below, the lost steer lowed. James had forgotten all about the roundup, and he didn't give a second thought to the steer. It might be frightened, dead-ended in one of the dark crevices. The storm had finally hit. Snow fell hard, coming down in white sheets. Thunder cracked — so loud it could split the rocks. Sticking the three Polaroids into his pocket, James hardly heard.

"Shit," he said, so loud his voice echoed down the canyon. "Don't snow. Just don't snow yet . . ."

He holstered his pistol and fell to his knees. The snow fell faster than he could look. He brushed it aside, wanting to keep the ground clear. The snow would blanket the canyon, the trail, this abandoned camp, and James would lose his chance.

*An early winter,* his father had said. *Three feet this week,* Paul had predicted. James's wrist bled onto the white ground, and his thigh seared from where Chieftain had fallen on him before, but he just kept looking for signs.

# Chapter Seventeen

Daisy hunched over her makeshift worktable, candles burning all around the room. Sometimes she knew she was just making jewelry — just stringing objects together, creating adornments for women to wear — and other times she had the sense of making magic. Her touch was quick and hot, her fingers hovering over the bones.

Outside, the snow came down. The wind howled through the rafters of her small cottage, and sparks flew up the chimney. She had made a tape — many years ago, when she had lived here before — of Shoshone chants. She had brought them from home, and they played now on the portable tape recorder, competing with thunder coming down the mountain.

She hadn't slept much, but staring down at the bones had a hypnotic effect on her. Work, she thought. Make something, use your hands, stop thinking. Yesterday she had carefully picked burrs from Scout's tail, and the rhythm and feel and mindless repetition had made the time pass.

She knew it was strange, but when she worked with bones she tried to be gentle, as if she could somehow avoid further injuring the animal from whom they had come. Daisy willed herself to imagine the creature: From the size of the bones, she guessed they'd come from a wolf. She thought back to the Bear Mother necklace she'd made for Louisa, and now she conjured up the wolf's spirit.

Pulling her tools from a case inside her travel bag, Daisy used a scalpel to loosen the remaining tendons from the bones. She separated the metatarsal bones and claws; she found where the ankle had been attached to the shin. Feeling love for the animal, she prayed for the release of its spirit.

The region abounded with Coyote-Wolf stories. Wolf, considered good and benevolent, was believed to have created humans and stars. Coyote was a trickster, harming people and impeding Wolf's efforts. Louis Shoulderblade had once told her that wolves were born of the Long Snows Moon, that they were quick, serious, and devoted to their young.

Devoted to their young . . .

As Daisy worked, she thought of other Shoshone myths. They taught of a time when humans could transform themselves into animals. Before written languages, the adornment of jewelry had been an important element of Native American communication. Hunched over her table, Daisy's body was taut. Her hair fell over her eyes, glinting red-gold in the firelight. She thought only of the wolf spirit, of bounding across long distances to reach her brood, of devotion to her young.

Using her stylo, she etched markings in the bare bone. Initials for each child, a heart around "S" for Sage, a star around "J" for Jake. She would fill the grooves with black India ink, like scrimshaw. She would add polished beads from the streambed, and she would attach them with braided strands from Scout's tail. Scout, the horse who had carried her and the twins on so many happy rides . . .

Daisy worked on the wolf bones, carving the faces of a man and a woman. The surface seared her fingertips. Back in Silver Bay, she had made necklaces that brought love to the wearers. Deep love — strong enough to hold magic — had been given to Daisy first by her parents, then by her sister. The daughters of English scholars, they had read Shakespeare and Austen and Bronte — all the great love stories — and these had seeped into their souls. Then Daisy had come out here to Wyoming, and she had met James. And the love stories had come to life.

The candles flickered in the wind. Daisy paused, pulling her sweater tighter. She wondered whether the men were back from their day, and she walked to the window. The snow was coming down so hard, Louisa had decided to stay at the hospital another night. Daisy thought of Sage out in that weather, then of James. She drifted back to her worktable, but the ability to make magic had temporarily left her.

Burying her head in her hands, she listened to

the Shoshone chanting. She thought back to her first time here, searching for inspiration in the wilderness. Every part of Wyoming had seemed huge, extreme, and magnificent. The story of Sacagawea had moved her heart and soul. She had immersed herself in Native American lore, visiting the Crow and Shoshone reservations.

Girls from other eastern establishment families might have tried backpacking through Europe, baby-sitting for families on the Vineyard or Nantucket, crewing on schooners sailing the Maine coast. Daisy had grown up sheltered and loved. Being from a close family was the best thing in the world, but Daisy knew it could stunt her if she let it. At twenty-two, she had never gone anywhere alone. At art school in Providence, she'd lived in a house with six other girls, and returned home nearly every weekend. She had started to feel like someone walking miles in shoes that were too tight. She knew she had to do something.

Daisy had an artist's temperament and training — there were plenty of artists in the nearby colonies of Rockport, Newport, and Old Lyme — but something in her spirit had pulled her west — alone. Her luggage had been cumbersome: riding clothes, a down jacket, binoculars, cameras, her easel, top-quality drawing paper, her jewelry-making tools. But she had no protectors or chaperones, and when she reached Wyoming, she had felt like a bird soaring free from the nest for the first time.

The rocks had astonished her: black mica, green hornblade, crimson sandstone, rose quartz, chalky white feldspar. The Wind River mountains soared above the plains, and from the minute she saw them, she knew she had to go deeper into their land. She wanted to make jewelry like the Native Americans — she knew she had something primal inside that needed to be unleashed, and she knew that wasn't going to happen if she went home to Connecticut too soon.

She decided to go panning for gold. She found a dude ranch near Lander, and they gave her western riding lessons and a sense of how it felt to be a cowgirl. Her hacking jacket, canary breeches, and velvet hat stayed in the bag: She wore ranch clothes, just like everyone else. She stopped trying to post and learned to sit in the saddle. After two weeks, Daisy felt confident enough to ride off on her own. She packed up for the day, picked a spot on the map, and rode out to Midsummer Creek.

Wearing chaps and a Stetson made her feel like part of the landscape. Her red sleeveless shirt was all cotton, bought at the country store in town. Daisy had followed the trail, keeping watch on the sky — they'd told her thunderstorms blew up fast in the Wind Rivers, and although she had a poncho in her pack, she wanted to stay alert.

She rode through meadows of buckwheat and mountain sorrel. Buttercups and primroses bloomed everywhere. Her horse stopped to graze, but she'd learned enough to pull his head up and make him walk on. The sky was so big and blue overhead, the clouds pure white billows. Daisy was in heaven, and it was called Wyoming.

Panning for gold had been fun. Crouched by the cold stream, she had pulled her hat low over her eyes to keep the sun out. She had filled her saddlebags with a few bones left behind by an owl, a ram's horn, and a handful of quartz. But here on the riverbank, she felt the thrill of prospecting. Easterners had been coming west for a hundred years, hoping to strike it rich. Maybe she would be next . . .

She had heard the rattle just in time. Reaching into the water to scoop up a pan of pebbles, she had nearly put her dry hand down on a rattlesnake. The snake was huge and coiled. It had slithered out to sun itself on the rock, and its camouflage was perfect. The gold and brown diamonds looked just like stones, and Daisy wondered how long it had been sitting beside her.

"Don't move," said a deep voice.

The snake rattled its tail. Daisy was frozen in place, wondering what the rattles actually looked like. This was happening in slow motion, as if another, braver girl was panning for gold and Daisy was just watching from afar.

"I won't," she said softly.

"This is gonna be loud," the voice said.

"Uh-huh," Daisy said.

The snake opened its ugly mouth to strike — the throat deep and black, the fangs curved and sharp as needles. A shot rang out, blasting Daisy's eardrums, and the snake's head disappeared — leaving its thick, disgusting, and impossibly long body writhing on the rock.

Daisy clapped both her hands to her mouth. She jumped up, knocking over all the maybe-gold pebbles she'd panned from the stream. A stranger walked out of the shadows across the way. Daisy smelled the gunsmoke and saw him sticking his pistol into a holster. They stared at each other across the narrow stream.

"You didn't scream," he said.

"What were you doing, watching me?" she asked.

"Not for long," he said. "But, yes."

Daisy tilted her head, gazing at him. He was a cowboy, tall and so lean he looked like a hard, straight line. He wore tight jeans and a dusty white T-shirt that said "Powder River Rodeo" in red letters. He held his black hat in his hands; the sun had bleached his brown hair, and although he wasn't much older than Daisy, he had lines around his mouth and eyes.

"Thank you for killing the snake," Daisy said.

"He was about to strike. I hope the shot didn't scare you too much."

Daisy nodded. She'd been having an out-of-body experience, taking in the beautiful parts of the scene — the sun, the blue sky, the handsome young cowboy — and blocking out the fact that she had nearly been bitten by a poisonous snake. Or that she could have been hit by the ricocheting bullet. Her hands began to shake, and she held them together to keep them still.

"Oh, brother," she said, looking down at them.

"It happens that way sometimes," the young man said. "It hits you later, when you think what might have —"

Daisy nodded, and she put her face down so he wouldn't see her start to cry. She cried very easily — her emotions always embarrassed her. She felt everything strongly, and tears came with the territory — when she was happy, sad, elated, sorrowful, frightened, disappointed, hurt. It didn't matter: Daisy cried.

Willows grew on Daisy's side of the stream, but across the way was a thicket of pines, cedars, and stunted junipers. The smell of pitch carried on the wind, fresh and sharp. The cowboy watched Daisy bury her face in her hands, and then he walked right through the water with his boots on. It must have been deeper than he thought, because the water poured into his boots and nearly pulled them off. But he kept coming.

"You're okay," he said, putting his arm around her shoulders. "Don't be scared."

"I didn't see it," Daisy said, shaking. "I stared right at the rock, and I didn't see the snake."

"That happens all the time," he said. "It's

happened to me."

"Really?"

"Yes."

"And you're from around here?" she asked, unsure of whether to believe a real westerner would be so blind.

"Yeah, this is my land."

Daisy jumped back. She felt even more embarrassed now. "No," she said. "I'm staying on the dude ranch, and they sent me here. They gave me a map, showing me the good spots to pan for gold . . ."

"They always do." He laughed. "They only own a few acres, and they figure we won't mind a few tourists taking our stones. They're not real gold, though. Hate to disappoint you."

"I'm sorry," Daisy said. "God, I can't believe they'd do that —"

"It's okay. I'm James Tucker, and you're on the DR Ranch."

"I'll leave —" Daisy said, backing away.

"No, stay," he said. "But tell me your name first."

"Daisy Lambert. From Silver Bay, Connect-icut."

"Prospecting for gold?"

So Daisy told him about going to art school, designing jewelry, being fascinated by western materials and designs. When she told him she felt curious about the snake's rattle, he cut it off with his knife and stuck it in her saddlebag. He told her if she made something with it, he'd buy it from her. Daisy asked if she could keep the pebbles she'd panned, and he said she could. But when she showed him, he picked one mis-shapen stone out of the bunch.

"It's real," he said. "I take back what I said before. You found real gold."

"Honestly?"

Together they examined the small rock. It looked dull and dark, no different from any of the other stones she'd picked up. But James had seen the value, the sparkle under the river moss. Daisy knew she'd carry the small gold nugget home with her, use it in her first western-inspired necklace. The breeze blew, and she felt the first rush of wilderness inspiration — exactly what she'd been after on this trip to Wyoming.

"Oh!" she said, the force nearly knocking her over.

James had been holding his hat in one hand, and he took Daisy's right off her head, letting her coppery hair blow in the wind. Cupping the back of her head in his hand, he'd let the hats fall to the ground and kissed her till she saw stars. She clutched the gold in one hand and gripped his forearm with the other — she had never known a man's body could be so hard. It shocked her more than seeing the snake on the rock, and she dropped the gold.

James didn't stop kissing her for a long time. He made it slow and gentle, the way he tangled his fingers in her hair, moved his lips from her mouth to her neck. The sun heated their bare heads and arms; every time Daisy felt a new muscle on his biceps or back, her knees went weak, and if she'd had more gold to drop, she would have.

When they stopped, James crouched down to find the nugget. Standing above him, Daisy looked at the shape of his narrow bottom in his tight jeans and wondered why she'd never looked at a man like this before. He handed her the gold, closing her hand in his fingers. His calluses were so rough, they scraped her skin.

"Cowboy hands," she said softly.

"What?"

"Oh, nothing —" She wanted to think of something else to say, so he wouldn't go. "Just that I like being here. Riding. Everything."

"Cowboy hands," he said, grinning. "You can have them, too. Just stay on the dude ranch for a while. Keep riding, panning for gold, you know?"

"I'm staying on a ranch that's not a ranch," she said. "It's just a bunkhouse with a barn and a map of someone else's land."

"Come stay on the DR," James said. "We have room."

"Thanks for offering, but I couldn't."

"Why not? You can make your jewelry, ride when you want. It'd be nice to have you. Are you in a hurry to get back to Connecticut?"

"No . . ."

"Then why not?"

Daisy shrugged, shaking her head. It seemed impossible, too much of an adventure for her to imagine. But then he kissed her again, tipping her face back toward the sun, covering her mouth with his soft lips. Once more, Daisy dropped the gold nugget; again, James picked it up for her.

And she moved off the dude ranch and went to stay on the DR. James put her right here, in the secluded cottage where she was staying now. He kept a respectful distance for a good long time. At least twenty-four hours. Daisy had eaten her meals up at the main house with James, Dalton, and Louisa. She had made friends with Paul March and the others. Louisa's nephew Todd had been working here back then; Daisy remembered the time he'd brought her a bouquet of mountain daisies and looked in her window. She remembered how James had nearly killed him.

Raising her head, Daisy looked around. She blinked at the window, almost expecting to see summer light instead of falling snow. The little place hadn't changed at all. Thinking of James, of their first meeting, broke something deep inside. The magic started again, and Daisy's fingers felt hot. The candles flickered, as if a ghost had just flown by. Daisy thought it might be the spirit of that rattlesnake, the hideous creature that had — for so many years — filled her with gratitude.

Her jewelry put the wearers in contact with the spirit world, suggesting the sun and moon, the earth's wintertime slumber and springtime renewal, and the reappearance of snow geese after their long migration. The division between the earthly and spiritual worlds was too mysterious for Daisy to fathom.

All she knew was, her fingers felt hot and the candles were burning down. The chants continued, and she wondered whether James was home from the range. Sage and Jake were in her heart, and for the moment that was enough. These spells of work brought her peace and serenity for as long as they lasted.

Picking up the bones, she heard a wolf call in the snow outside. It barked again, then poured out its heart in a full-throated bay. Something shook, like the ghost-rattle of the long-dead snake that had carried Daisy into love. She started, looking around, then realized it was just a loose pane of glass in the old cottage window.

Wind blew down the chimney, swirling the embers and making the candle flames jump. Daisy kept working, the magic and inspiration delivering her from worry. Sage was coming. She was traveling west, just as Daisy had done herself so long ago. Sage's parents' love and the spirit of the bones she wore around her neck would keep her safe. And bring her home.

Taking shelter from the storm, David and Sage had found another old cow barn. Two nights on the road, and this was getting to be a habit.

269

Outside, the snow came down. Three inches had fallen already, and David said they'd have six more before it was over.

"More in the mountains, where we're heading," he said. "Three, four times that in Wyoming."

"But it's not even Thanksgiving," Sage said, thinking of how the ski areas in New England would love this.

"It'll melt as fast as it falls," he said. "It won't last. The real snows don't start till later. December, January."

They were settled in a back corner of the barn, the dogs and kittens sleeping on their laps. Petal chewed her stuffed toy, staring with devotion at David's face. Sage tried to arrange herself comfortably on the hay; the baby was active today, and she couldn't find a position where his feet weren't tapping on her organs. Once, David had stared hard at her belly, as if trying to see whether she was really pregnant or just fat. But he'd been too polite to say anything.

"You know a lot about Wyoming," Sage said.

"Yeah."

"Is it nice there?"

"Same as anywhere. Nice some places, bad others."

Sage heard the cows mooing, and she looked around. She felt a thrill of memory, smelling the farm animals and hearing their big bodies rustle in the straw. This was a living, breathing herd, and she wondered whether it was anything like her father's.

"We have cows," she said.

"You do?"

"At my father's ranch."

David let out a quick, scornful snort. "He's a *rancher?*"

"Yes, he is."

"I hate ranchers," David said.

Sage felt shocked, as if he'd spit on her feet.

"With a passion," David continued.

"I don't see how you can say that," Sage said. "Considering where you picked for us to sleep. If you hate ranchers so much, why do you stay in their barns?"

"This is a dairy farm," he said, glowering. "Not a ranch. There's a big difference."

"Cows," Sage said, holding out one hand and now the other. "And cows. Big difference."

"Milk," David said, turning his left palm up, then his right, "and hamburger. Ranchers get the cows to trust them, and then they slit their throats."

"Oh —" At some level, of course Sage knew that beef came from cattle and cattle came from her father's ranch. But she had never liked to dwell on the particulars. She preferred to wash the picture in softness and light, mountain vistas in sunset colors. The idea of hamburger made her gag, and she covered her mouth.

"Sorry," David said.

"My dad doesn't do that part himself," she said.

"You sure?"

"Yes," Sage said, even though she wasn't.

"It doesn't make a difference anyway. It's cruelty to animals. You get them to love you, take food from your hands, and then you make them suffer. It sucks, and I hate anyone who does it."

Sage watched him as he spoke. His face twisted up like a wet washcloth, turning bright red. He took a cigarette out, held it in the palm of his unhurt hand. His teeth were clenched, a lot like a vicious wolverine's. Sage actually felt a little scared of him; she could see there was nothing casual about the way he felt.

"Did you grow up on a ranch?" Sage asked after his face unknotted.

"No."

"Then why do you hate ranching so much?"

"I've seen plenty."

"Where did you grow up?" Sage asked, thinking it would be better if they got off this subject.

"Hollywood."

"Really?"

"No."

Sage's feelings were hurt, but she wasn't going to show it. The kittens were asleep, curled into six purring balls in the hay between her and David. The Scottie and spaniel stared at the cows, and Petal licked her shredded toy as if grooming a puppy.

"Why don't you light that if you want it so bad?" she asked, gesturing at his cigarette.

" 'Cause this is a barn, and there's hay around,

and I don't want to kill us and the cows," he said. "You'd better get clear on barn behavior if you're gonna live on a ranch."

Now Sage's feelings were worse than hurt. Her throat felt tight and her eyes filled with tears. She was just like her mother, she cried very easily.

"Shit," David said.

Sage wished she had never met him. Her lower lip shaking, she bit it hard and tried to see through her tears. The snow was only three inches deep — she could walk back to the main road and find her way to Wyoming. She wouldn't even hitchhike. Her legs were strong and solid, and they'd carry her there. She would walk, Sage thought, starting to sob.

"Sage," he said, coming up behind her. "Hey, Sage."

"Leave me alone." Sage shook her head. She stepped in a big clump of cow manure, and crying hard, she tried to scrape it off. "I don't need a ride from you," she said. "I'll make it on my own."

"What, in the snow?"

"Yes."

David stood there. The more Sage tried to clean her boot, the worse the manure seemed to stick. Her stomach churned, and she knew she was going to be sick. She could almost read his thoughts; he must be feeling disgusted by her pregnant condition and that her father was a cruel rancher and the fact of cow manure on her shoe. And now she was going to throw up —

She did — all over her other shoe.

David didn't even move. He didn't turn away or make sounds of revulsion. Sage retched until her stomach was empty, crying between spasms. Leaning against a wall of worn barnboard, she felt overtaken by depression and loneliness.

"Here," David said, taking her hand. He guided it to his shoulder, propping her up as he used a handful of straw to clean off first her left boot, then her right. Sage gripped his slender shoulder bones, trying to stifle the sobs that rose in her chest. Then easing her hand away, he stood up.

"Don't cry," he said, looking into her eyes.

Sage and David stood face-to-face. She shuddered, feeling the emotion pour through her. David wiped her tears with his thumb, and again she noticed the owl tattooed on his wrist. The color was vivid and lifelike, as if the tattoo artist had used magical pigments to make the bird come alive. Staring at the creature's yellow eyes, Sage avoided David's.

"Sage . . ." he said.

"What?" she whispered.

"Hey . . ."

He was waiting for her to look at him. She felt her heart beating, and for a minute she wondered if he was going to kiss her.

Right now, standing in front of David, she had some of the same physical sensations that went with kissing: the flush in her face and neck, the tingling in her arms and the back of her legs, the building sense that something was about to happen. But as Sage raised her head to gaze into David's eyes, she knew that she was wrong about the kiss.

His expression was blank, as if he was sleep-walking. His mouth was half open, his eyes wide. Sage watched how he just stared at her, as if he needed her to say something. When she didn't, his mouth moved. He seemed to be trying to form words, and then he finally spoke.

"I would never have let that guy hurt you," he said.

Sage bit her lip, afraid she might start crying again.

"No matter what. I don't let things get hurt. Dogs, cats, cows, people. I wouldn't have let him hurt you."

"I know. You rescued me."

"I saved the dogs from puppy farms," he said, as if reminding her and himself. "I've known Petal since she was a puppy herself. She was my mother's favorite dog."

"You lived on a puppy farm?" she asked, shocked.

David nodded. As if he'd missed a tear, he used his hurt hand to wipe her cheeks again. His gaze was blank, as if he had long since decided it was better to feel nothing than to remember the details.

"What was it —" she started, wanting to ask what had made him run away.

"That's why I save things," he said. "Why I

don't let them get hurt, no matter what. Okay?"

Sage said okay.

"So don't worry anymore."

"I won't."

"You need to eat," he said. Although he didn't mention her pregnancy, Sage realized then that he knew: the second person, after Deenie, to notice. She didn't care; she was kind of glad, because she felt close to David in some way she didn't quite understand — that was as important as kissing but didn't need it. Good friends, potential best friends, she thought. The kind of friends that went through bad times together, feeding kittens with baby bottles. The kind of friends that helped each other find shelter from all sorts of storms.

"I know," she said, patting her belly. "I need to eat."

"Sit down," David said, walking her toward the dogs and cats. "I'll be right back."

Settling herself in the nest they'd made before, Sage let the animals gather around her. Their body heat warmed her, and their beating hearts comforted her. Closing her eyes, she felt almost peaceful.

She heard the sound of liquid hitting tin. At first she thought someone was spraying a hose at the roof, but then she saw David halfway down the barn. In the dim light coming from tracks overhead, she watched him crouching in the straw, milking a cow. Sage could see he knew what he was doing; it took him less than a minute to fill the small pail.

Carrying it through the barn, his face was dark and shadowed. She couldn't read his expression from here, and for some reason she was afraid it would be that blank stare. But when he handed her the pail, his eyes were soft and eager.

"Is it good?" he asked.

"It's good," she said, trying to hand him the warm pail.

But he wanted her to have it all. She felt suddenly ravenous, but she had to be careful and not take too much too fast. The animals must have smelled the fresh milk; they all began to stir, waking up from deep sleep. David opened the bag he had brought in from the car, filled the dogs' bowls with food and water.

As he sat down to feed the kittens, Sage drank some more milk. A feeling of contentment started deep inside, beneath the fear and anxiety that had been with her every day for months.

# Chapter Eighteen

Louisa wished Emma and Ruthie were with her. When you were Louisa's age and sitting in a hospital room by the bedside of your infirm beloved, you wanted your family by your side. You wanted to remember that you were loved and cherished, that you had made a difference in this world, that your spirit would live on. Crises made you realize that no one goes on forever, that this precious life was over in a snap — just like *that*. And it made you want your offspring to reassure you that they would be there and love you till the end.

Two days after his fall, Dalton, sleeping, looked horrible. Louisa peered over the *People* magazine she was reading and thought his color was worsening. He lay on his back, tubes running into his wiry arms, his mouth wide open. The nurse had taken his partial plate, and he looked like a toothless vagrant. It shocked Louisa so much to see her Dalton looking so bad.

"Sweetheart," Louisa said, grabbing his arm and shaking him awake. "Darling —"

"Huh?" he asked, not opening his eyes.

"Darling, it's me."

"Rrrrr . . ."

"Isn't this place awful? I know you must hate it so much . . ." Louisa looked all around, at the ugly yellow walls, the nylon curtain around his bed, the heart and blood-pressure machines, the way his lower body was suspended in traction. If only they hadn't given him so much medication: She wished he could join her in loathing the hospital. She would give anything to hear him crabbing and yelling for the doctors to let her take him home.

They hadn't shaved him that day. A snowstorm had started yesterday and many nurses and aides had arrived late or not come to work at all. If Louisa had him at home, this wouldn't have happened. She'd have gotten him ready — washed, changed, fed, happily installed at the big window overlooking his ranch: snow quilting all the corrals, barns, troughs; elk and bison trailing down the mountains in search of food; red-tailed hawks soaring on their daily hunts. Dalton would be wide awake, groomed and watching the world. Staring at Dalton's grizzled face, Louisa knew what she had to do.

Rolling up the sleeves of her soft cherry wool dress — soft challis, cut on the bias so the skirt would swing like she was on the dance floor — Louisa rummaged through the bedside cupboard — tacky hospital-issue furniture, made of plastic and particle board — and found a basin, soap, towels, and a razor.

Louisa knew how to make a man feel right. She ran the water in the bathroom till it was scalding hot, and she soaked the towels for a good while. Then, wringing them out, she rushed them to Dalton's bedside and wrapped them lovingly around his face to soak his beard and make him feel all swaddled and warm. Didn't matter that he was eighty-two years old — he was all man and hurting bad. Louisa knew the best medicine for the toughest ranchers was sometimes letting them feel like a brand-new baby.

"There, sweetheart," she whispered into his ear — other than his nostrils, the only part she'd left uncovered. "Relax, Dalton love. I'll shave you better than any young nurse can."

She unwrapped the towels, started up the lather. Working the cheap hospital soap into a rich lather took some doing, and she was mindful of the sensitive condition of Dalton's skin. He flinched from the touch. Although he seemed asleep, he kept trying to talk.

"Sssh, love," she said, rubbing the creamy suds into his beard. "I'm here, giving you your morning shave. Don't know why I'm bothering, though. Always did like the way you looked after a night on the range, kind of low-down and grizzly . . ."

"Rrrr," he said.

She began the actual shaving. She had done this before, many years ago. When she was young, before she'd met Dalton, she had worked as a dancer in a Cheyenne rodeo revue. She had been poor and broke, with an iffy career and a baby to support. So she had done outside work. There had been a men's club, the Rod and Rifle. Louisa had worked there some nights, giving rubdowns and shaves — nothing cheap or unrespectable. She had learned to think of the razor as a feather, the man's face as a balloon. She'd earned the biggest tips of anyone there because she'd had the lightest touch.

"That feel good, honey?" she asked, drawing the blade up his neck. She stroked the razor in a gliding upsweep, dunked it into the basin of clean water.

"Yes, feels good," Dalton said.

Louisa's heart leapt. She almost upset the water. "How are you feeling?"

"Like hell," he said, but his eyes glinted through the lather. They stared right into Louisa's, and she dropped the razor to clasp his hands.

"It hurts?"

"Not so much," he said. "Can't feel much of anything, as a matter of fact. Just like I drank a tub of bourbon. Where's Jamey?"

"Fall roundup. He told me to tell you he's coming as soon as he gets the cattle shipped."

"Fall roundup." Dalton closed his eyes again. "I should be there."

"Let the boys take care of it," Louisa said. "You rest up and let your sweetheart give you a nice shave."

"My sweetheart," he said. "Rosalind."

Louisa gasped. She jostled the water basin,

spilling it all over the side of Dalton's bed. He had made that mistake exactly two times at the beginning of their time together — Louisa had told him if he wanted her to stay, he had better never, *never*, call her by the name of his dead wife again. And he had kept that vow all these twenty years. To hear that name here and now filled Louisa with such sorrow and rage, she had to walk away from his bed.

"Jesus Christ," he said. "I'm all wet, Louisa!"

"It's Louisa now, is it?" she asked, more sadness than anger in her voice.

"What're you talking about?"

The doctor and nurse picked that exact moment to walk in. The nurse exclaimed over the sloppy mess and the doctor came over to stand by Louisa. She knew her mascara was in railroad tracks under her eyes. The doctor was already talking about a discharge date, how Dalton was stabilized now and what he needed was a place to convalesce and regain his strength, how Louisa would have to make arrangements.

Louisa licked her lips. She felt like crying more, and she thought she knew why. Making medical decisions for Dalton felt like skating on thin ice. They had never discussed their health-care desires with each other. She had once mentioned living wills to him — you'd think, with his high-risk life as a cattle rancher, he'd have thought once or twice about the possibility of falling off a cliff — but he'd just about snapped her head off. The fact was, she wasn't

282

his wife, and she didn't have his health-care proxy. She sniffled, holding back the sobs.

"Listen," the doctor said. "I understand how hard this is. May I make a recommendation?"

"Please do," Louisa said stiffly.

"A few weeks in a nursing home would be the best thing — to let him heal and get him some physical therapy. If you can afford to keep him at home after that, and it won't be too hard on you, you might hire a nurse's aide. Insurance sometimes covers it, and there's a lot of people around looking for work."

"Thank you for the suggestion."

"He's strong. His muscles are in good shape, and he —"

"Thank you," Louisa said again, cutting the doctor off. She was hugging herself tightly, wishing James was here to help her make the decisions. The nurse, who was young and quite pretty, was changing Dalton's wet clothes and sheets behind the curtain. Louisa could hear him flirting with her, and suddenly it cut her like a knife.

"See you tomorrow," the doctor said.

Louisa nodded. She thought of the name Rosalind, of how easily it had slid off Dalton's tongue. Did he think of her all the time? What did Louisa mean to him, after all? He had never asked her to marry him. The fact had stung her when she thought about it, but she had honestly never realized, not once, how it cut her to the core.

Rosalind of the DR Ranch.

What if Louisa wasn't in the will? James would kick her out in a second. She shook her head, unwilling to think such negative thoughts when Dalton was about to be ejected from his hospital bed. Nursing homes, physical therapy . . . at least the young doctor hadn't mentioned senility or dementia today.

What had Todd said about a friend who worked in the nursing field? Something concerning home-care . . . a cousin or an in-law who looked after people in their own homes? Louisa would give Todd a call. She'd wait for Dalton to fall back to sleep, and then she'd take a walk down the hall. She had seen a pay phone around the corner from the nurses' station.

# Chapter Nineteen

While Daisy worked with the wolf bones, strange things began to happen.

The snow fell deeper and faster than any early November storm on record. Wolves circled down from their mountain lairs, howling outside Daisy's window as if they could free the spirit of their fallen brother. Swallows left the barns and took shelter on the house porch rafters. By night, owls hunted during breaks in the storm, droves of burrowing owls, saw-whet owls, and screech owls flying low across the deep drifts.

The wolves yipped and bayed. Exhausted from working through the storm, James wondered what the hell they were doing so close to the houses. He and Paul had gathered the cattle, and now it was weaning time. The wolves stayed hidden, but James could feel their presence by the way the cows were acting.

Under the snow, mud sucked at everyone's feet. The semis were parked by the gate, waiting to be loaded up with calves. Two drivers sat in one cab, smoking and telling stories while they waited. They'd been driving stock trucks for a long time, loading up DR cattle and taking them to market.

Those Polaroids were burning up James's pocket. Who would want to take pictures of DR cattle? He kept looking at the photos, the corners flaking ash, wishing something new would emerge. Louis Shoulderblade and Daisy had talked about spirit pictures, where ghosts and clues to the past would appear in photographs that had been taken long ago. Every time James looked, he half-hoped and half-feared he'd see an image of Sage shimmering out.

"You seen anyone hiking around the canyons?" he had asked Paul.

"Nope," Paul had answered. "Why?"

James had shown him the pictures, asked if he thought they might have something to do with the dead cows. Paul had stared hard, suggested they show them to the sheriff, but thought it was probably some tourist from the dude ranch taking pictures of life in the Wild West.

James forced himself to concentrate on the task at hand. It was time to separate the calves from their mothers. Already the mothers were feeling it. They'd been nervous all morning, and now they were starting to cry. Animals had the same emotions as humans, James was convinced. He hated this part of his job.

The cow dogs were black and slick with mud. They nipped at the calves' heels, urging them left, into the sorting corrals. The cows were directed right. Confusion reigned. At first the cows thought they'd just lost sight of the babies — nothing drastic, nothing permanent. They looked uneasily from side to side, the panic growing.

The snow had tapered off. Thirty-two inches were on the ground, but the heat of the herd — all packed into this one small area — had melted it clean away. James rode his black horse through the crowd, shouting for the mothers to move away.

"Yah!" he called, waving his arm. "Get on!"

The truck drivers threw their cigarettes down, came around back. The doors opened wide, and suddenly the mood changed. Those trucks had carted many herds off to slaughter, and their walls held the stench of fear and death. The scent carried on the storm wind. The cattle began to shift: The mothers knew.

James heard the bellowing start. The mothers lined the fence of their sorting corral, craning their necks. Their big open faces mooned toward the trucks where the calves were being loaded. The lowing turned to grief.

In their midst, James nearly got knocked off his horse. Chieftain slipped in the mud, banging through the herd. James watched the mothers climbing on top of each other to reach their off-spring. But the fence was in the way. The mothers crushed each other, bellowing with unbridled agony.

Thirty times: James had weaned and shipped cattle thirty times. It had never been easy, but he couldn't remember it ever being this hard. His stomach churned, reacting to the animals' noise.

When Dalton was here, James stayed focused on being a good rancher, making his father proud. This was what it meant to be a Tucker on the Wyoming range: James was just the latest in a long line.

Today he felt sick. He didn't know why. Maybe it had to do with his father being gone, with Daisy being here. He didn't want to think of her hearing this. A cow charged in front of him, crying mournfully. Barging straight into the pack, she lost her footing and went down in the mud. The other cows climbed on top of her, as if she wasn't even there.

James jumped down from his horse. Fighting through the herd, he wrapped his arms around her.

"Come on," he said. "Stand. Get up."

She cried, her eyes wild, the herd stepping over and around her. James was in danger himself, but he was tough and his first priority was the cow. He quickly saw he couldn't yank her to her feet, so he took a few turns of rope around her neck; mounting his horse, he lost a boot in the slurping mud. Taking a turn around his saddle horn, he backed Chieftain into the herd and pulled the cow free.

With all the clamor, he almost didn't hear the woman's voice. It was higher than the cows', but it contained all the grief and terror of someone who was losing her child. Up on his horse again, above the boiling herd, at first James thought he was hearing a bird.

Wearing a dark green jacket, Daisy blended with the stand of pines and cedar at the far end of the corral. She had climbed up one rung on the fence, staring at the cows and stock trucks. With hundreds of calves being led away and four hundred cows bellowing to follow, Daisy had come to watch.

James felt his heart tighten, filled with inexpressible sorrow and rage, and he tried to hide it by kicking his horse, driving him into the mass of cows. He wanted to unknot the herd, keep the cows in the back from trampling the ones in front.

Daisy's cries came over the herd's noise, and he couldn't stand it anymore.

Galloping through the mud, James felt the black spatters all over his face. He pulled up in front of Daisy, but she didn't even see him. Her arms were outstretched, as if she could embrace all the calves and mothers.

"Jesus Christ," he said. "Go inside, Daisy."

"Listen to them." She wept.

"It's weaning time," he said. "That's all it is. Happens every year."

"They're crying," she said. "Can't you hear them?"

"It's a roundup. They always make a lot of noise. Go inside and close the door. It'll be over soon. You won't have to hear them anymore."

Daisy closed her eyes. Her face was pale and radiant. She threw her head back, as if she was having a vision. James shivered, staring at her bare wrists. They were so delicate and fine, he could see her blue veins through her skin. He had always thought her the most vulnerable creature alive, and it drove him crazy to think of the weight she'd had to withstand.

"For God's sake, Daisy!" he exploded. "Go inside."

"I can't," she said.

"Why do you put yourself through it? Isn't it bad enough we don't know where Sage is? Do you have to listen to this —"

"I know how they feel," Daisy said. "I know what they're going through."

"And watching them is gonna make you feel better?"

"Nothing's going to make me feel better till Sage comes home," she said, gulping. "But I'm not going to leave them alone. I'm staying here till every calf is gone. Till —"

"Till they lose hope?" James asked, tormented and not knowing where the words came from. "That it?"

"I just want to be with them," Daisy said. "That's all. I can't explain it." She took a deep breath, and suddenly she wasn't crying anymore. A great calm seemed to have overtaken her, and she looked James straight in the eyes. "This has nothing to do with you," she said. "I'm fine. I mean it. Go back to work, James."

"Nothing to do with me." James furiously turned Chieftain and galloped away. He saw Paul watching him, but he didn't care. His bare foot — without the boot he had lost in the mud — felt cold and wet. The cows were louder than ever. James didn't understand the woman who had once been his wife, and he wondered whether he ever had.

The calves stumbled up the ramps into the trucks, bleating like sheep, not knowing what was about to happen. Like life, James thought. Youngsters trusted their parents to take care of them.

"Shit," James said, just before he got within earshot of Paul. He didn't feel like explaining anything, and he could see Paul wanting to ask questions. Paul rode over.

"Got a gallery," he said. "Fans watching the action."

"No fans here," James said.

"No? She looks pretty riveted."

"I didn't say she wasn't riveted," James said. "She's just not a fan."

"Ladies don't like this part," Paul said.

"She wouldn't like you saying 'ladies,' either," James said. "She's not very happy."

"We're almost done," Paul said. "The cows'll be quiet soon. They'll forget what just happened, and they'll settle down to a long winter's rest. Till we get 'em bred again, anyway."

"Hey, Paul?" James asked, trying to be heard above the cattle.

"Yeah?"

"Would you shut up?" James asked. Then he rode away to pull another downed mother out of the mud.

291

Driving Dalton's truck — it had the best traction, in case she got stuck in the snow — Louisa pulled in midway through the weaning operation. She had gotten used to it over the years, the god-awful screaming of the cows — but today it hurt her ears and made her breasts ache. There were James and Paul, leading the cowboys as they separated the herd. And there was Daisy — watching the whole thing from the far end of the main corral.

Louisa shook her head. Daisy knew enough about loss without watching the goddamn cows bellow for their babies. She felt like pulling the girl right off her rung, but if someone wanted to be a martyr, far be it from Louisa to stop them. Folks knew what was best for them, and they followed their own inner compasses. Louisa had never claimed to know what made people tick, but she tried to respect it even when she couldn't understand.

Once inside the ranch house, she breathed a great sigh of relief. It felt good to be home, instead of cooped up in that awful hospital. Dalton was all medicined up, calling her Rosalind and thinking he'd been shot by sheep men. Then he'd get straight, call her Louisa, ask her when he could go home.

It was enough to drive her crazy. Louisa went to the sideboard, poured herself a glass of neat whiskey. Her father had taught her how to drink a long time ago. Do it like a man, he used to say:

nothing sweet, nothing creamy, nothing but straight. She didn't believe in drinking alone or before sunset — but today was a day to break the rules.

Flopping down on the living room sofa, she looked around the room. Handsome portraits of Tucker ancestors glared down from every wall. Mama Tuckers and Papa Tuckers. Louisa sipped her whiskey, letting her gaze travel to the silver tea service Dalton's wife had inherited from her dear departed grandmother.

Louisa knew the story. Rosalind had been well-bred. She had come from Boston, from one of those Brahmin families that had sailed over on the *Mayflower* or the goddamned *Santa María*. She had gone to finishing school, she knew which fork to use for every occasion, she spoke with a New England accent.

But the kicker — the thing that had made Dalton fall madly in love with her — was that Rosalind had been a crack shot. She had entered a competition back in Boston, moved into the next round and beaten everyone in New York, traveled by rail out to Cheyenne, where she'd shot an apple off the head of a horse, and won first prize in the competition. Won the gold medal and won Dalton's heart.

"The gold medal," Louisa said out loud. She heard the venom in her voice, took a nice long sip of whiskey. By the time she'd drifted across the living room, to the case where Rosalind Tucker's gold medal was displayed, her voice was softer. "First prize," she said.

Louisa could afford to be kind. Rosalind was dead, and she had been for many years. Since James was fifteen years old. They had been in the pony barn, mother and son, after a snowstorm just like this one. The snow had been heavy, and the weight had collapsed the roof right on top of them.

James, hurt himself, had pulled his mother out. Oh, what that must have been like. Louisa had imagined it many times: the young boy with his broken leg, holding his dying mother, the life flowing right out of her. Her blood had soaked into the snow — Louisa knew exactly where, because Dalton had placed a stone cross on the spot.

Touching the glass, Louisa couldn't reach the gold medal. Rosalind had been so many things Louisa was not: eastern, well-born, rich, a champion. Louisa couldn't hit the broad side of a barn with a full load of buckshot. Louisa was sex and Rosalind was class. She was the girlfriend; Rosalind had been the wife. Drifting over to Dalton's desk, Louisa began to casually tidy the papers on top.

As she did, she settled into the comfort of the room. Louisa had decorated the place herself, using pictures as inspiration. She had pored through back issues of *House & Garden*, looked at photographs of great ranches in Texas, Montana, and British Columbia.

She had wanted to keep the flavor of the Old West, using the pieces Dalton had inherited from his parents and his wife. So she had kept the mission tables, the cracked leather armchairs, the portraits and rolltop desk, the big Oriental rug that had lain on the dining room floor of Rosalind's parents' Back Bay mansion. But from there, Louisa had veered off.

She had covered the sofa and settees in elegant sage-green velvet. She had chosen green brocade drapes, floor-length and lined with cream. She had picked out brass lamps, crystal decanters, a funky mahogany bar from an old saloon in Lander. She had mounted Dalton's father's barbed-wire collection — a sample from every fence he'd ever strung. Louisa had done that without any pride whatsoever: The fences had been erected to keep out her family and their sheep.

Sighing, she realized what she was doing: looking for the will. She was full-blown nuts, all upset over zilch. Of course Dalton would take care of her. She knew the man, believed he loved her with all his heart. Calling her "Rosalind" was nothing more than drug-and-pain talk. Thinking of her own family, she picked up the phone and called Todd's wife. Tammy was a nice girl, very loving and devoted to Todd.

"Well, hi, Mrs. Rydell," Louisa said into the mouthpiece. "Mrs. Todd Rydell."

"Hi, Aunt Louisa," Tammy said, laughing at the pretend formality. She asked about Dalton, and they talked for a while about his condition and prognosis.

"Listen, your big, handsome husband told me your sister does health care, and I'm thinking about hiring her."

"She's good," Tammy said. "She's caring, and she needs the work."

"Which sister's this?" Louisa asked, trying to keep Tammy's family straight. "The one with kids or without kids?"

"They both have children," Tammy said, sounding confused.

Tammy gave Louisa her sister's name: Alma Jackson. A wayward husband and two boys to support. She had worked in hospitals and nursing homes, and she did private duty work somewhere up north. Louisa thanked her niece-in-law and promptly dialed Alma's number. The voice on the answering machine sounded plain but nice, and Louisa left a message.

Then Louisa tried her own daughter. With all those bellowing cows, she wanted to talk to her baby. She let the phone ring a long time, to no avail. That girl had a life and a half, Louisa thought, shaking her head. Just like her mama. Trouble from the get-go with a capital T. Hanging up, she looked around. The house felt strange without Dalton in it.

Almost as if it still belonged to Rosalind.

*Kids run away all the time, every day of the week.* That's what Detective LaRosa had told Daisy, and that's what the police said in every department she called. Staring at a map of the United

296

States, Daisy had been working her way across the country. She drew a line from the town in Iowa where Sage had gotten off the train, to the ranch. Choosing towns along the line, she'd call information and get the numbers for the local police departments. Some had received bulletins about Sage; most hadn't. None had seen her.

She couldn't get the sound of the cows out of her head. She telephoned police department after police department. It was nighttime now, and most of the places she called sounded quiet. No, everyone told her. We haven't seen your daughter. Kids run away all the time.

Outside, the night was silent. The semis had pulled out, taking the calves to their deaths. The cows stood huddled in the corrals, their noisy grief subsided. Daisy felt washed out, as if she'd been crying for days. The snow had started again. Colder and drier than before, it tapped against the windows. Daisy cringed, thinking of Sage in the snow.

She called another police department. The dispatcher was rude and brief. She tried another, hung up when she heard the recording: "Due to the storm, all lines are temporarily out of service . . ." Shaking, she turned to her workbench. The wolf claws lay before her. Her carving was almost complete; the male and female faces nearly defined.

The howling started up again. Had she conjured it? Daisy felt powerful in her work: If she could bring love without intending to, perhaps she could call wolves down from the foothills. Worried about the mother cows — too distracted by missing their babies to take care of themselves — she wished she could drive the predators away instead.

When the knock came at the door, she nearly jumped out of her chair. The candles flickered as she crossed the room. Halfway to the door, thinking it might be news of Sage, she started to run.

Flinging open the door, she gasped.

James stood there, scraping snow off his boots. Daisy's eyes flooded with tears. His stare was hard, and he didn't smile.

"What are you doing here?" she asked.

"That's what I want to ask you," he said. "Can I come in?"

Daisy stood aside. Her arms hugging herself, she looked down at James's feet. She saw his boots, one of them encrusted with mud, and she remembered how when he had ridden over to her at the corral, he'd had one bare foot. She hadn't laughed then, and she didn't laugh now.

"What the hell are you doing?" he asked.

"Right now?" she asked. "Calling police stations." She showed him her map. Running her finger along the line she'd drawn, she pointed out the towns she had already called. Even if they hadn't seen Sage, at least she could put them on alert. They'd be watching out for her.

"You can do that from home," he said, interrupting her.

"What?"

"You can call every goddamn podunk police department from back east. From your own house. Go home, Daisy."

She held herself tighter, staring up into his face. The lines were sharp and deep, his jaw square and set. He looked like the land, she thought: all rock. His cheekbones were angular, his eyes dark and sunken. Oh, the color, she thought. Those eyes were hazel, the shade of sagebrush in October sun. Blinking, she tried to look away, but he grabbed her wrist.

"You don't belong here," he said.

"It's where I have to be." She tried to pull away.

"I heard you today, we all heard you."

"Crying? So what?"

"This is a ranch, Daisy. It's not a zoo. It's not a park, where you take the kids to pet a calf, play with the ducks. You know? Jesus, you've never let it be. You always wanted it to be something it's not."

She shook her head. "You don't know what you're talking about."

"The calves," he said. "They went off to slaughter today. You heard their mothers."

"So did you," Daisy said.

James exhaled. He paced around the small room. Seeing him in here, the first place they had made love, was almost too much for Daisy. She took a deep breath, exhaled slowly, unable to take her eyes off James.

"Fuck it, Daisy," he said. "Go home."

"I'm waiting for Sage."

The fire sputtered, and James stared at it. He shook his head, opened his mouth, closed it. "I don't want to be mean," he said. "But you don't belong here."

"Sage is coming — I belong here."

"Shit goes on here," he said. "You can't believe. You can't take it, and I don't even think you should. What good does it do you, hearing the cows cry?"

Daisy felt something happening. Sometimes when she sat down to work, when she passed her hands over the bones, she could feel the creature's spirit enter her fingertips. Ready, willing to take it on, Daisy would open her heart; the ghost of whatever love the dead had ever felt would flood inside her. Oh, she felt it now. Staring at James, hearing the venom in his voice, she felt the rock inside her break like a dam.

"What good does it do you?" she asked.

Surprised by the gentleness of her tone, he looked up. He wiped some imaginary dust from his cheek, the corner of his eye. His gaze was bitter, but for one moment it looked desperate — as if something was hanging in the balance, as though he had some secret life-and-death conflict going on inside.

"Sending those babies off to get killed," she said. "It hurts you, James. And don't give me that stuff about being a rancher."

"I'm a cattle rancher," he said. "It's the biggest part of what I do."

"No," Daisy said, her throat aching. "The biggest part is taking their temperature when they get sick. Feeding them from bottles when their mothers die. Riding onto thin ice when you think one's going to fall through. Giving them your last water when the drought's too bad and you find them thirsty —"

"I have to keep them alive," James said. "Till they're old enough to die."

"And you love and care about them."

"That's beside the point."

"I don't think so."

"What's the difference?" he asked.

"It's torn you up," Daisy said. She wanted to touch his cheek. She wished she could take him to a healer, see if what was broken inside him could be fixed. For a long time, back when Jake had first disappeared, Daisy had wanted to be that healer herself. Now she knew she didn't have that much power.

"I'm fine," he said.

She shook her head. "No, you're not."

He stared at her, but nothing about him softened. His expression was just as hard. He looked straight through her, as if he hated her, as though nothing would make him smile until she was gone. Yet she had come upon him brushing Scout — currying that old horse till she gleamed like fine gold.

"You've got to get out of here," he said. "I'll get Sage home to you. Don't you believe me?"

"I believe you."

"You don't," he said. "You can't, after what went on with Jake. You think it's the same."

"It's not —"

"But you think it is. It must feel that way —"

"Kids run away all the time," Daisy said. She couldn't believe it, how easily those policemen's palliative words tripped off her tongue. Wanting to strangle whoever said them to her, she now said them as if they made the most sense in the world. Sage had run away; suddenly, the facts seemed clear and comforting. That's all — she was sixteen, a dauntless rebel, pregnant and scared. She wanted her father, and she had run away to be with him. Nothing about this was James's fault.

"I don't blame you," she said quietly. "For any of it."

"Fuck. *I* do," James said.

"I know." She wanted to take his hand, but she couldn't make herself do it. She felt electricity under her skin, and she was afraid he'd feel it. "You always have."

"You said kids run away all the time," James said. "What if they do? What if it's the most normal thing in the world? You can't stop bad things from happening to them."

"I know. I'm trying to have faith."

"Faith," he said, somewhere between a snort and an outright spit.

"And hope."

"That's even worse," he said. "Hope. I saw you at the corral. You know better than anyone

302

how it feels to lose hope. That's why you were crying for the cows."

"I do have hope, James," Daisy said quietly. "I wish . . ." You did too, she wanted to say. She wished she could give it to him — put her arms around him, feel their hearts beating together the way it used to be. He was so handsome, the man she'd fallen in love with. But she was frightened by the hardness in his eyes. She and he had lost faith over Jake, but she never would — never — over Sage. "Sage is on her way, and she's going to be safe. Wherever she is tonight, she's out of the snow. She's safe and dry, and she's going to make it to the ranch —"

*Alive.* The word hung in the air between them, and it took flight like a bird. Daisy felt it go. This night felt like a séance: She was calling up all sorts of creatures and ghosts, filling the air with them. Closing her eyes, she felt tears running down her cheeks. She heard birds' wings beating, and she moved to the window.

Outside, the night was full of yellow eyes. They peered from every branch, every fencepost. They crisscrossed the ranch, flying on their wild hunt. Owls had come down from their nests and burrows, scouring the snow-covered ranch land for mice. Daisy gasped. She stared out, wanting James to come look. But she couldn't speak.

"I'm going to say it again," he said, his voice breaking. "Leave, Daisy. Go home. I know you believe Sage is safe, and so do I. I have to. But what happens when she gets to the ranch? This is where things happen, not out there."

"We're here," Daisy whispered. "Her parents."

"What good did we do before?" James asked, like a man whose life was over, whose life had been over for a good long time.

"Our best," Daisy whispered back.

She turned to face James Tucker, and their eyes met and held. She watched his expression soften — his muscles were so taut, it looked unbearable. He had to let go, she knew. She wanted to help him, to rub his tense shoulders and back, to whisper the things she said to the bones. Daisy felt herself wanting to love him again, and that scared her even more than the hardness in his eyes. Instead, she pointed out the window, wanting him to see the owls.

But they were gone. The night was dark and empty; not a creature stirred. A wolf called from the hills. The cows were silent. The owls had disappeared, and Sage was nowhere in sight.

But the magic was still in Daisy's heart, and so was the hope. She closed her eyes, wishing that James would take her in his arms. Her heart was pounding, and her skin tingled. She needed comfort from her babies' father, but she didn't know how to ask. With James standing at her side, their arms close but not touching, Daisy's hands began to shake. The night was dark, and Sage was out there alone.

# Chapter Twenty

After the snow stopped, the stars came out. They showed through cloud scraps, sparks in the night. James sat on the fence rail, staring at the sky. The cows were just across the corral, so quiet he almost didn't know they were there. Night birds called, and owls flew low above the chaparral.

James felt torn down the middle. What was happening to him? Standing so close to Daisy, he'd had to hold himself back from holding her tight. She still smelled like lemon spice, her skin still glowed from within, she was still the same girl he'd fallen in love with long ago.

Especially there, in that little house. That was where they'd made love the first time, after days of kissing on the range and along the stream. He had been so crazy by then, so ready to undress her, touch her, ravage her, be part of her — the desire had come flooding back tonight.

But his mind knew better. James felt in his pocket for the charred Polaroids. He had almost shown them to Daisy, to shake some sense into her and chase her off the ranch. Didn't she understand that evil things happened in this world? After all this time, what did she tell herself about Jake? Whether accident of nature or malice of humans, it didn't matter: James didn't want it to happen again. He wanted Daisy and Sage far away from here.

That night, after he'd left Daisy alone in her cabin, he'd ridden the inner perimeter of the ranch — the fenced-in part around the houses. Looking for footprints — any prints that didn't belong — he had wanted to reassure himself that he was wrong. The pictures didn't mean someone was planning more harm to his family; Paul was right, they'd been taken by some tourist wanting souvenirs of Wyoming ranch land. Those tracks in the canyon had been brushed out by wind and blowing leaves.

He'd kept his eyes peeled, but he hadn't found anything. His chest hurt now, breathing in the cold air. He kept staring at the cabin, where he'd left Daisy an hour ago, and that wasn't doing him any good at all. Her lights were off, but he could see the fire glow. Candlelight flickered on the ceiling, driving him wild.

James jumped off the fence and headed up to the main house. He was ready to walk in, wake up his father, and show him the pictures, before he remembered Dalton was in the hospital. The roundup and weaning had kept James from going to see him — a little blessing, considering how much he hated the thought of seeing his father in the hospital.

So James went to wake up Paul. Told his wife it was an emergency, waited in their living room for Paul to get dressed. Glancing around the room, James realized he hadn't been inside the March house in years. It was smaller than he remembered, not much larger than the cabin where Daisy was staying. Long ago he had dropped the twins here for the Marches to baby-sit. Ancient history.

Pictures of the four March kids — born after Daisy had taken Sage back east — stood on top of the upright piano. James was staring at them when Paul finally came down.

"What's wrong?" Paul asked. "Is it Sage?"

"No," James said, taken aback by the question.

"Then what?"

"The pictures," James said. "Who'd take pictures of a bunch of cows?"

"Come on," Paul said. "Let's walk."

They went outside, and the clouds had cleared a little more. The moon had risen, cresting over the mountain. On their way across the yard, James laid out all his arguments for why the pictures were weird, why there was danger on the ranch. He wanted Daisy gone tomorrow.

"There's no danger," Paul said. "It's campers."

"She shouldn't be here," James said, glaring at the cottage.

"That's for her to decide."

James scowled, shaking his head.

"You want me to take your side," Paul said, grabbing his arm. "And I am. You just can't see it."

"My side?"

"I'm on your side, James. She's here because she needs something," Paul said. "Something she lost a long time ago."

"Something I took away," James said, thinking of Jake.

"No, you're wrong. You did nothing to hurt her or anyone. I was there, remember? You searched till . . ."

James hardly heard him anymore. An owl swooped down, feet thrust out, talons extended. It grabbed a gopher from the snow, flew off toward the moon. But James wasn't watching. All he could see was Daisy thirteen years ago, rolling in the dust where Jake had last been seen.

"Talk to her," Paul said gently. "She needs you while she waits for Sage to get here."

James closed his eyes.

"You're not listening to me, are you?"

"You make it sound like there's something I'm not doing for her," James said. He glanced at Daisy's cabin.

"Maybe there is."

"We're on our own now. You don't just undo divorce."

"Hey." Paul gave James a friendly chuck on the shoulder. "The next time you want to wake me up at midnight, at least pretend you care about my words of wisdom."

*Kids run away all the time,* Daisy had said.

"You okay?" Paul asked.

"My kid's on the way here," James said.

"Where do you think Sage is?" Paul looked

around as if he could actually see anything in the dark.

"That's what I'd like to know."

"Me, too," Paul said.

"Once we find her, Daisy can go."

"If you're from Wyoming," Sage said, "what are you doing driving through Nebraska?"

"If you're from Connecticut, what are *you* doing driving through Nebraska?" David retorted with a devilish grin. He lit a cigarette and threw the match out the window.

"I told you. I'm on my way —"

"To the Emerald City," David said.

"And you're the tin man." Sage was feeding one of the kittens as they drove along. "I'm going to look for a father, and you're going to look for a heart."

"You think I'm mean?"

"Only to me." Sage smiled. "By not telling me why you're driving through Nebraska."

"Okay, I'll tell you," David said. "I'm on a mission."

"Wow! Big revelation!" Sage said. "No kidding!"

"You figured that out?"

"Well, yeah!" Sage laughed. That kitten fed, she placed it on the seat between her and David. She let the next hungriest kitten scramble into her lap, start sucking air before it could get to the baby bottle nipple. "The fact you're a teenager and driving a car full of animals instead of going to school is a dead giveaway."

"How old do you think I am?" David asked.

"Seventeen? Sixteen?"

"Well, sixteen," he said. "But most people think I look a lot older."

"You look older," Sage said. "Slightly. Like seventeen."

David blew out a long, authoritative stream of smoke. "Slightly, no way. I get served in bars. I can buy . . . started driving when I was fourteen, and I never got stopped. I cruised right by troopers, and they never gave me a second look."

"Troopers? Where are they when people need them?" Sage said. "Nothing but crows and cornstalks and rusted-out cars and perverted insurance salesmen. I think you really are a tin man."

"Don't get disrespectful," David warned.

"It's your tattoos," Sage said. "They'd make anyone look older."

Sage's heart felt light. Joking with David made her feel better than she had in a long time. The snow was piled high along the sides of the road, the shorn-off cornstalks poking through, looking like stubble on a man's chin. The sight made Sage laugh harder, but when she told David, he just scowled.

"You're in a good mood today," he said.

"Getting closer to home."

"Right. The *ranch.*"

"I already know you're not going to kick me out," Sage said, "so quit putting down my dad."

"Whatever you say."

They drove along, stopping to let the dogs and kittens — and Sage — relieve themselves. None of the animals had ever seen snow before, and they stepped with caution and trepidation through the cold and fluffy substance under their paws. They all kept stopping to sniff every few feet.

"First snow," Sage said, making a snowball with her bare hands.

"First everything," David said. "You should have seen Gelsey the first time she set foot on solid ground. After living in a cage her whole life, when she got free she thought she was on another planet."

Sage watched the dogs walk along the road. They all had curved spines, bowed legs. Life in cages had crippled their bodies. When David said this was like another planet, Sage could only imagine their time without space and light. Sage loved how much David cared about them: He had called the Scottie "Gelsey" because it sounded Scottish, the spaniel "River" because the breed loved water.

"What happened to River's face?" Sage asked.

"She stopped breeding — wouldn't let the sire mount her. The owner got pissed and threw hot water at her. That's when I took her away."

"You put the bandages on?" Sage asked.

"Yeah."

"Tell me how you know where the puppy farms are."

"I have a list," David said. "The owners all know about each other. I took the list from my mother's desk."

"Is that your mission?"

"Let's drop it," David said.

Sage nodded. She was curious, she wanted to know, but she also wanted to maintain the good feeling she had inside. After being snowbound in a cow barn for ten hours straight, the fresh air made her feel free and light. She sensed David watching her.

"This time next year," David said, nodding toward Sage's belly, "it'll be first snow for him or her."

"Him," Sage said. "I'm having a boy, and I'm naming him Jake."

"When's he going to be born?"

"End of January," she said.

"Then he won't have to wait a whole year for his first snow."

"He'll see it in three months," Sage said.

David nodded. He threw his cigarette down; it burned a hole into the snow. The animals must have sensed that it was time to get in the car, because they all turned at once. Sage watched them bound back, thronging around David's feet as he opened the door. They weren't going to let him get out of their sight, not for a minute. Neither was Sage.

Louisa met Alma Jackson at the kitchen door and thanked her for driving all the way to the ranch in the snow.

"It was bad," Alma said woodenly.

Louisa didn't know quite how to respond to that.

"Well, I guess we could have postponed our meeting. Dalton's not even home!"

"Dalton?"

"Mr. Dalton Tucker. The man you'd be taking care of. Good care, from what your sister says."

"Well," Alma said, not corroborating the accolade one little bit. She licked her lips and looked around, seeming very nervous.

Louisa tried to smile at the woman standing before her, but her lips got stuck in a straight line. Could Alma have replied with one iota less enthusiasm? Was it possible that this little mouse could actually be related to Todd's Tammy — of the warm smile and twinkling eyes? Did she want the position or was she just wasting everyone's time?

"You have done home care before?" Louisa asked, getting down to business.

"Oh, yes."

"Why don't you tell me a little about your résumé?"

They sat at the kitchen table. Louisa gave Alma the hard once-over. She looked about forty, forty-one, with pasty-pale skin and a burnt-umber dye job: neither brown nor red, but somewhere in between — just a serviceable rinse to cover the gray. Didn't she have a husband, someone whose eye she wanted to catch and please? Alma mentioned working at hospitals in Laramie and Lander, rest homes in Cheyenne, Dubois, and Three Peaks. She listed six private home-owners she had cared for after strokes, heart attacks, a broken hip, and frostbite.

"So you see," she said, "I'm very qualified."

"You sure sound it," Louisa said, feeling somewhat reassured.

"Nice of Todd to recommend me." Alma looked around the kitchen. "This seems like a nice place to work."

"I drive my help hard," Louisa said. "Sorry to be so blunt, but that's how it'd be. I pay well, but I expect a lot."

"A lot?"

"Yes. I'm a roll-up-your-sleeves kind of person. If you're on my nickel, I want my money's worth. Besides which, you'll be taking care of my sweetheart. All the gold in Fort Knox wouldn't cover . . ." To her dismay, Louisa felt herself choking up. She couldn't express to this stranger or anyone else how she felt about Dalton.

Alma's eyes were oddly flat, but seeing Louisa's emotion, she reached over and patted Louisa's hand.

"It's very hard, in times of illness," she said. "When the people we love are laid low."

"It is," Louisa gasped. "Oh, it is."

"Tammy and Todd speak very highly of you."

Wiping her eyes, Louisa thanked her. They

discussed salary, and Alma's expression brightened when she heard the exact amount. Louisa said she'd want Alma to live in, for at least as long as it took Dalton to get on his feet. She might be very shy, Louisa thought. That could explain her initial dullness. Suddenly Alma seemed warm and friendly. Her dark eyes darted around the kitchen, taking everything in.

"You didn't mention any names I recognize," Louisa said. "I hope you won't mind, but I'd like to check your references. Nothing personal, of course —"

"I don't mind," Alma said quickly. "But I don't know many people around here. I'm from the other side of Dubois. I've hardly even been here to visit."

"Except to see your sister?"

"That's right," Alma said. "Tammy and Todd have such a nice house. It's a showplace, compared to my old . . . oh, never mind. I don't want to get complaining about my sorry old life. It's just fine, it really is."

"So, assuming your references check out, you'll take the job?"

"I will," Alma said, flashing the closest thing to a real smile Louisa had seen. They shook hands, and Louisa told her what the doctors had said: that Dalton could return home in a few days. He would need physical therapy, but Louisa had arranged for someone else to come in for that.

Outside, Daisy came loping into view. She sat

315

atop Scout, the old mare's gait livelier than Louisa had seen it in many years. Daisy's cheeks were rosy, her coppery hair streaming out in back. The snow was deep, but James had plowed out tracks and trails for riding.

Alma watched Daisy too, a slight frown on her face. "Does she live here?"

"She's visiting," Louisa said, not wanting to explain the relationships. It caused her embarrassment — pain — to have to say Daisy was Dalton's daughter-in-law but not her own. "Don't worry — your duties won't involve anything but taking care of Dalton. I'm not going to hire you for one thing and expect you to pitch in everywhere else."

"It's just, she looks familiar," Alma said.

Louisa didn't reply. There had been so much publicity back when Jake had disappeared. Maybe Alma recognized Daisy from the news accounts — the TV stations and newspapers had plastered her all over the airwaves and front pages. Thirteen years had passed, but Daisy looked pretty much the same — even the worry was the same, only now it was for Sage.

Daisy waved at the house, then cantered toward the barn. Alma watched her disappear inside; when she turned back to Louisa, her blank eyes flickered with something like worry. She said she had to leave, to get home and put her husband's supper on the table.

Louisa had said good-bye, grateful she didn't have a man in her life who'd make her worry like that. The strange thing was, she'd gotten the feeling that maybe Alma was having second thoughts. That if she could have, she would have withdrawn her offer to work on the DR Ranch, taking care of Dalton Tucker.

The most bizarre thing of all, Louisa thought as she watched Alma drive away, was that seeing Daisy had had something to do with it.

# Chapter Twenty-One

The snowstorm was followed by several days of brilliant sunshine, and by the time the doctors had okayed Dalton to continue his recuperation at home, the snow was melting away. James went with Louisa to drive him back. Picking her up at the main house, he saw Daisy standing on the front steps, waving as they pulled out. She was wearing tight blue jeans and a soft yellow sweater. Staring, James nearly drove the Suburban into a fencepost.

"It's sure nice having Daisy here again," Louisa said.

James fought to concentrate. A photographic image of Daisy waving, of her curves backlit by the morning sun, had imprinted itself onto the backs of James's eyelids.

"You're sure Dad's ready to come home?" he asked instead.

"Of course I'm sure. You think I'd bring him home if it was the wrong thing to do?"

"No, Louisa, I don't," James said, calmly.

"Well, thank you. My God —" she sputtered.

James couldn't help smiling. As much as she brought out the devil in him, he brought out the worst in her. They sped along the highway that

318

traversed a quarter of DR ranch land. The Wind River mountains rose to the west, snow-covered peaks soaring into the blue sky. He hoped Sage, wherever she was, was seeing this sunny day. It was a hundred percent better than picturing her in the storm.

Three times on the way, Louisa told him he'd have to take care of Dalton's paperwork. "I'm not authorized, you know," she said. "Only a wife or a family member is able to sign."

"What about Dad?" James asked finally, wondering what she was getting at. "He can sign for himself, can't he?"

"They're going to have him sedated for the ride home," Louisa said. "Maybe we should have hired an ambulance to drive him — I don't want him bouncing around back there."

"I'm driving my father home," James said.

Louisa sighed, but she didn't argue. She knew that James hardly ever left the ranch for any reason. A beer at the Stagecoach, a trip to the grain store — that was about it. But that morning, he and Paul had washed the big ranch wagon. They'd folded the back seats down, placed a thick bunk mattress in the cargo space. Daisy had brought out quilts and pillows. Making up the bed, her hand had brushed James's.

He wondered if maybe they were both thinking the same thing — about the time they'd taken the kids to the rodeo in Cheyenne. A whole caravan of ranch families had headed down for the two-day fair. They had camped out, barbecued together, watched Paul and James compete in the team roping event. Driving home, the twins had slept on a mattress in the back of the Ford wagon.

James had held Daisy's hand almost the whole way home to the ranch while she'd kept his trophy on her lap. Halfway there, just past midnight with a full moon painting the mountains and range with white light, James had stopped the car. He'd walked around the front, opened Daisy's door, lifted her in his arms. It was summertime, and the air was hot and dry. The land was bright as day under the moonlight, and he'd carried his wife through the sagebrush to a spot twenty yards from the car.

"We can't leave the kids," she'd whispered into his neck.

"We'll hear them if they wake up."

"And they'll hear us —"

"I'm the rodeo champion — I want my own way." James laughed, kissing her hard, sliding his hands down her full body.

"Then you'll get it —" Daisy said, undoing his big brass buckle. They pulled each other down on the ground, undressing each other as they went. The ground was hot and dry, but James had spread his shirt so Daisy wouldn't get dirty. Back then, the feeling for each other would be so wild and intense, they'd stop everything to be together. Her body was pearl-white in the moonlight, her nipples dark and sweet.

James tensed up, thinking about it now. The kids had been two at the time. They hadn't woken up. For the rest of the drive home, holding Daisy's hand with the windows open, James had smelled the musk of their bodies mingled with the spicy scent of sage swirling through the car. His thighs had ached, and all he'd been able to think about was loving her again the minute they got home.

He still couldn't look at that old rodeo trophy — a gold-plated cowboy on a rearing horse — without remembering the burn in his thighs, the smell of that night, Daisy's eyes full of mischief in the moonlight.

"You sign your father out," Louisa directed now, as they pulled into the hospital lot. "And I'll make sure he's ready."

"Whatever you say." James wanted to get home fast. He wanted his father safely installed in bed, and he wanted to be there with Daisy, in case . . . He heard Louisa's bitterness, her unspoken gripe about being Dalton's mistress and not his wife, but James had never considered that his problem. He'd let his feelings be known long ago, when he was just a boy missing his mother. Dalton was his own man; he'd had decades to propose if he wanted to. Shaking off Louisa's guilt trip, James went into the office.

Finally — papers filled out and Dalton in a wheelchair — they were ready to go. Louisa held Dalton's hand while James pushed the chair. He was shocked by his father's pallor, by the fact he'd lost so much weight. When Dalton talked, his voice sounded light and weak.

"What a good son," Dalton said. "Coming all this way to drive me home."

"I felt bad, not visiting you," James said. "But —"

"I know, I know," his father said. "You had the roundup, and you wanted to keep an eye out for Sage."

Louisa let out a huge exhalation, and she dropped Dalton's hand.

"Louisa!" Dalton called, but she didn't turn around. "What's she mad about?" he asked James.

"I don't know," James said.

"Louisa . . ."

She just walked faster. James couldn't imagine what was eating her — getting temperamental at a time like this. James watched her walk ahead, arms held tight around her chest as if she might fall apart. Dalton's head nodded from side to side — the effort of transport from hospital to car, coupled with Louisa's bad mood, too much for him.

With the back cargo doors open, James bent down. He had never done this before — picked his father up. Slinging Dalton's arm around his neck, he slid his arms under the old man. Dalton rested his head against James's, and for a second James went back to the days with his son. Jake had done the same thing — touched his temple against James's when James would pick him up.

"Ready?" James asked. "I don't want to hurt you."

"Don't worry," Dalton said weakly.

Carefully, James transferred his father from the chair to the mattress. Dalton clenched his teeth, but he didn't cry out. As James covered him with the quilts Daisy had supplied, Dalton's face was pale and set. By the time they hit the highway, he was asleep. Driving, James kept quiet as long as he could. He looked across the front seat, saw Louisa fixing her hair with a comb.

"What was that about back there?" James asked. "In the parking lot?"

"Nothing," Louisa said.

"Didn't look like nothing. What were you thinking of, getting him upset when he has this ride ahead of him?"

"Getting him upset . . ." she began.

"Yeah. What were you —"

"Do you ever think, James, that I might be upset?"

"He's the one coming home from the hospital —"

"He's the one, she's the one." Louisa tried to laugh, but her voice was full of tears. "That's how you think, isn't it?"

James just gripped the steering wheel, not hearing anything she had to say right then.

"In families, there is no 'he's the one,' " Louisa said. "When one person suffers, everyone does. Your father's pain is my pain."

"I never doubt that you care about him."

"No, you just doubt that I'm good enough to be his wife. And now, with the Alzheimer's, he's started forgetting who I am. Forgets my name and thinks your mother's still alive. Think that doesn't hurt me?"

"He does?" James asked with a start.

"Just sometimes. Recently. He knows I'm his sweet Louisa. In his heart he does and always will."

James glanced in the rearview mirror. His father lay flat on his back, the white quilt pulled up to his chin. He hadn't moved, and for an instant the quilt looked like a blanket of snow. James remembered the snow falling on his mother's body as he tried to pull her out. So many years ago: It surprised him to hear what Louisa was saying.

"He calls you by my mother's name?" James asked.

"Yes, he does. Once in a while. But you don't want to hear what I have to say, do you?"

"Tell me," James said, trying to be patient. "I'll give it my best shot."

"He's the one coming home from the hospital," Louisa said, "but it affects me, too. I love him."

"I know."

"I have to watch him learn to walk all over again. I have to open our home to a live-in aide, get used to a stranger at our breakfast table. When I sing at the Stagecoach —" She twisted the handkerchief into a tight ball. "I have to get used to him not being there. I want his arms around me. James . . . I still want him so much!"

"I'm sorry," James said, shocked by the force of emotion.

"Old age can go to hell!" Louisa shouted.

"Rrrrr . . ." Dalton mumbled in his sleep.

"You're not old," James said.

"I'm old enough to know more than you do," Louisa said. "So listen, and listen good. Get it the hell out of your head, this business about 'my part and your part, I'm the one and you're the one.' "

"You mean with —"

"With Daisy! You're *both* the one — you loved your babies and she loved your babies. You're worried sick about Sage and *she's* worried sick about Sage. For right now, till that girl gets herself home safe, you and Daisy are family. You're in this together."

James held the wheel. He wanted to snap, to tell Louisa to stay out of it, to tell her about the mutilated cattle, the pictures — he was trying to protect Daisy and Sage, the same as he'd always wanted to do. But she just kept talking.

"You don't know the first thing about staying together."

"I *what?*"

"You blew your own world apart. After Jake got lost."

"You don't know what you're talking about."

"You felt unworthy," Louisa said, suddenly

325

sounding exhausted. "I saw it — we all did. You thought you lost your son, you might as well drive off your whole family. But there wasn't any talking to you then. You were determined to bear the whole weight yourself."

"Jesus Christ —" James muttered, glaring at the road.

"And the weight wasn't all yours to bear," Louisa finished.

She didn't say anything more. The land slid by, snow-covered peaks and pastures melting down to rocks and mud. James looked up at the blue sky, saw a flock of geese coming down to land. They angled down, an arrow pointed at the earth. James saw the lake, wide and blue. A thin layer of ice had formed, but the lead goose broke through with his landing; the others followed safely behind.

"Rosalind . . ." Dalton called from the backseat.

James glanced across at Louisa, to see what she would do. An hour ago, he might have felt happy to hear his father say his mother's name. But right now, he felt sorry for the woman sitting beside him.

"Rosalind . . ." his father said again, his frail voice plaintive and afraid.

Louisa half turned in her seat. Then, unbuckling her seat belt, she got up on her knees and reached back to take Dalton's hand.

"I'm right here, darling," she whispered. "Don't you fear — I'm with you all the way."

James watched the geese in the lake as long as he could. Then, both eyes on the road, he drove his father and Louisa due south, straight home to the DR Ranch.

David and Sage had run out of money, so they stopped at a truck stop in the middle of nowhere and signed on to wash dishes for a few nights. In return, they got minimum wage, plus lodging in a ramshackle bunkhouse out back. Sage was amazed by the fact that no one asked questions: They didn't have to give their names, addresses, or Social Security numbers. They were just shown the kitchen and told not to break any-thing.

While David scrubbed the big roasting pans, Sage loaded plates and glasses into the dish-washer. She was glad to stop moving for a little while. Wearing an apron, she pretended she was the mother and she was cleaning up after a very big family. She imagined it was a holiday — Thanksgiving, maybe — and she had just cooked a turkey for Ben, their son, her brother Jake, her parents, and Aunt Hathaway.

That made her homesick, more than she'd felt since leaving Silver Bay. A telephone hung on the wall, and every time she went near it to grab another stack of dirty dishes, she felt a pang in her heart. She hadn't called home once. Thinking of it hurt too much; she'd hear her mother's voice and go to pieces. Her mother would talk her into flying back east, and she'd never get to see her father. Sage would miss her chance to get to know the man who'd given her life.

"What's your dad like?" she asked David.

"He's nice," David said. "He has a nice twinkle in his eye, and he spends his days petting the dogs and smoking a pipe. I love him a lot."

"You do?" Sage asked, beaming.

"No."

Sage's heart fell. She never knew when David was kidding her. When it came to his home and family, it was best to assume that when he said something good, he was being sarcastic. But Sage wanted to know the truth.

"I mean it — what's he like?"

"I hope your kid has a good father," David said. "Because I hate mine. Is that what you want to hear?"

"I don't *want* to hear it," Sage said kindly, "because why would I want that for you? But tell me more. I'm all ears."

"No. Why don't you tell me more?" David asked, using steel wool with all his might to scrub black stuff off the broiler pan. "Tell me about your two wonderful parents, one east and the other west. If they're so fantastic, why don't they live together?"

"Because my brother died," Sage said. "And they couldn't take it. It broke them up."

"Your brother died?"

"Yes. My twin. We were three. His name was Jake."

"Like your baby —"

"Yes. I'm naming my son after my brother. His father said I could. Ben. My son's father's name is Ben."

"What if the kid's a girl?"

"I might name her Jake, too. I like the name. I loved my brother. We never wanted to be apart. Sisters share rooms, right? Well, I wanted to share a *bed* with him — I mean it. We were buddies, buddies, buddies. Do you —"

"Have any brothers?" David asked. "Yeah, one. But I don't want to talk about it, okay? Let's just wash these dishes and get paid so we can feed the animals. They're probably wondering where we are by now. Besides, I want to leave tonight."

"Tonight? I thought we told the manager tomorrow —"

"As soon as we're done with these," David said. "There's something we have to do."

Sage nodded. She had saved some scraps of roast beef for Petal, Gelsey, and River. She wondered why David refused to talk about home, but she wasn't mad. People sometimes kept a lot inside — that's what her mother used to say about her father. You couldn't make someone talk before he was ready — but you could be patient and keep listening. You never knew what you might hear.

And she wondered what he had planned for later.

He had a list. He had things to do, items to

buy. Still, he kept watch for the girl. Her family was ready for her, making everything nice. Just the way a family should be: sticking together, looking after each other. He watched her mother pace the small white house; he watched her father ride the range waiting for her to arrive.

It had never been like that for him.

*Home.* What a place.

There had never been people waiting, keeping the home fires burning. He had known yelling and silence — one or the other. Rarely laughter, hardly ever warmth. Not that he held a grudge. The adults had certainly had their worries. It was hard to raise kids right when you had to worry about the roof leaking and cupboards being bare and heat being turned off.

Cattle ranchers: They were the ones with happy families. They were the ones with new shingles and full pantries and hot water. Their children had new toys to play with and horses to ride. When their children cut themselves, their mothers put on Band-Aids. They wouldn't make their kids take care of their own wounds.

The Guardian's scar itched. Sticking his hand down the back of his jeans, he felt it with his fingertips. Raised and half-round, like a length of wire, it ran across his left buttock and down his thigh. The touch of it made tears fill his eyes. He thought of scrambling over that fence when he was little, catching his butt on that rusty nail.

The scar no longer hurt — it hadn't for years. But just the same, scratching it with dirty fingernails, he gulped back sobs as tears rolled down his cheeks. He thought of how alone a person could be — a little boy, a grown man, it didn't matter. Being abandoned felt the same no matter how old you were. And someone could be abandoned even when there were people all around.

He cried in the snow, because he was alone, and he always had been.

# Chapter Twenty-Two

Sunlight poured through the cottage windows. Finishing her latest round of calls to police departments, Daisy sat back in the rocking chair and wondered what to do next. Suddenly she heard a whistle. Opening the door, she found James on his horse, leading Scout by the reins.

"Come on," he said. "Get your boots on."

Daisy hesitated, thinking of all the reasons why she shouldn't go, each one better than the other. But James was smiling, an honest smile so full of hope it made her think of that young cowboy who'd asked her to come stay in a cabin on his ranch.

"I'll be right there," she said. Running inside, she pulled on her boots and jacket and grabbed sunglasses, because the snow still on the ground made the sunlight seem twice as bright.

James climbed down to help her mount. First, he put a white hat on her head: *her* hat. It was dusty with age — more gray than the pure white it once had been: the old Stetson he'd bought her that first year on the ranch. She had left it hanging on a hook in the front hall, and she felt surprised — touched — that he'd kept it all this time.

"You'll need to keep the sun out of your eyes" was all he said.

"Thank you" was all Daisy said back.

She stuck one foot in the stirrups, and James gave her a leg-up. Scout whinnied and pranced in place. Stroking the horse's neck, Daisy leaned over to whisper in her ear. Then James was atop Chieftain, and they headed out.

Daisy rode about ten yards behind. She knew these trails by heart, and she concentrated on their beauty, instead of thinking about why they were doing this. The questions came through anyway: Why had James asked her to go riding? Why had she said yes? Daisy pushed them back by staring at the full sweep of mountains and sky, the jagged peaks and endless blue.

Riding along the stream, she saw pines and junipers sending their roots straight into the rocks above the water. The creek tumbled over a small chute, spraying rainbows into the air. Golden grasses poked through the melting snow, waving in the breeze. Feeling warm in the sunlight, Daisy unbuttoned her jacket.

They passed beneath the Rydell Cliffs, so named because supposedly James's grandfather had driven an entire herd of the Rydells' sheep to their deaths from the range five hundred feet up. Daisy believed the legend; she used to come out here to find bones to use in her work. She had never liked imagining her husband's ancestors acting with such cruelty, and she nudged Scout now, urging her into a canter.

James kicked the black horse to keep up, and they rode through open meadows toward Daisy's favorite trail. With Scout beneath her, drinking the wind, Daisy felt her worries slip away. This was how it was to ride, the part she had loved most about living in the West: the way space would surround her and pull the thoughts from her head. Her mind dissolved in nature and the wind.

They came to a clump of aspen, and James and his horse began to climb.

"That way?" Daisy asked, surprised. Their usual route took them farther along the trail, into the mountains through the red rock canyons. James began to answer, but just as quickly Daisy realized what he was doing: He didn't want to take her past the place where Jake had disappeared. She just nodded and kept following.

A huge cottonwood had fallen across the trail, dead leaves clinging to the branches. Years ago Daisy would have jumped it, but today she rode Scout the long way around. Hanging back, she watched James take the stallion over. Their bodies taut, his arms and the horse's legs extended, Daisy knew she would have to carve that image someday.

James turned, the shadows of some aspen leaves falling across his face. They looked like the circle-dot pattern some shamans tattooed across their cheeks and foreheads to represent supernatural vision. Daisy squinted, but then James passed into full sunlight and the shadows disappeared.

"What is it?" he asked, riding closer.

"I just — never mind," she said.

"You look upset."

"The shadows on your face — they made me think of Louis . . . Is he still alive?"

"No," James said. "He died last winter."

Daisy nodded. It made her sad; she hadn't heard. Louis had been a shaman, and he had believed in the cycles of nature, that burial illuminates a person's life and brings him into contact with the spirits of those he loved. He had befriended Daisy even before Jake . . . he had helped her find the spirits in bones and feathers. *In death, we are given ever-seeing eyes,* he had told her.

James gave her a long look, as if to make sure she was all right to continue. She nodded, and they turned back to the trail. Sunlight blazed off the melting snow, as they climbed higher. At one point James began to ride slower. And slower still, until they were side by side along the gradually climbing trail.

"I don't know this way," Daisy said. "I don't think we ever rode here together."

"We've had some trespassers down back: I want to keep away from there . . . and anyway, I want to show you something new."

Daisy nodded. The mountain scenery was wild and romantic, with odd-shaped peaks jutting into the sky, but she couldn't see it. Hearing about Louis had thrown her. She couldn't stop thinking of him; he had tried to give her peace, spiritual guidance, during the time of Jake.

James's knee brushed hers as the horses rode side by side, and she tried to block the electricity from passing through her body. They bumped again, and the contact felt so intense, she nearly fell off her horse. She couldn't think; she was all emotion and instinct right now.

Riding Scout had always had a strange effect on Daisy. It turned her primitive. All the "shoulds," "shouldn'ts," and "what-ifs" went straight out of her head. There was something about being borne by a big, warm creature up a craggy and dangerous mountain trail, being filled with the smells of sage, pine, and wind, that stripped away one thousand years of civilization.

So when James reached across the space between them to take her hand, Daisy turned into a molten river and just about poured herself all over the rock-strewn ground. His hand felt so familiar — so lean and rough and scarred. She pulled her hand away. Daisy wanted to scream: *Why?* Why had all of it — any of it — happened? Why had he abandoned her and Sage?

They moved apart, scrambling up a particularly steep part of the trail. Daisy heard the rushing water before they rounded the bend. Gnarled cedars clung to the rocks, and through their sharp needles, she saw the slender column of water pouring down. Her throat began to ache, and it spread to her heart.

Rounding the bend, they scared a pair of bison. Daisy watched them bound off the purple rock ledge and disappear into a cleft. A golden eagle had made its nest on the cliff face across the chasm; Daisy knew this was the source of some river, one of the best hunting grounds around. The eagle glared with yellow eyes, then soared in a free fall into the treetops.

Climbing off Scout, Daisy pulled herself up the rock chimney. James had gone before her, and he turned to offer a hand. Hardly winded, Daisy let him pull her up. Her heart was pounding, and she was afraid to look — not from vertigo or fear of falling, but of what she felt inside. The water flowed clear at her feet, so cold and transparent she could see every stone and twig on the pool's bottom.

The clear waters gathered here, one last moment of serenity. Then they plunged over the precipice, three hundred feet down in water as white as snow. The red rocks were nearly vertical, and the mist rising a hundred feet from the foot was flecked with pink.

Daisy stared down, inching toward the edge. Her boot slipped, and she steadied herself by grabbing a juniper whose roots were growing straight into the rocks. She must have gotten too close, because she felt James's arms come around her from behind. Her face was wet, from her own tears and not the spray.

"Washakie," she said.

"Why do you say that now?"

337

"Remember how we taught the kids to say his name?" she asked, as if she hadn't heard him.

"I remember."

Daisy closed her eyes. She could see her children staring up at her, holding hands, trying to pronounce the chief's name. But they had done it easily, as if the spirit had come over them: "Washakie. Washakie." She could hear them both, Sage and Jake.

"You're crying," he said, nearly touching her face. "I thought you'd think the falls were beautiful."

"They make me think of things I've lost," she said, her voice thick.

"Sage'll be here — don't give up on her."

"I never will."

"Any day now, she'll come —"

"She's been pining for you every day," Daisy said. "She's needed you all this time . . . I couldn't let her go!"

"I'm sorry," James said. "I wish —"

"And I'm so worried," Daisy said, the words rushing out, spilling over James's.

"She's strong, she'll be —"

"She's pregnant!" Daisy said.

"Pregnant?" James asked, shocked. His face went pure white, and he backed away from the falls. "She's only sixteen —"

"Sixteen," Daisy said, "is old enough."

They stood there saying nothing, just listening to the falls roar at their feet. Daisy looked up and saw the shock and sickness in James's eyes.

"I was never there to protect her," he said.

"She needed you —" Daisy said, swallowing hard. He was asking, and she wanted to tell him. All the sleepless nights she and Sage had had — Sage crying for her father and Daisy hurting for Sage. The waterfall sounded like rage: crashing, anguish, destruction.

"Did I ruin her life?"

"I don't . . ." Daisy began, biting down on the words.

"Did I, Daisy? Tell me —"

"I don't know yet!" she screamed. "She's not here! I don't know if she's coming back!"

"It's my fault," he said. "It is. I know —"

"Tell me why you never saw her," Daisy said. "Not once, not one single time, in all these years."

"I can't."

"You can't tell me?"

His face turned hard again. The lines were deep around his sage-colored eyes, and Daisy could see how much he had invested in aloneness, in keeping it all inside, in never letting another person in. She had long ago stopped wanting to shake it out of him, but the old feeling came back again.

"Tell me!" she screamed. "I'm her mother — I deserve an explanation!"

He grabbed her arms and held her so tight she felt her bones bruise. She didn't care. His eyes were full of hate, and for a minute, she thought he was going to throw her over the falls.

"I stayed," he said through gritted teeth, "to kill whoever it was that took our son."

"Kill?"

"Kill, Daisy. Tear him apart."

"But we don't know —"

"I know," James said.

"You can't! The police never said anyone — there weren't any clues — he just disappeared. James! He must have died — that's what happened — he just —"

"We never found his body," James yelled, without loosening his grip on her arms. "We never found him to bury!" She was too frozen to break away. The look in James's eyes was intense, passionate, and borderline crazy.

She nodded, finally understanding exactly what he was feeling. The tears ran down her face for the only bones that really mattered, the lost body of her three-year-old son. She had heard James's reason before — that he had stayed on the ranch for Jake. Before, it had seemed like an excuse. Standing here, a mile from where he'd disappeared, it seemed like a good idea.

Daisy felt a strange sense of peace and forgiveness come over her. Her eyes must have softened, because something happened to James. He was tall and lean, nearly a foot taller than Daisy. But suddenly he let go of her arms and he bowed his head level with her shoulder.

They stared together at the calm water pouring itself into tumult, and Daisy let James spin her around and hold her tight. Her face was

340

crushed against his shirt, and his arms felt like iron bands around her back. They had made two children together, and both of them were lost. When she glanced up, she could see that his face was crumpled, and tears were pouring from his eyes.

"I'm sorry, Daisy," he said, the words cracking and ripping from his throat. "You should have both your children — there was nothing I could do."

"I never thought there was," Daisy cried, clutching him. "I never did!"

"They're gone," James said, wild with disbelief.

The water fell at their feet, pulling everything out of them, taking it all away. A gold leaf swirled in the current, then disappeared over the side. Daisy heard the roar, and she knew it was the sound of sorrow.

Grieving is a learned skill; she and James had not been taught it. They both knew the dark place where prayer couldn't enter or help. Clinging to each other at the water's edge, the parents of Sage and Jake Tucker did what they had never done before. They cried together for what they had lost, what had been taken from them: their chance to be a family. Standing there for a long time, until the eagle returned to its nest and mistook them for a tree, the Tuckers held on.

Paul March met James in the barn. He had a handful of papers in his hand, feed and maintenance bills with checks to be signed. James had just finished putting the horses away and was filling the troughs with water.

"Have a good ride?" Paul asked.

"Yep."

"Where'd you go?"

"To see the headwaters."

"Solstice Falls?"

James nodded, not really wanting to talk about it. His mind hadn't yet made sense of what had just happened between him and Daisy — he wasn't sure it ever would. He still felt the imprint of her head against his chest; it burned like a scrape or bruise. The ranch odors were strong, but all he could smell was Daisy's perfume. His eyes burned from the tears he'd shed. The knot in his chest was smaller than it had been in years. And his daughter was pregnant —

"I thought you were worried," Paul said, handing him a pen and the first check. "About intruders on the ranch — I'm surprised you took her out riding. I thought you wanted her to leave."

"I took her away from the canyons," James said. He looked down, signing his name on a check to Thompson & Sons Saddlery.

"Where the bad guys are?"

James heard Paul wanting to joke around. His time with Daisy felt dead serious and raw. He wasn't in the mood for this, for talking to anyone.

"Don't push it," James said very quietly.

"I'm just glad you took her out." Paul smiled. "It's good for both of you."

"Thanks. What else do you want me to sign?" James asked.

Paul handed him the sheaf of papers. This had been their way for years: Paul would catch James when he could — on the run, in the barn, by the corrals — and get him to take care of business. Paul was an efficient foreman. James hated paperwork, and neither man liked desks or offices. When James finished, he sensed Paul wanting to say something else.

"What is it?" James asked. "What's going on?"

"Just —" Paul began. Eyes narrowed, he looked like a man trying to solve a crime. His brain seemed to be working overtime, trying to figure James out. Maybe he wanted to be a friend, more likely he wanted to offer advice — something about him and Daisy, probably. James wasn't going to hear it.

"Leave it," James said. "Just leave it for tonight."

Paul hesitated, frowning, but he nodded. Taking the papers, he walked away. And James drifted over to the barn door and stared across the darkening fields at Daisy's house. Then he grabbed the door handles and shut the barn up tight.

By nightfall, David and Sage had left the main highway. The old black car was bouncing along a rutted farm road, with Sage reading a map by flashlight. David had made an X on the map, but wouldn't tell her where they were going. The closer they got to the X the angrier his face got.

Without warning, he stopped the car and went to the trunk. The animals whimpered with anxiety. Sage turned in her seat, trying to see what he was doing. She heard a bag being unzipped, and she saw the glow of a light as things rustled mysteriously. He was back there a long time — at least fifteen minutes. When he got into the car, he kept his head averted, as if he didn't want her to see his face.

"I'm not going to navigate if you won't talk to me," she said.

"Don't be a jerk," he snapped.

"I'm not. You are. Is this the mission? Is that what we're doing tonight?"

"Sage —"

She flipped the switch, flashed the light directly in his face. What she saw made her gasp. He had drawn all over his face: seven black dots in a line across his cheeks, concentric circles and dots on his forehead and chin, four thin black lines streaking down his neck. The markings looked like tattoos.

"David, what are you doing?" she asked.

"It's the tradition," he said. His voice sounded odd, as if it wasn't his own. Wind blew outside, making dry leaves scuttle along the road. Sage's hair rose on her head and the back of her neck.

"What tradition?" she whispered.

"Do you know about messengers between

realms?" he asked.

She started to shake her head, but for some reason she stopped. Her mother talked about such things: When she carved bones, she imagined calling forth spirits of the dead. Lambs, birds, cows, deer. Fingers trembling, Sage reached into her blouse and felt for her two-sided amulet. She felt the back-to-back faces, the boy and the girl, the twins.

"Yes," she said.

"Do you know what these dots mean?" he asked, pointing to his cheeks.

Sage shook her head.

"Savings," he said.

"Savings?"

"Each time I've been able to save things. One of the dots is you."

Reaching out, Sage touched David's face with her index finger. She traced the dots across his cheeks, counting them as she went: one-two-three-four-five-six-seven. This was the most bizarre experience of her life, yet she somehow understood and wasn't afraid. She was the seventh dot, David's seventh saving. Without being told, she knew what the other six represented.

"We're going to a puppy farm, aren't we?" she asked.

"Yes."

"Can I come in with you?"

David hesitated. He started up the car again, so he wouldn't have to answer right away. Sage held all six kittens on her lap, curled into sleeping balls. The dogs lay still in the backseat, and the only sound was Petal licking her ragged toy.

They drove for half an hour more. The road was straight, and it ran due north. Shadows rose in the west, blocking the stars, and Sage knew they were the foothills of a mountain range. It looked like a long, shallow, black hole in the bottom of the sky. She heard an explosion of air and realized it had come from her: She'd been holding her breath.

A cluster of lights showed up ahead. David turned off the headlights and checked the map, holding the flashlight close to the paper so no one outside the car could see. He slid a battered hacksaw from under the seat and turned to Sage.

"You can come," he said.

"Thank you," she said, suddenly unsure of whether she really wanted to.

"But you have to wear something if you do."

"What?"

"The owl," he said.

Sage cocked her head. What was he talking about: wear an owl? Opening the glove compartment, he pulled out a small leather case. The light was so dim, she could barely see. He told her to turn on the flashlight and hold it very close. She saw a case of needles, thread, and ink. Her heart pounding, she watched him extract colored pens. He took hold of her right hand.

"Where did you get your tattoos?" she asked in a high voice.

"I do them myself."

"Is that — is that what you want to do to me?" she asked, trying to pull back her hand.

"Not tonight," he said. "Not ever, unless you want me to."

He licked the tip of the brown pen, and very gently he licked the back of her right hand. His tongue felt soft and warm, and Sage closed her eyes, wishing he wouldn't stop. But he did, and he started to draw. The pen point was fine, and it tickled. He seemed to be drawing each individual feather.

"Why an owl?" she asked. "What does it mean?"

"It sees."

Changing pens, he took out a bright yellow one and drew two piercing eyes. When he was done, Sage had an owl on her hand. It was perfect, tiny, and fierce, exactly like the one on David's wrist. Staring at it, Sage felt braver than she thought possible. It seemed like magic, just like wearing her mother's jewelry. Although she never took it off, she found herself pulling her necklace from around her neck. Her heart was pounding; her hands moving almost by themselves, she handed the pendant to David.

He peered at the carved bone, turning it over and over in his hand. Nodding, he seemed to accept its power. He touched the faces to his forehead, then to his heart, then to the knife he carried in his pocket.

"Who made this?" he asked.

"My mother."

"Is she Shoshone?"

"No, are you?"

"Maybe." He grinned. "Or maybe I'm a wolf. Ready?"

Sage reached for her necklace, but he held on as if he wanted to keep it. "Don't you want to know who the faces are?" she asked. "It's the only two-sided one she's ever made."

"I know who they are," he said. "They're you and your brother. Come on. Let's go." He handed it back to her.

Sage took a deep breath. She felt like saying a prayer, chanting a spell, somehow blessing her, the baby, David, and all the animals. No words seemed right — nothing that made any sense, anyway — she tried to remember the word her mother used to say, the Indian name that meant bravery. It was too elusive, like a feather in the wind, so she just crossed her fingers instead.

There seemed to be two farms on either side of the dirt road. One looked bigger than the other, with a tidy white farmhouse, a red barn, and a silver silo. The other farm had an old brown house, a brown truck, and several brown sheds. Sage could hear barking, and the closer they got, the louder it sounded.

David crept low to the ground, like an Indian brave. He held Sage's hand for a while, but then he dropped it and began to run ahead. She had a stitch in her side, and she needed to stop and rest. Circling back, he looked furious.

"What's the matter?"

"I'm out of breath," she said, feeling her baby change position. She supported his weight with her hands, wishing he'd keep away from her bladder.

"Do you want to wait here? We have to be ready to run fast when we finish inside."

"Can't you tell me what we're going to do? So I can be prepared? I'm wearing the owl —"

David paused. She couldn't see his face in the dark, but she sensed that it was grave and unsmiling. "Then you already know," he said.

They moved on. The house was nearly all dark — except for a dim light in the kitchen and a blue glow from the TV room. A tilting, peeling sign by the road showed a picture of a hunting dog proudly pointing at a dead pheasant. "Purebred English Setters," the writing said.

Now, from inside the house, Sage heard yelling. A woman's voice raised in anger, and a man's voice in response. Some kid was crying, and another joined in. She heard a smack, then a door being slammed, then silence. The barking went on in the shed, as loud as ever.

"They're sick fuckers," David whispered.

"The English setters —" Sage said, pulling toward the house. She wanted to rescue whoever had just gotten hit.

"No, the people. All the puppy farm owners are the same. Exactly the same — nightmares. They beat their wives and they both beat the kids. This is how they spend their nights. It's no big deal. Come on . . ."

"No big deal . . ." Sage gulped, staring up at a second-floor window where a light had just gone on. The curtains glowed from within — they were pink, and a young girl's sobbing could be heard through the glass. Through a space in the curtains, Sage could see a poster of Ariel, the Little Mermaid.

"He hits her, and he probably fucks her, too," David said, glaring. He pulled Sage's arm, and she turned to follow him. They plodded through a muddy yard. David whispered, "Don't worry about stepping in dog shit — they're not allowed out."

"Never?" she asked.

"Never."

David had stuck the hacksaw in his belt like a sword, and he removed it now and sawed off the flimsy lock. Gingerly, he opened the creaking shed door. Sage slipped in behind him. The space was pitch-black and very cold: She couldn't see a thing except for clouds of breath in front of her face. The dogs had been yelping; smelling humans, they yelped a little louder. David disappeared. Sage felt petrified, as if she was standing in a dark cave all alone. But then, as her eyes grew accustomed to the darkness, she began to see.

The shed was about fifteen by thirty feet. Cages lined the long wall, two high. Each cage was made of wood and wire mesh, about two feet square. David moved methodically along the wall, opening all the doors. He had his flashlight out, his bandaged hand hooding the beam as he trained it into each cage.

Sage went to be beside him. She saw the dogs cowering against the back walls. Although they were long of bone, they were curled into snail-like balls. Some had puppies nursing on their teats. The stench of excrement was strong, and Sage held her forearm over her mouth and nose. Some cages contained mother dogs and several dead puppies. No one had bothered to remove them.

"Poor things," Sage said, reaching in to pet one trembling dog.

The dog bared her teeth and snapped.

Sage stepped back. She tripped over something and fell backward into a pile of fur. It was cold, and it smelled horrible, and when David reached down to pull her out, she realized she had fallen into a heap of dead dogs.

"Oh, no," she cried.

"Sssh," David said, moving. "Be quiet."

Trembling, Sage watched him. He was looking for something, going up and down the row again and again. Some of the dogs had started to creep forward. The bravest ones stuck their noses out, sniffed the air outside. They jumped down, trying to straighten out their backs and legs — perhaps for the first time in their lives. Sage watched them try out their legs, taking steps like new colts.

David was going to set them all free.

"You can't," Sage said, grabbing his arm. "Where will they go? What will they eat?"

"They're hunters," David said. "They'll survive."

"They don't know how," Sage said. "They'll die!"

"You think that's as bad as this?" he asked, his voice as much a snarl as any animal's.

Sage looked around. Very slowly, one by one, the dogs had all hopped free of their cages. Many of them had dragged their puppies out, one at a time, holding them in their mouths the way Petal carried her toy. Others had abandoned their litters, and when Sage checked, she saw that most of those babies were already dead.

One wasn't. He stood on four solid feet, wagging his tail as Sage bent down to see. He was no bigger than her hand, with brown-and-white spots and a friendly red tongue. "Hi," she whispered.

He yapped at her, hopping friskily.

"Here you are," David said from a cage at the far end of the row. "I've been looking for you."

With all the dogs free, the barking had just about stopped. The silence was deafening, more frightening than anything Sage could think of — it would bring the farmer very soon.

Sage stared at the tiny puppy. She counted to three, then stuck him in her pocket. "Hurry," she said to David, but he was one step ahead of her. She saw him wrapping his jacket around the dog in the cage, lifting her into his arms, heading for the door and easing it open. Across the driveway, the yelling had started again. Sage heard banging, and someone crying hysterically. She watched as David pulled his knife, went to the brown truck, and slashed all four tires.

The dogs slipped out the open door. Some of them stopped to sniff the grass, but most of them limped for the hills — puppies in their mouths. They didn't stop for anything, didn't even slow down. Their legs were bowed, their gaits were crooked and crippled, but their desire to escape was great.

"Come on," David said, carrying his bundle up the road.

Sage hung back. She had the owl on her hand, helping her to see souls in all worlds. Her vision intensified, and she could almost see through the farmhouse walls. The young girl was huddled on her bed, hiding from her father's blows. Sage and David were saving things: Why couldn't they save her?

"Can't we help? Can't we take her with us?" Sage implored.

"No. Come on."

"Please, David —"

"Our mission is the dogs," he said. "She has to save herself."

"But what if she can't?"

"She can," he said sharply. "I know from experience. Hurry."

By the time they got to the car, the farmer had

353

noticed the silence. The porch lights blared on, and the screen door slammed. David didn't even take time to place the dog — wrapped in his jacket — in the backseat. Starting up the engine, he kept her on his lap. He turned the car around and pointed it down the road. Then he waited.

The farmer was yelling for his family to come outside and catch the dogs. His wife came running out, followed by two children. Sage saw the girl standing on the porch, and, petting the puppy in her pocket she felt a lump in her throat imagining the girl was glad that the mothers were free. David thrust the dog onto Sage's lap and threw open his door. He leaned on the horn.

"Hey," he shouted. "Asshole!"

"What? Did you steal my dogs?" the farmer screamed, running for his truck. "I'll kill you —"

"You're gonna burn in hell," David yelled. "You're gonna go to a place where the animals are cruel to you. Your kids are gonna hate you! They'll run away and they'll tell everyone who you are and what you did! Live with that, you asshole!"

The farmer started his truck, but the tires just flapped around the axles as if he were driving on pancakes. He jumped out again, pointing a shotgun as he started to run toward the car.

David climbed back in and did a long burn-out. Sage's heart was racing as she heard the shotgun blast again and again. They were out of range, but it sounded like fireworks in her ears. Expecting David to drive back the way they'd come, she felt afraid they might be stopped by the police. But half a mile down the road, he turned right and began traveling west.

The road wasn't marked or paved. Pine trees grew right down to the edge, the low boughs brushing the car's roof. Sage looked over her shoulder, but the trees seemed to have closed the path behind them. The puppy squirmed free from her pocket and jumped into the backseat to make friends. The other dogs growled suspiciously, and the kittens hissed.

"Do you know where we're going?" she asked.

"Of course I do."

"How do you know —"

"I've been to that farm before. My mother traded them a bitch for a sire one time, back when we used to have setters."

"Is this —" Sage asked, her heart in her throat, feeling the trembling dog on her lap. "— Is this the same dog your mother traded?"

"No, she'd have died a long time ago," David said. "They don't last very long. This is someone else, someone new. Let her out . . ."

Sage unwrapped David's wool jacket as if she were taking the blankets off a baby. The dog inside was shaking like a leaf; her spine protruded from her back, and it was twisted like a corkscrew. She had only three legs, and when she tried to bare her teeth, Sage saw that they all were gone.

"What's wrong —" Sage asked, horrified.

"She's been tortured," David said. "They all have."

"Why her?" Sage asked, petting the ragged, patchy fur.

David didn't answer right away. He kept his eyes on the road, which Sage had just realized was a logging trail. She stared at David, saw the way he was struggling to keep his face and eyes blank. The markings on his face were still there, black and precise.

"Why her?" Sage repeated. "Of all the dogs, why did you take her?"

"Because she was the worst one." David's voice cracked. "She wouldn't have been able to get away. I always take the worst one."

"What's her name?"

"It's up to you. I named the others."

"Jamie," Sage said, thinking of her father waiting in Wyoming, of all the hardships she had gone through on her way to him. "Jamie" came from "James," but it sounded pretty enough for a girl. Petting the scared dog, she thought of the young girl back on the puppy farm and prayed that she would get away, that maybe somewhere she had a real, better home to run away to. "Her name's Jamie. And my puppy is Maisie."

It rhymed with "Daisy."

# Chapter Twenty-Three

Daisy walked up to the house to visit Dalton and came face-to-face with a stranger in the kitchen. The woman looked about forty, with brownish hair and eyes, and a pink sweater over a white uniform. She had tea and toast on a tray, but when she saw Daisy, she jumped and spilled it all over.

"Oh, I'm sorry," Daisy said, crouching down to help.

"Not your fault." The woman kept her head down and away, as if she didn't want Daisy to see her face. Daisy noticed a scar above her right eye and bruises on her inner arm.

After they'd wiped up the mess, the woman set about making more toast. The kettle had just boiled, and she poured more water into a clean mug.

"I'm Daisy Tucker," Daisy said.

"I'm Alma Jackson."

"Have we met before?" Daisy asked, trying to remember. The woman looked so familiar: a broad face with triangular cheekbones, furtive dark eyes, a high forehead. Plain ordinary looks that Daisy had seen before.

"No. Louisa just hired me. Just this week."

"I'm sure, at least I think we've met before — oh, never mind," Daisy said, smiling and shaking her hand. "It's nice to meet you."

"Thanks," the woman mumbled, turning back to her task.

Daisy walked into the living room, wondering about the bruises on Alma's arm. Dalton sat in his wheelchair by the window, watching a line of antelope cross the hillside. When he heard Daisy, he put down his binoculars and tilted his face up to kiss her.

"Daisy, you're a sight for sore eyes," he said.

"So are you."

"Have you come to stay?" he asked.

"For now," she replied. She wasn't sure exactly what he meant — how much he remembered about where she'd been — but she didn't care. She had always been inordinately fond of Dalton Tucker, and she felt content just to sit by his side and hold his hand.

"Have you met the Hun?" he asked.

"The Hun?"

"Old what's-her-name, out in the kitchen. Louisa hired her from somewhere way down in the Rydell family gene pool. A nasty one, isn't she?"

Daisy smiled. "She looks tired. You're probably working her too hard."

"She's here spying for Todd. Don't think I don't know it, either. How Rosalind got herself born into a clan like that —"

"I think you mean Louisa," Daisy said gently.

Dalton looked stricken. "Did I say Rosalind?"
She nodded.

"Jesus, hit me next time I do that. You're Daisy — I got that right, didn't I?"

"Yes, but it doesn't count as much." Daisy laughed.

"Very true, very true. She's gone downtown to rehearse with her new guitar player, wants to make me jealous. Should I be?"

"I haven't met the guitar player," Daisy said. "But Louisa is gorgeous. She gets better as she gets older. Forget about my name and just remember hers."

"Hard to forget yours, Daisy," Dalton said. "You're my only daughter-in-law."

"You're my only father-in-law," Daisy said.

"You gave James a run for his money. Never brought anyone around the ranch after you left."

"Never?" she asked. She knew it wasn't her business, but she couldn't help wanting to know.

"Nope. Never. You were it. Maybe still are. I don't know. He doesn't talk. Just rides and ropes and works . . . maybe he talks to Paul. Go ask him."

"That's okay . . ." Daisy's gaze moved from Dalton to the room. She saw Rosalind's shooting medal, her violin, and all the family pictures arranged on the wide stone mantel: Daisy and James's wedding picture, the twins' birth pictures, Sage wearing her red cowgirl hat, Jake smiling from up on Scout.

"My grandbabies," Dalton said, following Daisy's gaze. "I miss them. More every day."

"I couldn't let Sage come back to visit," Daisy said. "She wanted to, but I just didn't want her coming this close to where . . ."

"I gave them toy cows when they were born. Sage still have hers?"

"She does."

"Good."

Daisy nodded, looking into her children's eyes. They looked so happy. Smiling into the camera, loving their life on the ranch. Growing up with horses, cows, dogs, a grandfather in the next house. Life had been so perfect, as close to paradise as a human family could get. Unable to bear Jake's smiling face, she laid his picture facedown.

"Come here," Dalton said.

Turning slowly away from the pictures, Daisy walked across the room. Dalton looked so old and feeble, a plaid blanket wrapped around his legs. But when he reached for Daisy's hands, his fingers felt surprisingly strong.

"You can't erase the past," he said. "Or close the door on it. You shouldn't even try to. You know how my Rosalind died?"

"Ssh," Daisy said. "I don't want to talk about this."

"The roof caved in on her. It was a snowstorm, and she was out in the pony barn with James. They were bringing oats and water, feeding the animals. Snow was falling, half sleet — full of ice. Two feet fell, and it was so heavy, the barn collapsed."

"Stop, Dalton."

"They were both trapped inside — my wife and my son. Where was I?"

Daisy blocked her ears. She thought of the day Jake had disappeared. She'd been playing with Sage, teaching her how to paint watercolors of meadow flowers.

"I was hauling some dumb calf off thin ice — didn't want him falling through. You think I give a damn about that calf now? James crawled out, fifteen years old with a broken leg, and pulled his mother free. She was alive then. She lived a good long time — over an hour while he tried to get help — before she bled to death."

Daisy pictured herself wetting the brush, showing Sage how to paint foxgloves and buttercups. She could see the dot-dot-dots of gold, stamens and pistils in the flowers' centers. Her own voice came drifting back, telling Sage how inspiration comes from anywhere, from close by, from the ground around their feet. Daisy and Sage painting while Jake evaporated into thin air . . .

"You think I don't wish I'd let that calf drown? That hour made the difference between her life and death. Oh, I hated that calf. Hated myself — for letting Rosalind die, letting James sit there and watch her."

"You didn't let her die. It wasn't your fault."

"That's right," Dalton said. "That's how I see

it now — but it took me a long time to get here. God must have needed her more than we did, me and James. She used to call him Jamey — did you know that? I stopped the nickname, though. Couldn't stand how it made me think of her. Put that picture right, why don't you?"

Daisy reached up on the mantel, took Jake's picture in her hands. She dusted off the glass. Then she propped it up, facing straight at Dalton.

"Good girl," Dalton said, his watery eyes boring hard into hers. "Don't shut the door on the past."

"I won't," Daisy whispered.

"It's why I keep Rosalind's medal out, even though I love Louisa."

Daisy nodded.

"Louisa's got a gig down at the Stagecoach tonight," Dalton said. "Do me a favor and go for me? Take James along and make him give her a big wolf whistle. She likes it when the young guys go wild."

"Don't you get jealous?" Daisy asked, smiling.

"I turn green. But I let it continue because it makes her so happy."

"I think it does make her happy."

"Tell James to make it loud. Tell him your father-in-law said so."

"Maybe I will."

Alma walked in at that moment, setting the tray down by Dalton's side. Dalton winked at Daisy, put a finger to his lips. She knew it was because he didn't want her talking Tucker business in front of a Rydell, and she figured the only reason he'd allowed Alma's hiring was to make Louisa happy.

Lifting her eyes, Alma glanced at the pictures on the mantel. She did a double-take, nearly spilling Dalton's tea a second time. Daisy watched her, unsure of why she looked so stricken. One thing Daisy *was* sure of: Those bruises on Alma's arm had come from a man's hand.

"That's my grandson," Dalton said, seeing her stare at Jake's picture.

"I was looking at the girl," Alma said quickly. "In the little red hat."

"My granddaughter," Dalton said.

"Oh," Alma said. "She's cute."

Dalton agreed, asking Alma if she had kids of her own. "Two boys," Alma answered. Dalton asked her their names, whether they liked to hunt and fish, and Alma began to answer. But Daisy hardly heard. Alma had barely been able to take her eyes off Jake's picture.

Why had she lied? Daisy wondered.

Try as she might, Daisy said, she couldn't see herself going to the Stagecoach Tavern while Sage was still out there alone. She wanted so much to be in the audience — and not just because Dalton had asked her to. She said she had always loved Louisa's music, hearing her sing, being part of the excitement of a performance. But she wanted to stay near the phone — on the ranch, at least — in case Sage called.

Louisa listened to the younger woman, touched by the things she said. *And* by the fact that Dalton had put her up to calling. Louisa had her makeup on and her hair done, and she was letting a third coat of polish dry on her fingernails — an alluring autumnal shade called "Pumpkin Frost." She had the phone wedged between her ear and the bar wall, trying to ignore the guys making a beer delivery behind her.

"You should listen to Dalton," Louisa said, "and get yourself down here."

"I'm sure the place'll be full to the rafters without me."

"Well, it will." It wasn't immodest if it was true, and she knew for a fact the place would be packed tonight.

"Dalton was so alert," Daisy said. "I guess he's having a good day."

"He has them now and then," Louisa said. "Not as often as before, but we're grateful when they come."

"I wanted to ask you something about Alma."

"Oh, did Dalton put you up to that, too?" Louisa asked, frowning. "Honestly, just because her sister is married to Todd —"

"It's the way she looked at Jake's picture," Daisy said. "Do you know why she'd even notice him?"

"Well —" Louisa began, but she bit her

tongue. Didn't Daisy know how everyone had talked way back then? Jake's disappearance had caused a huge stir. This was Wyoming, where everyone knew everyone else. There was so much communal worry and anguish over the missing boy — posters hanging on shop doors, tips he'd been spotted everywhere from Lander to Salt Lake City. There was also a fair share of vicious talk and terrible suspicion, and for a long time, most of it had fallen on Daisy and James. People always suspected the parents: Louisa was sure Daisy had known.

"Tell me, please," Daisy said urgently.

"Well." Louisa made the words sound as kind as she could. "From what Tammy told me, Alma's boys would be about the twins' age. I'm sure she remembered the news about Jake and she was just looking at his sweet face, thanking her lucky stars . . . that something bad hadn't happened to one of hers. That it was him instead of them."

"Oh," Daisy said after a long silence.

"She's a simple soul." Louisa wished she could give Daisy a hug, wanting to chase away this most recent pain. "She doesn't mean you any harm. Her home life is ugly — they live in some squalid little place up north, too many animals and not enough money to feed them. The family suffers for it. Her husband drinks. She comes off a little unpleasant because she has a hard life."

"Thank you for telling me," Daisy said.

"I wish you were coming tonight." Louisa heard her guitar player start to tune up. The drummer brushed the cymbals, and they began to rehearse the music. She felt a thrill and a sadness — both at the same time.

"I'm sorry."

"Tell Dalton this night's for him." Louisa choked up, wondering whether he'd ever sit in her audience again. He seemed to be getting better, but he was aging before her very eyes.

"I will."

"Dedicated to the one I love," Louisa said. "Tell him, will you?" She saw Todd walk in, give her a big wave from the saloon doors. Louisa turned, pretending not to see him. He had really opened a Pandora's box, asking her about Dalton's will. Now she found herself cleaning drawers and boxes, straightening papers, doing everything to avoid the place she knew it had to be: Dalton's safe. When Dalton asked her for a kiss, she wondered whether he had ever really loved her at all. Louisa should have insisted on a proposal instead of just moving in all those years ago. She had thought their love would lead to marriage. Dalton had wanted to spare James thinking someone could take the place of his mother. But even now, Louisa wanted nothing more than a ring on her finger.

"Have a good show," Daisy said, her voice flat.

"You bet I will," Louisa said, with all the false cheer she could muster. She wiggled the fingers of her left hand. A diamond would surely look nice. The pearly amber shade of Pumpkin Frost on her long nails would really set it off.

# Chapter Twenty-four

James stood outside in the dark for a long time. That in itself wasn't strange. He'd spent half his life standing outside these buildings — walking from one to another, leading a horse, hauling a wagon of hay, waiting for Daisy or the kids or his father. But this was different. James had taken a shower and changed his clothes, combed his hair, left his hat on a chair at home.

He stared at Daisy's windows. He saw the flicker of candlelight, and he knew she was home, working. Telling himself he'd just stay a minute, he moved toward the door. He thought back many years, to the summer she had come to stay on the ranch. She'd been a lodger — that was the best way to describe it, he guessed. They were strangers who had kissed on a riverbank, that was all.

A long time ago.

He nearly turned to walk away when he saw her come to the window. She peered out into the darkness. She wore a chambray shirt — all he could see above the window ledge. Then she let the curtain drift back down.

There were a hundred excuses he could make about coming to see her. His father had told him she'd wanted to go see Louisa sing tonight; he could offer to loan her the truck or drive her himself. He could ask her questions about Sage, help her call the police stations she hadn't gotten to yet. His mind raced with good-enough reasons to knock on her door.

But when he actually did it, his head was empty. There wasn't a thought going on up there; the way his heart was pounding in his chest, he swore it must have knocked them all out.

"Hi," she said, opening the door. He was glad she didn't sound disappointed to see him, even though he knew she had to be hoping for Sage.

"Hi," he said back.

"Come on in."

James nodded as she smiled a little and opened the door wider, and he walked in. A lot like how it used to be, way back when.

"This reminds me of that summer," he said.

"What summer?"

"When you were our lodger."

"Lodger," she said, smiling as she said the word. "That's what I was . . ."

James nodded. "Long time ago . . ." He'd been younger then, and less shy. Words had come more easily. He'd known how to present himself: the brash cowboy. What was he now?

"That was the summer all this started," she said. She'd walked over to her workbench, and she seemed to be looking down at the wolf bones he'd brought her.

"All this?" he asked, just touching her hair, wondering whether she meant them — him and her.

"My work. Making jewelry from the things I found on the ranch. It came to life when I came here."

"You made me this," he said, pulling from his pocket a money clip set with one gold nugget. The first one she had ever found, panning for gold in the river.

"You still have it!"

"Yeah."

"People think I bring them love." She flashed him a bright smile, but it quickly faded.

"How do you do that?" he asked.

She shrugged. Her shoulders were thin, her arms long and graceful. James picked up the piece she was making, looked at the faces she'd carved into the bone. They stared at each other from within a ring of concentric circles, and he guessed they were a man and a woman.

"Who are they?" he asked.

"I don't know. It's only the second two-faced piece I've ever made."

"What was the other? Who'd you make it for?"

"Sage," she said. "I did it of the twins."

James nodded. He ran his thumb over the tiny faces. They felt smooth under his skin, and when he stopped rubbing he looked again. Their eyes were alive and full of longing, and he suddenly knew they were of him and Daisy.

"What do they want?" he asked.

"Each other."

"Why can't they have that?"

"I don't know," she said, staring.

"It's us, isn't it?" James moved closer, until he was standing right beside her.

She smiled. "Maybe that's why these things work. People see themselves —"

James watched her gather a pile of stones in her hand, and he knew she was avoiding him — she hadn't even answered the question. The candlelight flickered, throwing shadows around the room. Outside — close by — a wolf bayed. Louis Shoulderblade had said Daisy had power, that James was lucky to have her. James didn't know if he believed such things, but he couldn't deny he'd heard a lot of wolves recently, ever since he'd given her those bones.

She was still holding the stones. James said her name out loud, and she looked up. He took her in his arms, and he heard a pebble fall to the floor. Just as when he'd kissed her the first time, in the streambed, when she'd dropped the gold nugget. He kissed her now.

"James, don't."

"Remember this place?" he asked, his mouth against hers. "I don't think you could be staying here now if you didn't still think of us, if the memories weren't good —"

"This place." Daisy shook her head. She pulled away, and she stared at the small bed. He wondered whether she was remembering the first time they'd made love, when they were young and full of passion and it had all been like . . . a summer adventure.

He asked her: "That time, the first time? Or later, when we —"

"Don't!" she said as she pulled away.

A year and some months later, after they'd gotten married, when they were possibly even more full of passion, when their own bed had felt too big, and they'd wanted to squeeze their two bodies into the place where it had all started —

"Remember?" he asked, taking her hand, kissing the back of her neck from behind. "We left our house —"

"Our bed was too big." She resisted, but the words, or the memories they evoked, unlocked something inside her. "Our bed was too big," she said again. James felt her take his hand, and he kissed her soft, smooth cheek. Arching her back, she let him kiss the side of her neck, her shoulder, her collarbone.

"This one wasn't," he said, leading her to it now.

"No, it wasn't." She raised her lips for his kiss. He braced himself against the wall, leaning down to touch his lips against hers. She tasted like spice, and he wanted more. Fumbling with her buttons, he started to undo her shirt.

"Tell me," he whispered. "Those faces are us, aren't they? Your carving —"

"They are," she whispered back.

"The woman looks like you. So beautiful and delicate, that face in the bone." He was reeling from touching her, from having her say she'd been carving him and her together, one of her pieces that brought people magic-love. It was what they'd always had, what fate had taken away, what James had known he wanted back the minute he'd stood beside her at the waterfall.

"It feels like you," she said, running her hands up his biceps, around his back. She pulled him closer, until they were looking into each other's eyes. James's heart pounded, knowing he would have died for Daisy any time during the last thirteen years and before — that every mistake he had made — even the worst of them — had sprung from the fact that he loved her so much.

"I never stopped," he said, kissing her hard and lying against her on the small bed. "Never stopped loving you."

"It was you," she whispered, her breath hot against his ear. "In every single thing I did. All those necklaces I made . . ."

James moaned, feeling her touch his stomach, run her hands around his waist and down the back of his pants.

"The necklaces that brought everyone else love . . ." she murmured.

"Daisy —" He felt her hands trying to undo his belt, brushing against his zipper.

"They have you in them. Nobody but you."

They kissed hard, taking the rest of their clothes off. James wanted to pull back, to see her alabaster skin in the candlelight, but he didn't want any space between them. He felt their hearts pounding together, as if their skin had disappeared and they were one body.

"All those people," she whispered fiercely. "I gave them our love because I couldn't have you. Because we lost what we had."

"Get it back, Daisy," he said, stroking the side of her face. "Take it back for us."

"It doesn't work that way."

"How does it work?"

"We . . ." she whispered, starting to cry. "We would have to start over. Begin again."

He inched back a little, just enough to lean on his elbow and look at her. The insides of both her arms looked so tender and vulnerable, his throat tightened. Loving him had brought her so much suffering, yet he wanted her to try again. Bending his head, he kissed her shoulders and arms now.

He kissed her breasts. They were full and beautiful. He saw the stretch marks, remembered they had formed after the twins were born. She had nursed their children; they had conceived them right here, in this bed. This bed had been better than theirs, because it was so small and they could touch every part of their bodies together. Some afternoons, Daisy would bring the babies over to sit on the bed and nurse them right here — where she and James had brought them to life.

"Daisy," he said, his voice breaking. "You put our love into your carvings, circles one inside each other. We don't have an end. We just go on loving each other," he whispered, bending his head down to touch hers.

"The circle," she whispered.

"We can't get back what we never lost."

"James," Daisy breathed, touching his erection. It felt like fire, as hard as the bone she carved. She bit his shoulder — not hard, just enough to let him know she was there. He entered her, feeling her slippery wetness envelop him like a river.

"Do you believe me?" he asked, cradling her in his arms. He had to hear her say "yes," that she believed in him. It meant as much to him as seeing their faces in the carved bone.

"I believe you," she said, holding his gaze with hers. Letting him take her in a rhythm, in a dance, on the bed where they had found love the first time, and where they'd started their family.

The surge shook him, the force shaking his body like the waters of Solstice Falls. He poured out his love for her, every bit he'd kept stored inside all these years, moving together like the Wind River, running over rocks and boulders and fallen trees — obstacles that were nothing to a river.

"James . . ." she said, encircling his neck with her arms.

"I've got you," he whispered into her ear.

They'd fallen into the river, and they were clinging to each other. The water swirled around them, carrying them downstream, down the mountain from the land of snow. The riverbed was ancient, and the flowing water made everything in its path worn and smooth.

"Right now," he whispered. "Get it back."

He had her in his arms. He could save her from anything. They were swimming to shore, making love in the small bed, getting back all they had lost. As long as they held on to each other, he could keep her safe. She covered his mouth with hot kisses, saying his name again and again. Her nails gripped his back, digging into his skin as if she feared he'd be yanked away.

"I'm here," he said. "I have you, Daisy."

"Don't let me go," she cried.

"Never," he said. "I never will."

She felt so amazing and wet, her body so hot and slippery. James felt himself getting lost in where he ended and she began. Her breasts slid against his chest, and he lowered his head to kiss her nipples, hold them in his mouth. He slipped out of her, and he felt her hand seize his erection, guide it back inside her. He held his breath, drawn up on his knees. He watched Daisy meet his eyes. Their gazes held for a long minute, and then James knew it was all over.

"I love you," was all she had to say, and he shuddered in an explosive climax, her words pounding in his brain, the same words pouring from his lips. "I love you, Daisy. I love you, I love you . . ."

A wolf howled, or maybe it was James himself. Daisy held James and he held her, their eyes steady with old — or maybe new — understanding, rocking with the rhythm of their beating hearts, listening to the animals outside, being the river together for just a few minutes longer, resting in the circle they had never left.

*Mother and Father. Mother and Father.*
They were in there together, in the nice warm house with candlelight bouncing off the walls, the fire keeping them toasty, everything cozy and romantic. While he was on the outside looking in, freezing cold, all alone on the snowy path, feeling his lungs ache with every breath.

What were they doing? He adjusted the binoculars against his eyes, trying to see. She had drawn the curtains. But there was a spot where the fabric didn't quite meet, and through that gap he was able to see bodies and shadows, so close together they had to be kissing, on their way to ~~fucking~~.

The Guardian crept closer, trying to see. Information was his goal, but he caught himself being a Peeping Tom, and he almost laughed. Wasn't this what kids tried to do? Spy on their parents in bed? Well, he'd missed his chance when he was young. Parents who didn't get along didn't spend much time in bed.

A noise in the underbrush made him freeze. Someone was coming down the path. The Guardian darted into the chaparral, and he held his breath as the person came closer. Staring at his own tracks in the snow, he hoped they would be invisible in the darkness. It was almost pitch-black right here. He didn't carry a flash-light, for obvious reasons, but neither did the person coming along.

The boots came crunching through the snow, and then they stopped. Just a few feet away, so close he could hear the person's breathing, in the exact spot where the Guardian had been standing a moment ago, the perfect vantage point for trying to peer through the woman's windows.

*Peeping Tom,* the Guardian thought derisively: Although he had his reasons for wanting to gather information, this new watcher was just a voyeur, standing very still, getting off on peeking into the woman's bedroom.

After a brief interlude, the watcher walked back the way he came — so focused on the cur-tained window, he hadn't noticed human tracks leading into the brush. Typical, the Guardian thought. He had left trails everywhere, evidence right out in the open, and they'd found only a fraction of it. In time, they would find more

Shivering in the cold, he knew it was time to go. He slept in the barn some nights, in the base-ment of the big house on others. But he had his main camp set up on the nearby cliff, his tent pitched and his stove ready to fire. Just thirty feet up a gently sloping mule track, the Guardian had the best lookout a person could want. Oversee the ranch, the herd, the people, everything. His museum.

Keep watch.

He liked to be able to see his museum. That was important to him, his collection of artifacts. A little of this, a little of that. From his lair, he could see the whole display. And they all could see him, if they'd just decide to look up.

He yawned, feeling tired and hungry and ready to crawl into his bedroll, but first he had another mission. The Guardian wanted to follow the other tracks, the ones made by the other watcher. It had to be someone who lived on or near the ranch; wouldn't it be interesting to find out who that might be? Peeping at the good rancher and his lovely ex-wife?

*Good night, Mother and Father. Good night, happy family.*

*Look up, assholes.*

# Chapter Twenty-five

The logging road ran through a deep ponderosa pine forest. Sometimes the road would break free of the trees and climb, and from the hill's crest, the woods looked endless and black and full of secrets. The surface had been packed dirt at first, then gravel, and now a rough black pavement that sounded loud under the tires. During the night, while David drove and Sage slept with her head resting against the door, they crossed the border from Nebraska into Wyoming.

She must have known, even in her sleep. Dreaming of home, of her parents and brother, Sage had felt dizzy with joy. They were all on horseback, galloping across the range, holding hands in an unbreakable formation. When she woke up, dappled sunlight was coming through the pine boughs. Without sitting up straight, she turned her head and looked at David.

"We're almost there, aren't we?" she asked.

"Wyoming's a big state," he said.

"We're in Wyoming?"

"We're here."

Struggling to come fully awake, she peered out the window. The scenery looked the same as yesterday: thick trees everywhere. David must have traveled this remote road before, because most people would have gotten lost fifty miles ago. Sage's mouth felt dry, and she wished they had something cold to drink. The baby must have felt her anticipation — being in the land of her birth and her father — because he began bouncing up and down.

"Whoa," she said, grabbing her belly.

"What's wrong?" David asked.

"Nothing. He's just playing."

"They don't play," he said.

"Babies?"

"Before they're born," he said. "They're just floating around inside."

"How do you know?"

David didn't answer, and his silence had weight and impact. Glancing over at him, Sage was glad to see that he had washed his face. Last night, after they had been driving for about half an hour, he had stopped to add his eighth and ninth dots — representing Jamie and Maisie, his latest savings. While Sage slept, he must have wiped all the marks off. He was glowering at the road ahead, his shoulders heavy with some invisible burden.

"Are you mad?" Sage asked.

"No. Leave me alone."

"That's a little hard, considering — ow!" Sage said, feeling the baby give her a double-footed kick. David cast a scathing look at her belly, as if he wished it — or she — would disappear. Sage felt an unmistakable shiver of fear. Here she was, on a deserted logging road in the wilderness, with a person who, last night, had drawn dots and lines all over his face.

"Where's your father's ranch?" he asked, as if he wished it was around the next corner and he could drop her off.

"The town's called Solstice Falls," Sage said. "I have the exact address —"

"I know those falls." David cut her off. "I've camped up there."

"Why are you mad at me?" Sage asked. "We were friends last night. You let me name the dogs. What's wrong?"

David shook his head. As she stared at him, she could see shadows of the lines he had drawn. He wasn't actually frowning — but the rubbed-off lines were slanted down, giving him the appearance of a bad mood, a mean streak. She must have been staring for a long time, because he finally looked over at her.

"What?" he asked.

"What did you mean yesterday?" she asked quietly.

"About what?"

"About being the messenger between realms." Just saying the strange phrase made her feel self-conscious and afraid. "What does that mean, anyway?"

"That was last night."

"I know, but I've been wondering ever since you said it. What realms?"

"Sssh." He steered around a fallen branch.

"What's the tradition?"

"Don't talk about it now," he said. "While the sun's up. It's better to wait till dark."

Sage gathered the kittens around her. She began to feel spooked, in a way she probably should have last night. There she'd been, driving up a stranger's driveway with a madman with paintings on his face, getting shot at by a man whose dogs she had just set free. The thing was, last night it had all made sense — they had been doing good deeds, saving helpless animals. Last night, the lines on David's face had reminded her of the Native American motifs her mother worked with.

But today — he seemed so angry. He was driving too fast, skidding around fallen trees, upsetting the animals in back. Sage thought of her mother, the Shoshone designs she used — evoking the spirits of bears, owls, loons, and caribou.

"When you marked your face last night," Sage said, "were you calling up the spirits of the dead?"

David looked shocked, then apprehensive. "How do you know?"

"My mother's an artist. She does it, too. I recognized the dots and lines."

"Maybe I was," he said.

"But which ones?" she asked. "Which spirits?"

David looked around, giving Sage the idea they were being watched as they traveled through the forest. David shivered, and Sage caught it: The hair on her arms stood on end. Two of the dogs began to whimper, and Sage felt as if she had just invited a ghost into the car.

"Not during the day," he said. "I told you — they don't like it."

"Tonight, then?" she asked. He was making her afraid, but one of Sage's main qualities was an insatiable curiosity; she had braved many fearsome things to find the answers to her questions.

"You're just going to leave, anyway," he said. "What's the difference why I do things? Why even ask me?"

"We can still be friends, right?"

He brushed the air with his hand, making an impatient noise. "Why say that?" he asked. "You'll go live on the ranch, and I'll keep driving around. I don't exactly have a phone in the car. What're you going to do — write me care of General Delivery?"

"I've had a long-distance relationship with my father since I was four," she said. "I don't forget people easily."

"We just met. You'll forget."

Sage tugged her necklace out of her shirt and leaned across the seat to put it in his face. She made him touch the amulet, run his thumb over the two faces. "I don't show this to just anyone," she said. "But I showed it to you, remember? I let you hold it."

"People do a lot of things," he said. One of the dogs had started barking, as if she was really hungry or had to go to the bathroom. David pulled over into a clearing, and began the ritual of feeding the animals. Sage watched him for a while, then got out to help. His eyes looked tight, and his shoulders were tense as he settled down with an armful of kittens.

"I really don't show my necklace to anyone," Sage said, sitting beside him and taking two of the kittens. The ground was cold and hard. "Maybe four people altogether."

"Four people," David said, as if that was a large number.

"You, my mother, my aunt, and Ben."

"The father."

Sage nodded, clearing the nipple so the kitten could get more milk. Maisie would be next. She felt David watching her. For a man on the road, a rescuer of animals, he seemed very young and vulnerable, someone who'd been left. Sage knew how it felt to be left — she had been left by her brother, by her father, and by Ben. It was more than an event in a person's life. It was all-encompassing, a way of being, who you were. David had been left; Sage would have bet her necklace on it.

"So we can be friends after you drop me off at the ranch," she said, watching his face.

"What makes you think I want to?" David asked unkindly, but the fight was gone from his voice.

"You made me a dot."

"Excuse me?"

"On your face. Last night — I was one of the dots, things you've saved."

"Yeah, well —"

"We'll stay friends. You don't just abandon someone you've rescued."

"Some people do," he said harshly.

"Not you," Sage hesitated, then reached over to touch his shoulder, take his rough hand. He let her hold it, and they held hands while managing to balance the nursing kittens between them.

"No?"

"You're not that kind of person," Sage said.

David snorted. He had mucus running from his nose, and tears from his eyes. It was fluid and terrible, and he didn't seem able to stop it. The dogs had finished eating, and one by one they began to climb back in the car. Sage reached in her pocket, but she didn't have a tissue. She offered her sleeve, hoping to make him laugh, but he didn't even smile.

He just sat there on the hard ground, crying into the kittens' fur. Sage held on to his hand; she wouldn't have let go for anything. Maisie snuggled against her thigh. The sun hid behind the trees, and she tried to judge how far it had to go before it set. Many hours. Usually she didn't wish the days away, but right now she couldn't wait for night.

They would have driven many miles by then, and they'd be that much closer to her father's ranch. And once the sun was down, once darkness had fallen, David might be willing to tell her about the tradition of being a messenger between realms. Maybe he'd tell her about the spirit he'd been trying to call by painting his face.

Sage could tell him more about her family — about her mother and father, about her twin brother, Jake.

"We should go," David said, gazing down the long road ahead at the exact instant that Sage, starting to push herself up off the ground, spoke.

"We should go." The words fell from Sage's lips at the same time as David's, as if they were speaking lines from the same play, completely in sync, being directed and spiritually guided by someone from beyond. The coincidence seemed funny to Sage, but David didn't laugh.

He offered his hand, to pull her up. Sage thanked him, but he didn't reply. The sun slanted through the thick pines, and Sage shivered — from something scary that was coming from inside David. Something had happened to him last night, something that Sage didn't understand. His eyes looked hard, as if going to the puppy farm had brought back a terrible memory.

Crossing her fingers, Sage tried to remember that name . . . the Shoshone name her mother used to say, such a long time ago Sage could hardly remember, the name to call upon whenever one needed courage the most.

*Wesh* . . . Sage thought. *Wash* . . .

The name was right there, on the edge of her memory and the tip of her tongue, just out of reach. Taking a deep breath, she held the kittens on her lap while David drove them down the lonely road. They were in Wyoming, on their way to her father's ranch. It wouldn't be long now.

*We're almost there,* she whispered silently to her baby while David gripped the wheel in silence. *Almost there . . .*

Daisy and James sat at the table in her small house, drinking coffee. The curtains were open to the mountain, and they watched snow clouds slide down from the north. Herds of migrating elk and antelope followed the trails south, just ahead of the bad weather. Observing nature seemed safer than talking, so they sat by the fire, staying quiet as long as they could.

"Where do you think she is?" Daisy asked, when she couldn't hold it in any longer.

"Somewhere safe," James said. "On a bus, coming here to us."

Daisy bit her lip, wishing that were true. "She hopped a freight train. The night before she left, she capsized in a canoe. She takes risks —"

"So do we." James squeezed her hand. "We always have."

Daisy wished that made her feel better. "I know."

"When did you find out she was pregnant?" James asked.

"After she left. I found the test."

"She didn't tell you?"

"No," Daisy said, her voice small.

"And that's why she left?"

"She wants to see you —"

"I know," James said. "But I've always been here. Why right now?"

"We fought," Daisy said. "Not a lot, but sometimes. She wanted me to be different, the way she thought I used to be. More fun, more adventurous. She wanted to go out west, and she wanted me . . ."

James waited, not blinking as he stared across the old wood table.

"To want to, too," Daisy continued. "She used to look at our yard, and ask, 'Can it *be* any more suburban?' "

"You didn't want to come?" James asked, running his index finger over the back of her hand. Daisy had felt liquid since they'd ridden to the falls, and she wasn't sure she'd ever get her center back.

"I was trying to be a good mother," Daisy said. "I thought we belonged at home."

"This was your home," James said. "Once you left, you never thought about it that way?"

Daisy closed her eyes. "I was afraid to."

"Afraid of what?"

"That we'd have to come back," Daisy said, eyes closed. "If I missed it too much."

"And you didn't want to?"

She shook her head. "No."

389

"You never used to be afraid." Now he stopped tracing her skin. He clasped her entire hand in his and held it until she opened her eyes. He was sitting across from her in a T-shirt, and she gazed up his chest to his broad shoulders and finally to his face. He hadn't shaved that morning, and she saw that he had gray in his dark stubble. But his face was still as lean and handsome as ever, and Daisy thought it was poignant and strange and somehow confusing to be having this conversation with the man who had been her husband.

"I know," she said.

"That first week here, you'd hike into the mountains to look for stones," he remembered, "and Dad I and would try not to worry about you. You were fearless."

"Fearless." The word seemed wonderful but foreign. It applied to other people — her ex-husband, her father-in-law, her daughter. But not, anymore, to Daisy. She'd still hike the mountain, ride Scout up steep and narrow trails. But she was no longer fearless.

" 'She's like a cowboy,' I said to Dad. 'A cow-girl,' he corrected me. But that wasn't right. It was too different, too rodeo-prissy or something. I thought of cowgirls in red skirts with white fringe, dancing onstage with white lariats — nothing like you." James came around the table, placed his hands on Daisy's shoulders.

"I'm not the white lariat type," Daisy said.

"So you weren't a cowboy," James said, easing

his arms around her back and pulling her up out of the chair so she was standing there looking up at him, "and you weren't a cowgirl. You're the cowboy girl."

"The cowboy girl . . ." Daisy said, remembering the odd phrase, how James had said it of her and Daisy had said it of Sage.

"Do you think I still am?" Daisy said, needing to know.

"Tough enough to ride a trail, but all girl," James said, folding Daisy in his arms.

"But not fearless," Daisy said. Not since Jake . . .

"I know." James held her tighter. "But being brave doesn't mean you don't feel afraid." Outside, the snow began to fall. The first flakes fell hard, a sudden, fast-moving squall, obscuring everything in the window. As if he could protect Daisy from seeing, he wrapped her head and body as much as possible with his bare arms.

"I want her home," Daisy said, the panic building in her chest. "James, I want Sage home."

"You're the cowboy girl," James said, stroking her head. "And she's your daughter. She'll be here soon."

# Chapter Twenty-Six

Louisa had to give it to Alma: She didn't look like much of anything, but she was expert when it came to caring for Dalton. She hefted him from bed to his wheelchair, his wheelchair to the living room sofa. His cast was cumbersome, covering his entire right leg, and moving him was no easy task. She worked without small talk or unnecessary questions. Watching her closely, especially when her hands were touching Dalton, Louisa saw that she was very gentle.

When Alma gave him his morning grooming, she kept one hand on his shoulder while softly washing his face or combing his hair — the way a mother might steady a child. She clipped his fingernails and toenails, taking her time and making sure not to snip a piece of skin.

Getting him ready for the day, Alma always wheeled him over to his closet, so he could pick out whichever clothes he felt like wearing. Louisa admired Alma's patience, the way she was treating Dalton with respect. On the other hand, Louisa wouldn't have let Alma stay if she was acting any other way.

While Dalton was sleeping in his chair and the snow was coming down hard, Louisa waited for

Alma to settle down with her coffee and a book of crossword puzzles. It was time she got to know this woman — who was getting so intimate with Louisa's sweetheart — a little better. Pouring herself a mug of coffee, she drifted over to the kitchen table.

"Dalton's sleeping like a baby," Louisa said.

"I wouldn't leave him alone if he wasn't," Alma said defensively.

"No, I can see you're very conscientious," Louisa said. "Mind if I sit down?"

"No," Alma said, although her eyes and reluctant tone showed that she probably did.

Louisa pulled out her chair, acting oblivious. She had bought a book on nutrition and Alzheimer's, and she paged through it now. She looked for examples of people with the disease, searching for ways they differed from Dalton; she wanted the diagnosis to be wrong. She read: "a progressive loss of function in the section of the brain responsible for memory and behavior." Her eyes focused on the word "progressive," and she closed the book.

"Tell me about you, Alma," she said.

"Me?" Alma asked, as if it were a foreign concept.

"How'd you get into this line of work?"

Alma shrugged. "Took care of my mother for a long time. I was good at it, doing it for free. So I figured, why not get paid?"

"That's smart of you. A woman needs to value herself high in this world."

"No one else will," Alma said. "Unless you get good and lucky."

"Like me," Louisa said. "My Dalton treats me like a queen." Her heart felt heavy even as she spoke. The words sounded right, but she knew that as soon as she left the table she'd start another round of searching for Dalton's will.

"Tammy said —" Alma began, then stopped herself. "Never mind."

"What?" Louisa asked.

"I don't want to get too personal."

"Go ahead, Alma. We're practically family," Louisa said. "Your sister being married to my nephew and all."

"Well, she said it would just be you and the Tucker men here. She didn't mention nothing about the daughter-in-law."

"Daisy? What difference does Daisy being here make?"

"No difference." Alma looked more closely at her crossword puzzle.

"Well, you must have mentioned her for a reason."

"Just —" Alma laid the book down hard, "— she seems to have trouble with her kids. The boy getting killed, and now the girl running away. A rich girl like her, and her kids ain't any better off than . . . anyone else's."

"Life's not easier for one mother than it is for another."

Alma thinned her lips and looked over with cynical eyes.

"Mothers have it rough," Louisa said. "You hear about the joys and the love, you think if you have enough money for bunny wallpaper and a nice white cradle everything will turn out just fine. But you know the fairy tales? They all happen in magic castles with jewels and crowns, and those queens are just as heartbroken as the rest of us."

"Bunny wallpaper," Alma said. "My kids didn't have none of that."

"But you love them anyway, right?" Louisa asked.

"Always did." Alma shook her head. "But they are sorely testing my patience these days."

"Your sons?"

"One in jail, one on thin ice. He knew I was working here, he'd come drag me out with a rope. Takes after his father and does things the mean way."

"What would he have against you working here?"

"He used to listen to his Uncle Todd tell stories about the Tucker cows and how they ruined the Rydell sheep. Guess he thinks we'd be part of a big ranching fortune if the Tuckers hadn't been so high-handed about the land."

"That feud is long done," Louisa said.

"Some men like to fan the flames."

"Todd's one of them," Louisa agreed. "Your sons and he are close?"

"Yep."

"Tammy must've known that when she recommended you to me," Louisa said. Something was making her feel nervous, and she wasn't sure quite what it was. "I wonder why she suggested you work here, if it would make your family uncomfortable."

"Tammy knew I needed the work," Alma said. "And no one else needs to know nothing about it."

"You didn't tell your sons you're working here?"

Alma shook her head. "How would I tell them? Like I said, one's serving time for damage he did in a bar fight, and the other never comes by. He dropped out of school. He drinks, just like his father and brother, and he lives in the hills."

"In the hills?"

"Somewhere in the Wind Rivers," Alma said. Her eyes turned red, tears pooling on the lower lids. Two bright pink patches appeared on her cheeks. "He's a teenager, but he thinks he's a mountain man. One of those survivalists, you know? Thinks the whole damn world is against him. I didn't do enough for him when he was young, so he's gonna pay me back by living like an animal now. Sometimes I wish I'd never —"

"I'm sorry," Louisa said. "What about your husband?"

"Never mind him." Alma shook her head hard, as if she was angry at herself for showing such strong feelings. When she looked up, her eyes were blank again. "I take care of myself."

Louisa stared at the salt and pepper shakers: corny, brightly colored ceramics of a boy and girl on horseback. She felt disturbed by the way Alma had wiped the intense emotions off her face as if she were a chalkboard. But something else was nagging at her, pulling from down in the pool of that morning's memories. She had it —

"I was wondering," Louisa began, almost as if she was going to say something about the weather, "why you said that about Daisy's son being killed. No one knows that for sure, you know. He's still considered missing."

"Missing? They still look for him?" Alma asked, the bright spots on her cheeks reddening.

"Well, no. Certainly the police stopped long ago," Louisa said.

"Because I'm sure he was killed," Alma said quickly. "Todd was there that day. You know? He's always told us there was no sign of any living boy, that the rescue party would have found him if he was there."

"I sometimes forget Todd was there," Louisa said. "That Dalton had given him ranch work that year . . . to make me happy, I guess."

"Todd told us the whole thing," Alma said. "How the boy must've gotten dragged off by a wolf or a bear. Or how he might've crawled into the canyon and found a secret cave. Fallen into a crevice and not been able to get out. A million things could have happened. But he's dead. He's got to be."

"Tell that to James," Louisa said. "He's barely

left the ranch in all these years, thinking his boy's gonna come walking out."

"He won't." Alma had spoken too fast and loud, and her eyes widened as if she'd shocked herself. "The family should let him rest. Sometimes you just have to give up."

"I don't think this family believes that." Louisa wondered about Alma's vehemence.

"Being a parent's hard enough," Alma said bitterly. "Without torturing yourself over the impossible."

Louisa didn't speak. She clasped her hands on the table, resting them on the Alzheimer's book. Louisa could only imagine what Alma's home life had been like, with one son in jail and another living out his angry fantasy as a mountain man — plenty to torture herself with.

Perhaps that's what Alma's outburst had been all about. On the other hand, Louisa thought, why had she seemed so adamant about Jake being dead? Outside, the snow was falling hard. That couldn't be easy on Alma, her son living somewhere in the Wind River mountains. Watching Alma stare out the window, Louisa wondered whether he was somewhere in sight: perhaps living right up there, on one of the peaks bordering the DR Ranch; in that haunted, mysterious country. "Fanning the flames," as Alma had said, of whatever resentment kept him going.

With snow falling, James found it hard to leave

Daisy's side in the morning. He had been spending nights at her cabin, and the sound of snow hitting the window made him want to pull her close under the quilt and stay warm in bed all day. But he made himself get up, go to work, just like all the other days. Someday soon Sage would come, and she and Daisy would leave. Or maybe they wouldn't.

He rode along the river, scanning the range with binoculars. He needed to find his daughter, and he still wanted to learn more about whoever had left those pictures behind. His life had been filled with mysteries for many years. With Daisy waiting in the cabin down below, he told himself that if he could just find Sage for her, answer some of the old questions, maybe she would stay.

He saw the birds at three in the afternoon.

The snow had been coming down hard, but now there was a break in the weather. Patches of blue sky showed through gray-white snow clouds as he trained his glasses over the canyon land. The birds wheeled in circles with glints of sunlight shining on their black wings, and James felt his heart stop. Scavengers were common on the ranch, but seeing the birds now — while he was looking for Sage — set his teeth on edge.

Spurring his horse, he took off through foot-deep snow. Paul and some of the others were mending fences, and James flew by them without a word. He galloped roughly westward. High above, the cliff tops glowed gold with the strange mid-storm sunlight, but as he entered the canyon it became almost dark.

The vultures cawed like witches, and their black shadows fell over his face. Some had landed on something a hundred yards ahead. They were big and ugly, their folded wings giving them the appearance of humpbacked monsters. James yelled and waved his arms, scaring them off. His voice echoed around him. The birds circled up and around, their wings thundering with every flap.

This was where he had found crows on the dead wolf, where he had looked for birds to lead him to Jake. James rode over to where they'd been feeding. His head felt light, and his heart was pounding as hard as the birds' wings.

James had found the missing steer. The animal lay out in the open, ten yards from the closest canyon wall. Obviously he had been dead for a few days now; predators had been at him. Chunks of flesh had been torn from his side; holes had been pecked in his skin. His head had been cut off.

Climbing off his horse, James crouched by the animal's shoulders. The snow was covered with bits of black fur, and the area around its neck was stained dark with blood. James heard hoofbeats. When he looked up, he saw Paul galloping into the canyon and waved him over.

"Jesus," Paul said.

"Did you see the birds?" James asked.

"Must have," Paul said. "But I didn't think

anything of it. They're out here all the time. You found the steer —"

"The birds found him last week."

"Yeah," Paul said, staring at the bloody neck. "Jesus."

"Someone did this since the roundup. A fucking butcher."

"The heads —" Paul said, and James nodded, seeing them, too. He remembered riding the range, coming upon fenceposts with four cow heads stuck on.

"He doesn't know what he's doing," James said. Touching the ragged skin, he could see that whoever had done this had used a serrated blade: a jagged hunting knife, a rusty hacksaw. The slicing was uneven, and flecks of rust lay on the bloodstained snow.

"That's a big steer," Paul said. He was ranch foreman: It was his job to figure out how much money they had just lost at the market.

James was thinking about how long it would have taken someone to saw the head off a two-ton steer. The snow would have been falling, but he would have been sitting out here in the open. Someone could have passed by and seen him. The steer had been shot. James looked at the wound; although it had been pecked at by birds, the evidence of 30-30 shot was imbedded in the flesh.

"Who did it?" Paul asked.

"I don't know."

"It's got to be the same guy," Paul said.

James looked around. Someone had taken pictures of his herd. He was killing his cattle, taunting him: Where would the head show up? Daisy talked about the land being home to spirits, but James knew this canyon had a butcher. James smelled blood and pine, and he wondered if ghosts knew how to use knives.

"Someone who hates animals," Paul said.

"Someone who hates me," James said.

The will had to be in Dalton's safe. Louisa had been resisting the temptation to look there. Checking the desk and the bureau had been one thing, but now she was about to get serious. Louisa stood in their bedroom, staring at the portrait of Rosalind. It was very old and beautiful, and it had been painted by someone famous back east. Dalton had often said the painting belonged in a museum, that when James was ready he'd donate it to the Laramie Museum of Fine Arts — she'd have liked that.

Now, with Dalton asleep in his wheelchair, all the way down the hall in the study, Louisa gazed into the portrait's eyes. Rosalind looked back at her with arrogance and hauteur. Her chestnut-brown hair was piled high on her head; her elegant neck was long and stately. Rosalind had sharp blue eyes, like a pair of priceless, exotic sapphires. They were adversaries, old enemies, Louisa and Rosalind. For years, Louisa had slept with this long-dead snob staring down at her, and now she had the guilty feeling Rosalind was staring straight into her soul.

"What's it to you?" Louisa asked, her own eyes flashing. "This is my house now."

*No, it's not,* Rosalind seemed to say. *Just look inside, and I'll prove it to you.*

Dalton snored in his chair down the hall, crying out in his sleep. Alma was downstairs, getting his dinner ready. Louisa glared at Rosalind. The woman had died young — in her mid-thirties, not much older than she'd been in this portrait. Rosalind hadn't lived with Dalton nearly as long as Louisa; she hadn't taken care of him through illness, hadn't had to watch him lose ground to Alzheimer's. She hadn't even been there when his grandson had disappeared.

"I deserve this," Louisa whispered, touching the gold picture frame.

*See what you get,* Rosalind seemed to smirk. Louisa swung her smug face right out of the way, pushing the painting aside and revealing the safe behind it. Her hands were trembling — just as if she was the thief Rosalind thought she was. Louisa blew on her fingers, trying to remember the combination.

Dalton had given it to her years ago, after he'd gotten hurt falling down a cliff. *In case anything ever happens to me,* he had said. Then he had told her the numerals 53-43-82 and a half-turn back. Taking a deep breath, Louisa dialed the combination. The heavy safe door fell open.

Inside, Louisa saw many things. Deeds, blueprints, and topographical maps for the ranch buildings and land; James's birth certificate; gold bricks; rodeo medals; a pearl-handled Colt .45; a box of rifle shells; a satin case of Rosalind's jewelry that Dalton hoped one day to give to Sage; and the last will and testament of Dalton Tucker.

"Oh, shit," Louisa said, her fingers shaking so hard she couldn't hold the paper still. She had been looking for this all month. Now she would unfold Dalton's will and read it. She would set her mind to rest. One way or another, she would know.

*It won't change anything,* she told herself, staring at the document. *No matter what this says, I'll love Dalton just as much. He'll still be my knight in shining armor. I'll still be the luckiest woman alive, and I'll go down to the Stagecoach Friday night and stick my face right in Todd's, singing love songs for Dalton Tucker —*

"What's that you got there?" Dalton asked.

"Oh!" Louisa jumped. He had wheeled his chair down the hall, the Oriental rug muffling the sound. "You scared me! I thought you were asleep —"

"What's that in your hands, Louisa?"

"Why, it's nothing . . ."

"You wanted something in the safe?"

"Just . . ." she began. "I felt like looking . . ."

"That's my will," he said. "Isn't it?"

"Yes, it is."

"Something got your curiosity going?"

"Well, with Daisy being here and all," Louisa began. "I got to thinking about family and the future, little Sage on her way here to the ranch."

"Goddamn it!" Dalton shouted.

Louisa stepped back, shocked. His voice reverberated through the room, and she swore it shook the prisms hanging on the hall chandelier. He wheeled his chair painfully across the room. Even though his head was only about even with her breast, Louisa felt as if he was towering over the scene.

"Goddamn it!" he yelled, even louder than the first time. He snatched the will right out of her hands, leaving them empty and trembling.

"Dalton —"

"You go there to that bar," he said, his eyes and voice ferocious, "every Friday night. Every weekend, as long as I've known you, and other nights, too."

"I know —" She wanted to add: I sing for you. But he just went on as if she hadn't spoken, as if her next thoughts didn't count.

"They circle around you like buzzards, their tongues hanging out. They watch your body, they want to touch you — don't think I don't see!"

"But I don't want them —" she said.

"Every single one of them wants to dance with you. Friday night after Friday night — whether I'm there or not. Whether I'm by your side or here on the ranch. Before I fell —" he slapped his side, as if he could patch his brittle bones together. "I forget, but I still have feelings. I'm still a man!"

"I know," Louisa said, her eyes filling with tears.

"I trust you," he said, his eyes blazing. "I watch you go off to that bar, I think about those cowboys, but I trust you — no matter what!"

"Dalton —"

"And this —" He shook the document in his thin hand. "This is how you show your trust for me?"

"I have to see," she implored.

"Have to see with your two eyes what you can't see with your heart?" Dalton asked. "Is that it?"

"After you went to the hospital," Louisa said, desperately wanting to explain, "Todd asked me where I would live, if something ever happened . . ."

"Todd Rydell?" Dalton asked, his tone dangerous.

"He's my nephew. He cares about me —"

"That son of a bitch," Dalton said. "That no-good little shit . . . you'd listen to him instead of — goddamn it, why didn't you just ask me? Why'd you have to go poking around the safe, looking at lawyers' papers? Aren't I worth talking to anymore?"

"Oh, Dalton. You're worth —"

"I'm worthless, that's what you think. I'm an old nothing. No-good legs, no-good brain, no-good love. That's it, isn't it?"

"I love you," Louisa said.

"This is how you show it." Dalton bowed his head. Alma had heard the ruckus. She'd come bounding up the stairs, but Louisa held up a warning hand. Alma skidded to a stop in the hallway, not venturing into the room. She just stood there, frozen and listening, unsure of what to do.

"I love you," Louisa said again.

Dalton's head drooped lower. He was holding the will so tight, it was just a crumpled ball of heavy bond paper clutched in his hands. His shoulders shook, and Louisa knew he was crying.

"Look at me," Louisa said. "Dalton, please . . ."

"Rosalind," Dalton said.

Louisa's heart sank. This was it, the horrible disease that had started the whole thing. She couldn't trust his heart, because now he called her by his first wife's name. Dalton was breathing hard, but his brain was dying. Louisa must have let out a sob, because Dalton looked up. His eyes were alert, stricken.

"I mean Louisa," he said.

"I know you meant that," she said, taking his hands.

"I said the wrong name."

Louisa nodded. Rosalind's portrait was staring down at them, having the last laugh, but Dalton seemed not to see it. He dropped the will in his lap, holding Louisa's hands. His body seemed so thin, and his face was gaunt.

"I'm sorry I said the wrong name."

"Don't be sorry, love," she said. "Don't be sorry."

"Don't leave me, Louisa," he said, his voice cracking, his eyes filmy with tears and cataracts.

"Never," she whispered, laying her head on his lap. His legs were covered with a blanket, and the crumpled-up will had fallen to the floor. Louisa didn't pick it up; she couldn't even move. Dalton's hand felt so good on her hair.

Wind whistled down the chimney, and snow tapped at the windows. Alma shuffled her feet in the hall; after a few minutes she retreated back downstairs. Louisa heard Daisy call hello from the kitchen door. She heard Alma and Daisy talking quietly, their voices muffled. Dalton seemed not to notice. He just sat in his chair, stroking Louisa's hair as if the touch gave him comfort.

"Don't leave me, Dalton."

He didn't reply, but just kept brushing her hair.

# Chapter Twenty-Seven

Daisy wished that feelings were linear; that once she had decided to forgive, to grow beyond the hurt and pain of the past, her emotions would cooperate and follow the same smooth path. Life would be like an anniversary card, with pictures of a sunset and sweet words of love in calligraphic script. She and James would hold hands and gaze into each other's eyes. That *had* happened — the last few nights. Today was another story. She sat at her workbench, frozen and upset, unable to touch her work.

Outside, wet snow came slapping down. She heard the ice crystals hitting the roof. The wood she had used to stoke the fire must have been wet, because the smoke had a damp, acrid smell. Daisy didn't care. James had kissed her that morning, his eyes bright with promise. At the time, Daisy had seemed to believe him. Hugging herself, she tried to figure out what was wrong.

She decided to do the thing that always worked best at home, when she felt depressed, dark-hearted, or even slightly off-base. Picking up the phone, she called her sister at the shop. But she reached the answering machine.

"Hello, you have reached the Cowgirl

Rodeo," came Hathaway's voice. Daisy listened until the message ran out, then hung up. She could have tracked Hathaway down at home, but she decided not to.

Ice coated the fences and trees outside, turning them to glass. Daisy sat very still, looking out the window, afraid she herself might break.

That night, with the snowstorm covering the entire state of Wyoming, David, Sage, and the animals sought shelter in an abandoned wildlife observation station about fifty miles from the DR Ranch. The walls were thin and uninsulated, and the air inside was bone-cold and damp. The snow outside was so wet it stuck to the station as it fell, blocking all cracks and holes in the wood, forming a sort of natural insulation.

*Like an igloo,* Sage thought, sticking her finger through a knothole in one board, feeling three inches of snow on the other side. The dogs and cats surrounded her, keeping her warm. Inside, her baby adjusted himself. Sage sat quietly, watching the light fade as David built a fire in the black potbellied stove.

"Dinnertime," she said.

"I know," he said. "Roast beef and mashed potatoes."

"Oh, I was thinking of lobster and french fries." She laughed. She watched him start to feed the animals, and she pulled out a package of cereal they'd brought from the truck stop.

Arranging everything in front of the stove, they sat together. The sounds of hungry animals eating comforted Sage as she munched dry wheat puffs.

When everyone finished, David rolled toward his pack leaning against the wall. He pulled out his cigarettes and a pen. The kittens were purring, their full stomachs round and happy. With Maisie sleeping on her lap, Sage watched as he began to trace lines on the back of his right hand. Only then did she notice that he had taken the bandage off, from where he had punched the pervert's teeth.

"Is your hand better?" she asked.

"Yeah," he answered. She leaned over to look, holding his hand to see better. She saw the fading bruises, two scabs where the teeth had pierced his skin. Sage shivered, remembering how the man had touched her. She looked at David's tattoos, and the owl's yellow eyes seemed to blink.

"What are you drawing?" she asked, touching the pen.

"Pictures," he said. "Want one?"

"I don't think so."

He began to trace tiny feathers on the back of his own hand. Then he drew a series of dots and circles. They passed the time for a while, listening to the storm outside while David drew designs on his skin. Sage leaned close, her knee touching his. The fire glowed warm and red.

"The circle," he said quietly, drawing, "pro-

411

tects the dot." Then, drawing a larger circle around the smaller. "And the circle protects the circle."

"You like protecting things," she said.

"Someone has to," he replied.

"Who's the first person you ever protected?"

"Wasn't a person," he said. "It was one of the dogs. Aunt Thelma — that was her name. I protected her from my 'father.' "

Something about the way he pronounced the word "father" made Sage turn her head. "Why do you say it that way? As if he's not your real father?"

"He's not," David said. "I'm adopted."

"Oh." Sage tried to imagine what that would be like. "But once people adopt you, they become your real family. Right?"

"That's what they say."

"It's not true?"

"If real families treat you like shit —"

Sage thought of what they had seen at the puppy farm, where they had gotten Jamie and Maisie. Sage had wanted to rescue the little girl, and David had said she would have to make her own way. Sage had known then that he was talking about himself, that all his rescuing and tattoos and strange spirit magic had to do with whatever his own life on a different puppy farm had been like.

"What did they do to you?"

He shrugged, bending closer to his hand, seeming to concentrate as he drew circle after circle. She watched as he reached into his case for a needle and thread. He licked the thread, then coated it with black ink from a short bottle.

"What did your family do to you?" she asked again.

"Ssh," he said. Then, "Are you going to give your baby up for adoption?"

Sage slid her hands down to her belly, cradling her baby. She was only sixteen, she had no job and no money of her own, but she knew there was no way on earth she would ever give her child to anyone, anywhere. He was hers, and she was his. "No," she said. "I'm not."

David frowned, but he nodded with approval. "I think . . ."

"What?"

David rolled back his left pants leg and pushed down his sock. He lifted the skin with his right hand, and with his left hand passed the needle and inked thread through it. Sage cringed, but he didn't even flinch. He just bent down, concentrating on his work. She watched him create one wavy line. Then he drew out the thread and began the process over again until he had three lines about an inch long, one on top of the other.

"A river," he said.

"Why?" she asked.

"A river ran by our house," he said. "I used to make boats from fallen logs and imagine I could float back to my real family."

"Stop," Sage said, touching his skin. Dots of blood appeared where the needle had passed in and out. The skin itself was inflamed — bright red. "What do you mean, your real family? The people who gave you up?"

"I miss them," he said, once again not seeming to hear her question. "I didn't even know them, but I miss them." He let out a crazy laugh, shaking his head. "You don't get it, do you? With your two good parents in two different places?"

"I get it," Sage said, her voice thick. "I know more about missing someone than *anyone*." Suddenly she got something else: The tattoos were company. The pictures, the symbols, even the sensation of pain. Reaching inside her shirt, she held her necklace in her palm.

"My brother and I were in our mother's belly at the same time," Sage said, closing her eyes. "We were made from the same blood."

"And you missed him when he left —"

"I felt half-gone," Sage said.

"Half-gone," David repeated, staring at his tattooed arm and ankle, as if he knew exactly what Sage meant. David had tattoos to fill the emptiness; now Sage had the baby growing inside her. She rocked gently, feeling his heart-beat mingle with hers.

"Where —" Sage and David began at the same time. They laughed, and Sage continued, "Where did your real family live? Wyoming?"

"Guess so. The people I grew up with — my family — hardly ever left the state, except to trade dogs in Nebraska . . ." David stared into the stove. "Half-gone . . . I know what you mean. Missing someone so bad you can't even live right. Like Petal and her toy — missing her babies so much she went nuts."

"You think Petal's nuts?"

"Just half-gone," David said. "Like me."

"Who're you half-gone for? Your real family?" Sage asked.

David didn't answer. The fire sputtered, and they threw more wood on, just to keep it going. Petal lay beside them, resting her chin on her stuffed toy. Sage stared at it, trying to make out what it once had been. A teddy bear? A toy dog? The brown fabric was shredded and torn, the button eyes chewed off.

The other dogs and cats had settled in various parts of the room. Remembering how she and David had started their questions at the same time, she said, "What were you going to ask?"

"Where do you think your brother went?"

"I don't know." Sage felt prickles behind her neck. "Into the earth."

"Into a cave?"

Sage tilted her head. "Why do you say that?"

David shrugged. "Those mountains are full of caves. Maybe he crawled in . . . I got lost in one once. Fell down a crack headfirst and had to get pulled out by my foot. It's how I got this —" Pushing back his brown hair, he showed Sage a thin white scar that ran along his hairline.

"How old were you?"

"Little," he said. "Four or five. Small enough

to fit down the crack."

Sage closed her eyes. The image was so terrible — a little boy, curious and brave, scuttling into a cave to investigate the mysteries inside. Maybe he was pretending to be a bear, a wolf, a Shoshone scout. Bright-eyed and full of mischief, then tumbling straight into a chasm of hell. She couldn't bear to think of that happening to Jake. At least David got rescued.

"Who saved you?" she asked quietly, petting Petal.

"My uncle," he said. "My fake uncle, I mean. My adopted mother's brother. He hauled me out, got me stitched up."

"That's good," Sage said. "That he was there."

"Yeah. He's pretty nice — the best part of the family. Once when my dad was making me ax a litter of puppies, he almost killed him. Punched him out, knocked him into the dirt —"

"Your father was forcing you to kill puppies?" Sage asked, horrified.

David nodded. "Yeah. That's the kind of thing my family does. My uncle's different, though. Real good compared to the rest of them. He said he was gonna haul me out of there, take me somewhere better. I heard him yelling. He said he was sorry he'd ever pulled me out of the cave, brought me back to the farm, if that was how they were gonna treat me."

"Couldn't he take you away?" Sage asked. "Couldn't you go live with him?"

David shrugged. "He stopped coming around. He and my parents quit speaking after that."

"Go find him," Sage said. "Move in with him."

Frowning, David began to draw on his skin again. Choosing a new spot on his right arm, he drew another owl. Dots, dashes, owls, and circles: the markings David seemed to like most. Sage watched, listening to the storm grow more ferocious outside.

"I saw owls in the cave," he said. "Yellow eyes watching me."

"Scary."

"No, I knew they were my friends."

"You're a good artist," Sage said, suddenly missing her mother. "You must have inherited that from someone in your real family."

"Yeah, maybe. My brother can't draw worth shit."

"Your brother — is he from your real family, too?"

"No," David said. "He's theirs. Their real son. My adopted brother."

Sage nodded. Her baby kicked inside her, and suddenly she felt strange — as if she was going to be sick. The wind howled outside, rocking the small cabin. The structure seemed to move, as if it was teetering on a cliff edge. Sage clutched Petal, Maisie, and Jamie closer, feeling afraid.

David held her hand. Without asking this time, he started to draw a bird — this time she let him. His touch sent tingles up and down her spine. Just then, a branch fell on the roof, and she jumped.

"This is just a Wyoming storm," he said. "Don't be scared."

"I can't help it."

"We're warm, we have food."

The wind howled, picking up velocity. A downdraft sent sparks jumping in the stove, and David held her hand tighter.

"The baby," Sage said. "What if something happens and we can't get out? The wind's scaring me —"

"We could always call for help." David's face was perfectly serious. He began to draw circles and dots on her hand. "You could call the spirit."

"The messenger between realms?" she asked, trembling at the words. It was dark outside: David had told her he wouldn't talk about this during daylight, but night had long since fallen.

"Yes."

Panes of glass rattled in the windows. Sage felt scared by the weather, but excited by what David was saying. This reminded her of her mother: the studio filled with feathers, bones, rocks, and gold wire. Dream-catchers — netted hoops she had once hung over her infants' cribs to catch the good dreams floating by — hung from the ceiling. Her mother was the most spiritual person Sage knew, believing in seeking spirits for their dreams, visions, and help.

"What spirit?" Sage asked.

"The bravest one," David said. "It's a magic name that can keep you safe. If you say it, no one can harm you."

Again, swimming up from Sage's memory came that word, the Shoshone name her mother used to say — she didn't feel strange now, because this was so familiar. "What?" she whispered.

"Washakie." David said it once, then again louder.

Sage's eyes clouded as a memory came out of nowhere. She could see red ranch trail dust and four small feet. Two were hers and two were her brother's. The boy had eyes the color of David's, and like many twins, he and Sage often said the same word at the same time. She could hear their mother's and father's voices telling them about a Shoshone chief, how his very name meant bravery and courage. She and her brother were holding hands.

"Oh, my God."

David looked over at her, his expression calm but curious.

"Jake." Her voice croaked, tears filling her eyes.

David stared at her. "What?" he asked.

"Is it possible?" She fumbled for his hands as the salt tears poured down her cheeks. "Is there any way? I think you're my brother . . ."

# Chapter Twenty-Eight

Just before dawn, the ranch was cold and frozen. White stars were brilliant in the blue-black sky, hanging low over the ridge, caught in branches of the stunted cedars. Last night the temperature had dropped hard and fast, freezing the wet snow solid. James knew the cattle wouldn't be able to break through the crust, so he went to the barn to saddle up and ride out.

He found Daisy brushing Scout at the tiedowns. She didn't see him at first, so he hung back in the shadow. Last night he had gone to her house, as he had been doing since they'd gotten together, and her lights were off. At first he had thought she might have turned in early. Thinking of her warm and sleepy, waiting for him in bed, had excited him more, so he had climbed the steps.

Ready to knock, he happened to look through the front window. There she was, wide awake — huddled on the floor by the fire, arms wrapped around her knees. Her hair hung over her eyes, but from the way her shoulders were shaking, James could see she was sobbing. Wanting to help her, he put his hand on the cold doorknob, and at that moment their eyes met. Her gaze was anguished; with a small shake of her head, she sent him away.

So now, seeing her so soon, James hesitated. He didn't want to force something that shouldn't be there, to make her uncomfortable or upset. But he wanted to hold her. That's all, he told himself. He wanted to walk across the barn and take her in his arms. To smell her hair, kiss her skin, feel his arms encircling her body. To feel he could do something to make her better; make up for all the years they had lost.

Instead, he cleared his throat. When she turned her head, he approached from the other side of Scout, standing with the horse between them.

"You're up early," he said.

"I couldn't sleep."

"Did the storm bother you?"

She nodded, and he could see the tightness around her eyes and mouth, as if she were holding something inside that just might make her burst. Her cheeks were rosy, though, and that made James feel better: The ranch air was doing her good.

"I stopped by last night," James said, watching her carefully.

"I know," she said. "I was having a bad time of it."

"You saw me."

She nodded.

"What was wrong?" he asked. "I thought we —" He trailed off, too hurt to put it into words.

"It was about Sage," she said. "With this weather — I can't stand it anymore. She's all I can think about. Last night I sat up, praying and watching the snow . . ."

"We could have done that together."

Daisy's face crumpled, as if she was in the most terrible pain. "Together . . ."

"Is that bad?"

She shook her head. "I've just gotten so used to doing it alone."

"So have I." James took a step around Scout. He waited to see what Daisy would do; she just stood there looking up at him. The barn was chilly: Their breath came out white and dissolved in the air. Daisy wore chaps over her jeans, a pale yellow sweater, and a dark green jacket. James focused on the pink in her cheeks, told himself her time here was good, really good for her.

"So much has happened," she said, looking down at her boots and shaking her head. "Last night I sat in that house, thinking back. When we first found out I was pregnant, all I could think about was how lucky we were."

"We were." James didn't feel right about touching her, even though he wanted to. So he tickled Scout's velvety muzzle instead, staring into Daisy's eyes.

"That our kids would get to grow up on a ranch. That I got to live in such a beautiful place. That you and I found each other . . ."

"We could still have that," James said. "Sage

will come. She can have her baby."

"We can be grandparents?" Daisy asked, trying to smile.

"We will be grandparents," James said it out loud for the first time. "Wow." Just then, he noticed that she had gotten Scout's bridle and saddle out of the tack room.

"You're not planning to ride, are you?"

"Yes," she said. "I can't stay inside today. I'll go crazy. Maybe if I head out toward the main road I'll meet her coming in."

"There's ice on the ground," he said. "I don't think you should go. It might be dangerous."

"It's dangerous out there for Sage, too," Daisy said. "I'm going."

They saddled the horses. James gave her a blanket coat, took one for himself, and they rode out. The snow was two feet deep, and there was a thick crust of ice on top. The horses' hooves cracked it, leaving a marked trail behind them.

James had intended to head northward to his cattle, taking a shortcut through the Rock Springs Pass. Thinking it might be dangerous for Daisy, he decided to go the long way around. The sun was just starting to rise, turning the darkness from black to gray. Stars began to fade, millions every second, leaving only the brightest constellations and planets visible.

Daisy seemed to relax as they rode. Scout's gentle gait rocked her, and the ride gave her the feeling she was doing something to find Sage. James watched how she turned her head from left to right, staying vigilant, even though it was still too dark to see much of anything. She wore her grease-wool muffler pulled up over her mouth and nose, to keep her face from freezing.

They plodded along the riverbed. Snow covered everything, making the willows and junipers droop low under its weight. The water had frozen solid in places, but around this bend it rushed over rapids, the boulders slick with ice. Crystal Lake spread off to the right, frozen and white with snow. It should have been smooth, but as they got closer, James could see the surface was covered with bumps.

"Look," he said in a low voice, reaching over to grab Daisy's wrist.

"What?" she asked.

"There." He pointed at the lake. The horses stood still, their breath puffing into the frigid air. James saw Daisy's eyes narrow as she tried to make sense of the lumps. The lake looked like a field covered with tiny boulders.

"What are they?" she asked.

Light from the rising sun reflected off the red cliff, pouring pink light over the snow-covered land and lake. James held Daisy's wrist for over a minute, waiting for the sun to rise a little more, illuminate the bumps. He kept the horses still, not wanting them to crack the ice crust and scare the wildlife before he was ready. His heart was beating fast, because he had seen this several times over the years, each time dreaming he could show it to Daisy.

"Do you believe in signs?" he asked, his blood pounding.

"You know I do." She was smiling behind her scarf. He could tell by the way her eyes crinkled.

"What's the totem for marriage?"

"The what?"

"The Shoshone totem for marriage?"

"Louis told me the Shoshones believed it was snow geese," Daisy said. "They mate for life."

"If I can make the snow geese appear," James asked, "will you marry me again?"

Daisy didn't answer, but she kept smiling. James assured himself of that, watching her eyes very carefully. The tiny lines at the outside corners deepened slightly, and their expression was full of affection and mirth. The sun was coming up fast, its red reflection sliding down the cliffs and spreading light all over the snow. He decided he'd better not wait another second.

Kicking his horse hard, he took off at a full gallop toward the lake. Chieftain flew, black and sleek and hell-for-leather, loving the strange weather and his rider's mood. Frozen air rushed past them, filling James's lungs till they wanted to burst. James kicked again, waving his arms and yelling wildly.

"Yah!" he yelled. *"Yiii-ahhhhh!"*

The bumps began to move. They wriggled like thousands of cats hiding under a pristine white comforter. Then the snow began to break, and the first heads and necks appeared — hatchlings in the new dawn. The first stirrings of wings as one goose rose in flight, and then another. As James galloped to the edge of the lake, the entire flock of snow geese took off.

Turning to grin over his shoulder, he watched Daisy's reaction. She stared with delight and amazement, both hands held to her scarf-covered mouth. The migrating snow geese had scattered on takeoff, but now they remembered their formation. Following their leader, they created a gigantic V and wheeled southward. Daisy rose in her stirrups, throwing her arms up as if she could catch the geese that flew overhead.

As if she could catch what they had, James thought, watching her. As if she could harness their resilience and endurance and devotion, as if she could have her marriage back. Or maybe that was just what James wanted for himself. His heart was pumping, so full of love for her he thought it might knock him off his horse.

"Marry me!" he yelled across the long expanse of dawn-pink snow. It was punctuated by Chieftain's hoofprints — the mark of one rider.

Daisy didn't call back, but as James watched, she began to ride toward him. Scout was old and slow, but she had always loved to run. The palomino began a slow canter, her hooves cracking through the crust, and as James watched, Chieftain's prints were joined by Scout's. Their trails merged until Daisy was sitting right beside him.

He said again, straight to her face: "Marry me, Daisy."

"I love you, James."

The snow geese had disappeared from sight, but they could still hear the beating of a thousand wings, the loud honking that echoed off the mountain walls.

"Devoted for life," he said. "That's what I want to be to you."

"It's what I want too."

"You couldn't have felt it, being so far away," he said, his throat tight with cold and incalculable passion. "But it's what I've been all along. I never stopped."

She nodded, her eyes shining and bright. Reaching over toward his saddle, she took his right hand and squeezed it tight.

"I know that," she said.

"For you and Sage. For Jake, too. For our family. Marry me, Daisy."

"So we can be a family again." Daisy clutched his hands.

"Say yes —"

"When Sage comes home." Daisy's eyelashes were frosty with tears. They froze there, just under her eyes, and they stayed. "Ask me again then, James. I can't say yes until our daughter is safe."

"I understand," James said, his voice thick with tears because he understood so well.

They stayed by the edge of Crystal Lake for a few minutes more, not speaking again, listening for the snow geese. But the flock was gone, continuing on their migration to warmer, safer lands. Holding Daisy's hand, James waited for his heartbeat to return to normal. It never did, and it probably never would while she was right there. But after a while, when the sun had cleared the mountain and turned the sky bright blue, he let go of her hand and started to ride.

Toward the main road, away from the lake and river, away from the canyons and range. The cattle were hungry, waiting for someone to break the ice and let them graze, but James decided to let them wait. Paul would get to them, or some of the punchers.

Right now James was going to ride with Daisy to the highway, where there was no livestock at all. Maybe a few cars and trucks would pass by, ranchers with business to take care of after the storm. James and Daisy would be watching for the one with Sage inside, bringing her home to her parents.

Bringing the Tucker family back together.

From his bed, Dalton had watched James and Daisy ride off before dawn, and now he sat by the window, hands folded on his lap while he dozed and dreamed of being young. He had such strength! He could ride all day, his muscles as strong as the horse's. The landscape was washed with colors, a hundred shades of green in a single leaf, the canyon walls a palette of reds. Winter came fast in Dalton's dream, in the time it took to draw one breath. The snow was heavy, and it broke houses apart. When the roof fell in, all Dalton had to do was move the timbers, pull

Rosalind and James out to safety.

"Oh, God." Dalton woke with a start. "Oh, dear God. Rosalind, my Rosalind."

"What's that, Mr. Tucker?" Alma, the nurse, asked.

"Nothing," Dalton muttered, wiping his eyes.

The dream had seemed so real. That sense of strength and ability — the power to save the people he loved most. He hadn't had to leave the job to his young son — to try and fail to rescue his mother. In the dream, Dalton had been able to be the strong one — the father and husband — and lift those broken roof beams right off his beautiful wife.

"Want a tissue?" Alma asked, thrusting the box at him.

"What for?"

"Your eyes are watering. So's your nose." She wadded up a tissue and dabbed at his face, exactly like his mother used to do.

"Stop that, young lady," he said sternly.

"Why are you crying?"

"Ask me that again, and you're fired." What had life come to, that this nurse-lady could walk through his ranch house like she owned the place, asking Dalton Tucker why he was *crying?*

Already the dream was fading. He stared down at his withered hands and wrists, trying to bring back the shimmering strength he'd had in his dream — and his youth. As he sat there, watching the morning sun flood through the windows, he thought of how quickly life had passed by. In the blink of an eye!

So much love — first for Rosalind, now for Louisa — and even with all of passion's power, he wasn't able to guard his youth. How could it all go so fast? His broken leg stuck out straight in front of him, mocking him. It told him there wasn't going to be a happy ending to this story.

Dalton was going to keep getting older. More of his bones might break. He would forget Louisa's name more often. His days of making love were over, and the most he could hope for was a little hugging and kissing now and then. Tenderness — all that crap he'd shunned like the plague as a young man full of spit and vinegar. That was all that was left to him now. Much more than he deserved.

"Good morning, darlin'."

At the sound of Louisa's early-morning voice — sexier and sandier than at any other time of day — he glanced around. She stood there, lush as a tropical oasis in green silk and maribou mules, messing her long chestnut hair in a big overhead stretch. Knowing she wasn't needed, Alma walked away.

"Good morning," Dalton said.

"What're you doing up at the crack of dawn?" Louisa bent down to embrace him from behind, kiss the side of his neck. Oh, her lips still felt so good. Dalton closed his eyes and wished she wouldn't stop.

"Just watched James and Daisy head out for a ride," he said.

"Pretty early," Louisa said. "Maybe they're eloping."

"Now, there's a thought."

"Nice, how they're getting along. I wasn't sure how that would go — her coming out west and all." Louisa rubbed her cheek against Dalton's.

Just then, in the midst of him getting all ardored-up, he remembered: He was supposed to be mad at her. She had rifled through his vault, searching for his last will and testament. His woman didn't trust him to leave her fixed after he kicked the bucket! Recalling that moment of shock, he pulled away.

"What's the matter?" she asked.

"Damn nasty business, you not trusting me."

She jumped back. "Do you have to start that up again?"

"I just remembered it."

"I apologized," she said. "Are you so ornery you've got to hold a grudge for the rest of your life?"

Dalton narrowed his eyes, staring out over the frozen fields. The horses had been dark dots on the snow, and he watched the direction they'd gone, wondering when they'd be back. *The rest of his life.* He wondered how long that would be. He felt the haze closing in, taking his memories away. Right now he felt clear, but before the hour was out he'd be asleep again. He had something he wanted to say, but he couldn't quite get to it —

"The rest of my life?" he asked, buying time.

"Yes. You plan on being mad all that time?"

"Maybe," he snapped. "Maybe I will."

Louisa exhaled. She strode away, giving Dalton time to rack his brain. What had he been about to say? As he gazed across the snowy fields, he saw a formation of snow geese flying south. They were dark silhouettes against the sky, and he knew if he was on horseback out there, they'd sound like thunder going over.

Snow geese.

He thought of his old friend Shoulderblade. He had told Dalton snow geese were the luckiest creatures — they married once, and that was that. Dalton had taken it to heart. Louisa thought he had never proposed because of James and his loyalty to his mother. But Dalton had another reason: He believed in snow geese, in their devotion and love for each other, that you only got one real love in this world.

For Dalton, it had been his first love, his only wife — Rosalind. He had spent a lifetime telling himself that. He kept her portrait on the wall, her shooting medal in the dining room, her initial on the ranch's name: the DR Ranch.

Dalton-Rosalind.

Snow geese. Staring outside, Dalton wondered about James and Daisy. Were they smart enough to realize they'd been given a second chance? That fate had brought them back together for one last try — that they had all the love they'd ever need; all they had to do was decide to stay with each other?

For better for worse, for richer for poorer, through sickness and health . . .

Dalton blinked, trying to stay alert, trying to push back the haze of age. Sickness and health: Would Rosalind have loved him the way Louisa did through this miserable decline? He had to admit, when he looked into Louisa's eyes, he saw the same mad desire he'd noticed way back when he was a young buck. She couldn't possibly want him, but she still knew how to treat him like a man.

Snow geese.

As he watched, the great V circled around and landed in the field. He wondered about their ages, how many migrations they'd taken together. If he was a gander, he'd have passed twenty-eight winters with that goose in the next room. He and Louisa had had many more migrations together than he and Rosalind.

"Louisa!" he called.

She took her sweet time coming. Probably mad as hell at him, letting him cool his heels till she got good and ready. A fat three or four minutes ticked away — more and more of life passing every second. "Louisa!" Dalton bellowed.

Finally, she showed up. She was still in green silk, still had her hair down, still had those sultry bedroom eyes. Maybe she'd been at the makeup mirror, because Dalton hadn't noticed her in eye shadow and mascara before — but she was now.

"You called?" she asked frostily.

"C'mere," he said, sticking out his gnarled old hand.

She ignored it, like the elegant lady she was. Dalton left it there, the effort of holding his arm out straight just about toppling him out of the chair. He thought of his will, and shame filled his heart. Thank God he had stopped her before she'd read it. He wouldn't have wanted to hurt her like that for anything.

"Hold my hand, sweetheart."

"Why should I?"

"Because you're the love of my life."

She gazed down with full lips and steady eyes. He stared up at her, praying that he would remember to call Wayne Harding — his lawyer in Dubois — at the stroke of nine, the minute his office opened. Maybe he just hadn't wanted to consider his own death, imagine Louisa going on without him. But where had he thought she would live?

"Life is long," Dalton said, "but it's over in a lightning flash."

"Your life's not over," Louisa said.

"I'm a tired old rancher."

"And I'm a tired old saloon singer."

"You're my beautiful Louisa," he said.

She shook her head, but he could see he had pleased her: She was hiding a small smile. He thought of Daisy and James out riding the range: Let *them* be the snow geese. Some people were given more than one love in their lifetime, if they weren't too foolish to miss it.

As Louisa took his hand, Dalton was filled with peace. They were going to be okay; he knew it deep inside — as long as he remembered to call the lawyer. But James and Daisy: They were another story. Dalton stared out at the ranch, the land that he and his son had kept going all these years, and he hoped that their family would carry it on: James and Daisy and Sage.

And whoever would come after.

# Chapter Twenty-Nine

Treacherous driving lay ahead, but David had convinced Sage they should dig out of the wildlife station and try to get to a main road. He was a Wyoming local and he said that even though the sun was shining today, they shouldn't be fooled: Another storm was right behind the last one. Silver threads of thin cloud told the story, way up in the blue sky.

They found shovels in a utility closet. Sage helped the best she could, but every time she lifted a shovelful of heavy snow, she felt a twinge in her belly. After a while, she sat down to rest, letting David do the work. It was hard not to follow him around: Sage wanted to ask him a million questions, prove that he was actually Jake.

Once he had the car dug out, he brought all the animals outside and loaded them up. Then he went back to help Sage. The heater was on, blasting like a furnace. David checked the gas gauge; it had been a while since he'd filled up, and they would need to find a station soon. Sage let him get them started — backing onto the logging road, getting stuck, engaging the four-wheel drive, pulling onto the flat surface. Then she took up her theory again.

"Everything fits," she said. "You have brown hair, I have brown hair. You have green eyes, I have green eyes."

"You have two legs, I have two legs," he said.

"See?" she asked, laughing. "That's exactly my humor! We're both sarcastic!"

David lit a cigarette, scowling.

"You're him," Sage said. The more she stared, the more she became convinced. She adored him, every bit of him: his eyes, his nose, the scar on his forehead, his long fingers, his thin arms, even his tattoos. Would she feel this way about someone who wasn't her twin brother?

"Why are you staring at me?" he asked.

"You're him, you're him!" She touched his sleeve, the back of his hand.

"You're crazy."

"Just start with the coincidence!" she said. "*What are the odds* that two people the same age would meet on a dark road in Nebraska, one of them being attacked? And there you were to *rescue* me?"

"So that makes me your brother?"

"That fact, plus others."

He exhaled smoke, shaking his head as if he wished she'd just quit talking. But his curiosity must have gotten the best of him, because he glanced over in spite of himself. "What others?"

"Your tattoos —"

"Your family likes tattoos?"

Sage shook her head. "No, but they remind

437

me of my mother's work. Wait till you see. She makes these necklaces that everyone wants. They're very mystical, made of bones —"

"You showed me."

"That's right." Sage started to reach inside her shirt to show him again. But just then, two of the kittens who had been burrowed in her jacket woke up and began to circle around and around her arm, wanting to be petted.

"She likes Shoshone legends, and she uses circles and dots all the time. That owl on your hand? She's drawn the same owl — the exact same bird! Identical eyes, feathers, wings — wait till you see!"

"She draws owls?"

"And dots and circles and hawks. She's magic. I know you think that sounds strange, but all the women in our town say it's true. She can make love happen for other people, just by concentrating on the bones."

"Love?" he asked skeptically.

"Yes. For other people," Sage said, feeling momentarily sad. "Not for her and my dad. They ended back when . . . you disappeared. Oh, God." She put her hands over her mouth, overcome by emotion. "Those tattoos you draw — they're how she stayed connected with you."

"*What?*"

"It's true!" Sage exclaimed, shimmering with the magic. "If you knew some of the people my mother brought together — why couldn't she do it with her own son? Wherever you were, even though we thought you were gone forever, she sent you those owls and hawks and circle-dots!"

He grimaced in disbelief, shaking his head.

"Well, how did you learn to draw? Did you go to art school?"

"No. I just pick up a pen and it happens. No big deal."

"Why owls? Why circles around dots? I'll tell you: They're messengers from her to you."

"Messengers . . ." David said, the word striking a chord with him.

"Between realms," Sage said. "Her realm and your realm."

"You're crazy. I don't even know her."

"You do, you do."

He frowned, shaking his head. Holding the wheel, he pulled out of a bad skid, steering around the next patch of blue ice.

"How is it we both know about Washakie?" Sage demanded, her adrenaline flowing from the skid and from the emotional current running through her body. "Is it one of your earliest memories, learning his name?"

"So what?" David glanced over.

"Our parents talked about Washakie. Our father's spiritual but doesn't know it — that's what Mom says. He just works the land, runs his ranch, looks for you. He passed certain legends on to her, and she gave some to him. She uses them in her jewelry. Just like you use them in your tattoos. You'll see how similar your designs are when you meet her."

"Like that's ever gonna happen."

"Oh, it will," Sage said confidently, re-arranging the kittens to reach across and take his hand. "Jake, Jake."

"Stop calling me that."

"I have your booties! Blue booties — yours — hanging in my room. Oh, my God." She was gazing down at his boots. "They were on your feet, those feet right there — this is incredible."

"You saved your brother's *booties?*" he asked, as if such a thing was unbelievable, too senti-mental and corny for words.

"Jake," she said again. "Does that sound familiar? Do you remember hearing us call you that? Jake — that was my first word. Your name."

"Stop."

Sage closed her eyes. The joy and pain were almost too much to bear. To be reunited with the boy she had loved so much. What could have happened to him? How had he stayed alive, yet failed to return to her family home? She was pos-itive she was right — about her mother magically sending him images and talent, about their father teaching everyone about Washakie because they would need so much courage in their lives.

Tears pressed against Sage's eyes, but she willed them back. She touched her heart, felt it thudding. Her heart felt full — yes, that was the truest test of all. Sage's heart felt fixed, after all these years.

"I've missed you so much," she said throatily.

"Don't say 'you,' " he said. "Say 'him.' You've missed your brother —"

"I've been half-gone."

"Half-gone —" His eyes were bright and sharp, his mouth open.

"You feel it too, don't you?" she asked through glistening tears, her smile widening. "You know it's true."

He didn't reply, but she could see the flush starting in his neck. It rose into his face, the back of his ears. Sage watched him recognizing what she knew by instinct, way down in her gut: They had been together before birth. They were part of each other, separated all these years, together again. No longer half-gone, but whole. Feeling for her necklace, she worked it free and stared down at the faces.

Sage looked at the girl's face first, then turned the carved surface over and looked at the boy's. Now she glanced at the boy sitting beside her: His profile was sharp and handsome, the planes of his face even and noble. Same forehead, same cheekbones, same nose, same chin.

"It's you," Sage said. "You're Jake."

"That's wishful thinking," he snapped.

"No —"

"It is." The blood in his face made him look angry, rageful. "You're a dreamer, Sage. Just a fucking dreamer."

"Jake —"

"Shut up! Don't call me that!"

"But you're him! I swear, just look at my mother's carving — it's you! And I'm not a dreamer — I'm being practical. This is evidence!"

"A goddamn dreamer," he said. "Hitchhiking across the whole fucking country to a father who didn't want you that much in the first place."

"He did —" Sage said, aghast.

"Bullshit! He let you and your mother go just like my first parents let me go. You're nuts if you think someone like that wants you."

"He wants me."

"They want you to think that because it makes them feel less guilty. But parents are only out for themselves. You're tricking yourself, just like you're trying to trick me right now. Give it up."

"Never." She was trembling.

"Did he invite you?" he asked. "Did your wonderful, perfect father *ask* you to come out? Go home before he tells you to."

"He loves me," Sage said.

"So much he never wanted to see you."

"He loves me," Sage screamed, pounding the seat. "He adores me! He only stayed on the ranch to be there, in case you — in case Jake — ever came back! That's the kind of man he is! The kind of wonderful father!"

"So wonderful he lost both his kids," he yelled back.

"Lost us! Never —" Sage started to shake. "Someone took you. Kidnapped you — it's the only explanation."

"Don't say 'you,' " he warned.

"Kidnapped!" Sage yelled. "He would never lose us! He only let me go because my mother couldn't stand being there anymore. Hanging around the place where my brother was taken from her . . ." The emotion was so great, she began to cry. The sobs poured out of her as she pictured her mother and father, as vague memories of those horrible days without Jake came pouring back.

"Sage," he said. "Calm down."

"Calm down? You say something like that, about my father, and . . ." She gulped, choking on tears.

"The animals are getting upset. Petal's hiding under the seat."

"I'm . . . sorry . . ." Sage sobbed, trying to reach back and touch the dogs. She heard Petal whimpering, and she realized that the animals had probably heard many people crying and yelling; that's the kind of place puppy farms were, the kind of home Jake had been delivered to. Sorrow and compassion made Sage weep harder.

Outside, the road was dangerous. The four-wheel drive worked, taking the car through two feet of ice-crusted powder, but in some places the land fell away in sheer drops. Sage clung to her seat, noticing for the first time that the topography had suddenly changed to rocky terrain, with big craggy bites taken from the road's shoulder.

"You okay?" he asked.

"Yes . . . Jake," she said defiantly.

"Call me David, okay?" he asked. "That's my name. I gotta concentrate on my driving right now, and you calling me that screws me up."

"Jake . . ." she whispered so low he couldn't hear.

"What?"

"Okay," she said. "David." But she kept hold of her necklace, rubbing her thumb over Jake's face, just to remind her of the truth. The car skidded slightly, and she grabbed Maisie. This part wasn't fun; she didn't want him to feel any more nervous than necessary.

"Thanks," he said.

They didn't talk. He gripped the steering wheel with both hands, driving one mile at a time. The gas gauge had dipped below a third, and there didn't seem to be any sign of a main road anywhere. The logging trail just kept winding along. Although they were on flat terrain, the mountains rose all around them.

"What are these mountains?" Sage asked, looking at the red rock ridges and soaring purple peaks. She was certain she had a poster of this exact scene hanging on her wall; her father had sent it to her.

"We're in the Wind River Range."

"How far away are we?" Sage asked.

"Twenty, fifteen miles . . . I'm not sure."

"The DR Ranch," Sage whispered to the baby inside her. "We're almost there. Almost there!"

If David was her brother Jake, what would she call the baby? She could still name him "Jake," or she could call him "James." Suddenly, it seemed possible that the baby was a girl; Sage could call her "Rosalind" after her awesome target-shooting grandmother.

"Oh!" she said, feeling a twinge. "What a strange coincidence."

"Don't start again." David's eyes looked tired from staring into the blinding snow. More storm clouds had started to gather over the mountains, boiling up into dark anvil shapes. He was right — another storm was coming. "No more about me being your twin brother."

"That's not what I meant." Sage reached beneath her.

"Then what?"

"Just that, I was thinking hard about my baby and his name and being so near the ranch, being almost home . . . and I'm pretty sure that my water just broke," Sage said, bringing out a wet hand.


James and Daisy had spent an hour cantering along the main road, keeping their eyes open for Sage. A snowplow sped by, spraying wet snow ten feet in the air, creating drifts a story and a half high. James waved at the driver; he had once been employed — as had many local men at one time or another — as a hand on the DR Ranch.

Daisy wanted to ride slowly, taking it easy on Scout. Every so often she would stop, so Scout could rest. Daisy would dismount, shading her eyes as she looked around.

She'd watch and listen, taking in the cloud patterns in the blue sky and cedar formations on the sandstone ridges. Wind rushing through the pine boughs would bring her hope and peace. The white moon in the daytime sky meant protection and watchfulness. Drawing circles in the snow with a broken stick, she put a dot in the center of each one: James knew they symbolized members of their family. Daisy had magic in her heart, and she never gave up. James wished he could say the same for himself.

James didn't know what he believed. For years he had been operating on autopilot. It had been a long time since he'd found meaning in clouds or snow — if he ever had. For over a decade, running the DR Ranch, he'd been phoning his life in — showing up in body only, leaving the details to Paul March.

But this morning, something had happened: Seeing the snow geese, a part of him had cracked open. Making them fly hadn't been his idea; it had come through him from somewhere else. Was someone — God, the Great Spirit, a higher power, the ghost of Louis Shoulderblade — telling James to wake up? James had never been big on prayer. His mother had taken him to church when he was young, but he'd stopped believing in God — in anything — round about the time the roof had caved in on her.

He hadn't been planning to ask Daisy to marry

446

him that morning, but the words had come out of his mouth — and she hadn't said no. Right now, watching Daisy write in the snow — circles around circles, letters spelling "SAGE" and "JAKE" — James hung on to his saddle and felt hope spreading through his body.

Just then, a blue pickup passed by, headed in the direction of the ranch. James watched it drive past about fifty yards, hit the brake lights, and turn around. Sensing danger, without really thinking, he gave his horse a light kick. The big black began to move slowly, and James maneuvered himself between Daisy and the road. The blue pickup came back.

The truck seemed to gather speed, but as it approached Daisy and James, it slowed down. James watched the driver's window roll down. His stomach tightened, ready to react. Todd Rydell poked his head out, and James wasn't sure whether to relax or get ready to fight.

"Hey, James," Todd said. "Hi, Daisy."

Shielding her eyes against the sun, Daisy smiled. "Hi, Todd."

"What're you doing out here?" James asked. "Thought you were doing deliveries for some outfit in Lander."

Parking his truck, Todd climbed out. He wasn't dressed right for the weather — not even for driving around. He wore boots too low to do any good, a lightweight jacket that would have him frozen to death if his truck ever decided to break down somewhere remote. James knew that was why he had never made it working on the DR — why he'd never make it as a rancher anywhere: He didn't have any common sense.

But right now, the thing James noticed most was Todd's pallor. He had a jellyfish look to him — pale and soft and somehow floppy, as if whatever backbone he had, had gone right out of him.

"Got something I need to talk to you about," Todd said, looking upset and guilty.

"What's that?" James asked.

"Maybe you and I —" Todd began. He was going to suggest the men stand aside, talk out of earshot of Daisy. But James shook his head.

"Whatever you want to say, say it in front of Daisy."

"James —" Daisy backed away. "It's okay."

But James crossed his arms, shaking his head. "What, Todd?"

"Shit," Todd said, as if he didn't really want to talk. "It's about Alma."

"Alma?"

"Tammy's sister," Todd said. "Does health care — Louisa hired her to help out with Dalton's recuperation."

"The woman at the house," Daisy said.

"Yeah. Alma." James had done his best to block out the fact they had one more Rydell — or near-Rydell — living under his family's roof. "I know her. What about her?"

"Look," Todd said. In spite of the cold, sweat was pouring down his face. He wiped his sleeve across his brow. His eyes had always been evasive, and right now they darted around, everywhere but James's face. "You and I haven't always gotten along. The sheep and cattle stuff, and you and me personally —"

"We haven't always gotten along," James repeated, squinting. Something bad was coming: He could feel it inside. The way Todd was talking, trying to squirm out of whatever had happened — James thought back to the months after Jake had disappeared, how Todd had constantly apologized for not finding him. He had been on the scene, one of the men riding the roundup. Part of the search party, he had stayed out two solid days looking for the little boy.

He had apologized to James, and Tammy had asked forgiveness from Daisy. It had struck them as strange and upsetting, and they had done their best to steer clear of the Rydells from then on.

One time — about a year after Daisy had left him — James had gone to the Stagecoach and run into Todd. The recriminations had started up: *If only I'd looked harder. I'm sorry. Can you ever forgive . . .*

The emotion had shot through James like a freight train and he'd asked Todd: *If it's not your fault, why do you keep saying you're sorry?* Right there with Louisa singing down from the stage, James had decked him. Todd had fought back, bottles breaking and fists flying. Then Todd had asked the real question: *How do you live with yourself, knowing you lost your kid?* The fight had ended fast after that — James knocking Todd to the ground, trying to kill him with his bare fists like the godless man James had turned into.

"Todd," Daisy asked now, sensing the same trouble brewing. "What have you come to tell us?"

"Alma Jackson has two sons," Todd said.

"So what?" James asked.

"They're bad kids," Todd went on. "They both are, both brothers. Been in juvey hall for drugs and stealing, one's there right now. Alma thinks the other one worships the devil, wants to be a mountain man. When she took this job, taking care of Dalton, I told her — make sure he doesn't find out you're here. She needs the money bad, or I wouldn't have told Louisa to call her."

"How old are they, her sons?" Daisy asked, her voice soft.

"Teenaged." Todd couldn't meet Daisy's eyes. He was even whiter than before, as yellow pale as dirty snow.

"They're young . . ." Daisy said.

"Well, he found out she's working on the ranch. His father spilled the beans, I guess. He called his mother, and Alma told Tammy."

"What's his problem with us?" James was staring at Todd across the top of Daisy's head.

"The kid's had the idea for a long time now that the land should belong to Rydells. I know he's not family by birth, but with me and Tammy being married, I guess he figures he should have a piece. Calls himself the Guardian — guardian of Rydell land."

"How'd he get that idea?" James asked, feeling hot as he imagined Rydell holiday dinners, the whole crummy clan sitting around the turkey, grousing about how the Tuckers had run them out two generations ago, plotting how to get even.

"Never mind that." Todd wiped his brow. "The point is, he's here right now."

" 'Here'?" James thought of the Polaroids, the tracks, the campsite, the dead steer.

"Somewhere on the ranch. Hiding out, I guess."

"How long's he been here?" James asked, thinking back to problems last spring and summer.

Todd shrugged. "I don't know. The only reason I heard anything is that Alma talked to Tammy. Her boy — his name is Richard — knocked on your father's kitchen door one night."

"What'd he want?"

"Food, I guess. To go in and look around."

"Did she let him?" Daisy's voice was thin.

"Let him?" Todd asked nervously.

"Let him in — give him food."

"No." Todd was vehement, and he shook his head for emphasis. "No, she did not. She sent him packing."

"I wish she had let him in," Daisy said, gazing up at the mountain. "How old is he?" she asked again.

"I dunno — sixteen, I guess."

"I hate thinking of him out there, being hungry," Daisy said, scanning the trees along the ridge.

James had seen the brutal evidence: If this kid was responsible for killing the calf and steer, he wasn't going to worry about him being hungry. Instead, his concern was for Daisy. Even now, he didn't like her standing out here in the open. And where was Sage? If they had an enemy, James wanted his family inside, where he could keep them all safe till the kid was caught.

"So." Backing away, Todd seemed as uneasy and nervous as before — as if he couldn't wait to get going. "I just wanted to let you know. It's not my fault — he's her son, he's always had problems — if I'd known —"

"Not your fault." James stared at him . . .

Tripping over his own feet, Todd went down on one knee. His useless boots had submerged, and now he sank into the snowdrift. Pulling himself out, he scrambled into his truck and drove off. James watched him go, hearing the tires hiss over the plowed pavement.

"That was strange," James said. "Is it my imagination, or does he feel more guilty than he should about all that?"

"I wonder . . ." Daisy held out her hand, so Scout would come closer. The horse nuzzled her from the other side, as if she wanted to keep Daisy safe. A white stream of exhaust trailed behind Todd's truck.

"That kid is here, somewhere on this ranch,"

James said. "And he hates us, wants what we have. Guardian for the Rydells — God. Is that enough for Todd to feel guilty over?"

"Alma was staring at Jake's picture," Daisy said. "I saw her."

"What?"

"She couldn't take her eyes off him."

"That doesn't mean anything." James wondered why Daisy would mention it now.

"Remember how we suspected Todd, back when Jake —"

James didn't like the wild look in her eyes, the direction she was heading with her question. "Daisy," he said, holding her hands.

"Remember, though?"

"We didn't have any answers," James said calmly. "That's all. I didn't like Todd, he didn't like me — it was easy to look at him. What reason would he have had to take our son?" But Daisy had started him thinking.

Images of bullet holes and blood filled his mind: This month alone, someone had butchered one of his calves and a steer. James knew a lot about hate, and he understood that that was what it had taken to pull the trigger, wield the knife. Don't let it be true, he thought. Don't let the truth of what happened go this way . . .

"I'm thinking something crazy," Daisy said, trembling harder as she raised her eyes to James's.

"Don't," James continued, holding her hands. "Just think about Sage. She'll be here soon."

"What if?" Daisy asked. "That's all. What if?"

453

"Daisy, don't do this."

"The age is right —"

"Don't."

"Oh, what if . . ." Daisy whispered.

James grabbed her hard, held her against himself till she stopped talking and he started asking the questions of himself, the what-ifs, one after another.

What if Daisy was right, and Alma had been staring at Jake's picture? What if Todd had only pretended to search, had taken Jake away? What if Todd's nervousness today — the guilty look in his eyes — went all the way back thirteen years? What if he'd had that much hatred and resentment inside him, passed it to the kid who was out there now — somewhere on the ranch?

Daisy was electric. James could feel the tension filling her body, making her quiver against James's chest as if she were being electrocuted. Running his hands down her back, he felt her buzzing. She was charged — on fire — with the idea their son might be — could be — alive. The possibility gripped her, shaking her from the inside out, and now that the thought had her, it wasn't going to let go easily.

Clutching Daisy, James knew what it was like: He had lived with that electricity, the constant possibility of Jake Tucker one day walking out of one of the canyons, for every minute of the last thirteen years.

What if their son was alive? And he hated them?

# Chapter Thirty

David held the wheel and tried to focus on driving. That was all he cared about right now. The kittens were mewing, hungry as bears, and he hated to hear hungry animals. Petal was still whimpering from him and Sage yelling before, but he couldn't stop to comfort her right now. He had a pregnant girl sitting beside him, the snow was about to close in again, he didn't know how passable the roads were up ahead, and her water had just broken.

"Maybe I just peed," she said, her voice high and excited. "I was so keyed up, I just didn't even notice — I should have asked you to stop."

"You didn't pee."

"Are you sure? How do you know — I think maybe —" She chattered nervously.

"I'm sure," he said. Growing up on a puppy farm had taught him many things, not least of all what amniotic fluid smelled like. The barns had been soaked with it, and many nights since he'd left there, David had dreamed the odor in his sleep.

"It can't be," she said, clutching her belly. "It's too soon."

"I know." He gave the car a little more gas, as

much as it could take on this ice.

"But what will happen," she asked, letting out a panicked whimper, "if the baby comes too soon?"

"Don't think about it," David said, reaching into the backseat, fumbling for the paper bag containing the kittens' things. If he kept Sage distracted, maybe they'd get to help in time. He figured they were closer to the DR Ranch than any medical center. He hoped someone there would know what to do.

"Here," Sage said, clicking her tongue for the kittens to come. She was trying to fill the bottles, but in her anxiety, she'd spilled most of the formula on her lap. The cats didn't care — they began lapping right off her coat. Maisie scrambled up to join them.

"Are you okay?" he asked.

"I'm fine," she said. "And I'm sorry to say this, but you're wrong. It wasn't water breaking, it was something else. So let's get back to other things, Jake. Like your memories . . ."

"Let's not," David said, pushing the car a little faster. Sunlight sparkled on snow and ice, hurting his eyes. The mountains loomed high on the right side of the car, and he knew that within the hour, shadows would fall and make the driving worse. Plus, clouds were starting to form overhead. Sage was breathing hard, as if she were exerting herself in some new way. Her body knew what her mind would not admit.

"Jake," she said. "I've been thinking."

"Stop calling me that."

"Listen, okay? Just for a minute — you're adopted, right? And then when you were three or four, you got lost in a cave?"

"Yeah, so what?" He still remembered the cave — the darkness full of yellow eyes, the sound of his own voice echoing against the rocks as he called for his mommy and daddy.

"What if those two memories are the same? If they happened at the same time?" Sage asked.

"They didn't —" David didn't want to hear her stupid theory anymore. The idea of coming from her perfect family was too nice to even consider — when it turned out not to be true, he'd feel like driving this old car off a cliff. On the other hand, the more she kept talking, the more distracted she'd be.

"What if they did?" Sage pressed. "What if you weren't an infant when you got adopted by the puppy farm family — but older? Three or four."

"I was a baby when I went to live there. They —" He had been about to say "they told me," but his memory stopped him short: He had been calling *Mommy, Daddy!* in the cave — he could hear it now, ringing in his ears — but he had never called his adoptive parents by those names. He had called them by their Christian names, same as he did now.

"Tell me," Sage said. "I know you remember something."

"Nothing."

"We're twins — I know you're remembering."
But she let it go. She just held the kittens, trying
to feed them, a scared look on her face. "Oh,"
she said suddenly.

"What is it?"

"Aaahhh!" she cried. Bending double, she
nearly crushed the kittens and Maisie. They
scattered, jumping into the backseat with the
dogs. Sage rocked back and forth, moaning in
pain. David checked the road, the sun in the sky,
and he put the pedal down harder. Sage
moaned, her breath tangled in her throat. He
wanted to reach over, help her through, but he
was afraid to let go of the steering wheel.

"Sage, breathe."

"I am." She was crying.

Straight ahead, he could see a real road. Cars
and trucks were going by, slowly, but at least
moving. The logging road had another hill in it
— a long slope down, on the dark side of the
mountain's shadow. David tested the brakes.
They caught, making the car fishtail a little.
Good — if he could just steer straight and not
panic.

"Oh, Jake," Sage cried.

"We're almost there," David said. He gripped
the wheel. This had been his uncle's vehicle. His
uncle was well-off compared to his family, and
he seemed full of guilt or something about the
way they lived. He hadn't been back since the
time he'd threatened to take David away, but he
did things like send them money, clothes, and

458

this old four-wheel drive.

"Owww," Sage breathed.

David remembered looking out in the driveway one day, seeing the car parked there. He'd been so excited — thrilled to think his uncle might have come back to visit. Hope had been scarce on the puppy farm, but David remembered his uncle as kind and fun. Someone who used to play with him, to ask if he was okay, who wanted to protect him from the bad stuff. Also, who had saved his life in the cave.

David had taught himself to drive in this car. At fourteen — way too young, but that far out in the boondocks, who was going to know? His parents hadn't minded — they had liked the fact he could now haul sick and dying animals to the burial ground, go on late-night puppy runs, drive errands to places he wouldn't likely be stopped. The terrain was often muddy or icy; he had learned to use four-wheel drive the way other kids learned to ski.

They had made him kill the runt litters and sick mothers — too old or used up to reproduce anymore. Whenever David closed his eyes, he saw those plaintive faces, heard their whimpering pleas, heard the whack of the ax. He had been his parents' executioner, killed more dogs than he could count.

As soon as he could — in August, when he'd saved enough money and hoarded enough food — he had taken Petal out of her pen. Then he'd stolen his uncle's car and run away. He hadn't planned his crusade at first; all he had known was he was never going back to the farm. But the more he drove, the more he saw Petal looking at him with gratitude for saving her, the more David had known his mission in life was to help dog mothers.

And girl mothers, he thought, glancing at Sage . . .

"This hurts." She met his eyes across the seat while bent nearly in half. "I'm having bad cramps — the worst I've ever had."

"Contractions."

"No, it can't be!" she said, her face knotted with emotion and pain. "It's too soon. It takes nine months. I'm having cramps — from something I ate. I'm having terrible, terrible gas. Those wheat puffs —"

"You're having the baby." David kept his eyes steady on the real road as his uncle's car cruised them safely down the washboard slope, the last quarter mile of logging trail that had taken them through the central wilds of Wyoming. *Mommy! Daddy!* It was weird, how his own distant voice seemed to be getting louder in his own head.

Dalton thought of those frontier movies, where the mortally injured hero — arrows sticking out of him, blood pouring from the gashes — drags himself home through the canyons and across the range, hanging on through the last half-reel in order to save the goddamn family farm. Well, that's how Dalton felt today. Clinging with every shred of memory he had left to the fact that he had to talk to the lawyer at nine A.M. and make things right for Louisa, dragging himself — bleeding — through the morning.

His thoughts were slippery things, like trying to hold an armful of snakes — serpents slithering off into dark corners the more he tried to hold on to them. And just about as nasty, too: Wills, death, and memory loss were not pretty thoughts. But if he didn't take care of this now, he might forget forever.

Alma came skulking in, her washbasin sloshing with water. Dalton sat upright in his chair, resenting the intrusion so much he damn near lost his purpose. He had been holding a slip of paper on which he'd written, in his spidery hand, "lawyer." With Alma setting up her portable barbershop, Dalton stared at his note and forgot what it meant.

"What the hell's this?" he asked, staring at the word. When she tried to read it, to help jog his memory, he grabbed it away. "Never mind," he said. Then he remembered. "Bring me the phone," he said.

"I have to get you shaved."

"Well, that's nice of you, but I've got business to attend to first, young lady."

Alma narrowed her lips, biting them from inside and drawing her mouth in like an inside-out purse. She wasn't a looker, poor woman, and biting on her lips like that just made things worse. She had sallow skin, overplucked eyebrows, and an unfriendly disposition. Dalton hoped maybe being around Louisa would help her out disposition-wise. Right now Alma looked about ready to collapse.

"The thing is," Alma said, twisting her hands, "I have a family emergency. And I'd like to attend to you first off, so I can —"

"First off," Dalton said, interrupting her, "hand me the goddamn phone. You want to see a family emergency, I'll show you one if I don't make this call."

Her lips thinning even more, Alma let out a volcanic sigh and went to drag the phone across the study. Dalton kept staring at his note, just to stay clear-headed. His broken leg stuck out in front of him, symbolic of those arrows from the frontier movies — reminding him that every minute counted. Dalton had to do this last half-reel right.

Alma came over with the phone, and Dalton had to send her straight back to the table to get his address book. He told her to look up Harding & Powell, and if she knew that was Dubois's finest law firm, she gave no indication. Directing her to dial the number, Dalton waited for her to leave.

"Water's getting cold," she said, testing the shave basin.

"Make it nice and hot again," he suggested, killing two birds with one stone — getting rid of her and assuring himself of a hot shave. "That's a girl."

Wayne Harding and Dalton Tucker had been doing business for fifty years, and Dalton's father had used Wayne's father's services for fifty years before that. Wills, trusts, contracts, deeds, commercial transactions, it didn't matter: Tuckers called Hardings. Just as, on the ranch, the Tuckers had always used Marches for foremen: Paul now, his father, Asa, before him. Some partnerships endured. Although Wayne had recently been elected probate judge, he still did work for Dalton.

"Dalton, it's good to hear your voice," said Wayne Harding.

"Good to hear yours," Dalton agreed. They made the requisite small talk about snow, cattle, court, and families. And then Dalton explained what he wanted. Wayne listened carefully, not interrupting once. He knew about Dalton's loyalty to James and his love for Louisa, and he understood the complicated history between the Tuckers and the Rydells.

"Let me make sure I have this straight," Wayne said. He had been taking notes, and he read some of them back. "You want to give Louisa a life estate in the DR Ranch — that is, the right to stay there for as long as she lives."

"Yes," Dalton said. Although his mind was fuddled, he trusted Wayne completely, and he knew that Wayne would carry out his wishes to the letter. He felt he could start to relax a little now, not hang on to every detail so tightly.

"She will have no actual ownership, no right to sell or pass it on to her heirs . . ." Wayne allowed himself a chuckle and a little aside. "That'll be sure to delight Todd and Tammy Rydell."

"Let's make sure of that," Dalton said. "No Rydells smiling at the reading of my will."

"None?" Wayne asked.

"None!" Dalton pounded the arm of his wheelchair for emphasis.

"Well, Dalton, Louisa's a Rydell."

"Damn." Dalton loved her so much, he always almost forgot.

"You could change that," Wayne said, chuckling again. "Make an honest woman of her and marry her."

Dalton squinted. He'd thought of that, only about fifty million times. God, he knew how happy it would make her: the ring on her finger, the walk down the aisle . . . she'd make a beautiful bride. But then Dalton saw himself — the groom — withered and be-casted, sitting there in his wheelchair in a morning coat and top hat, his scowling son James standing at his side, holding the ring and Dalton's dentures on a little pillow.

"Bull crap," Dalton said. "You had to bring that up, didn't you?"

"Got you thinking," Wayne laughed.

"Shit-fuck." Dalton's heart was heavy as he swore: Rosalind's portrait was glaring at him from the bedroom down the hall. He wished he could walk right over and close the door.

"You're an old romantic," Wayne said. "Jennie's always said so. Every year she's a little more disappointed not to get a wedding invitation. See you and Louisa properly married off."

"Twenty-eight years she's waited," Dalton said. "Now she'll have to wait twenty-nine."

"Okay," Wayne said, laughing. "Let me draw up a draft, and I'll run the new will out to you this week."

"Make it Tuesday rather than Friday," Dalton told him. "I'm not getting any younger. And listen, Wayne. There's one more thing . . ."

Dalton lowered his voice, explaining the details. Wayne wrote everything down, repeating it word for word. He promised to be in touch with the proper tradesman, have the document drawn up to be signed along with the will.

Hanging up the phone, Dalton was ready to be shaved. He saw shadows down the hall, caught sight of Alma with someone — a young man. She was pleading with him — holding her hands out. Her family emergency, Dalton thought; she's brought it here. The young man's posture was familiar to Dalton: brash, arrogant, too busy to listen. He brushed her off, trying to walk away. Dalton had acted the same to many women many times.

"Young fellow!" Dalton called.

The man turned to look.

"Come here!"

"Richard . . ." Alma begged, tugging the

stranger's sleeve.

"I'm the boss around here," Dalton said. "Come here when I call you."

The young man stood straight and tall. Even from ten yards away, Dalton could see the sneer on his skinny face. His hair was long, brown, and dirty; he was dressed in layers of filthy woolen rags, and he was holding a gun.

"What do you want?" he asked.

"Who are you?"

"Mr. Tucker," Alma said helplessly. "This is a family matter — between me and my son."

"I'm the Guardian," the young man said, pushing past his mother to tower over Dalton. "That mean anything to you?"

"No, should it?"

"You've taken what doesn't belong to you." The young man looked wild, his green eyes glinting. Staring at his gun, Dalton lunged forward. Imprisoned by his chair and the cast on his leg, he couldn't reach the intruder.

The young man laughed.

"You're an old fool," he said. "I could shoot you if I wanted, but why waste a good bullet?" Turning, he strode away.

"Richard!" Alma wailed, running after him.

"Get back here!" Dalton roared.

Launching himself out of the chair, Dalton tackled the stranger. His leg was on fire, but he had to defend his home and family. They rolled across the floor, the gun between them. Dalton gripped the intruder's arms, but the man broke away. Swearing, he punched Dalton in the head.

To Sage, the rest of the trip was a blur. She had never known such pain. With an epicenter low in her torso, it radiated outward in searing, agonizing tidal waves. This was unnatural! People weren't made to withstand such a thing! However horrendous it felt to Sage, it had to be worse for the baby inside: How could a tiny infant live through such a human earthquake? Trying to grip the door handle just for something to hold, her fingers wouldn't even close. Attempting to say the name "Jake," she could only manage "Aaaaarrrrrgh!"

"Hang on, there," he said, speeding them down the road.

"I can't. I can't."

"Breathe, Sage."

"Oh, God," Sage said through clenched teeth. She was in the middle of what Jake claimed was a contraction, and right now she was inclined to believe him. It felt like being bitten by a bear, shaken from the inside out. "Remember the bear?" she asked, spitting out the words.

"What did you say?"

Sage gritted her teeth, tears rolling down her cheeks. She couldn't speak just now, but she was thinking of her scariest little-kid memory: Once she, her brother, and their parents had gone camping in the mountains. Their father had gone off to get water or something, and a grizzly bear had started attacking the tent. Sage had been tiny, but she still remembered the grizzly's teeth: huge, dripping fangs coming through their tent flap. She could feel them chomping down now, right on her insides.

"Thought you said something about a bear," he said.

*I did,* Sage thought, biting down on her sleeve as the car hit a frost heave. "Aaaa!" she cried.

"Ever seen a grizzly?" he asked, talking fast as if he could distract her from the contraction. "I got attacked by one once. Almost, anyway. I barely remember, but it was a mother grizzly with her cubs. She was meaner than spit. I'm not kidding. She had claws as big as bananas. Fangs that looked like spikes."

"I was theeeeerrrrrre," Sage wailed, picturing the exact same terrifying sight. Of course they would both remember it. Three-year-old twins seeing an angry grizzly bear — that would haunt their nightmares forever!

He didn't understand, or at least he chose not to reply. He just kept driving, passing slower-moving pickup trucks. Sage had the impression of great speed, of flying down a road between mountains. She thought of Ben, wept because he wasn't with her. Their baby was going to be born, and he should be holding her hand, brushing her hair back from her face. Like families on TV: where the father cares and the mother gets to cry — but not too much, because there is so much to be happy for.

"Oh, Ben," she moaned.

"You calling me 'Ben' now?" he asked, trying to joke. "Better than 'Jake.' "

The contraction passed, thudding away like horses disappearing through a distant pass. Sage gripped her belly, wondering what could possibly be happening down there. It still hurt, but not like before. In spite of the deep snow outside, she was soaked with sweat. And she couldn't stop crying.

"My baby's father," she explained. "I wish he was here."

"I'm sorry," he said.

"We didn't get to go to Lamaze classes," she said.

"What are those?"

"Classes," Sage said. "Where parents learn how to have babies."

"Huh."

"I wanted us to be together," Sage cried, rocking in her seat. "I wanted him to be my birth coach."

"Your *what?*"

"My birth coach." Sage wept. "If these were really contractions, he'd be timing them with a watch, telling me how great I'm doing. He's the father, he cares about the baby more than anyone but me. Oh . . ." She gritted her teeth again, feeling the epicenter starting to rumble.

"They're really contractions," he said solemnly. As Sage glanced over, she saw that he was concentrating almost as hard as she was, watching the road and flooring the accelerator.

"I . . . wish we were there," Sage said. "This is happening fast. I need my father. I need him now . . ."

"We're almost there," he said. "Look —"

Sage blinked, through tears and increasing waves of pain, and there she saw: the gates of the DR Ranch.

Stone pillars flanked huge white gates, swung open to the world. Sage scanned the horizon for a house, but all she saw were boulders and trees. She knew the ranch was huge, but she needed home right *now.*

"Help," she gasped, panicking, fumbling across the seat for something to grab.

"I'll help," he said.

"You can't," she sobbed, the contraction getting ready to dig in. "You don't know what Lamaze is. You never even heard of a birth coach before. You don't believe you're Jake. I need my father!"

Still patting the seat for a handhold, Sage felt his hand. He thrust it into hers. "Squeeze. Squeeze hard."

"Ooooh, what if we don't make it?" Sage wailed, afraid of the contraction. It was really starting. It might be as bad as the last one, or it might be worse. But she squeezed his hand with all her might, and somehow that made things a little better. The animals were silent, Maisie and all six kittens lined up on the seatback behind her, as if they were her cheering section.

"I've brought you this far," he said. "You

think I'm gonna drop you here? God, Sage. Hang on, we're —"

"Almost there?" she asked, crushing his hand.

"Not almost," he said, hitting the gas. "We're *there* —"

She hurt so much and felt so scared, she almost forgot to be grateful he was with her. She thought of her bear memory, wondered whether it really had been the same grizzly as his. Suddenly, somehow, it didn't matter whether David was really Jake or just an amazing stranger. She didn't care. He loved animals, he called good spirits, he was bringing her home. Angels came in all sorts of packages.

That's why, when she looked at him now, she knew it was somehow going to be okay.

"I'm not going to make it," she said.

"Sure you are —"

"Now." She felt everything shift inside, knew that her baby was going to be born fast, right this minute. "I'm having the baby right now."

He stopped the car and stared down. As if she had done this before, Sage was already spreading her legs when the contraction took hold.

# Chapter Thirty-One

After James had gotten Daisy safely to her small house, he rode out again. Shielding his eyes, he scanned the land for the kid Todd had told them about. James had found the Jackson boy's prints in the canyon twice before, so he rode through there now.

Riding under the Rydell cliffs, James stopped to look up. He tried to picture his grandfather driving another man's sheep to their deaths below. When spring came, the cattle loved to graze here — seemed to think the grass tasted better than anywhere else on the ranch. Those sheep bones had flavored the grass with calcium, and the cattle couldn't seem to get enough. Dalton had been a little boy, helping his father kill the sheep. Paul's father, Asa, had been there, too.

James sat on his horse, staring up at the rocks. They were red and craggy, forming ledges, chimneys, and chutes. As he scanned the cliff, he imagined the sheep hitting those ledges on the way down, wondering how his grandfather could have done it. He thought of his own father seeing the lambs' eyes, hearing their screams. And just then, James Tucker saw the steer's head.

It was impaled on a dead cedar tree, about twenty feet up the cliff. The birds were at it — he had seen them, thinking they were flying to a nest. The head, pecked half-clean by crows, gaped at the DR Ranch with hollow eye sockets. James gazed up, tracing the route the kid had taken to put it there: He had trekked the original sheep trail along the eastern side, across a narrow rock bridge, along the steep ledge to the gnarled tree. The perfect spot for a self-appointed guardian.

Shaking his head, James thought about climbing up to knock it down. Ice slicked every rock surface; it would be like trying to climb glass. He saw other things hanging up there, objects he hadn't noticed before: a calfskin tied to a branch, two large animal skulls, a pair of longhorns, and a "No Trespassing — DR Ranch" sign that James hadn't even noticed missing.

"Jesus Christ," James said. The kid had put a lot of effort into his display. James wondered how many times he, Paul, or the others had ridden past here and not looked up. He thought of the bloody history of this land: tribal battles, the slaughtered sheep, now this Rydell-revenge show. Having seen the dead steer and calf, he knew the kid had a gun, and he felt exposed and uneasy, out here in the open.

His stomach ached, and he knew it wasn't just because of his butchered livestock. He kept thinking of Daisy's eyes, the hope and brightness he'd seen in them when he'd left her at home:

"What if . . . ?" she kept asking.

Asking himself the same question, James couldn't stand the answer. What if the boy was Jake? Staring up at the skulls and sign, James tried to imagine his son putting them there. The effort it would take to kill the animals, steal the sign, assemble the shrine: hours and hours of intense work. Fueled by hatred poured into him by Rydells, talking against Tuckers and the DR Ranch all these long years . . .

"Help!"

The word echoed down the rocks, and at first James didn't know where it came from.

"Help, anyone!"

He heard it again: a boy's voice, strong but frantic. Behind it, the ungodly wailing of what he first thought was a wild animal but then decided was a young girl. The recognition shot through him, primitive and powerful: The voice was his child's. *Sage*. He kicked his horse and galloped around the sharp red promontory toward the ranch's main drive.

He saw a familiar old black car stopped dead in the middle of the road, the windows fogged up, the front passenger door open. Heart pumping, James galloped across the frozen snow. He saw small animals — dogs and cats — cowering by the back tires. A girl's legs protruded, and a boy stood between them, looking wildly over his shoulder. His pose was that of a doctor or a rapist. Gritting his teeth, James went for his gun.

Daisy was too excited and stirred up to sit home alone, waiting for James to return. She needed to talk to someone about Todd's warning, about her own dawning hope. She ran up to the main house and walked into the kitchen, where she found Alma Jackson talking to a young man.

"Oh," Daisy said, putting the brakes on her boot heels.

"Richard, go —" Alma said quickly.

The teenager froze, eyes darting around for a hiding place. But once he saw it was too late, he stared straight at Daisy.

Daisy stood still. She stared at him, her pulse racing. He was about five nine, with a thin face and a sparse reddish-brown beard. His brown hair was shaggy, but looked as if he had cut it himself recently. He wore ratty clothes that hadn't been washed in a long time, several layers of long underwear showing under the sleeves of his brown corduroy shirt.

"He's just leaving," Alma said.

"He doesn't have to." Daisy took a step forward. "It's cold out there."

"Ma, I'm goin'," he said, head down.

"I'm Daisy Tucker." Daisy put out her hand. She told herself she'd know by his touch. Her heart was in her throat, waiting for him to extend his arm. Every heartbeat sounded like a drumroll in her ears.

The boy met her eyes. His were dark green,

hard and flat. Daisy felt afraid of those eyes, but she smiled at the boy and kept her hand out. Staring at his eyes the entire time, she searched for some sign that he could be her son. She wanted the eyes to soften and smile, to show some sign of life. But they looked like nail heads in a hard face.

"Tucker," the boy said, without shaking her hand.

"You must have been cold out there." Daisy finally dropped her arm. "Your uncle told us you'd been camping. You're the Guardian, aren't you?"

"The what?"

"The Guardian. Todd told us."

"My uncle —" he said. Confused, at least his expression changed. It didn't soften, but it transformed, sparking those dead eyes dark with rage. He directed it at Alma, speaking into her face. "You talked to Tammy?"

"When he knocked last week, I was so shocked. I hadn't known he was here, and to have him out in that weather," she explained to Daisy, terrified. "I only let him stay in the basement, never the rest of the house. And only a couple times!"

"Goddamn stupid woman." The boy shook Alma's arm. "I told you to keep quiet. Opening your mouth to Tammy — Ma!"

Daisy moved to pull him away from Alma, but then he wheeled and walked away. His face was bright red, and she could see the cords popping out on his neck.

"Mothers worry," Daisy said, swallowing. "That's all she was doing."

"Hell with that," he said, knocking into the table as he turned toward her.

"I should know." Daisy raised her eyes to his face, into his frightening, bleak, blank eyes. What made his eyes look that way? Daisy wanted to touch him: If there was any connection, she would feel it. "I have a son out in the mountains."

"Mrs. Tucker . . ." Alma said, her tone pleading, beseeching. "Leave us alone. Go back to your —"

Daisy blocked Alma out, and concentrated on the boy. She tried to forget the darkness of his eyes, tried not to imagine what had happened in his life to cause such a death of spirit. Rage showed in his muscles, his posture, the tendons in his thin neck; but his eyes were dead. Daisy tried to tell herself this could be her son, her baby, that she could love him no matter what, and love could melt anything. What if, she kept thinking . . .

"My son is lost in those mountains," Daisy said. "I think of him every day."

"You lost him," the boy sneered. "I know. My Uncle Todd told me the whole story."

"It wasn't on purpose. I wouldn't have lost him for the world. I loved my son with my whole heart. I still do."

"Tuckers love money and cattle," the boy

said. "Right, Ma?"

"Richard," Alma begged.

"Rydells and Jacksons know how to take care of each other," the boy went on. "We wouldn't have lost a kid."

"Richard, no." Alma's expression was wild, the thin skin around her eyes purplish. Standing between the boy and Daisy, she faced Daisy. "He's just talking. I need this job — Tammy set me up, and I rightly appreciate it. He doesn't belong here. He's going soon. His father drinks, all the time, ruined this family. But that's no excuse for him being here now . . ." Her voice trailed off.

"He was cold outside," Daisy said softly. "I understand." Then, turning back to the boy, she spoke directly to him. "Are you hungry? Wouldn't you like something to eat?"

"Ain't eating no Tucker food," he snarled. "And my dad never ruined our family. Least when he's around you don't talk shit against us —" He shoved Alma now, jabbing his fingertips into her collarbone. "Better stop it."

Daisy stepped forward. She couldn't stand seeing violence against anyone, even someone she liked as little as Alma.

"Stop," Daisy said. "Don't hurt her."

Touching the boy's arm, she felt coldness. The cold ran through her like icy stream water as she got him to turn toward her. She scanned his face, looking for any sign that he could be hers. Nothing — none of his features — appeared familiar. The twins had looked so much alike at three; nothing about this boy reminded her of Sage, told her he was Jake Tucker.

"Stay out of my family business," he said to Daisy.

"What did I do wrong?" Alma asked. "Rocked you in your cradle, sang you to sleep."

"Wasn't no singing I can remember. Shut up, Ma."

"Loved you from day one."

"You shouldn't be here, Ma." He pushed her again. "It's disloyal to Uncle Todd."

"You're just a Jackson, not a Rydell." Alma shook her head. "And in neither case do you have any place here. Now get yourself home before you turn out worse than your brother." Her chin began to wobble. "Here I am in a caring profession, just trying to help a person in need —"

"What about me?" he exploded. "What about when I was in need? Cut and bleeding, and I had to fix myself. Got scars so ugly no one can stand to look —"

"I know, honey. Lord, I wish —"

"Like a snake down my backside," he said. "Down my leg, thick and ugly because the cut never got washed out and I never got stitches. Where were you?"

"I should've been there."

"Damn right," he said. "But you had better things to do."

"I've made my mistakes." Alma spoke quietly,

as if she didn't want Daisy to hear these family stories. "I should have been there that time and others. Life with your father . . . sometimes I had to get out of there, Richard. I'm sorry."

"Don't go blaming him," he said, his face twisting into a snarl. "You could've made a nicer home and he might've stayed."

Daisy looked from Alma to the boy, and any last thought she had of his being Jake went out of her. She knew mother love when she saw it, and she saw and heard all Alma's sorrow and grief for having failed her sons, and she suddenly knew the boy was hers. Daisy looked at the boy's shark-flat eyes, and she shuddered.

" 'Stayed,' " Alma explained to Daisy. "His father was in prison half the time, drunk the other. Todd was a father figure. I let Richard get pretty attached to him, and look where it's led."

"Your Uncle Todd is concerned about you," Daisy said, still trying to smile. "He told us."

"Us?" the boy asked. "You and the rancher?"

"Yes," Daisy said. "We want to help you, James and I —"

"Wouldn't take your help" — the boy said, suddenly grabbing his parka and making for the door — "if I was dying."

"Don't die," Alma pleaded, starting to cry, pulling at his arm.

"Don't worry." Richard flung her off as he stormed out of the house. "*I* won't."

Watching him go, Daisy could have felt relieved. He was mean, and he frightened her, but as the door slammed, Daisy felt her heart drop. He could have been Jake. She had wanted it to be true. As troubled as he was, she believed that if he were her son, all the injustices and cruelties of the past could be set right. That's what love can do, Daisy believed: heal anything.

Anything at all. Hurt, sorrow, suffering, horror, loss, separation, torment — love could cure it all. She hadn't thought it would be easy or quick; she wouldn't expect results or returns. But Daisy Tucker was patient and steady, and she had faith in the power of love: If that boy — Richard Jackson — had turned out to be her lost son Jake, Daisy's love would have softened those hard, hurt green eyes.

But he wasn't Jake.

"Help! Mister, help!" the kid yelled.

The girl's wailing was high and horrible. James kicked harder, driving Chieftain faster, the horse's hooves smashing through the ice crust. The boy crouched down, intent on his work. Twice, calling for help, he had looked backward. But suddenly he was hunched over again, face-forward and focused, seeing that James was on his way.

David heard the rancher riding up, but he just stayed crouched between Sage's legs, giving all his concentration to getting the baby out. He had seen many puppies born on the farm, and he had been present for the birth of his mother's real son, so he had known, when these last contractions began, that Sage's time was now — that there wasn't any chance to get to any ranch house.

"Aaaaaah!" Sage moaned. "It hurts!"

"The baby's coming," David said. "You have to push now. Can you hear me, Sage? Can you do it?"

Sage didn't waste her energy on words. Her face red and twisted, she bore down, trying to have her baby. David had his gloves off, his hands cupped and ready. When he saw the tiny head, he took hold of it. The infant was as small as a puppy, tinier than any human child should be.

The horse galloped up, and then the hoofbeats stopped. David heard the big man jump down out of the saddle, come marching over through the crisp snow. He heard the sharp breath as the rancher saw what was happening.

"Sage?" the man said, his voice breaking.

Sage couldn't hear, or if she did, she couldn't look up. She just held on to the front seat, having her baby. David's heart was pounding. He didn't trust or like ranchers; their work was too close to what happened on puppy farms. They raised animals to trust them, then used them to make money. But this was the DR Ranch, and he was Sage's father — the man she had come three thousand miles to see.

"She needs help," David said, not wanting to turn around, let go of the baby's head.

"Let me help her, then," the rancher said. He

threw his leather gloves down on the ground and stood beside David. David waited for the man to get into position, moving his big hands toward the baby, hovering in place just long enough for David to see them shaking, then slide them around David's hands onto the baby's head.

"Oh," Sage groaned through clenched teeth. "Oh, God."

"You're doing fine, sweetheart," the rancher said. "Just a little more. That's right."

"It hurts. Daddy, it hurts."

"I know, sweetheart. Push if you can. Just a little more. There, there you go. That's it."

David took a step back. The animals were all huddled by the back wheel, keeping each other warm while not straying too far from Sage. David crouched beside them, letting the dogs climb onto his lap and the kittens inside his jacket. They squirmed around, wanting to get settled. David closed his eyes.

"Oh!" Sage screamed. *"Ouuuuuccccchhhhh!"*

"One more," the rancher said. His voice was so kind, full of love. David hadn't thought ranchers — or fathers — could sound this way. He heard him talking to Sage, her answering back, as if they had been together all these years instead of separated most of her life.

"My baby!" Sage cried. "Is he born? Is he okay? Oh, please . . ."

"Oh, God," the rancher whispered.

"My baby," Sage wept, holding out her arms.

"Give him to me. Oh, Daddy. Oh, Jake, I want my baby!"

David looked over. The rancher held his hands around the baby's tiny head and shoulders, and David could see what he had known the minute he had touched the baby's head: Sage's baby was being born dead. David's heart lurched. He had seen dead puppies, but nothing had ever made him feel like this. Sage was waving her arms, and he couldn't even bear to look at her.

The rancher had tears running down his leathery cheeks. He had the baby out, and he held it in his arms, trying to breathe into his mouth. The baby's head and limbs lolled, but the rancher hardly seemed to notice. He ripped at his own front, unbuttoning and pulling his coat and jacket off. Throwing the blanket and sheepskin to David to tuck around Sage, he kept trying to save the baby.

"Live, please," the rancher said, his voice cracking. "Please."

"Daddy, give him to me!" Sage breathed.

David jumped up. He wanted to help, but he didn't know how. Sage and the rancher seemed out of their minds. Now the rancher was pulling off the flannel shirt he had on. His arms got stuck, and he held the baby crooked in his left elbow, but he finally shook the shirt off.

"Did I have a boy?" Sage asked. "Or is she a girl?"

The rancher had pulled a knife from a sheath

on his belt. With it, he cut the umbilical cord. Swaddling the infant in his shirt, he kept trying to make it breathe. His arm muscles were huge, bigger than the baby. David felt afraid of the energy in the man's eyes. As he watched, the rancher knelt down in the snow.

"Sage," he said quietly.

The girl was nearly hysterical, but at the sight of her father holding the baby, she started to calm down. David watched their eyes meet, father and daughter, and he saw the smile of joy dawn in Sage's eyes.

"Daddy," she breathed. "It's really you."

"Sweetheart," he said. "You had a boy."

"I did?" she asked, her voice high and thin, reaching around the sheepskin jacket he had laid on top of her to hold the baby.

"He was too small," the rancher said, his arms trembling. David stood behind him, staring at the tense muscles in his back. It was frigid out, but the rancher didn't seem cold at all. He talked in a steady, quiet voice, taking his time. "He was just too small. He didn't make it."

"Didn't make it?" Sage asked in disbelief.

The rancher shook his head. David shuddered. He remembered his first puppy: When it had died, his father had told him to throw its body in the trash and stop bothering him, he was watching the Nebraska Cornhuskers. Staring at the rancher, bare-backed in the snow and not even flinching, David wondered about life.

"He's beautiful," the rancher said. "He looks like you."

"Can I hold him?" Sage reached out.

The rancher nodded. Leaning into the car, he placed the dead baby in Sage's arms. Once he was in there, it seemed too much for him. He kissed the top of the girl's head, embracing her and the infant. When he pulled himself away, he had tears all over his face. David watched him step back, giving Sage a minute alone with her baby.

"She needs help," David said again.

"I know," the rancher said. His cowboy hat had fallen off, and a gust of wind blew it skidding across the ice. He stared at David, assessing him. "Can you ride?"

"I can drive. This is my car."

The rancher didn't question him. "I'm not leaving her to ride home. Take my horse, and I'll drive the car."

"Forget it," David said, not trusting any rancher alone with Petal, Gelsey, and the others. "The animals need me. I'll drive, but I'll give you a ride. Is the ranch far?"

"Three miles."

David herded the animals back into the car, the rancher climbed in behind Sage, and they set off. This trip was almost over: David would get Sage to safety, and then he'd leave.

# Chapter Thirty-Two

Louisa loved to rehearse with the greats. She would choose a CD by one of her favorites — Patsy Cline, Loretta Lynn, Reba McEntire — and sing along with her headphones on. Sometimes she sang with Garth Brooks, sometimes with Waylon Jennings, occasionally with a recording of herself. Usually it picked her right up, but the fight with Dalton had her feeling downcast, and not even singing helped. Quitting her session early, she went into the kitchen for a cup of coffee and found Daisy and Alma standing there.

"Who's with Dalton?" was the first thing Louisa asked.

A guilty look crossed Alma's face, but only for a second. She was too busy staring out the window. "Where'd he go? Oh, I wish I could have talked him into going home, where it's at least *warm*."

Louisa watched Daisy walk over to Alma, put her arm around her shoulders. Together the two women stared out the window. Alma's posture was ramrod-stiff, as if she didn't want any part of Daisy's comfort, but Daisy was undeterred.

"He's so young," Daisy said. "To be out there

alone. I know, I know how you feel."

"It's a heartache," Alma said, breaking away. "That's all I can say. You do your best, work yourself to the bone, and it's not enough. He sees his father acting like a brute, and that's good enough for him. Excuse me, while I see to Mr. Tucker . . ." Bowing her head, she hurried out of the room.

"What was that all about?" Louisa asked.

"Her son was here," Daisy said.

"Doesn't seem to have lifted her spirits any."

"No."

"Yours, either."

"No," Daisy said. She looked so frail, standing by the window, looking out at those big, snow-covered mountains. Such fine bones, such sorrow in her posture, the attitude of waiting hanging on her like a black shawl: Daisy looked like a country-western-song heroine come to life.

"Usually I love snow," Louisa said. "But this is a downbeat day. I tried singing, exercising — nothing's helping."

"It's funny," Daisy said. "Riding with James, I felt happier than I have in . . ." She trailed off, as if counting back years. "I got my hopes up, I guess."

"About you and him?" Louisa asked.

"About everything," Daisy said, her voice low.

Louisa nodded. She knew all about that — blind optimism, Dalton used to call it. Louisa would expect the best without believing the facts. She would plan a picnic and count on the sun, no matter what the weather map said.

"I was hoping for a miracle," Daisy said. "That Jake —"

"Jake?" Louisa asked, confused.

"Never mind." Daisy shook her head. "Sage is my miracle. She always has been. I don't know what I'd have done without her all this time, and now — I don't know if I can wait another day. I really don't think I can —"

Looking out the window, Louisa saw the big black car come careening down the drive. It was old and rusty, with a reinforced bumper held on by baling wire. Fishtailing on the ice, it nearly crashed into a cottonwood tree. Louisa saw Daisy's back stiffen, watching the car's crazy progress.

Screeching to a halt by the main corral, the driver threw open his door. He jumped out and ran around to the passenger's side. Daisy just stood riveted, her eyes wide, watching. He was slight, brown-haired, in black jeans and boots. He grabbed the passenger door handle, yanked hard, got it open.

Louisa saw James climb out — shirtless, holding a small bundle. He carefully handed the package to the brown-haired boy, then turned back to the car. Very gently, as if he were handling a butterfly, he lifted a young girl from the front seat. He picked her up, held her against his chest, carried her toward the house. The girl held out her arms, and the boy placed the bundle in them. A parade of animals emerged from the car, thronging around the boy's feet.

"Maybe you don't have to do that," Louisa said to Daisy. "Maybe you don't have to wait another day."

But Daisy was long gone. She had flown out the kitchen door the second she'd seen the girl. Louisa remembered Sage from toddlerhood. She had seen many pictures over the years — the school photos, the holiday snapshots — and she would have known the child anywhere.

Louisa watched Daisy fling herself at James, getting as close as she could to Sage. She was kissing her face, her hands, as if she could climb right into James's arms and be carried along with their daughter. Louisa saw the strange boy, left out of the family group.

"Dalton, your granddaughter's here," she yelled, heading for the study. They had fought before, but if this wasn't cause to let bygones be bygones, what was?

She found him leaning against his chair, his cheek red and swollen.

"Sweetheart —" she began, running to him.

"Louisa." He grabbed her hand. "There's a maniac in the house."

"Alma's son — did he do this to you?"

"All I could think about was you," Dalton said. "Protecting you. Getting to the phone to call the police."

"Oh, Dalton." Louisa hugged his head to her

chest, too moved for the moment to tell him that Sage had come home.

Daisy clung to Sage. She wanted to hold, examine, and smell her child — fill her senses until she could believe it was true, that Sage was really here. James cradled her in his arms, meeting Daisy's eyes over Sage's head as they stumbled through the ranch yard. Daisy might have expected to see elation in his face, but instead she saw grief.

"What is it?" she asked, suddenly feeling cold.

"Inside," James said, striding through the snow toward the door.

So thrilled and shocked to see Sage, Daisy had barely noticed that James wasn't wearing a shirt. It was twenty degrees, snow was starting to fall again, and James was bare-chested. Now she saw Sage was wrapped in his sheepskin jacket, and her nose was buried in James's bundled-up flannel shirt.

"The baby?" Daisy whispered.

James nodded.

Daisy's heart stopped. She stood still, watching James carry Sage ahead, waiting for it to start again. Her breath caught, and her blood was frozen. Daisy had spent the last weeks sweating and dreading Sage's pregnancy, what this baby would do to her life, how it would rob her of all her chances. Now, watching Sage sob over the tiny inert bundle, Daisy felt cold sorrow pour over her.

"Sage." Daisy ran to catch up, her heart thudding again.

"Let's get her inside," James said, his voice rough.

They ran up the path — Daisy and James carrying Sage and the baby. When they got to the door, James paused, and Daisy was too wrapped up in Sage to grab the latch. Suddenly the strange young man stepped up, opened the door. James hurried in with Sage, and for one moment, Daisy and the boy came face-to-face.

Daisy stared into golden-green eyes. They were as hot as the other boy's eyes were cold, and Daisy could feel them wanting to look after Sage. Instead, the boy turned them on Daisy, and he took her in, starting at her hair and moving down to her feet and coming back to rest on her face. The sensation of being scrutinized was strange, but Daisy found herself doing the same thing to him. He had light brown hair, wide eyes, and the shadows of masklike markings on his forehead and cheeks.

"Are you her mother?" he asked.

"Yes," she said. "I'm Daisy Tucker. Thank you —"

"She talked about you," he said. "A lot."

Daisy opened her mouth. She had to get to Sage, but she couldn't take her eyes off the boy. His face was very solemn, tanned from the sun and wind, and for a moment he reminded her of a shaman. Peering at the marks on his face, she touched the dots above his left eyebrow.

She recognized the symbol. "Protection."

"Sage said —" he began, surprise lighting his eyes.

"What?" she asked, being pulled to Sage, but feeling compelled to know why he looked so shocked.

"Nothing." The boy was frowning now. "Just — Sage said you'd know." He backed away, getting ready to leave. As he touched the door handle, Daisy caught sight of the owl tattooed on his wrist. The yellow eyes were bright and mesmerizing, and for a moment she weaved, as if hypnotized.

Inside, Sage's voice became louder. She had been crying softly, and now she said the name "Jake" over and over again.

"That's what she named the baby," the boy said.

"Thank you for being with her," Daisy said, wanting to keep him there, needing to go to Sage.

"Tell her good-bye." The boy backed away from the door.

As Daisy moved toward Sage, she heard the door close behind her. James, sensing Daisy's approach, stood up and backed away from Sage. "She needs you," he said.

Daisy nodded, holding his arms as she moved around him.

"Where is he?" James asked. "The boy."

"He left," Daisy said, and for some reason saying the words made her feel empty.

"I've got to catch him." James grabbed a jacket off the rack and ran back out. His voice was anxious, as if the boy had something James needed to get back. Daisy hoped he'd be able to stop him, but she blocked out the wish and turned to their daughter.

Sage, still wrapped in her father's coat, was huddled on the daybed by the woodstove. She clutched the baby, whispering into his ear. Daisy sat beside her, not touching her, giving her this minute with her child. His features were perfect, waxen, tiny as a doll's. Daisy gazed at his lips, his nose, his ears.

"This is my son," Sage said.

"He's beautiful," Daisy whispered.

"I knew he was a boy," Sage said. "The whole time."

"You did?"

Sage nodded. She hadn't looked up at Daisy, wouldn't take her eyes off the baby. She touched his chin, kissed the soft dark hair on his round head. Now she smoothed the hair down, as if preparing to show him off. Glancing up, her eyes were wide open and expectant.

"I didn't know you'd be here," Sage said.

"I had to come," Daisy said. "So I could see you the minute you arrived."

"Would you . . ." Sage began, with some hesitation, "like to hold him?"

Daisy swallowed. She had to take a second to compose herself before answering, but she had already reached out her arms. "I would love to."

494

Sage passed the baby to her mother. Daisy took the tiny infant, warmly wrapped in James's navy flannel shirt, and held him to her heart. Oh, God, he was so small, but he felt so heavy to Daisy — he was a real little person, a true boy, a human being. He was her grandson, hers and James's.

"I love him," Sage said, leaning on her mother's arm to peer into the face of her son.

"I know you do, sweetheart."

"He was born too soon," Sage wept. "He's too small."

Daisy closed her eyes. She held the baby to her breast, kissed the top of his head. Old memories came flooding back, of holding the twins when they were born. They had come nearly a month early, and their birth weight had been so low — four pounds for Sage, four pounds, one ounce for Jake — the doctors had been worried.

They hadn't been much bigger than the baby Daisy held in her hands. Tears rolled down her cheeks, into the baby's hair, and she sobbed for what might have been. She had wished that Sage weren't pregnant, but she would never have wanted this to happen. She cried for herself and Sage, for their lost sons.

"I'm sorry." She wept, tenderly handing the baby back to Sage. "I'm so sorry he couldn't live."

"He was with me all this time, through so many nights — I thought we'd be together forever," Sage cried. "With him, I felt whole again.

I named him Jake, but . . . I wish I hadn't."

"Why?" Daisy smoothed Sage's damp hair. "I love that name."

"Because now it feels . . ." Sage burst out, starting to sob again, "as if I've lost him twice."

They cried together, holding each other with the baby between them. Daisy felt Sage clutching the body, grasping him tight as if she thought someone would come along to take him away from her.

"You have no idea," Daisy said, shaking Sage as she held her. This wasn't the time; she was supposed to be calm and steady and only sympathetic, but hearing Sage cry about her lost baby, Daisy was unable to contain herself anymore. "No idea how worried I was about you. I thought I'd lost you! God, Sage, I was so afraid I had lost you, sweetheart. Like I'd lost your brother — didn't you know?"

"Did you see him?" Sage gulped.

"Who, honey?"

"Jake."

Daisy was confused. Hadn't she just held him, given him back to Sage? Had her tirade mixed everything up? But when she asked as much, Sage shook her head. "The boy I was with —"

"The one who drove you home?"

Sage nodded.

"I saw him. Why?"

"Did he remind you of anyone?" Sage asked.

Daisy thought. She pictured his green-gold eyes, his brown hair, the shape of his head. Her skin tingled. Those beautiful eyes, staring into hers as he held her cheeks between his small, flat hands . . .

"He has tattoos," Sage told her, "that remind me of your drawings."

Daisy began to tremble, picturing the owl — his feathers, his startling eyes. Once again she pictured the boy's face, his own hazel eyes. Her heart began to race, and her mouth was suddenly dry.

"I kept telling myself he was *him*, Jake — but I must've been fooling myself. Like I had to believe it or something."

"But he reminded you of —"

"Mom," Sage said softly. "Don't be mad, but can I be alone with him?"

"With your baby?"

"Yes."

Sage stared blankly at her dead infant, as if she had absorbed all she possibly could, as if all the emotion had drained out of her.

"Of course," Daisy said, kissing her head.

"I wish David had been my twin brother. It doesn't matter now; it just seems crazy."

"What seems crazy?"

Sage spoke through exhaustion, still clutching the baby, the words tumbling out. "So many coincidences seemed to fit. We're the same age. We met in the West. We kept saying the same thing at the same time, and we look alike. He draws so much like you . . . I missed you so much. I guess I wanted to think he was my brother. But mostly, he knew that word, that name you used to say for courage . . ."

"What word?"

"The name. Washakie."

"Oh, God," Daisy said. And she ran outside.

James caught up with the boy as he was loading the animals back into the car. One of the dogs seemed to be sniffing the snow, finding the right spot to relieve herself, and the boy was just holding the door open, waiting. James relaxed a little and approached more slowly.

The teenager, aware he was being watched, raised his eyes slowly. He regarded James with suspicion and something just short of contempt.

"Hey," James called. "I want to talk to you."

"We're out of here," the kid said. "C'mon, Petal. Hurry up."

Now James focused his attention on the dog. It was a tricolored pit bull, white, black, and brown. Her big jaws were clamped down on a ratty old toy as she kicked back clumps of frozen snow, finished with what she was doing. Then she hopped up into the car. James walked over and caught the boy's wrist.

"She called you Jake before."

"So what? She was having a baby. She was mixed up."

"Did you tell her that's your name?"

"My name's David," the kid said coldly.

"David what?"

"Just David," he said, trying to yank his arm away.

Thinking of Todd Rydell, of what he had said about his nephew hiding on the ranch, James held him tighter. He didn't know the circumstances of how this kid had met up with Sage; he had seen him helping her, and he believed that he meant her no harm. Had he figured out who she was, grabbed the chance to present himself as her brother?

James didn't know — none of it made sense to him. But he could see from the kid's expression he didn't think much of James, and that was a Rydell trait. Plus, he was positive he had seen this old car before, years ago, that it belonged to someone he knew. Now the kid started to pull harder, clearly wanting to get away.

"Hey, man," he said as James tightened his grip. "What's your problem?"

"You like to hurt animals?" James asked, thinking of the butchered calves and steer.

"What are you talking about? I help animals —"

James stared into the car, at the cowering dogs and frisky cats. As James bent his head to look in, the Scottie and spaniel started to cry. The pit bull dove under the seat. Someone had beaten those dogs, to get them whimpering like that. "You're a liar."

"You're full of shit," the kid said, shoving James in the chest.

That was all it took: James felt the fight sizzling through him. He wished the kid were bigger, at eye level; he wished he were older than sixteen. The desire to deck him took hold, and he had to step back. Breathing hard, he looked hard into the boy's eyes. They were bold and green, flecked with gold fire. The boy was defiant, but wary, as if he sensed James's emotion.

"I had a son named Jake." James breathed the cold air, looking up at the mountains to calm himself down. "I don't like people using his name."

"I save animals," the boy shot back. "I don't like murdering ranchers telling me I hurt them."

"You kill a steer?" James asked.

"Kill a *steer?*"

"That's right."

"No."

"You shoot some calves this summer?"

"I told you — I don't hurt animals." David rubbed his wrist. Then, sounding like someone very young, he added, "You do."

"Me?"

"Yeah. You breed calves and treat them kind, and then you sell 'em off for hamburger."

"Not my favorite part of the job," James said, eyeing the kid in a new way. He sounded like a man of conviction, not someone who'd kill a steer and cut off its head.

"*You're* the liar," the kid said. "You just want to make money. Anyone who raises animals does it for the same reason. I know — my parents did it."

"This your parents' car?" James asked, leaning down again to look inside.

"Yeah," David said evasively.

"They know you have it?"

"Yes."

"They don't, do they?"

"They do."

"What are you doing out here on your own?" James asked. "I should call the police on you. This thing's so rusty, it's probably not registered. Is it? That, plus the fact you're — what? Seventeen?"

"Sixteen." The kid flashed him a thrilled, wicked smile — as if he'd put a big one over on James.

"Sixteen years old, and driving my little girl around in the snow. You could have run off the road."

"I saved her," David said.

"Yeah, you probably did. But you could have killed her."

James began moving around to the other side of the car. The kid's mouth was half open. He looked upset, probably trying to think of something to say, to convince James not to report him, too distracted to notice James opening the passenger door.

"Hey, what're you doing?" David dove into the car to grab James by the forearm. "Stop — put that back!"

But James had pulled open the glove compartment, started rifling around for the registration.

He found it, long expired, he was sure, in a yellowing envelope. David's fingers scrabbled, trying to get him to drop it. James was tempted to let the kid go. He obviously wasn't the butcher, and James was grateful to him for helping Sage. But James was thinking of his parents. Whoever they were, wherever they lived, they must be missing him. They might be half crazy with worry.

"You're going home, buddy." James stuck the old registration in his pocket. He grabbed the car keys at the same time, climbed out of the car.

"Don't, mister," the kid said, chasing him.

"Sixteen's too young to be on your own. Your parents deserve better."

"You don't know." David's tone was dangerous and pleading at the same time. "Gimme the keys. Please —"

"Come on in here," James said, opening the barn door. There was a phone in the tack room. He thought of Sage and Daisy up in the house, didn't want to disturb them with this. He wanted to go to them now, but this seemed so important, he had to make this call first. If he could save another set of parents one more sleepless night . . .

"I don't want to go back," David pleaded. "Don't send me back."

"Things can be worked out." James fished the registration out of his pocket. "You can talk to them. They'll be mad you took the car, but —"

David grabbed for the registration, extreme

strain showing in his face. James held the paper out of reach, wanting to open it so he could read the name, call information for the right number. David was grunting, trying to reach the envelope, but James caught sight of something happening behind him.

Paul came driving into the yard, talking on his truck radio. Gesturing at James, he beckoned him over.

"Give it to me," David said, climbing James's arm to get the registration. "Come on, please."

"James!" Paul called, climbing out of his truck. "There was trouble up at the house. Dalton called the police, and —"

James turned slightly to face Paul. "Trouble?" he called.

"Some young guy with a gun. I'm thinking it's the one who —"

James must have dropped his arm along with his guard, because suddenly he felt David grab the registration and keys from his hand and bolt. He fled out the barn door toward Paul.

Right on his heels, James expected Paul to do the honors: with all the trouble they'd been having, what choice would he have but to stop a fleeing boy cold? But instead, it was David who stopped himself. The snow had started falling harder — James knew it was time to go inside with his family, finish the business with strangers — but David's voice stopped James in his tracks.

"Uncle Paul," David said, sounding shocked. "What are you doing here?"

# Chapter Thirty-Three

James couldn't believe his ears. He stopped short, watching David look up at Paul March. Paul's color drained away and his expression was pure shock. His eyes had been trained on David; suddenly they wanted to look everywhere but at him.

"We've got to get out there, James," Paul said, as if David wasn't standing right in front of him. "Search the ranch."

"What did you call him?" James asked David. When the boy didn't reply at first, James looked at Paul. "What did he call you?"

"Nothing. I don't know." Paul was ashen.

David said nothing. James's pulse picked up — just a little. He stared at David for a long time, and his heart began to pound.

"It's a mistake," Paul said. "Mistaken identity, whatever. Right?"

James watched David's face. His eyes had looked happy for a moment — seeing Paul had made him start to smile. But now the happiness was gone, replaced by an angry scowl, and then a stone mask. Watching him shut off his feelings, James knew: He'd done it himself all these years. In counterpoint, James's own emotions were running high. His throat hurt — too much to swallow or speak. He had just remembered where he'd seen the black car.

James looked at Paul. His voice wavered. "That old Willys you had. What'd you ever do with it?"

"What the hell's that got to do with anything?" Paul asked, slapping his thigh. "The guy's out there, James — the one's been killing our stock. I told you. Dalton saw him with a gun."

"The Willys Jeep," James said, the fire starting in his chest. He tried not to look at David. "You gave it to your sister, didn't you? Lives up Appleton way?"

"James . . ." Paul said, licking his lips.

"Your sister June — her husband's some sort of farmer?"

"Raises dogs," Paul said. "Marshall raises dogs. Never mind about that old car — it was shit. The kid made a mistake, calling me that. Now, about —"

James's arms were shaking as he lifted them to take hold of the boy's shoulders. He could hardly breathe: The fire was banked, and his body was charged with the urge to kill. But right now, turning the boy called David around, James looked into those cool green eyes and, feeling his own heart crack open, asked, "What's your father's name?"

"Marshall Crane," David said, staring down at his feet.

James could barely speak. His hands were

shaking and he stared into the sullen boy's face. He saw faded lines and dots on the skin, like faded warpaint. "You called Paul your uncle. Is that what you meant to say?" he asked when he could.

"Yes," the boy said. "He's my mother's brother."

Was it possible? James began to tremble. He thought of Sage's story, and he held the boy at arm's length, remembering the day he'd lost Jake: He had been sitting on that rock in the canyon, smiling and waving as James rode off after the stray. James's last sight of his son had been over his shoulder, riding fast after a charging steer. He would know him anywhere. Suddenly, the color of this boy's eyes, the shape of his face, the curve of his mouth all came together in James's mind into the face of a smiling three-year-old boy.

"Sage called you 'Jake' on her own, didn't she?" James asked, his heart pounding out of his chest.

"Yes," he said, frowning.

"She knew."

"Knew what?" the boy asked.

"Hey." Paul was pure white now. "The kid admitted he made a mistake. Now let's —"

"They told you you were adopted, didn't they?" James asked.

"Yeah," the boy said, raising his eyes.

Thinking of Daisy, of his two children, knowing everything they could have been — all of them, to each other — James couldn't stand it anymore. The fire was raging, licking his skin and his eyes and his organs. He stared at Paul, and he threw his head back and shouted: "WHY?"

"James," Paul said. His tone was steady; he had talked James out of rage, grief, near-insanity so many times before. He had been a friend — James's best and sometimes only friend. He still thought he was going to pull it off; James could tell.

"You took our son," James said, the feeling boiling over.

"James, quit this —"

"You took Jake." James grabbed Paul by the throat, trying to break his neck.

"Stop. Jesus Christ — James, let go." Paul choked, trying to get air, fighting back. He threw a punch, but James caught his arm and threw it down. He shoved Paul down on the ground, slamming his head into the snow. Paul clawed at his eyes, but James just slapped his hands down. He pounded Paul's face, seeing it smile all these years, seeing it offer comfort and friendship and solace.

"You . . ." James said, smashing Paul's mouth with his fist.

"James, stop." Paul's voice was garbled with the blood he was swallowing.

"You killed my family, Paul," James yelled, "and I swear I'm gonna kill you."

Paul broke his grip, smashed a fist into James's

ribs. He tried to scramble out, but James was filled with superhuman strength, and he knocked him back down.

James grabbed for his knife. As he did, blood came off on his hand. He stared at the hilt: It was sticky and red, and now so was James's hand. It was the blood of Sage's baby, her boy who'd been born dead, the other Jake, and the sight of it stopped James from killing Paul. Because even though that little boy was dead, there was another who was still alive.

Pushing himself up from the ground, James stared down at Paul. His face was bruised and bloody, and he lay there in the snow without trying to move. James knew there was a story to get out of him, but he also knew it didn't matter now. He turned to the boy.

The kid just scowled. He looked tough, as if he'd been living in that old black car for a long time. James took a deep breath and stepped forward. The boy kept trying to look away. His eyes would dart down to Paul, then to the mountains, then to snow falling into the trough of running water. Everywhere but at James.

"Jake." James's throat was so tight the name barely made it out.

"No," the boy said.

"Yes."

The boy shook his head harder.

"Your sister knew," James said.

The boy stood taller, not speaking.

"Sage knew."

"Just thought she did," the boy whispered. "Jake."

The boy just stared at the trough. Snow was coming down hard now, and it hit the water's surface. He stared as if mesmerized by every flake, as if the water was his enemy. James walked over to the trough, scooped up a handful of water, and drank it. Paul had put the bubbler in three winters ago, to keep the water from freezing.

"Drought's over," James said.

"What?" the kid asked.

"You should have been here this summer. So dry, we had to truck water in."

"Huh."

"But the drought's over now," James said. "It's over, Jake." He put his arm around the boy's shoulder, to walk him toward the house.

Right then, Daisy came flying across the yard. Her cheeks were pink, her coppery hair streaming out behind her, no coat and no hat. She flew toward the boy, but she stopped short as she caught sight of Paul lying in the snow. Then her gaze returned to the boy, and she looked expectantly up at James.

"Daisy . . ." he murmured, just saying her name. His mouth was dry, and he couldn't quite look from her to the boy.

"I have to tell you something," she began, her eyes glowing, edging toward him.

"So do I," he said, folding her into his arms.

"I like your tattoos," Daisy said, staring at his arms.

"Huh," he said, frowning. His expression said he bet she didn't, that she was just saying so to make conversation. Hunched over at the kitchen table, he let the kittens walk across his shoulders and the dogs curl around his legs. The animals seemed anxious in this new environment, frightened of the unfamiliar sights, sounds, and smells.

Daisy put her hand down, trying to get the dogs to come to her. They wouldn't even look, hiding their heads in the boy's shoes. The animals looked shaggy and matted, as if they'd spent weeks or months in that black car. Trying to call them, Daisy's heart was pounding. Making friends with shy animals was much easier than trying to talk to the boy she was starting to believe was her son. She had asked him what he remembered, begged him to tell her about what his life had been, but he wouldn't say a word.

"I had a Scottie when I was little," she said, holding out her fingers.

"Huh."

"Did Sage tell you?" Daisy asked. She wanted him to say more: She wished to soak in the sound of his voice, see what it did to her heart. Close up, he looked like Sage, like Jake might look if he was sixteen. But it was too incredible, too much of a miracle even for Daisy.

"What's her name?" Daisy asked.

"Gelsey."

"Here, Gelsey . . . here, girl. . . ." Daisy said. The Scottie ignored her.

"When can I go?" he asked. "When's your husband gonna give me back my keys?"

Daisy swallowed, not answering. James had given her this time alone with the boy. He was with Sage, waiting for the midwife to arrive, and he had called the police and told them what had happened. The boy — David, Jake — refused to talk. He kept staring angrily at the table, smoking cigarettes, sighing audibly like a captured man. Daisy's skin tingled, but no matter how much she wanted to hold him, she wouldn't move till she got a sign.

"I meant what I said," she repeated. "I like your tattoos."

He shrugged. Shaking another cigarette out of the pack, he stuck it between his lips and lit it. Throwing the match into the ashtray, he missed, retrieved it. But as he brought his hand back, Daisy saw him glance down at the circle-and-dot markings on his right wristbone.

"Circles are important," she said. "They're symbols of protection — but you know that, right?"

Again, he shrugged, shaping his cigarette ash on the edge of the ashtray.

"Encircling," Daisy continued. "Native people practiced it, to protect against spiritual invasion. Like, they'd walk around strangers in a circle, so their footprints would enclose any evil spirits that might have entered with the new-comers."

He stared at his hand, at the circle-dot image, then turned his arm over so she couldn't see it anymore. Daisy closed her eyes. She was repeating this First People legend as if it had no bearing on her, as if she hadn't wished a million times that she had drawn a magic circle around Jake, to protect him from being taken. When she opened her eyes, they were bright with tears.

"*Ellam iinga*," she said. "It means 'the eye of awareness,' " she said. "The circle-and-dot image."

"Yeah?" He frowned at his knuckles. They were creased and dirty, as if he hadn't bathed in a while. Daisy stared at them, remembering when they were tiny, when she had held her son in the tub, scrubbing the ranch dirt off his hands. One of the dogs started to cry, and he reached down to scratch her.

"I like your owl." She leaned over to see his wrist better. "Your feathers are so precise, and the eyes — God, they look real! As if he might swoop down —"

"He's not real," he said harshly.

"But you've studied owls," she said. "Watched them carefully. You know owls, don't you?"

He shrugged. "They're everywhere in Wyoming." That was as much as he had said so far, and Daisy's heart soared. They were going to have a conversation: She could tell him how she was an artist, how she believed he had inherited her gift, how they were mother and son and they never had to be apart again. But just then, raising his eyes to meet Daisy's, he asked, "Can I go now?"

Daisy winced, but she tried not to let him see. He was sixteen; they weren't about to let him drive away. The police were going to question him, arrest Paul, learn the whole truth of what had happened thirteen years ago. But if the boy didn't want to stay, if he wanted to go back to where he'd been living, or if he chose to go into foster care, nothing she said or did would be able to stop him.

The dog who had been crying now began scratching the floor at Jake's feet. Her claws scrabbled on the wood, as if she wanted to burrow somewhere very safe, far from sight. Leaning over, Daisy took a second to still her racing heart. Her mouth was dry, and she felt the panic of knowing that the boy sitting across from her was her son and a stranger at the same time, that he was just counting the minutes until he could get away.

But as she bent down, her head under the table, she caught sight of the crying dog, and she held her breath. It was an old white, black, and brown pit bull. Her eyes were brown, encircled by pink, and she held a filthy brown toy in her strong jaws. Breathing with the stuffed toy in her mouth was difficult, and she seemed to shudder with every exhalation. But as Daisy watched, she saw that the shudders came from emotion. The dog's eyes were red with grief.

"That dog with the toy," Daisy said, looking at Jake. "What's her name?"

"Petal."

"Why . . ." Daisy began, staring at him. "Why does she have the toy?"

He shrugged, glaring at his cigarette. Blue smoke rose to the ceiling.

"Please tell me."

"She needs something to carry," he said sullenly.

"Why?"

He shrugged. Brown hair fell in his eyes, and when he pushed it back, she saw the scar along his hairline.

"Did you give it to her?" Daisy asked. "The toy?"

He frowned harder. But after a moment, he nodded. "Yeah. So what?"

"Why did she need something to carry?" Daisy asked, her throat aching. "What is she missing?"

"I don't know."

"James said your father — the man who adopted you," Daisy's voice was soft and thin, "ran a puppy farm. Is Petal missing her puppies?"

The boy stared at the ashtray so long, Daisy thought he was hypnotizing himself. She watched him reach inside, pick up a cigarette ash, rub it on the back of his hand. She knew that if he had a needle, if he pricked his skin where the ashes were, he would have a new tattoo.

"Maybe she is," he said after a very long time. "So what?"

Daisy's eyes felt hot with tears, and her heart felt so heavy she wished she could lie down. She looked under the table again, saw Petal holding her stuffed animal, digging into the floor. Daisy reached out her hand, but Petal just cowered behind the boy's legs. Then Daisy got down on her hands and knees and went under the table with her.

"Petal," she said. "Here, girl."

Petal whimpered.

"Here, Petal." Daisy held out her hand.

"She doesn't like strangers," the boy said from above. His voice sounded nervous and curious. "She bites."

Daisy just kept her hand steady. "I don't think she wants to bite me."

Petal's eyes were wide and red with blind grief. Her toy was covered with saliva, and although she held it in her teeth, her hold on it was gentle, the way a mother dog carries its babies. Daisy remembered her first days as a mother, and she thought of Sage down the hall. But right now, her eyes were focused on the old dog behind the boy's legs.

"You miss them," Daisy whispered. "Don't you?"

Petal stared, the ragged toy in her jaws.

"You miss your puppies so much, you can't

stand it," Daisy said. "You wake up at night, and you think they'll be there. You want to feed them, and there's no one to feed. When you roll over, you expect to feel their warm bodies. That little toy — what is it?"

"Don't get too close," the boy warned. "She'll snap at you —"

"What is that old toy?"

Daisy gazed at Petal. The two mothers crouched under the table, eye to eye. Daisy stared into those red, weeping eyes and saw herself. She wondered how long it had been since Petal had last had babies, and she knew it didn't matter. Right now her gaze was fixed on the toy, as her heart started to pound harder.

The fabric was brown felt, and Daisy could see the place where the animal's eyes had been. And there, on top of its head, right where a small toy cow's horns would have been, were two tiny shreds of yellow.

"Let me see," Daisy whispered. "Please, Petal. I won't take it from you . . ."

Petal whimpered, getting a better grip.

"I knew a toy like that once," Daisy said, reaching out a shaking hand.

"Don't touch it," the boy warned. Alarmed, he poked his head down. "She won't let you."

Daisy traced the ragged old cow with one finger. Petal stared at her, all the horror in her heart pouring through her gaze, meeting Daisy's eyes. Daisy traced the seams on the cow's ruined face, the spots where its brown button eyes had once been sewn on, the dirty yellow rags that had once been proud horns.

"Jake's cow," Daisy said. "When he was born, that's what his grandfather gave him. No cute little bears or lambs or bunnies for our boy — just a stuffed cow. He loved it so much . . ."

The boy had been watching to make sure the dog didn't bite Daisy, but now his expression changed. He no longer looked alarmed or annoyed; suddenly, his mouth was half open, and his eyes were hazy with a gathering memory.

"It was covered with mud and jelly," Daisy said, still talking to Petal. "One of his horns was crooked — Jake had loved it right off. He'd use the horns for handles, to kiss the cow right on the face."

Petal had stopped digging, and she lay down, the cow still in her mouth, staring hard at Daisy. Daisy's heart was racing, and as she touched Petal's wet toy, she brought back a flood of sensation.

"Jake's cow," she repeated. "After he disappeared, I looked for it. When I couldn't find it, I knew he had to have it with him. Oh, that gave me comfort. You have no idea how glad I was to think he had his cow with him."

The boy grunted, shuffled his feet.

"But I was like Petal," Daisy said. "I needed to hold something until my son came home again. So I used his blanket."

"His blanket?"

Daisy nodded, face-to-face with Petal. "His

old baby blanket. Jake had slept with it every night. It smelled like him, it tasted like him. I held that blanket in my arms, and sometimes I'd wake up with it by my mouth. Oh, how I wanted my son back. I loved him more than anything in this world except his sister. I held his blanket and told myself that I was keeping it warm for him —"

The boy's breathing had changed. He sounded almost like Petal now, as if he was holding something in his mouth, as if he could hardly take in air.

"Holding that old blanket." Tears spilled from Daisy's eyes as she looked from Petal to the boy. "The way I hadn't been able to hold you. This toy was yours, wasn't it? You gave Petal your old toy cow."

"Yeah. But I'm not —"

"I loved you then," Daisy said from under the table, petting Petal on her head as she gazed into the boy's green-gold eyes, "and I've loved you every second since. I never stopped for a second."

"She bites," he said, watching Daisy scratch the pit bull's head.

"Not even for a second," Daisy repeated vehemently as Petal gazed on.

The boy stared at Daisy's hand on Petal's head, and he seemed to notice that Petal had gotten some relief from her terrible grief, that she was no longer huffing like a steam train, that — for this moment anyway — the understanding of another mother who had known loss had brought her some solace.

"Jake," Daisy whispered, in the dark under the table.

"I think you're wrong," the boy said, his scowl gone.

"I don't think I am."

He cleared his throat, seeming to gather his thoughts together. He petted Petal, then in turn each of the other dogs. When he looked back at Daisy, his eyes were wide, hesitant, afraid. As he stared at her, gaining courage for whatever he was about to ask, he swallowed hard twice.

"Where —" he started to ask.

Daisy waited, her heart pounding.

"Where," he asked, swallowing a third time, his voice so quiet she almost didn't hear the question, "is that old blanket now?"

# Chapter Thirty-four

Sam Whitney, the best midwife in the West, came out to the ranch to minister to Sage. Sam was thirty-five years old, with long strawberry-blond hair and warm, crystal-blue eyes. Gentle and compassionate, Sam had interned in the inner cities of Baltimore and Salt Lake City, helping many mothers even younger than Sage. She was also a superb skier and horsewoman, and she had spent a summer punching cows on the DR Ranch. She now lived on a ranch in Dubois, and when James called her, she came instantly.

Daisy had liked Sam on sight, and when Sam asked that she and Sage be left alone, both Daisy and James trusted her enough to do so. Now, while Daisy talked to Jake, and Sage was with Sam, James stood out by the barn talking to Curt Nash.

Curt was the detective in charge. While most of his officers had fanned out to search the ranch for Richard Jackson, two had driven up to Appleton, to question June and Marshall Crane. Paul sat in Curt's police car. Once James had checked the registration, found the black car still registered in Paul's name, Paul had told the whole story. He had seemed almost relieved to have the truth out.

"It's a shocker," Curt said. "You and Paul go back a long way."

"Our whole lives," James said.

"You think you know a person," Curt said, shaking his head. He was fifty-eight or so, fit and strong, a cowboy with a badge. Years ago, before he had joined the force, he had worked with Dalton and James, seeing whether he liked ranch work enough to do it fulltime. He hadn't, but he and James had stayed friendly — until Jake's disappearance. Then, for several months, Curt had considered James the main suspect.

"You thought you knew me," James said. "But it didn't stop you from thinking I'd hurt my son."

"I'm sorry about that now," Curt replied. "But Christ, we wanted to find him. Three years old, vanished into thin air: That's how it looked from our seat."

"Paul took him." James glanced over at the police car. The sight of Paul made his skin crawl. His best friend, his ranch-brother. Paul had sat with him at his mother's funeral. He had baby-sat the twins. He had helped him look for Jake . . .

"We'll know more when we question the Cranes," Curt said. "The story's hard to swallow. That he'd put you and Daisy through hell, just 'cause his sister couldn't have a kid."

James stared at Paul's profile. He had told the police that taking Jake had been almost an accident. The boy had been missing for three days.

The search party had gone through the canyon twenty, thirty times, looking behind every rock, in every chasm. Just before nightfall, while the others were beating outward from the canyon, searching in ever-widening circles other parts of the ranch, Paul had decided to ride through one more time.

He had heard Jake calling for help. The voice had been tiny and scared, far away. Paul had yelled back, told Jake to keep talking. The little boy had obeyed, doing what Paul had said, reciting his ABC's, singing "Old MacDonald Had a Farm." Tearing around, looking every- where, Paul had come up empty-handed. And then he had found the cave.

The cave's mouth was a hole one foot in diam- eter. Hidden behind a clump of sage, level with the ground, it angled down into the foot of the cliff. Rain had washed claw marks in the rock, and the hole had blended in. But Paul heard Jake's voice calling from that hole, and when he'd stuck his big hand in, a little hand had grabbed it.

Pulling Jake to safety, he'd slung him on his horse. Still hanging onto his toy cow, the boy was dehydrated, banged up from knocking into rocks, his eyes swollen nearly shut. Galloping back to the ranch, Paul had had to pass his own house. He'd been charged up, knowing the Tuckers would be overjoyed, and he'd started thinking about having kids, how they made the world go around and everything in life worthwhile. Thank God Daisy and James had had Sage, one kid to love while they kept their vigil.

Unlike Paul's sister June. She had been trying for ten years to get pregnant, and all she'd had were a string of miscarriages. Her marriage was miserable, Marshall blaming everything on her being barren. Paul had hated seeing his pretty, funny sister so disappointed with life, stuck on that puppy farm with no child to love.

Jake had passed out on the horse, and Paul had decided to transfer him into his truck — driving him the rest of the way would be easier than trying to hold an unconscious kid on horseback.

And that's when Paul got the idea.

Jake was bloody and hurt, crying in his sleep and clutching his cow from the terror of being in the cave, and Paul got to thinking how stupid it had been of James to take him on the roundup in the first place. A three-year-old kid — sticking him on a rock and expecting him to sit still. Of course he had wandered off, exploring — what the hell had James expected?

The Tuckers, Paul thought, had always had it all. Todd Rydell was right about that — but at least he hadn't had to live his whole life in their shadows. Paul's dad had been loyal to Dalton, but many were the nights he'd down a few beers and tell his kids about the shit Tuckers expected Marches to eat, warn them to find their own ways while taking the Tuckers' money.

June had left the ranch as soon as she was old enough, moved north to Appleton where Marshall's people lived. Paul and his wife were pregnant with their first at that time, and baby-sitting the twins had shown them how great kids could be. The Tuckers had everything — they were rich, they had the ranch, they still had a daughter. They were young, and if they wanted to have more kids, they could in a heartbeat. While poor June had nothing.

So, Paul had driven Jake up to Appleton. June had taken some convincing, saying it was wrong, but Marshall had been firm: He wanted a son. Both June and Marshall knew first aid, had the rudimentary veterinary training it took to raise dogs, and they had taken the boy in and cared for him like their own from that first minute. *Loved him with all their hearts,* Paul had said. Of course, as so often happens, a year later June had a child of her own. Paul had had a twinge then, thinking he should maybe bring Jake back home.

But by then it was too late. Jake had stopped crying for his parents in the night, he had started believing Paul was his uncle, that his real name was David Crane. And Daisy was leaving James, to take her remaining child back east, away from the dangers of the DR Ranch.

"He thought he was acting for good." Curt was looking over at Paul in the car.

"I don't believe that."

"What he told himself, anyway," Curt said.

James stared at Paul. For years, he had promised himself he would kill whoever had taken Jake, and for a few minutes, he had wanted to destroy Paul. He had pounded him with his fists, and he'd nearly stabbed him with his knife. A fire had been burning for thirteen years, searing James Tucker from the inside out, and Paul had started it.

But suddenly, in one day, the fire went out. Just from helping Sage, from holding her and knowing that she was his daughter, and from looking into Jake's eyes — those cool green eyes ringed with gold fire — just from being with his children, James had found peace beyond his understanding. He would never get those years back, but he no longer needed to kill the man who had taken them.

"He wasn't acting for good," James said.

"You made sure he knows that," Curt answered.

"I'm glad."

"Your side okay?" Curt gestured to where Paul had punched him. "Want to add assault to the charge?"

"Kidnapping is fine," James said. "Says it all."

"Daisy must be overjoyed."

"Yeah." James thought of how, just that morning, they had seen the snow geese flying over. He had asked her to marry him again, and she had said she would — when their daughter got home. Well, Sage was home, and so was Jake. Some things were beyond his wildest dreams, and he knew Daisy had magic in her she hadn't even touched yet.

Taking one last look at the police car, James

shook Curt's hand and thanked him. Then he turned his back, and he knew he wouldn't see Paul March again until his trial. He strode up toward the big house, where he had spent his boyhood and where his father still lived.

Every single person James loved was under that roof — right now. Daisy was there with Jake; the midwife was helping Sage say good-bye to her baby; his father was waiting with Louisa. James heard the police car's tires catch in the snow, then pull smoothly down the ranch drive. He hadn't known he was holding so much tension inside till it started to let go, as the sound of the tires receded and Paul was taken away.

As he headed toward the house, he began to run. He passed the barn, and he thought of Scout, Ranger, and Chieftain inside. He wondered if the kids would remember the horses, if the horses would remember the kids. As he ran faster, he began to sweat. He saw Daisy waving to him from the front porch, and as he waved back, he found it hurt to swallow.

James Tucker had been so cold for so long. He cleared his throat, trying to get rid of the lump. He thought of Daisy working with such intensity on her jewelry, talking to the spirit world through bones and gold. James had none of that — he had stopped believing years and years ago.

Daisy took a step off the porch. She reached for the sky, as if she could embrace it, and as she did, James saw her moving her hands, writing invisible words. Snow was falling, but at the same time, sunlight had broken through a crack of clouds, and it came pouring down.

James imagined that if Daisy's words could be read from a plane or from heaven, they would tell the reader that her daughter and son were back home. Her shoulders were wide open, her slender arms loose as she brought them up and down, around and around. The sun threw gold and copper lights in her hair; her face was glowing in the sunlight, glistening in the snow.

Watching her, the woman he still thought of as his wife, James felt peace spread all through his body. Borne by a river of his blood, it started at the top of his head and traveled down. It warmed his neck and his shoulders, his biceps and his forearms, his hands, his fingers, his spine and back, his heart and organs, his groin and thighs, his calves and shins. It radiated through the tops of his feet and the soles of his feet, his heels and his toes.

James was smiling. As he watched Daisy make signs of thanks to the sky, his smile widened. James had his family back. His children were home, and he and Daisy were getting married. He felt melted inside, and for the first time he could remember — since that day the snow crushed his mother, since his best friend had stolen his three-year-old son — James Tucker wanted to say thanks.

He didn't know how, and he didn't really know to whom. Daisy could tell him, but he didn't want to interrupt her long enough to call out and ask. Things weren't perfect — they weren't perfect at all. Sage had lost her baby, Jake didn't know whether he wanted to stay with them or not — but they were here. His family was together for now, for today; together, they were on their way. James wouldn't be this warm if life wasn't about to work out okay.

So all he did — while Daisy continued to draw in the sky and the cattle grazed on grass poking up through their own hoofprints — was to tilt his head back and take the snow and sun full in his face. The sky was white, but through that one cloud the sun was bright.

"James!" Daisy called, as if she couldn't wait another minute. "Hurry home!"

Dalton was in his wheelchair, with Louisa standing beside him, right there in their bedroom window, watching James run up the drive. Louisa had a look of warm pride on her face, as if she couldn't believe how fast James was running, as if he were her son and she loved him like a mother.

*Some things in life aren't perfect,* James Tucker thought. *And some things are.*

Staring up at heaven behind the curtain of a white sky, James searched for the words he wanted to say, and all he could think of were two, so short and so strong, straight from the spot he knew was his heart. James Tucker shouted as loud as he could, his booming voice echoing again and again off the dark red cliffs of the Wind River mountains:

"Thank you!"

# Epilogue

And when it was spring, the horses rode through the tall green grass and bright new wildflowers, down to the part of the ranch where the pony barn had once stood. The land was full of legends and mysteries, and while it would have been fun to grow up there, it was almost as great to rediscover it — as if for the first time — now, at the age of seventeen.

"It looks so different without snow," Sage said.

"Yeah," Jake agreed.

"You sure this is the way?"

He glanced over at her, his expression wry. "Want me to draw you a map?"

Sage shook her head. With more important things on her mind, Jake's teasing wasn't going to bother her today. She was on Scout, Jake on Ranger — the two oldest horses in the barn. Maisie, her puppy, ran along behind — she followed Sage everywhere.

Their father wanted them to take it easy at first. Although Jake swore he'd been riding all along — on horses at the puppy farm — their father wanted them both to get used to riding the horses that would move slowest, the horses that had known them when they were children.

He wasn't taking any chances, he said. And even though Jake did seem to know what he was doing on horseback, he didn't argue very hard.

The horses plodded along the well-worn trail, through thigh-high waves of new grass. As she rode, Sage leaned down to pluck every wildflower she could reach. The range looked like a riotous bouquet of flowers, and she already had an armful of buttercups, primroses, kittentails, and saxifrage. Burying her face in them, she inhaled the heady fragrance.

"Got enough?" he asked.

"Not quite."

"You're big on flowers."

"I know."

"You act like it's the wedding of the century."

"It is," she said. "To me."

He did what he always did when he thought something was stupid or he didn't want to think about it: lit a cigarette. Sage felt like reaching between the horses and snatching it out of his lips. What was tolerable in their mad journey down the logging road, when he was just a savior-stranger, seemed much less so now that he was her bonafide twin brother, making everyone's life miserable by threatening to move to a foster home every ten minutes.

"They were already married once," he said. "Why even bother having a wedding the second time? They sleep together —"

"Like that's the important thing."

"Then what is?" Jake asked.

"You're not planning to attend the ceremony," Sage said coolly. "So what do you care?"

Jake blew a stream of smoke into the brilliant blue sky and rode on in silence. Sage kept picking buttercups. He was right: She did go a little overboard with flowers. As her parents' wedding day — today — kept getting closer, she had gotten her mother to order zillions of white roses from the florist in Dubois. They had arrived just before breakfast that morning, and she and Daisy and Louisa had spent hours placing them in vases all over the house.

She slid a glance over at Jake. He had that intense I-don't-belong-here look on his face. She was getting to know the expression well, so well that it hardly triggered her anger or frustration anymore. Her mother had explained to Sage that even though Jake was her brother, part of the family, he had grown up apart in such a horrible place that it would take him a long, long time to feel okay again.

But she wished he would go to the wedding. He had decided not to go at all. Making everyone upset, worried that he was even more troubled than they already knew — they wanted him to see a psychologist, and he said the psychologist could kiss his ass. He had the option of living with a foster family — his so-called adoptive parents, the ones Sage referred to as the scum-sucking kidnappers, were in jail — and he frequently said he was planning to exercise his option.

Jake never seemed very happy. He kept to himself, taking care of the dogs in their corner of the barn. He skipped school half the time and didn't even pay attention in class the other half. He had six new tattoos, and it infuriated Sage that her mother had let him give her one — a tiny wolf, baying at the moon, on her right shoulder. At the puppy farm, he had often slept in the barn — first as punishment, then by choice. He liked the smell of animals and straw; he preferred his bedroll to a mattress and soft sheets. So that was where he slept here — in the barn.

Even though Daisy didn't allow him to drive, he took off on the ranch tractor whenever possible. Lately, James had been letting him drive the pickup, but only after school when his homework was done, out of sight of their mother's window. After a life of having her mother all to herself, of worshiping her father from afar, there were days when Sage truly resented the intrusion of this ungrateful, unwilling boy and wished she and her parents could just be happy and love their lives without him.

But those days were few and far between.

Now, riding Scout through the meadow, Sage stared at Jake's back. He was just a few paces ahead, leading the way down to the pony barn just because she had told him she was coming here. He had been her protector from the day they had reunited on that dark Nebraska road, and although they didn't talk about it, she knew he considered himself her protector still.

"Aren't you gonna be late for the wedding?" he called back.

"No," she said, holding her huge bouquet. "There's time."

He exhaled, as if he disapproved, but he didn't try to talk her out of it. He wouldn't: Of that she was sure. Jake had learned those first few days together what meant the most to Sage: her parents, her brother, her baby. Nothing had changed.

When they got to the ruins of the old barn — just a few gray timbers sticking up from the tall grass — Sage put her free arm around Scout's neck and slid out of the saddle. Jake had already dismounted, and he held the horses' reins as Sage led them all to the spot. She paused, gazing for a minute at the old boards, imagining where the ancient barn had stood.

"Our grandmother died here," she said.

"Don't let Louisa catch you saying that," Jake said. "She thinks she's our grandmother."

Sage nodded. She knew Jake loved Louisa. He had taken to her right away — her brash manner, her tough-talking, showy don't-mess-with-me style. Although Sage loved her, too, she felt the fine threads of family stretching back through far generations, to the sharpshooting Bostonian who had given birth to James Tucker. Sage had deep respect for the bond between any mother and the child she carried, and her throat tightened as she stared down at the broken roof beams.

"Right there?" Jake asked, following Sage's gaze.

"Yes," Sage said. "Right there."

"And Dad tried to pull her out?"

"Tried to save her life," Sage said, gulping. "But he couldn't. His leg was broken."

"Man," Jake said.

Sage was thinking of mothers who died too soon and babies who died too soon. Pushing aside the tall grass, she found the thin, new path that led to the two small crosses. The grass had been scythed along the path, and the clearing had been mowed. Sage knew her father came here once a week to keep the crosses clear.

The crosses were made of stone. On one was chiseled the name "Rosalind," and on the other, "Jake." Sage knelt in front of them, and she kissed the ground in front of the cross where her son lay. The grass smelled new and sweet, and she imagined it was the skin of his shoulder.

He had died before he could open his eyes, but to Sage he was her son, the real little boy who had brought her home. If she hadn't had this baby, she might not have come out to Wyoming. She might not have met her brother on that lonely road; she might not have brought him home to the ranch. Her mother might not have decided to follow. Sage might not have finally, after all this long, long time, been reunited with her father. And her parents' wedding might not be happening this afternoon.

Squeezing her eyes shut, Sage pictured her

father's face. It was lined and tan, and at times his blue eyes were so sad — as if he couldn't quite forget, or let go, of all those years he'd spent alone, scouring the canyons for Jake. But her mother loved him so much, and so did Sage, that some mornings her father would smile across the breakfast table, and the sadness would be all gone.

"Jake," she whispered. "You brought us all together."

The tall grasses swayed in the spring breeze, whispering like the voice of a tiny child. Sage had a little of her mother's gift, and she heard her son's voice saying, "I love you. I love you. I love you forever."

She thought of Sam Whitney, the midwife. She knew midwives were supposed to help babies be born, come into this world, but Sam had been good and wise enough to help Sage let her baby leave. If only Ben could have been there. Sage knew they were too young to be married, but she still loved him so much.

She could hardly think about him. He was her first love, and sometimes it seemed he would be her only love. At night she dreamed of his face, staring at her. He had such deep regret and longing in his face, and Sage would reach out to touch him, and he would be gone.

"Ben, Ben," she would say in her sleep, but nothing could bring him back.

She had written him a letter, to tell him about the baby. Such a long time passed without

hearing anything that she thought he had forgotten her. But then, one day two weeks ago, a
letter had arrived.

He was sorry, he said. He had never meant to
hurt her, never meant for any of this to happen.
He said he was sorry to hear she'd lost the baby,
but that it was probably for the best. For the
best; how those words had hurt! Sage had crumpled up the letter, thrown it into the garbage.
But then, after a little while, she had taken it out
again.

She had stared at his writing. The way he
wrote her name with such careful, precise letters. The way he had referred to their son as "the
baby," as if that was as close as he could let himself get. He had signed the letter "Ben." Just
"Ben." No matter how long she gazed at that
wrinkled sheet of paper, Sage couldn't make the
word "Love" appear anywhere.

Sage still loved him, though. The love wasn't
growing any smaller yet, but every day it hurt a
little less.

"Hey," her brother said, touching her
shoulder. "Are you okay?"

"Yes," she whispered, wiping her eyes. "I'm
fine."

When she was ready, she knelt and separated
two small bouquets from her enormous bunch of
wildflowers. She handed one to Jake, watched
him lay it down on her son's grave.

"Your nephew," Sage said.

"I know," Jake said. "I remember."

Sage placed the other bouquet at the foot of her grandmother's cross and prayed that Rosalind somehow knew how happy her own son — James Tucker — was that very day.

The snows had melted weeks ago, but some of the birds and animals of Wyoming had not yet finished their spring migrations. Herds of antelope and elk scrambled up mountain trails, flocks of songbirds gathered in the cottonwood trees. Watching them for a minute, Sage reached for the two gold cords that hung around her neck. One held the twins, her two-sided necklace. The other held the Owl Child.

Sage's mother had made it for Sage's baby. Carved from wolf bone, marked with circles for protection, it bore a carving of the same owl Jake had tattooed on his arm. He had sat still while their mother had copied his drawing, as patient as it was possible for him to be.

"An owl for the baby Jake," Daisy had whispered to Sage that morning, wanting to remember her grandson on her wedding day. "Because he is wise and sage as an owl, because our family owes him so, so much." Her mother had handed the medallion to Sage, placing it in her palm. "I made him the Owl Child."

Sage had cried for a long time. Holding the amulet, she thought of the years of comfort her mother's necklace had brought to her. For so long, half-gone because her twin was missing, Sage had hung on to those bone faces. Her mother told her she could keep the Owl Child, wear it around her neck with the other. But Sage had known what she wanted to do: The amulet belonged with her son, to be with his spirit and remind him of his wisdom, of what he had done for his family.

"I love you," she whispered now, kissing the amulet and hanging it from baby Jake's stone cross.

"Are you ready?" her brother asked her. He frowned, looking at the bright blue sky, as if he thought the sun was moving too fast toward the appointed hour.

"Why?" Sage teased, wiping her eyes. "Are you afraid I'll miss the wedding?"

"It's just a wedding."

"Ever been to one before?"

"No."

"You might like it."

"I think I'm gonna hitchhike to Lander," he said. "Look at cars to buy. So I can get out of here."

"You could do that another day," Sage said, climbing back on top of Scout.

"I could," Jake said, mounting Ranger and immediately lighting up.

They circled back through the long grass. When they got to the main drive, Sage saw the ranch sign shining in the sun. Brand new, bright blue with gold letters, this sign replaced the old one that had been standing since before her father was born.

"JD Ranch," she read.

"Can't believe Granddad changed the name," Jake said.

"James-Daisy," Sage said, holding on to the saddle horn. "Dad and Mom."

"At least Louisa's happy," Jake said. "She sure didn't like having old Rosalind's initial out there."

"I still can't believe she and Granddad eloped — in their own house."

"It's how they wanted it," Jake said.

"We were all there! It could have been so great!" Sage said. "Granddad's idea of being romantic is calling a judge and telling him to change the ranch's name, then 'By the way, can you marry us?' — when he was signing the papers! Poor Louisa."

"Louisa's all right," Jake said. "She's taking me down to the Stagecoach soon, let me hear the new song she wrote about it. Her and Granddad and the new sign. Louisa's name's not even on it, and she's happy anyway."

"What's the song called?"

"It's called 'I'm Mrs. Tucker.' "

"I want to go with you," Sage said. "To the Stagecoach."

"Just me and Louisa this time. She said."

"You get your way too much. Everyone just wants to make you happy, and you won't even go to the wedding —"

"What, you're not happy?"

Sage shrugged, trying not to smile.

"Look at you on your horse," Jake said. "Six months ago, you didn't even know how to ride."

"That's bull," Sage said. "I've been riding since I was born."

Jake snorted. "Not like me. You were just a suburban kid."

"It's in my blood," Sage insisted.

"Huh," Jake said. "That's why we have to ride the oldest horses in the barn, because you're such an expert."

"You know what Dad says about me," Sage blurted out. "I take after Mom, and I'm the cowboy girl."

"Mom is," Jake said, barely able to hide his smile. "Not you. Okay?"

But Sage just rode in silence, letting her brother think what he wanted.

Daisy sat in her bedroom, by the dressing table, letting Hathaway brush her hair. It was her wedding day, and she had a semi-serious case of jitters. While Hathaway smoothed each strand, weaving it into a French braid, inserting daisies at appropriate intervals, Daisy stared at her face in the mirror.

"Is that too tight?" Hathaway asked.

"Hmm?" Daisy was gazing into her own eyes.

"The braid. Am I pulling too hard? Am I stretching your face into your ears?"

Daisy laughed. "No, it's fine."

"Okay, then. I want James to recognize you when he says 'I do.' "

"Are we crazy, having a real wedding, Hath?"

"As opposed to what? A sham one? No, Daisy.

Believe me. If two people deserve to pull out all the stops, it's you and James."

"That's what I think," Daisy said. Now her gaze slid to the picture on her dressing table. Louisa had taken it just three weeks ago. It showed Daisy, James, Sage, and Jake standing by the paddock, smiling into the camera, everyone except Jake with ear-to-ear grins on their faces. "I hope he comes."

"Jake?"

"Yes. I want him to be there."

"He's his own man," Hathaway said. "An excellent tattoo artist. He's been offering to do one for me ever since I got here."

"Are you planning to take him up on it?"

"Maybe yes and maybe no," Hathaway said.

"Hathaway —"

Dropping the braid she was working on, Hathaway came around in front of Daisy. Wearing a long, full yellow skirt and off-the-shoulder white peasant blouse, she looked beautiful, ready to stand up for Daisy at the wedding. She wore turquoise rings and bracelets from her own boutique, as well as one of Daisy's necklaces and their mother's pearl earrings. The combination of patrician eastern style and rugged western style suited Hathaway, and Daisy smiled as she watched her pull up her skirt to reveal a tiny tattooed cowboy hat.

"Jake did that?"

"Yes, he did," Hathaway said, admiring her ankle. "I told him he could visit me in Silver Bay.

541

We'll set up a tattoo booth, something out of a western frontier town, for one day only. My customers will love it."

Daisy smiled. Hathaway was a good sister, a loving aunt. She had always adored Sage, and now she would have a chance with Jake.

Staring at the little cowboy hat, Daisy thought of her son covered with tattoos, refusing to go to school, sleeping in the barn. She imagined the life he had led at the puppy farm, and she hated the time they had lost. So many years of pain for both of them — all of them. And now Jake had to bear the scars. Just because Daisy loved him didn't mean she could erase any of what had happened.

"Every so often," she said, "I'd like to kill Paul March."

"I don't blame you." Hathaway held her carefully, so as not to mess up the braid.

"I'm constantly telling James to forgive, it's all we can do, but sometimes the feeling is so strong —"

"Let it be as strong as it is." Hathaway's arms felt secure around Daisy's shoulders, as if they could absorb all the rage and fury she felt for the man who had kidnapped her son. "Feel it now, and then let it go."

"I want those years back," Daisy whispered.

"You're taking them back the best you can," Hathaway said. "By marrying James today. It's an affirmation of everything you believe in."

"Like what?"

"Well, love," Hathaway said. "An open heart."

"An open heart lets in so much pain," Daisy said, wiping her eyes.

"I know."

"You've been with me through it all," Daisy said. "I don't know whether I'd have survived it without you."

"You would have." Hathaway stroked her hair. "Because of the other things you believe in."

"What other things?"

"Well, hope and faith. Compassion. All these years you've used other people's love stories to sustain you — to give you hope and faith when you'd lost your own. It's in the work you do."

"Sometimes it's been easier to have it for other people than for myself."

"That's always the way."

"Hope," Daisy said. "That's all marriage really is, I think. I lost it last time."

"Not completely," Hathaway said. "Or I don't think you'd be here now."

Daisy wiped her eyes, and Hathaway scolded her for smearing her makeup. They touched up her mascara and blush, and Daisy took the time to pull herself together, enjoy her sister's closeness. Their faces were nearly touching.

"I'm going to be a westerner now," Daisy said.

"Mmmm." Hathaway was squinting as she tried to keep the eyeliner straight.

"Live on the ranch again."

"I know."

"Far from Silver Bay."

"You want to get me going, or what?" Hathaway asked, shaking the eyeliner.

"You'll come out to visit a lot."

"Well, yes. I know that." Hathaway snorted, as if Daisy had just stated the obvious.

Now Daisy gazed back into her own eyes in the mirror. She thought of Solstice Falls, Crystal Lake, the crimson cliffs, the stunted cedars, the silver-green sage, the snow-covered swans, the endless range, and the soaring Wind River mountains. Her heart beat faster, just thinking about such beautiful country. James was here, and so were their children. Daisy was a New Englander born and bred, but she had no doubt that she was home. That this was where she wanted to be, living on the land that inspired her work and dreams.

"I love you, Hathaway."

"I love you, Daisy."

"Can I ask you a favor?"

"Anything."

"If you see Jake before the wedding, will you ask him to come? Tell him — anything. Just get him to be there."

"He will be." Hathaway returned to the braid. "I know already. In fact, I'm positive."

"How?" Daisy looked past her own reflection in the mirror to see Hathaway's deep, knowing, humorous eyes.

"Because I'm the older sister," Hathaway said, breaking into a slow, wonderful grin. "And I know everything. Don't you know that by now?"

James stood out in the barn, adjusting his black tie. His father sat in a chair, dressed in his black dinner jacket with a string tie, and Todd stood beside him, wearing a bright blue tuxedo.

"Jesus," Dalton said, watching James fumble the tie for the third time. "Didn't I ever teach you anything? Bend down."

"I got it, Dad."

"You got it all wrong, is how you've got it. Bend down here."

James crouched in front of his father, feeling the old man's fingers grab the tie, fix it properly. James stared into his wrinkled face, the concentration in his eyes, and wondered why his father couldn't be this sharp and present all the time.

"Should have taken you to more formal occasions," Dalton said. "That's what your mother would have done."

"You did fine."

"Your mother used to talk about the balls back in Boston." Dalton laughed. "Didn't have many of those around here. Not much opportunity for wearing a dinner jacket and black tie."

James glanced over at Todd, wondering how he was taking this talk about Dalton's first wife. But Todd just seemed so glad to be here, part of the day, his face was placid and smiling. Who'd have believed he and Daisy would have a bunch of Rydells at their wedding? But they were here: Todd, Tammy, their kids; Emma and Ruthie; and, of course, Louisa.

It was Daisy's idea. After the feuds and hatred that had brewed between the two clans all this time, she had asked James if he would mind inviting the Rydells to their wedding. With Louisa an official part of the family now, it seemed right to her that there should be a larger gesture of peace.

How could James say no to her? And now, as if reading his mind, his father chuckled.

"Look at us here," Dalton said. "A bunch of Tuckers and Rydells all gathered in the same place, not wanting to kill each other."

"Will wonders never cease?" Todd laughed.

"Not with Daisy around, they won't," James said.

"I knew it wasn't your idea to have us here," Todd said. "But I'm mighty glad to be here anyway."

With Louisa directing the band to tune up outside, Dalton pushed himself out of the chair and, still chuckling, headed out to find his wife. Todd started to follow, but James held him back.

"Just a minute," he said.

"What?" Todd looked startled, as if his old reflex of suspicion had kicked in.

"I've got something to say to you."

"Look, James," Todd said, stepping back. "Dalton's right, and so's Daisy. Let's let the old stuff slide for today. We're here to celebrate —"

"I owe you an apology," James said.

"Excuse me?"

James cleared his throat. He pictured that day long ago, when Jake had disappeared. With all those men milling around, all the people he could have suspected, James had focused on Todd.

"I've been unfair to you."

Todd narrowed his eyes.

"All that time. For thirteen years. Thinking you were the one who took my son."

"I knew you thought that," Todd said. "Wasn't anything I could have said to you to convince you otherwise."

"There were other things," James said, "that made me see it that way."

"The feud."

"Tuckers and Rydells, cows and sheep. Good grazing and bad —"

"The old story," Todd said with a hint of bitterness. "You saw it one way, we saw it another. We carried it to extremes ourselves. I got two nephews in jail to prove that. Alma's sorry for what Richard did, and I know she wants to make restitution —"

"Forget it." James held up a hand.

"No, she wants to pay you back the value of the stock he killed."

"I don't want her money," James said sharply. "I have sympathy for Alma. She's lost her son, and I know how that feels."

"I fed Richard those old stories," Todd said. "He took them in, and I never knew how much they affected him. He wanted this land, and he set himself up to guard it for our family. You probably blame me for that."

"I'm sorry about your nephew," James said. "I hope he gets the help he needs. But I don't blame you, Todd. The fact is, I've blamed you for too much. I never stopped thinking you took Jake. Maybe I wanted to — there was never any evidence, but I had to blame someone. See, I believed those old Tucker-Rydell feud stories as much as your nephew. I wanted to hate someone for hurting Jake, and you were the easiest one around."

Todd waited.

"I'm sorry, Todd. I was wrong."

"It's okay, James. Lot of harm's been done on both sides," Todd said.

"I want to put an end to it. Daisy and I both want to do what we can to help Richard. You know, when you first told us about him, we got to thinking he might be Jake. It gave us a weird kind of hope."

"I'm glad you got your son back."

"Me, too."

The two men shook hands. James was glad he didn't have to say more. He didn't like talking about deep things to anyone but Daisy, and he could see Todd was relieved, too. They were men of few words, and nothing much more had to be said. But the spirit of forgiveness was in the air, on both sides. Daisy was right: They had had their faith strengthened by their experiences, and now it was time to practice forgiveness. They'd be working at it for the rest of their lives.

"He glad to be back?" Todd asked as they headed out of the barn into the bright day to wait for the wedding to begin.

"Jake?" James swallowed, because he wasn't sure how to answer that. He knew Jake loved his sister, that he was trying to get used to living in a real family again. But that could be a hard thing to do. James knew himself, from the way he felt inside. Letting people, especially such incredible women like Daisy and Sage, love them wasn't easy. It was hard enough for James; he knew it had to be nearly impossible for Jake.

"Yeah," Todd said. "Is he happy to be back?"

"I think so. I hope so."

"Where is he? Getting ready for the wedding?"

As James inhaled, he found he couldn't speak. Todd Rydell was standing before him, waiting for his answer, and the words stuck in his throat.

"He must be excited," Todd said as they walked outside. "Seeing his parents marry each other all over again."

James didn't answer, letting it go at that. He couldn't speak out loud, tell Todd Rydell that his son had led them to believe he didn't plan to attend the wedding. Daisy seemed to accept his decision, in her patient, loving way. James was trying, but he couldn't tell anyone, not even Daisy and certainly not Todd Rydell, that his heart felt almost broken.

That James Tucker's hard, crusty, unsentimental old rancher's heart felt like it might break in two because his son had decided not to come to their wedding.

Now that Sage and Jake were within sight of the ranch, riding up the trail, they could hear strains of music filling the air. A big blue-and-gold tent — the colors of the JD Ranch — had been set up, and its soaring peaks echoed the shapes of the Wind River mountains rising behind it. Their mother was probably inside, getting dressed for the wedding. Sage thought she glimpsed her veil — a long cloud of white tulle — flashing by an upstairs window.

"They're all here," Sage said.

"I know."

"Aunt Hathaway, the Rydells, Louisa and Granddad, Mom and Dad —"

"Gave Aunt Hathaway a cool tattoo," Jake said.

"She's the best aunt in the world," Sage told him. "You'll see. She's somewhere between a second mom and the coolest big sister you can imagine."

"I know," Jake said sharply.

"Did I say something wrong?" she asked, feeling anxious.

"No," he said. "You didn't. Except sometimes it pisses me off, thinking how much longer you've known all these people. You've spent your whole life with Mom and Aunt Hathaway, and I'm just getting started. I want my own relationship with Aunt Hathaway — and all the others — without you translating and interpreting every single thing."

"Okay," she said quietly.

"Sorry to sound so mad," he said, frowning as if he was actually furious.

"We're even with Dad. You have to admit that. Both of us getting to know him at the same time."

"You say that as if it's a good thing."

Sage just shook her head, momentarily unable to talk. She didn't think that part was a good thing — not at all.

"All there," Sage said finally, shading her eyes. "Everybody but us."

"Yeah," Jake said quietly.

"Your family, Jake." She knew she was walking a fine line, that anything she might say on the subject could make him mad.

"Quit it, Sage."

"As long as you know."

"I know." She thought his voice sounded thick.

"Don't mind me, watching out for you every minute," she said, trying to make light of it. "I'm your sister."

"Twin sister," he said in a joking tone, making Sage feel so happy that he got it, that he was ribbing her for a closeness he actually seemed to understand as deeply as she did.

The music sounded bright and festive, but suddenly Sage pulled back on Scout's reins to hear better. "Listen!"

"I hear it," Jake said, stopping beside her.

The band was warming up, and Louisa was rehearsing her wedding song. She had written it for James and Daisy, and it was called "The Forever Day." Jake started to smile, listening to her big voice singing across the lush meadow

"Not Louisa —" Sage said. *"Listen."*

It was springtime, very warm, too late for this to be happening. But as the twins tilted their heads back, shielding their eyes against the bright Wyoming sun, they saw a great, long V crossing the sky. Snow geese. The sun struck their feathers, turning them white as winter. They were honking as they flew, their voices and wings drowning out everything, even Louisa's song.

"The geese, Jake."

"I see!"

"How many are there? Can you tell? A hundred?"

"A thousand."

The twins knew the story of the geese, how their father had proposed to their mother the second time, how she had said "yes" when he'd sent them flying into that winter sky. The very sight of them now brought tears to Sage's eyes, and when she looked at her brother, he was standing tall in his saddle while Maisie barked at the sky.

"A thousand!" he said again.

"At least."

"Hey," Jake yelled, surprising Sage so much she nearly fell off her horse.

"The geese can't hear you." She laughed.

"Not them," he said. "I'm not talking to them."

"Then who?"

"Hey!" Jake yelled louder, standing taller in his stirrups.

Their father was standing by the paddock, talking to someone who had come to set up the food.

"They're back!" Jake called.

"You're calling Dad?" Sage said, her heart for some reason starting to race. Jake never seemed excited about anything. He never went to their father or mother to talk, never seemed thrilled about any of the good things in any of their lives. Sage knew it hurt both their parents' feelings, but their father's most of all.

"The band's too loud," Jake said. "He can't hear me."

"Louder, then." Sage was swelling with happiness. "Oh, Jake. Call louder."

"Dad!" Jake yelled, pointing at the sky. "Mom! They're back!"

At the sound of his voice, their father turned. Even from here, Sage could see the grin on his face, from hearing Jake call him "Dad."

Their mother leaned out the upstairs window, her veil billowing, as if she wanted to touch the wind. Sage smiled, waving her huge bouquet of wildflowers, but her parents had their heads tilted back, looking at the sky with the geese flying over.

"They're back!" Jake Tucker shouted with all his might. He was smiling, too, waving like someone who felt excited to be part of a family whose legend included snow geese and Washakie, exactly like someone who was riding home with his twin sister, on their way to the wedding of their parents: someone who very much intended to stick around and hear them say, "I do."

LUANNE RICE is the author of *Follow the Stars Home*, *Cloud Nine*, *Home Fires*, *Secrets of Paris*, *Stone Heart*, *Angels All Over Town*, *Crazy in Love* (made into a TNT network feature movie), and *Blue Moon*, which has been made into a CBS television movie. She lives in New York City and Old Lyme, Connecticut, with her husband.